THE QUEEN IS DEAD

The betties looked surprised to see us, but thanks to their friend's warning, they had a split second to react. I took a fist to the jaw. It was all I needed to bring the goblin to the surface – blood was a fabulous stimulant, especially my own. I reckon it was self-preservation.

"Put her down," I growled.

My betty pulled a shocker from his coat – a hand-held device that could incapacitate a half-blood for minutes at a time. He pressed a button and the prongs embedded themselves in my flesh. I felt the surge of electricity hit my body ...

I was not a halvie. I was not human. According to many, I wasn't even an aristocrat. And apparently, the amount needed to bring down a goblin was pretty freaking high. I felt the surge from the top of my head to the tip of my toes.

And it pissed me off.

By Kate Locke

The Immortal Empire

God Save the Queen
The Queen Is Dead
Long Live the Queen

THE QUEEN IS DEAD

KATE LOCKE

BOOK TWO OF THE IMMORTAL EMPIRE

orbit

www.orbitbooks.net

ORBIT

First published in Great Britain in 2012 by Orbit
Reprinted 2013

Copyright © 2012 by Kathryn Smith

Map by Don Higgins

The moral right of the author has been asserted.

A CIP catalogue record for this book
is available from the British Library.

ISBN 978-0-356-50144-4

Typeset in Times by M Rules
Printed and bound in Great Britain by
Clays Ltd, St Ives plc

Papers used by Orbit are from well-managed forests
and other responsible sources.

MIX
Paper from
responsible sources
FSC
www.fsc.org FSC® C104740

Orbit
An imprint of
Little, Brown Book Group
100 Victoria Embankment
London EC4Y 0DY

An Hachette UK Company
www.hachette.co.uk

www.orbitbooks.net

This book is for my mom,
who loved stories as much as I do, who taught me
how to dream, and who wore her eccentricities like
badges of honour. I didn't thank her enough.

And it's for my husband, Steve,
because he believes in me even when I don't.

PICCADILLY
CIRCUS

DOWN STREET
GOBLIN ENTRANCE

BUCKINGHAM
PALACE

WELLINGTON
ACADEMY

PALACE GUARD

VICTORIA
STATION

ST
PA

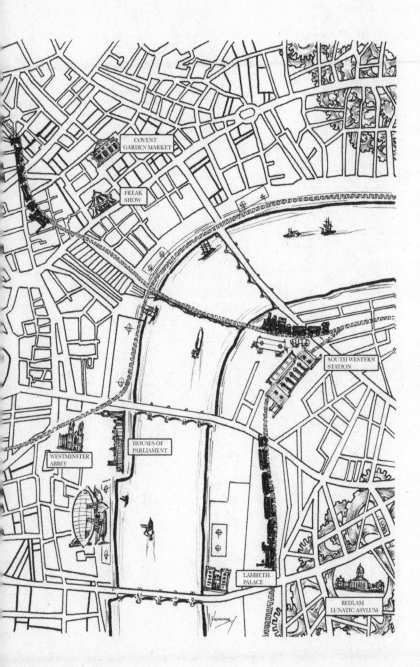

COVENT GARDEN MARKET

FREAK SHOW

SOUTH WESTERN STATION

WESTMINSTER ABBEY

HOUSES OF PARLIAMENT

LAMBETH PALACE

BEDLAM LUNATIC ASYLUM

CHAPTER 1

BATTLE NOT WITH MONSTERS LEST YOU BECOME ONE

There was a dead rat nailed to my door.

"Poor thing." I grasped the thick spike and pulled it free of the heavy wood. The small furry corpse fell into my hand. It was still warm. Left during daylight hours. Cowards.

Probably the Human League. They were the only ones who blamed rats for the plague responsible for vampires, were-wolves, half-bloods, and ... things like me. They also suffered from the mistaken belief that they were safe during the day. They weren't. No more than we were safe from them at night.

Underneath the murdered rodent was a copy of the front page of *The Times* from last Monday. There was a photo of me – now stained with rat blood – leaving the house, and above it the headline: *MONSTER IN OUR MIDST: Frightened residents want goblin "queen" away from their children.* Of course, no names were given, because I might decide to exact revenge upon those good citizens who hated me simply because of what I was.

In a way I understood – I was frightened of me sometimes as well – but the press, and the Human League, made me sound like some kind of bogeyman. A child killer. It was becoming a tad tedious, to be honest.

I buried the rat – and the paper – in the back garden, where I'd buried the last two to have been left my step. Since the neighbourhood of Leicester Square learned they had a goblin in their midst – to be exact, Xandra Vardan, the reluctant "Queen of Goblins" – they'd become a bit ... *enthusiastic* in their desire to convince me to pack my bags.

I was about to throw the spike into the hole as well when I noticed a small scrap of fabric attached. Part of a shirt sleeve if I wasn't mistaken. I pulled it off the iron and lifted it to my nose. Rat. Blood. Cotton. Newsprint ... Ah, there it was.

Human.

Sometimes a superior sense of smell was a disgusting affliction, other times it came in rather handy. This was one of those times. I took another sniff and walked around to the front of the house.

I lived in what had once been an old public house in Leicester Square – still had the sign above the door. I stopped on the pavement and took a deep breath.

West. That's where the little tosser went.

I set off down the street. The sun was still sinking in the sky, casting the city and its inhabitants in a mellow summer glow. I squinted behind my sunglasses. Unlike my furry subterranean brethren, I could brave sunlight, a fact that would surprise my rat killer. It didn't blister me or burn my eyes like it did to aristocrats – a term now used to describe vampires, weres and even goblins, though goblins thought themselves separate. I needed dark glasses and sunscreen, but I was okay.

All around me humans hurried here and there, either on foot or by motor carriage. I'd lived in Leicester Square for two months now, ever since moving out of the house I used to share with my sister Avery. She was still pissed off at me for keeping secrets from her, and for being a goblin. As if I had a choice in the matter.

Perhaps choosing to live in a predominantly human neighbourhood wasn't the most intelligent of decisions, given increasing human hostility, but it kept me reasonably far away from Queen Victoria's spies, and that was what mattered. I'd earned the disfavour of Britain's vampire monarch by being made queen by the goblins. Historically, the queens of Britain didn't look kindly on other queens infringing on their territory.

People looked at me as they passed by. A halvie wasn't that much of an oddity in these parts, though certainly not commonplace. Unfortunately word had got out, thanks to the rags, that there was a freaky new goblin in town. My photo had been in every paper a couple of months ago, first because of my love life, and then because of the scandal of my genes. I was something of a celebrity, though without the chat show appearances.

I had my guard up. This unusual heat was making people nervous, myself included. Some huey and halvie deaths over the summer, including Dede and a friend of hers from Bedlam, had the humans twitchy. The Queen's jubilee in May hadn't helped either. You could practically feel tension rising in the city.

A mother put herself between me and her child, as if she was any sort of protection if I decided I wanted to have the kid for tea. I smiled at her, but kept walking, following the scent of my rodent killer. I didn't want trouble – except with the person I was trailing.

I tracked him to an estate in Haymarket. It was one of those kinds that had terrace upon terrace of flats, but while his scent drifted up a set of stairs, it was strongest towards a small park area upwind, behind the three buildings.

I paused, stuffed my hair beneath my bowler hat so the unusual red didn't immediately give me away, slouched my shoulders and set off toward the boys gathered around a jungle gym. My thick-soled boots, short skirt, stockings and corseted waistcoat didn't look too expensive, and fitted in with current human fashion.

Six young blokes with hats pulled low over spot-riddled faces adorned with tatts and piercings looked up as I approached.

"Oi, what's this?" One elbowed another.

"Nice tits."

I rolled my eyes as they chuckled, thinking I couldn't hear them. I could hear them breathing, little wanks.

"Hullo," I said to the one whose stench filled my nostrils. He was probably seventeen, with sapphire-streaked blond hair that hung in his blue eyes and a silver stud in his cheek. He had spools in the sides of his nostrils, and cigarette smoke drifted out of them as he smirked at me.

"Hi," he said back. "What are you looking for, little merk?"

I didn't appreciate being referred to as a vaginal wig, no matter how trendy it was. "You, actually." I pouted. "Don't you recognise me?"

His friends chuckled when he did. "Should I?"

My left hand lashed out, catching him around the throat. His startled expression made me grin. The world brightened just a little as I let my fangs out – the goblin in me making my sight keener, my hunger sharper. I managed to keep the bones in my face from shifting, however. Didn't want the little lamb to pass out on me.

"Breaks my heart to think you might be murdering rats for other girls, my pretty boy."

"Fuck me!" yelped one of the boys, scampering higher on the metal climbing bars.

I ignored him. He wasn't a danger unless he decided to jump on me – which would just be stupid. The ones that needed watching were the ones who stayed close, even when they realised who – what – I was.

"Get lost," I snarled, all fang and spit. Out of the corner of my eye I saw them withdraw further. I didn't care if they watched, so long as they stayed out of it.

"It weren't nothing personal," rasped the boy.

I tilted my head, holding eye contact. He smelled good. Good enough to eat. I could take a bite from a place he'd never miss it . . . but I wouldn't. I had yet to give in to the craving for human flesh.

"Hard not to take something like that personally, my friend. Surely you can see how I might be . . . upset?"

He swallowed hard against my palm, jerked his head in a nod. I was impressed that he hadn't pissed himself yet. His face was turning purple. "He paid me."

I eased up on the pressure. "What's that?"

The kid drew a deep breath. "Some toff gave me a hundred quid to do it. He even gave me the rat." His gaze flitted briefly from mine. He hadn't liked killing the rat. It was something that was going to stick with him for a while.

I knew that feeling, though my moral code was slipping more and more every day. I wanted to kill this kid. His fear made my mouth tingle. It wasn't the violence that got my salivary glands all aflutter – it was the idea of the blood, the meat. He wasn't a prime specimen, and he reeked of drugs and stale fags, but he'd still taste ruddy good.

And I was starving.

"What did he look like?"

"I dunno. A toff." I squeezed his throat again and his eyes bulged. "He was blond – almost albino. And pale. Blue eyes. Real thin. Aristo."

My eyes narrowed, and I relaxed my fingers. "How could you tell?"

"Vamped out on me, didn't he? All toothsome. Threatened to kill me if I said a word about it."

"And yet here you are, telling me." Either this kid wasn't too bright, or . . .

"He weren't nearly as scary as you."

Well, that was something, wasn't it? I released him altogether. He sagged in on himself as his feet hit the patchy grass, like a rag doll, hand going to his bruised throat. "What else?"

The kid's expression was one of sheer panic. His friends had scattered, brave lot that they were. "There isn't anything else!"

Of course there was. "How was he dressed? What sort of vehicle did he have? What exactly did he say?"

"He wore a dark grey suit. Looked like a rag ad for cologne or something. He had a motor carriage and a driver, but I didn't see either of them, I swear. He said, 'I'll give you one hundred pounds to nail this unfortunate beast to the door of the goblin queen.' I took his money and that's when he said he'd end me if I told."

"If anyone's going to kill you, it's going to be me," I told him. His face went completely white. Fang me, he wasn't going to faint, was he? "I'm not going to kill you, you stupid git. No one is." Especially not me. I was stronger than that.

Poor thing was trembling now. "You got a pen?"

He seemed surprised by the question, but pulled one out of his jacket pocket. I took it and grabbed his hand, turning it palm up. "If he comes to you again, I want you to ring me on this number." I jotted my mobile number on the ball of his thumb. "If I start getting prank calls, I'll rip your tongue out and eat it in front of you, understood?"

He nodded, then shuddered a little, but still no piss. He really was a brave one. Being a hormonal teenage halfwit helped.

"What's your name?"

"David." His voice was hoarse. He'd barely be able to talk tomorrow.

"David, if an aristo or anyone else offers you money to do anything so fucking stupid in the future, I want you to be a good boy and say no, all right? Whatever they offer won't be worth it."

Another nod. "Yes, Your Majesty."

I rolled my eyes. "Sod off. Now go home. Tomorrow your cowardly friends will be impressed that you spent ten minutes alone with me and survived. Just don't tell them what we talked about. I don't want word getting back to your aristo friend that you betrayed him."

He nodded yet again, and walked away with his fists shoved in the pockets of his jacket. I watched him go, smiling when he finally gave in and started to run.

I walked home, stopping for a coffee and a box of

doughnuts along the way. The middle-aged human lady behind the counter didn't know – or maybe didn't care – who I was, and put a valiant effort into appearing friendly, but her indifference was written all over her slack features and sloped shoulders. It was actually nice to be treated with general disdain as opposed to abject terror.

A few months ago – when I believed I was nothing more than a regular halvie trying to make a name for myself with the Royal Guard – I thought I knew what it was like to be hated and feared. That was before I found out I was a monster. A pretty one, but a monster nevertheless, despite my barley-sugar-red hair and furless body. I was strong, very fast and generally considered ill-tempered. And as far as I knew, I was the only one of my kind. Not exactly something I aspired to.

I was eating the fourth of the doughnuts – bless my goblin metabolism – when I reached my house. It was still standing, which was good. Nothing dead on my step. No albino aristocrats.

There was, however, a halvie sitting there. I'd know her candy-floss-pink hair anywhere. "What the hell do you want?" I demanded.

My sister Avery rose to her feet. Her wide green eyes – the same colour mine had been before my goblin genes turned them slightly gold – were red, and her face had the haggard appearance of someone who hadn't slept recently. "I need to talk to you."

"You said enough when you kicked me out." I brushed past her and dug my keys out of the pocket sewn into the waistband of my skirt. Fang me, my fingers were shaking.

"It's important," she told my rigid back.

"I'm sure it is." I unlocked the door. "Why don't you send me a digigram instead?" I stepped over the threshold.

"Damn it, Xandy! It's Val."

I stopped, then turned my head to face her. Val was our brother, and Avery wouldn't have let go of her grudge to talk to me unless it was serious. Fuck it all. "You'd better come in."

I made tea because it was the civil thing to do. And I shared my doughnuts because, despite not speaking to me for two months, Avery was my sister and I loved her. And because she looked like shit.

We were in the part of my rented home that used to be the main room of the pub – equipped with original nineteenth-century bar and fixtures. I was behind the bar while Avery sat on a stool at the counter.

"What's going on?" I asked as I poured hot water into the pot. The scent of Earl Grey wafted up, delicious and sharp. This was like Dede all over again. Avery and I had had tea that night too. I didn't want to think about that.

She pulled apart a chocolate doughnut. "I haven't heard from Val in almost three days."

"And you came to me?" What, she couldn't just call? "How the hell would I know what he's up to?"

"I reckoned you and he would be tight again by now."

"Well, your reckoning is shit." I should have taken better care to hide how much she and Val had hurt me. "You certain he's not on a case?"

Val was Special Branch of Scotland Yard and worked all halvie and aristo-related cases. It wasn't unusual for him to disappear for days at a time. But Avery had said the same about Dede, and she'd got herself involved with traitors and then killed.

"I called his SI." She shot me a glance. "She thought I was you."

"Obviously you got over it. What did she say?"

"That she couldn't give me any details on Val or the case he was on."

"There, he's on the hunt. No big deal." Maybe Avery had invented all of this as an excuse to break the silence between us.

"She told me that his brother Takeshi had called as well."

"I fucking hate it when they call Penny by that name." Takeshi was better known as Penny Dreadful, one of the sweetest, most gorgeous trannies you'd ever meet. She was not Val's brother – not to me. She was his sister. She was practically family, even though she wasn't related to me by blood. She and Val shared the same mother, but not the same father.

"I know, but Penny said she found Val's rotary at Freak Show."

I poured tea into Avery's cup and then my own. "Not like him to forget his rote, but then he has a separate one for work, right?"

"Dunno. Perhaps." She dumped several sugar cubes into her cup. "Val never said anything about an investigation."

"Sounds like he wasn't allowed."

"And he didn't say anything to you at all? Nothing about a case involving the Human League or anything?"

I stared at her. Was she fucking mental, or just not listening? "I haven't seen Val for two months. You both decided to disown me, remember?"

She glared at me – she looked like a snarling doll. "You lied to us, about Dede, about yourself."

"I kept quiet so the two of you wouldn't get dragged down if it all went to hell – which it did. And I lied about me because I was just finding out the truth for myself. Thank you, by the way, for kicking me out when I needed you most."

"I didn't kick you out, you fucking left."

"Because you didn't want me in the house."

"Who the bloody hell told you that?"

"Vardan." Our father.

Her expression hardened. "He had no right."

I sighed and plucked a doughnut dripping with frosting from the box. "It doesn't matter now. Besides, Victoria made it clear she didn't want me in her territory."

She arched a brow. "Victoria, eh? On first-name terms, are you?"

I rolled my eyes. "Hardly. Regardless, what do you want me to do?"

Cheeks bulging with cakey goodness, my sister looked as surprised as a spinster matron in an all-boys shower. "Can't you … you know, talk to the goblins or something? Get his phone from Penny?"

"Why don't you go to Penny? And what makes you think the gobs know anything? Or do you think they've got him flavouring a stew as we speak?" I was going for a slightly more caustic tone that the incredulous one that clung to my words.

"They knew what happened to Dede, didn't they?"

Yes, they had. That would explain the déjà vu. "And look where that got me. Us."

Avery glanced up, cheeks normal, eyes wide. "Xandy, this

is Val we're talking about. Our brother, who always came running any time you or I called."

I refused to be guilted – mostly out of spite. "If something happened with his case, then the entire Yard is out looking for him."

"The Yard doesn't have access to the goblins, or to you. If anyone can find him, you can."

I ought to have been touched by the sentiment, and to an extent I was. I was still pissed off that Val had to get into shit for her to finally speak to me. "You going to help?"

Her cheeks flushed. "I can't. I promised Em I wouldn't go off courting trouble."

But I could. If it weren't for a promise to her fiancée, Avery would be out looking for Val right now, and I'd be none the wiser.

What a proper pair we were. At least I wouldn't go fooling myself into thinking I'd be accepted back into the family fold any time soon. Which was ironic when you consider that family was what had got me into this mess to begin with.

"Fine," I said finally, running my finger over the polished but scarred surface of the bar. "I'll ask around."

She opened her purse. "I can give you a few quid—"

My hand shot out and snapped the clasp shut. Avery squealed as the metal pinched her fingers. "You think I need money?"

Glaring and pouting at the same time, she shook her smarting hand. "I don't know. The RG fired you."

"I have my allowance," I reminded her, not wanting to think of how my supervisor in the Royal Guard had informed me that my services were no longer required. You had to be a half-blood to be an RG, and I was no longer a halvie. Never had been.

"Besides," I said lightly – I'd chew on silver razor blades before I'd let her think of me as a poor relation – "you know what they say about goblins and treasure."

She frowned. "I thought that was dwarves."

Albert's fangs. It was an old curse, a blasphemy of the late Prince Consort, and I used it without an ounce of remorse. "Dwarves," I ground out, "don't exist."

Avery shot me a droll look as she polished off her doughnut. "Until two months ago, neither did a furless goblin who could walk in the sun."

Touché. "I don't need or want your money."

"You're so fucking proud." She made it sound like a bad thing. "That's why I didn't want to come."

"Right, it's all my fault."

She slapped the flat of her hand down on the bar. "It is! If you hadn't been so afraid of what we'd think, or so dead set on protecting us, we could have helped you, Xandra. We could have been there for you, and for Dede. Now she's dead and you're living in an old pub in a human part of town, Val's gone and Churchill's supposedly on the run."

The mention of his name made my heart skip. "I haven't heard from him either." No one would. Not ever again.

"Just as well. They'd probably give him a medal for killing her."

At least that was something we agreed on. "Probably."

She checked her watch and sighed. "I have to go. You'll call me if you find anything?"

I shrugged. "Sure."

"Promise?"

"Ruddy hell, Avery!" I silently counted to ten and met her earnest gaze. "I promise. Now get the hell out, will you?" The longer she stayed, the more alone I was going to feel when she left.

As luck would have it, my sister seemed to understand exactly what I was feeling – the bitch. She nodded glumly, slipped off the stool and started for the door. I walked her out.

She paused at the threshold. "You'll be careful, won't you, Xandy?" She wasn't just talking about my promise to check up on Val.

I nodded. "I will be."

She smiled – just a little. "Good. If I hug you, will you hit me?"

"Not unless you want me to."

She was just a tiny bit shorter than me, so as her arms went around me, our cheeks brushed. Hers was wet. Hesitantly, I returned the embrace. Something in my chest twanged painfully.

Just as suddenly, she released me. "Goodbye." Then she ran down the few steps to where her shiny motorrad sat waiting. The two-wheeled vehicle roared to life and then sped off down the street. I hoped she'd stopped crying, because driving with blurry vision was hardly safe.

I closed the door, armed the alarm and went back to the bar. This time I poured something a mite stronger than tea. My heart was heavy but my eyes were blessedly dry.

CHAPTER 2

ALL HAIL THEIR QUEEN

There are only a handful of ways for humans to access the underside – one of them being the Metropolitan train service, the Met for short. There were barriers set up at the end of the platforms to discourage anyone who might think to follow the tracks into the dark. Of course, there was always the odd human who thought jumping the barriers was a sound idea. The lucky ones made it back to the lit areas, or maybe the surface, screaming. The unlucky ones didn't make it out at all. I've heard people talk about hearing blood-curdling screams while waiting for their train.

There's more beneath London than old train lines, catacombs, plague pits and tunnels. It's not so much the long-forgotten rooms and caverns that a body need worry about; it's the things living in them. I once heard that there's a species of mosquito that is found only in the dank dark beneath my fair city. Some stupid sod actually risked his fool life to go beneath and find the bloody thing.

If you willingly wander into goblin territory, you're considered fair game.

Since I was no longer RG, I was unable to come and go as I pleased in the walled neighbourhood of Mayfair, where the main entrance to the goblin – or "plague" – den was located. You either had to be a resident of the community, a registered visitor, or an employee of one of the three agencies given permission to enter – the Royal Guard, the Peerage Protectorate, and Special Branch. I was none of those things.

So I had to be a bit more creative in regard to gaining entry. I slipped goggles over my eyes and roared across town on my Butler motorrad, weaving in and out of traffic that thinned as I approached the West End. Not as many motor carriages where I was going. A lot of aristos preferred horse and carriage to anything with an engine. I thought it archaic, but my opinion didn't matter. Thank God Vex shared my sentiment.

He should be back soon, my alpha wolf boyfriend, but for now I was on my own in finding out not only which vamp paid my rat-killer, but just what Val was up to that was so important he hadn't told Avery or Penny.

I didn't want to go to the goblin prince. Every favour I asked dug me deeper into their culture, made it harder for me to put off accepting their crown. Part of me fought being a monster while another relished the opportunity. The part that wanted it frightened me, if I was truthful.

And if I became their queen, I would have to finally admit to being one of them. It was one thing for me to say I was a goblin; it was quite another to embrace it. No denying being a monster then.

I drove past Green Park on the A4, skirting my old neighbourhood of the Wellington district and the barbed gates of

Buck House – as the palace was sometimes called by old-timer aristos. One benefit to avoiding the Mayfair gates was that there'd be no record of my visit, and Queen V wouldn't know I'd been round. A decided disadvantage was trying to find a place to park. This area really came to life at dusk.

I found a place to stash the Butler not far from Hyde Park Corner. I checked for traffic and sprinted across the street, narrowly avoiding a collision with a Routemaster omnibus. Then I jogged down the stairs to the entrance of the Met station.

Most of the residents of this part of town didn't use the train, but the station was still fairly busy. Many humans and halvies worked in the West End in establishments that catered to aristos. Recently I'd learned that humans, like goblins, weren't quite as evil as I'd been taught. Still, they had tried to overthrow the aristocracy in 1932, and laid waste to much of Mayfair and its inhabitants. I'd been attacked by humans several times in the course of my life. That fear and prejudice was hard to put aside.

Hopefully the humans would never find out that we were as scared of them as they were of us, "we" being those of plagued blood.

A few of those waiting on the platform glanced in my direction, but halvies and aristos were a regular sight here, and I looked just like any other halvie. I had my lonsdaelite dagger sheathed in my corset and a pistol holstered in my bustle just in case someone decided to make a closer inspection of my person. The RGs had taken my Bulldog away from me after giving me the boot, so now I carried a smaller weapon – a pearl-handled revolver that fired bullets that fragmented inside their target, scattering shards of silver. It was almost as effective against aristos as it was against humans, which was why I carried it.

Across the tracks, pasted on the tiles, was a faded poster, the original slogan of which had been altered to read: *KEEP CALM AND PRAY FOR DAWN*. It was from after the Great Insurrection, when security protocols had first been implemented underside. Now, it was a reminder of just what humans thought of us.

The platform beneath my feet – scuffed and worn despite an attempt to keep it polished – vibrated as the rumbling down the track grew louder. A warm breeze brushed my cheek, filling my nostrils with the smell of hot metal, dirt and grease as the train pulled into the station. It dulled the scent of human that seemed to forever linger, teasingly, on the air.

I eyed the UV cannons set up at either end of the platform warily. If someone decided to smash the glass case and turn the light from one of those on me, how long would I last? I could still go out in the sun like I always could, but I was more sensitive to it than before, and these cannons were heavy-duty shit. They were most effective against "normal" goblins and aristos. I'd never seen one used, and hopefully I never would. They were there to give the humans a feeling of safety, but if someone were to go for the glass right now, I'd have their throat out before the last shards hit the ground.

The train doors opened – bodies out, bodies in. I stepped closer to the edge as a disembodied voice warned passengers to mind the gap between carriage and platform. A few people glanced at me, curious as to why I wasn't joining them, but they soon lost interest.

The train began to move and I tensed, waiting. My weight shifted to the balls of my feet, heart pounding out a count-

down. As the end of the long, wood-panelled train sped past,
I reached out and jumped.

My fingers closed around the bars and my boots landed on the
ledge. Clinging to the back of the carriage, I whipped past the
rest of the platform, into the semi-darkness of the next tunnel.

I wasn't on for long. As soon as I caught a glimpse of the
ruin that used to be Down Street station, I leaned my body out,
and when I spied the platform a track-width away, I leaped.

One brilliant bit about being a goblin was the reflexes, not
to mention increased speed and grace. One second I was hanging off the back of a train, and the next I'd landed in a crouch
on the dusty, debris-strewn platform of a station closed for
eighty years.

Down Street had many names, depending on whether you
were goblin, aristo, halvie or human. To some, its crumbling
cream and maroon tiles and grimy platform were a monument
to the duplicity of humans. To others, it was a giant tomb. To
the goblins, it was home.

Some brave – or stupid – human crew had come down here
after the Insurrection in the hope of clearing out the dead, but
only a handful of bodies were recovered – the rest had been
dragged even deeper below the city, into the plague den.

Halvies had been sent down to board the station up, but not
before a treaty of some kind was in place to make sure they
didn't suffer the same fate the humans had.

Despite the stories, the warnings and the precautions, there
were always a stupid few who thought they were too cool to
be goblin chow and risked sneaking in.

There weren't any lights here – the amount of dusty glass fragments that littered the platform, some cupped in the bones of a human hand, provided ample explanation. New bulbs were immediately broken. This was goblin territory, and light was not welcome. As it was, the ambient light from both the Hyde Park Corner and Dover Street stations would be hard on the average gob's sensitive eyes.

I was the exception, because I hadn't spent my life underground. However, I could see very well in the dark. *Very* well.

I followed the tracks for a little bit – maybe twenty or thirty feet – until I came to the hole in the wall that was the entrance to the den. Unlike my first visit, I didn't proceed with caution. I slipped through the hole and jogged down the rough-hewn stairs, deeper into under-London. Frescoes painted in blood decorated the walls, but I didn't stop to admire their macabre beauty. I heard the sound of music and I walked towards it, heart hammering even though I had no reason to be afraid. Old habits and all that.

The goblin den was a maze of crypts and tunnels and ruins running beneath the city, with this location at its heart. The entire underground was their kingdom, and all the treasures that came with it, such as Roman gold, and artefacts from the time before this city had a name.

I entered the great hall. Two goblins were playing piano and cello for the entertainment of what appeared to be the entire plague – give or take. Fortunately for London, goblins were few in number and had a low birth rate even for aristos. Unfortunately, one goblin was more than a match for two aristos – except maybe for a few of Vex's wolves – four halvies or a dozen humans.

The moment the performers spied me, the music ceased.

They fell to all fours, dropping their heads in supplication. The audience turned and did the same. It was like being bowed to by a very large pack of mangy dogs wearing accessories.

A few of them, I noticed, did not bow. In fact they didn't look very impressed by me at all.

"Xandra lady," came a low, familiar rasp. Goblin voices always sounded like they were on the verge of a growl.

I smiled as the prince approached me. He was tall for a goblin – about my height – and he wore a leather patch over one amber eye. He also wore a shabby dark blue Chinese silk jacket with a hole in the shoulder seam and frayed cuffs. Probably not many tailors that catered to gobs in the city.

The prince sketched a bow, and I let him, because this sort of behaviour meant something to him. Once he'd straightened, I asked the others to rise as well. It gave me the creeps to see them like that.

"Your prince hoped you might come," he said, taking my hand in his more paw-like one. It didn't bother me any more. In fact, it felt comforting. Other than Vex, I'd been sadly lacking in physical contact.

"I'm sorry I haven't been down for a bit. I'm ... " I didn't want to lie to him. "I'm still trying to sort things out."

He nodded sagely. "Big changes require little steps, yes." He escorted me towards the only chairs in the room. One was his throne and the other was mine, and they were both made of bone. Human bone. Although that fanged skull on the top of mine was certainly not human. I swallowed.

It was Church. I just knew it.

For a moment, I thought I might cast up my accounts all over the toes of my boots, but then came a flash of Dede, in my arms, dying from a gunshot wound inflicted by that bastard.

I sat down. The velvet cushioning on the seat and back made the throne surprisingly comfortable. I could get used to it.

And there was the rub. I wasn't sure about being the goblin queen, but the idea of being any other sort of queen was freaking brilliant.

"What brings the lady underside?" asked the prince, gesturing for the music to resume.

"My brother, Val. He's on a case and my sister can't find him. I thought maybe you might know what he's up to." It seemed like an odd question, but goblins appeared to know everything that happened in London.

Furry brows drew together. "Many you love get lost, my lady."

"The story of my life," I replied lightly. Were that it was actually a joke.

"Come," he said, rising to his feet. Goblins normally went about barefoot, as they had fur and tough leathery pads to prevent injury. The prince, however, sometimes wore boots. Tonight he was sporting a pair of highly polished but well-worn hessians.

"I'm sorry; am I interrupting something?" If incredulity had a taste, my tongue would be dripping with it. Music and entertainment happened all the time down here. Didn't it?

He ran a paw down one lapel – an oddly self-conscious gesture. "Dress accordingly, do gentlemen of rank." His gaze flitted away from mine, and I followed it to another familiar gob face. It was Elsbeth, a female goblin I'd met during the mess with Dede.

Fang me, was the prince courting her? She smiled at him – a terrifying sight. A goblin baring its teeth was never pretty, though the prince certainly seemed to like it. He smiled back. My stomach trembled, then growled.

This was so buggered up. "You had something to show me?" I prodded. The sooner he shared, the sooner I could leave. I wasn't ready for goblin mating rituals.

"Hungry is our lady."

And I wasn't ready to witness traditional goblin dining again. I'd seen what they did to Church.

What *I'd* done to Church. I swallowed the bitterness that coated my tongue. "I'm fine."

The prince barked – literally. It was a deep, sharp sound that got my heart kicking at my ribs. Seconds later, a small gob with horn-shaped barrettes on her head and metal rivets in her pointed ears appeared with a tray laden with fruit.

A similar tray had been offered to me the first time I came down here, and I'd resisted the temptation. It was a universally ignored fact in this city that goblins were also dealers of opium – junkies weren't usually missed when they disappeared. They owned a couple of legal dragon dens as well, but I reckoned most of their funds came from private deals and their little "soirées". I should probably be horrified, but I wasn't. You want to play goblin roulette with your life? That's your business. And your short little existence.

"It will not harm you," the prince said, as though reading my thoughts. He wasn't stupid, and my wariness was telegraphed so loudly Vex could probably feel it in Scotland. "What we give to the meat this is not."

Ah yes, the meat. My stomach growled again and I shrugged. I didn't want to offend and I was starving. Plus there was the dismal reminder that the goblins were the only friends I had. I might not be the brightest candle, but I wasn't completely daft. And I needed all the friends I could get.

The cherries looked bloody delicious. I took the entire

bowl from the tray. It had to weigh a couple of pounds. "Thanks."

The little goblin grinned. Sweet baby Albert, I hoped that stuff in her teeth was cherry pulp.

I ate as the prince led me from the great hall to the torch-lit catacomb corridor. I suspected this maze was mostly Roman in origin, but it was hard to tell in the dark. They might have been nineteenth-century tunnels or seventeenth-century sewers. I had no idea. The underside of London was such a hollowed-out thing, it was amazing the entire city hadn't fallen in on itself. There used to be a plague pit near here, but I had a sneaking suspicion that it was humans who'd been killed rather than mutated by the plague who made up a great deal of the furniture in the den.

"How big is this place?" I asked, glancing around at the rough stone and high ceilings.

"Big," the prince replied lightly as he stole a cherry from my bowl. "The pits, save them, please."

I spat the one in my mouth into the bowl. It was my spit, so I didn't care. The prince put his in his pocket.

"Thank you for accommodating me, I know you had plans for the evening."

He shrugged and shot me a myopic glance that glowed in the light. "You are our lady. Deny you I would never."

I frowned, chewed on another cherry. It split crisply between my teeth, sweet, wet tang flooding my mouth. "I don't want you to feel obligated to me."

"The lady feels obligation, that is why she is afraid to come underside, afraid her prince will expect her to wear the crown."

He was either terribly astute or I was simply transparent. "Yes."

The prince shook his shaggy head. "You are queen whether you want to be or not. We are yours whether it is pleasing or not. Only the lady does not seem to understand. Accept your crown or do not, it changes nothing."

"You'd swear fealty even if I didn't want it?"

His muzzle twitched. "Already sworn."

What the ruddy hell was I supposed to do with such blind devotion? I didn't even have a pet; how was I supposed to contend with several dozen killing machines determined to serve me?

"I'm sorry." It was all I could think of to say, bloody genius that I was.

"So much breath you waste apologising."

Really? I often thought I wasn't sorry enough. I bit into another cherry.

We turned left, and then right into a large room that made my jaw drop. Almost every inch of wall space was covered in screens of varying sizes. Instead of VBC channels, however, the images were of London streets and buildings.

No wonder the goblins knew so much. They had more eyes on the city than MI-bloody-6. Four goblins were in the room, watching the screens and recording information. A low-pitched alarm sounded and a small light flashed beside a monitor halfway down the far wall. One of the goblins immediately went to it and recorded what was on the screen. It looked like two men having sex in an alley.

"What is this?"

The prince stole another cherry from my bowl. "Knowing cobbleside business is necessary for the plague. We were ignorant once. Never again."

He was referring to the Great Insurrection, obviously.

Humans invading their territory en masse must have been a great surprise – one they hadn't seen coming. "Impressive."

"Plague knowledge is our lady's knowledge."

Ah, he knew how to play me. Imagine the things I could be privy to with this sort of set-up at my disposal. I peered at one monitor. "Is that the palace?"

The prince made a chuffing noise. Laughter? "Our lady's brother seen last when?"

"Two nights ago. He left his rotary at Freak Show."

It might have been my imagination, but the prince went very, very still at the mention of the club. "Roderick," he said.

A male goblin – and I could tell it was male not because of his name, but because he was very well endowed – strutted over to a large bank of buttons, switches and inlaid monitors. Had he never heard of trousers?

The prince inclined his head at the gob and I took the hint to approach. I kept my gaze firmly on Roderick's furry head. He bowed when I reached him. "Lady," he rasped. He didn't meet my gaze, simply gestured to one of the flat screens set into the console. As I watched, grainy footage of Freak Show's front and back entrances appeared side by side. A large furry hand with long-clawed fingers turned a knob that increased the speed of the images.

"There," I said after a few minutes, catching sight of my brother's familiar face and build. "That's him."

The time on the screen told me that Val had arrived at Freak Show shortly after midnight. Roderick reached for another knob – this one controlled the view of the back exit. I leaned close to the screen, even though my vision was beyond excellent. I wanted to make sure I saw my brother when he left.

Images flickered by – like one of those books where you

flipped the pages to create a moving figure. I watched with narrowed eyes ...

Fuck.

"Stop!" My hand whipped out and caught the goblin's arm. "Go back. There."

On the screen, in a million shades of grey, was the image of two bubonic betties – humans who injected themselves with plagued blood to enhance their speed and strength, and ultimately died from it – leaving the club. And between them, looking directly into the camera, was Val.

What the hell had he got himself into?

CHAPTER 3

NOR WIT ENOUGH TO RUN AWAY

Had Val gone with the betties willingly? They'd been known to attack halvies before, usually because that blood gave them almost the same rush with fewer side effects.

But Val didn't look hurt. He didn't even look concerned. It had to be part of his investigation, but what was he investigating? The betties? If they caught on to him, they'd kill him for certain. And they wouldn't be quick about it. They'd drain him first, the bastards.

I was *not* going to lose another sibling. There was nothing I could do. This footage was from two nights ago. He might not even be with the betties any more if he'd managed to fool and arrest them. Then again, he might be a prisoner somewhere, his veins being slowly milked.

Rage washed over me, hot, sudden and uncontainable. I lashed out, punching the rough wall with enough force to send little puffs of dirt and debris into the air. Some of it stuck to the inside of my throat.

None of the goblins said anything, even though my rage could have damaged at least one of their screens. Thankfully, the only thing I seemed to break was my own skin. Blood dripped down my fingers.

The prince very casually took my battered appendage in his, lowered his head, and before I could squeak in distaste, licked the blood from my skin. His tongue was warm, and slightly rough. It was like being licked by a big wild dog.

"Um, thanks," I said when he had finished. Would he be offended if I wiped his spit on my stockings?

"Healing has been quickened," he replied. I glanced down; the knuckles that had been torn up just seconds before already appeared to be mending themselves.

Creepy, yet freaking amazing.

Roderick appeared at my side, offering a photographic printout of the betties and Val. It wasn't terribly clear, but it gave me a place to start.

I slipped out of the monitoring room, pressed my forehead against the wall, and forced a deep breath into my lungs. Anger came in quick breaths, fear in shallow puffs. If I gave in, I'd gob out, and people tended to get hurt – or die – when I let my goblin self take over. I didn't want the prince to see me out of control.

Thoughts of Val filled my mind – from when we were children, growing up at the courtesan house, where our mothers had lived, to the Academy and later. He was my only brother – older than me by almost two years. He was one of the few constants in my life. It didn't matter that he was pissed off at me.

I couldn't lose him too. I just couldn't. I knew I was getting ahead of myself, but I couldn't help it.

A warm paw came down on my shoulder. I lifted my head and turned it to look at the prince. It was difficult to think of him as a monster when he showed me such kindness.

"Not the first halfing taken from the Freak Show," he told me. "The first to go willingly. Do not fear for him yet."

I placed my hand over his. My knuckles tingled, the wounds I'd inflicted continuing to heal. His fur was soft and thick. "Thank you. For everything."

He nodded. Sometime during this he had taken the bowl of cherries from me, and was carrying them against his ribs. We walked back to the great hall in silence. I didn't go in. I wasn't in the mood for music or a crowd.

"Your plague," the prince said. "What do you require of us?"

I folded the photo and stuck it inside my corset, just under my arm. "Nothing. You've already done so much."

He snorted – a sound that was a cross between a growl and a yip. "We serve our lady."

They weren't all keen on serving me, I reckoned. I hadn't asked to be their queen. Of course I hadn't turned it down either.

"I'll let you know if I need assistance," I told him. It was the best I could offer, even though he'd pledged his allegiance to me. Val could turn up at Avery's tomorrow for breakfast and this fretting would have been for naught.

The prince nodded. It was unnerving how well he seemed to understand me. "Grace us again soon, pretty."

"Pretty" had started out as a nickname, but now it felt more like a position, or a term of respect. A title, even.

My looks were camouflage. The realisation sent a little shiver down my spine. What carnage would follow if all goblins could come out of the dark? I'd been raised to have a little fear for humans, but goblins didn't fear anything. They were predators, and I didn't fool myself into thinking I'd be able to stop them if they wanted to treat the city as an all-they-could-eat buffet.

I left the den without making any promises. I hitched a ride back to Hyde Park Corner and exited cobbleside to a light rain. The neighbourhood lights brightened the night, blurred slightly by the wet. I ran across the street, leaping on to the kerb a split second before a speeding taxi made me a bonnet ornament. I shook my head. All these thoughts in my head made it hard to think straight.

Eventually I was going to have to decide if I was going to wear that crown sitting in a box in my bedroom cupboard. I couldn't be a goblin when it was convenient and then hide from it when it wasn't. I either had to embrace the truth of my genes or walk away from it.

But I didn't have to do it tonight, I told myself as I swung my leg over the Butler and started the engine. Tonight I would let Avery know what I'd found out. Hopefully she'd ring me tomorrow and tell me Val was fine. If she didn't, and it ended up that he was in real trouble . . .

Well then I reckoned I'd decide dead quick if I was a monster or not when I found the bastards responsible.

Avery didn't share the prince's optimism when I showed her the photo from the goblins' surveillance, and promptly burst into tears. Thankfully her Emma was there to comfort her, because I didn't have it in me to do it myself. Not that I was completely heartless, but I was still hurt that she had abandoned me when I needed her most.

I stayed long enough for a cup of tea – nature's cure-all – and for my sister to regain her composure. She sat across from me, her eyes and nose swollen and red, in a black corset, black shirt and black and white striped bloomers. It was an odd palette for her, much more my style.

"So what do we do now?" she asked me, voice low and nasal.

"We wait," I informed her. "If no one's heard from him by tomorrow night, I'll go poke around Freak Show and see what I can find out."

"If Penny doesn't know anything and she works there, how are you going to get information?"

I arched a brow – it was kind of an obnoxious habit. "Because I have a photo of the betties he left with. Someone might know who they are, or better yet, where I can find them."

She didn't quite meet my gaze. "I want to come with you." Realisation hit me between the eyes. This wasn't about Val; this was about Dede. Avery hadn't thought there was anything strange about Dede disappearing, so she was going full-on paranoid about Val.

I folded my arms and rested them on the tabletop. Countless times I'd sat at this table with her, but now I felt like a stranger in what had been my home for several years. "We don't even know that he's missing. If we both go around asking questions, we might do more harm than good. If he doesn't show up soon, you can follow up with Special Branch." That lot wouldn't confide anything to me now that I wasn't a halvie. "Say nothing to Vardan. And go have tea with Sayuri. Val might have told his mother what he was investigating. Then we'll know if we should worry."

"Why can't you talk to her? She's always preferred you over me."

If it weren't true I might have rolled my eyes at her petulant tone. "They won't let me in the courtesan house," I reminded her somewhat bitterly. "They'd never let a goblin close to the kids."

Avery visibly jerked. "But they've known you your entire life."

"Doesn't matter," I replied with a shake of my head. "I'm a goblin, Avery. A goblin who looks like a halvie, but still a gob. That changes things. Changes everything."

It was obvious from the furrow of her pale brow that this was something she hadn't considered. Avery was one of those self-absorbed types. It wouldn't have occurred to her that there would be prejudice against me – she was only concerned with what she believed I'd done to *her*. In her mind, and in her perfect little bubble of a world, everyone and everything was wonderful until she declared otherwise.

"I have his rotary. It's dead, but I'll charge it and see what's on there. I'll talk to Sayuri too."

"Thanks." I checked my pocket watch. It was after midnight. I'd only been up for eight hours, but it felt like an eternity. "I have to go. Vex is back tonight."

"Give him our best."

"I will." I rose to my feet. "I'll let you know what I find out. Ring me once you've talked to Sayuri or Special Branch."

"I could always come over," Avery suggested hesitantly. "Or you could come here."

A smile grabbed hold of my lips and yanked them upwards,

despite the day I'd had. "I'd like that." It might have been my imagination, but she looked relieved.

I didn't hug her as I left – I was still a little too fragile for that. I climbed on to the Butler once more and sped east to my little corner of Leicester Square, where humans still wandered about heedless of the dark, laughing and carrying on whilst enjoying the balmy summer night.

I steered the motorrad down the narrow alley between my building and the next and parked round the back. The lights weren't on, but I didn't need them. The ambient light was more than enough for me to see to unlock the door and step inside. I tossed my keys on the table and turned to address the alarm.

It had already been deactivated.

"I was wondering when you'd get back."

The familiar voice was a jolt straight to my heart – and my head. I'd been so preoccupied with my thoughts that I hadn't even noticed there was someone in my house! A very sexy someone, but it could easily have been someone else.

Vex MacLaughlin, alpha of Britain's wolves, was six-plus feet of brogue and muscle. He had dark wavy hair that was now just long enough that its natural curl was in danger of slipping out of control, and faded blue eyes that reflected a century and a half of living. He was at the hob, cooking up something that smelled like meaty heaven in my little kitchen that looked as though it hadn't been renoed in the last sixty years.

And he was wearing a black kilt with a white shirt tucked into it, and leather boots.

"You come straight from a caber toss?" I asked with a grin as I went to kiss him. His hand caught me behind the neck, holding me hostage as his mouth moved over mine. The man was a brilliant kisser, and for a few moments I didn't think of anything but how good he smelled and tasted.

"Actually I came from a wedding," he informed me. I'd missed the sound of his voice, and he'd only been gone a week. Most of the pack was in Scotland for the summer – safer during the longer daylight hours – and he tried to divide his time between London and there. He hadn't asked me to go with him yet, and I didn't blame him. It wasn't like I was his mate or anything.

I didn't ask about the pack. There were some who were giving him a hard time for being with me. And there were others who thought the goblins and wolves should join forces politically. There'd always been a little strife between vamps and weres, just as there had been between the Tories and Whigs of old.

"Is there enough for me?" I asked, peering at the pans on the stove. Sausages and eggs – all the protein a raw-meat-avoiding goblin could want.

"Of course." He watched me closely. "Don't you want to know about the wedding?"

I took a jar of almonds from the cupboard by my head and opened it. "Just because I'm a girl doesn't mean I'm wedding mad." Actually, I liked a wedding as much as the next girl, just not at that moment.

"Never said it did." He flipped the eggs. "It was two of my half-bloods. I performed the ceremony."

Ah, so that was why he wanted to talk about it. Half-blood unions had been frowned upon at one time because they could lead to aristocrat births that weren't of pure blood – or to goblins. Halvies had begun lobbying against them after the

Insurrection, but genetic screening had made it possible to assess the risk, and examine the foetus *in utero*.

"Big crowd?" I popped a couple of almonds into my mouth.

He didn't look up from putting sausages on to two plates. "Fair. Your sister was there."

All right, *this* was why he'd brought up the wedding, not societal politics. "Yeah?" I hadn't talked to Ophelia, my maternal sister, since I'd attacked and almost killed her. She had a fantastic way of pushing all my buttons.

"She asked about you." He plopped several over-easy eggs on both our plates. "Toast?"

"Of course. What did she ask?" I could pretend not to be interested, but what would that serve?

Vex switched the oven off before opening the door and removing a plate piled with toast. "Nothing specific – how you were, if you'd smacked Victoria in the mouth yet." He smiled. "I told her you kept your hands to yourself. She did say that she had some things of Dede's if you wanted them."

I frowned. "I thought they got rid of her things." It surprised me that they hadn't, even though keeping them was the polite thing to do. The humans and half-bloods hiding out at Bedlam weren't the first thing that came to mind when I thought of consideration.

He picked up our plates, so I took the toast and silverware and we sat down at the table – a small antique I'd moved in from the old pub room. "I think she hung on to them so you'd have an excuse to return to Bedlam."

Vex was the only person who knew that my mother, my sister and their insurrectionist friends practically lived in the Bethlehem Hospital for the Mentally Insane. It was the perfect hideout, where no one would think to look. My mother actually had a say in the running of the asylum as well. I'd seen some of the inmates, and she had my respect for taking a role in their care. Some of them had suffered horrible things.

"I won't be going back there for a while," I told him before attacking my food. The man knew how to cook. "I'm not ready."

I felt the weight of his gaze on me without looking up. "I know you're grieving, but those three words have become a regular part of your vocabulary of late."

Fork halfway to my mouth, I paused. "I know." I stuffed the egg and sausage into my mouth and chewed, then swallowed. "I realise I have to shit or get off the pot, but I have no idea how." Saying those words was like lifting an anvil off my shoulders.

"It doesn't all have to be done at once. One thing at a time." He took another piece of toast. "So, what did I miss while I was away?"

"Another rat was nailed to my door, but I found the kid. He says he was hired by an aristo to do it. And Val's dropped off the face of the planet."

Vex raised a brow. "Is he on an investigation?"

"Seems so, but the gobs got a photograph of him leaving Freak Show with two betties, and he left his rotary behind."

My wolf kept his expression neutral, but he had to know I was a little worried. "Has anyone checked it? A man like Val doesn't just forget his rotary, not unless he wants someone to find it."

"Avery said she'd charge it, but I haven't heard anything yet."

"I leave for a week and all hell breaks loose. Tell me everything."

So I did. I told him how I'd tracked the kid and what he'd said, and about Avery's visit and my trip to the plague den. Then I showed him the photo of Val and the betties.

"You need to take this to Special Branch," he said.

"I will, if I have to. Think you can do some sniffing around at some aristo functions for me? Maybe you can find out why someone wants to be a pain in my arse?"

Vex's expression was grim. He could look very intimidating when he wanted – it was sexy. "And if I find the bastard?"

Call me old-fashioned, but there was something romantic about the murderous glint in his eyes. I could always tell when his wolf was close to the surface, because his eyes took on a bit of a golden cast. "I'd like to talk to him and show him what I think of his piss-poor excuse for a sense of humour."

Vex nodded. One of the things I adored about him was he didn't go all chest-thumping on me and treat me like a delicate flower. I knew he'd rip apart anyone who tried to hurt me, but he'd give me first crack at it.

"Are you really going to wait until tomorrow to check up on Val?" he asked.

I wiped up egg yolk from my plate with a piece of toast. "He was last seen at Freak Show. Feel like going out?" It was the last thing I wanted to do. Tonight had already been one of the longest nights of my life and dawn was still several hours away. I was exhausted and wanted nothing more than to crawl into bed with Vex and rub naked bits. But Val's silence – and Avery's melodramatics – had my attention more than I liked.

I wasn't worried that he was dead. Not yet. First, he was a copper, which even a betty would think twice of ending. Second, if he *was* dead, we'd know, because when betties killed someone they either left the body in a high-traffic area where it was certain to be found and cause a stir, or tossed it to the goblins. Either scenario and I was going to hear about it.

And I'd tear the heart out of the chest of whoever had taken him. I might even eat it.

Churchill's heart in my hand, warm and still beating. Churchill's blood on my lips, coating my tongue. Warm sweetness sliding down my throat as my goblins ripped him apart. At least he had stopped screaming.

I swallowed. Hard. It wasn't guilt that had saliva flooding my mouth.

"Of course." Vex took a bite of sausage, seemingly unaware of what I was truly hungry for. "I don't want to poke a sore spot, but the goblins are going to want to know if you're ever going to wear that crown they gave you."

Made of an ancient skull affixed with metal and entwined with organic material, the crown looked like something a druid might have once worshipped. "I'm not ready for that either, but yeah. I know."

There was a glimmer of sympathy in his eyes, but it was a faint one. "Some things you'll never be ready for, sweetheart. You just have to do it. There are few people in this city – aristo or otherwise – who will tango with you when you have the gobs at your back."

"I know that."

"Hiding from it doesn't change the fact that you're one of them."

"Know that too." There was more bite to my words than I liked, but I couldn't hold it back.

Vex just chuckled. "Been thinking on it a wee bit, have you?"

I sighed and put down my silverware. "Second only to you."

"Nice to know I take precedence." He reached over and placed his much larger hand over mine. "It's going to be all right, love."

"You can't know that." I tried to pull my hand from his, but his fingers closed around mine like a vice – not painful, just firm. I could have forced it, but I didn't want to wrestle with him.

"You listen to me now," Vex said in that low growl of a voice that meant business. I went still, my gaze lifting to his. His eyes shone with a hint of gold, but I was more comforted than intimidated. "You make your decision and you stick to it. It will be all right because there's no other alternative. What isn't fine is jumping about like a skittish cat. Do you ken?"

I nodded. "Yes." He was completely right, of course. I always felt better once I put my mind to something. It was the indecision that made me hatters.

He smiled and gave my hand a squeeze. "I'll do whatever you need to help you figure it out, though I reckon you already know what you're going to do."

Was I that transparent? Or did he simply know me too bloody well? I opened my mouth to thank him, or perhaps whine a little, but the sound of the front doorbell echoed throughout the building.

Vex frowned. "Are you expecting anyone?"

I shook my head, already rising to my feet. "Not a soul."

I left the kitchen and walked down the corridor towards the front of the building, past the public room and the stairs leading to the upper floors. Vex slipped into the old bar and peered through the velvet curtains. When he came back to me in the hallway, he was frowning, but not in a murderous way.

He nodded at me, and I opened the door. Standing there in the narrow covered stairwell were two Special Branch officers. They weren't in uniform, but I knew a peeler when I saw one. They were halvies as well – all of Special Branch was. She had purple hair and his was dark green.

"Yes?" I asked as Vex came to stand behind me.

The female agent's brown eyes widened at the sight of the alpha. It was a typical reaction – he was unapologetically gorgeous. "Alexandra Vardan?" she asked, reluctantly dragging her gaze back to me.

I frowned and crossed my arms over my chest. "Quite."

She pulled her badge from inside her short, Mandarin-inspired jacket and flashed it at me. "I'm DI Cooke and this is DI Maine. Sorry for the inconvenience, but we'd like to ask you some questions."

"You couldn't call Her Majesty first?" Vex asked.

Cooke flushed. I fought the urge to shoot my wolf a rather pointed gaze. This was the first time I'd ever heard him refer to me with a royal title that wasn't a joke just between the two of us. There were so many things I could read into the remark, or wonder about it, that I chose to ignore any and all of it. Instead, I reached back, took his hand in mine and smiled at the officers.

"What about?"

"May we come in, ma'am?" she asked, in that tone that told me I really didn't have a choice. I might be a goblin, but I was still bound by the laws of the land. If I didn't cooperate, they could make my life very difficult, and it was already dodgy.

I summoned a false smile. "Of course." As they crossed my threshold, I couldn't help but ask, "Is this about my brother, Valentine Vardan?"

The male officer – Maine – shook his head. He had a solid, thick eyebrow that I reckoned he thought made him look stern. I thought it made him look like a puppet. "I'm afraid not ... Your Majesty. We're here to ask for your assistance in solving a rather high-profile murder."

I blinked, still holding the door wide open. "A murder? Whose?"

He turned suspicious dark eyes from studying my decor to me. "Lord Churchill's."

CHAPTER 4

OUT, OUT, DAMN SPOT

In some, panic inspires confession. In me it inspired the urge to rip the throats out of these two interlopers and suck the marrow from their bones.

Instead, I frowned. Tried to look innocent despite the metaphorical blood on my hands. "Murdered? I thought he left town."

"That certainly seems to be what someone wanted us to believe, ma'am," Maine informed me in a tone as flat as his gaze. "But new evidence leads us to believe Lord Churchill met a rather more sinister fate."

"Oh?" How indifferent I sounded. "What new evidence?"

Fang me, but it was as though the bastard could see right into my guilty soul with those suspicious eyes of his. "I'm not at liberty to discuss it."

"But you reckon I can help you in some way?"

Cooke answered this one. "We're told his lordship was last seen following you into the tunnels beneath Buckingham Palace."

"I suppose he could have," I lied. "I went straight to Yersinia. If Church did follow me into the tunnels, he didn't follow me there."

Cooke swallowed. "Yersinia. The goblin den?"

I nodded, resisting the urge to bare a little fang. If I intimidated them, it would make me look guilty – which I was, but they didn't know that. Or at least Cooke didn't.

"You're certain he didn't follow you?" Maine pushed. "You didn't see him, or hear him?"

I turned my head towards him. "I'm fairly certain I'd remember it if he had." Church hadn't followed me into the den. I'd dragged him into it.

"Ma'am, you should know that we've found evidence that suggests Lord Churchill was with you in those tunnels."

Fuck, fuck and fuck. "Church is an old family friend. He and I often spent time together. In fact, I spoke to him before the knighting ceremony." That was still a sore spot. I'd been about to be knighted for saving Queen V's life when the goblin prince interrupted and outed me as their queen.

"Was that before he killed your sister?" Maine asked.

Oh, I really wanted to eat him. I trembled with it. How dare he mention Dede's murder in such a practised, goading tone. Vex's hand came down on my shoulder, warm and calming. "Before," I replied coldly.

"It must have been horrible, seeing your sister cut down by a man of whom you thought quite highly."

"It was." I held his gaze.

"Personally, I might want revenge for something like that."

I arched a brow. "Perhaps you oughtn't to have chosen a vocation that requires you to carry a weapon."

"Did you come here to make accusations, DI Maine?" Vex

asked. "Because I'm sure you're aware that there are certain protocols involved in questioning a faction leader."

Maine's sharp gaze moved to Vex's. I noticed he had a slightly more difficult time holding the alpha's stare than he had mine. If only he knew which of us was the bigger monster. "But Lady Xandra isn't officially a faction leader, is she?"

I felt Vex stiffen, heard a low growl build in his throat. "Not yet," I said. Perhaps I had made my mind up more than I'd thought. "But if you want to ask me anything else, you can make arrangements for me to come down to the Yard. Meanwhile, please feel free to search the tunnels and Yersinia for any more 'evidence' of whatever it is you suspect me of having done."

Both inspectors paled, but Cooke was the one who surprised me. "Perhaps we will."

I smiled – a tight, pinched thing. "And now if you will please excuse me, I am still in mourning for my sister."

I could smell their shame. It wasn't enough. "Of course," Cooke replied. "Here's my card. Please ring if you think of anything that might be helpful in our investigation."

I plucked it from her fingers without looking at it, and stomped to the door. It took all my restraint not to rip it right off the hinges.

I wasn't afraid of these two, not really. They could make my life difficult, yes, but there was no way they were going to go into that den looking for Church. They wouldn't come out alive. The goblins didn't hold themselves to cobbleside law, and they would take such intrusion as an act of aggression unless an emissary was there to moderate things.

Besides, there was nothing left of Church to find. Even his belongings had been reduced to ash and scattered in the sewers. I didn't know what this "evidence" of theirs was, but it wasn't completely sound or they would have arrested me.

Cooke walked out first, but Maine paused on the threshold. "We all respect CI Vardan, but being his sister won't earn you any favours, right?"

I met his gaze. "Neither will respecting him."

For a second there was a glimmer of fear in his eyes. Delicious. Then it was gone and so was he, tramping down my steps with enough force to wake the dead. Cooke shot Vex an apologetic glance, but didn't bother looking at me. Cow. I shut the door – hard – and tossed her card on to the small table by the coat rack. Then I stomped into the bar and yanked back the curtain, watching the two of them until they got into their boxy motor carriage.

"Fucking brilliant," I muttered as I let the velvet drop. I rubbed my forehead and turned to find Vex leaning against the wall, arms folded over his chest. "Aren't you glad you came back?"

One corner of his lips tilted up as he lowered his arms. "Come here."

I went without hesitation, straight into his embrace. "If Val were here, he could find out what they have for evidence." One more reason I hoped he wasn't in trouble.

"It's not much," he said. I could feel the rumble of his voice where my head lay on his chest. "They wouldn't have left so quickly if they had anything concrete. They were just trying to throw you off. You did very well."

I snorted. "If you say so. I'm not going to Newgate for that bastard."

"You won't." He gave me a squeeze. "They won't brave the goblins."

"They braved coming here."

"Because they were told to."

I lifted my head to look him in the eye. "What are you saying?"

"You must be worried if you're not being paranoid." There was a touch of humour in his tone, but he was serious. I wasn't offended. I usually was quite paranoid. There was a stillness here that I'd never experienced before. I was a nocturnal creature, accustomed to living amongst others of my kind. The relative silence of the neighbourhood at this hour unsettled me. If I was honest, it was the humans who caused that silence that truly unnerved me. There were so many of them.

"Think about it. Who does Special Branch look out for?"

"Halvies and aristos," I replied easily, turning my mind from humans and their silence. As far as tests went, so far it was easy.

"And who do they answer to?"

"The PM."

"And?"

My shoulders slumped. How could I have been so dense? "Victoria."

He didn't give me a condescending look or pat me on the head. "It's the perfect way for her to fuck with you and keep her own hands clean."

Because I didn't have enough going on without the most powerful woman in the world out for my throat. "She might send them into the den."

Vex shook his head. "I've known her for a century and a half, and she's always been a decent strategist. She knows what's in her best interests, and risking war with the goblins isn't."

"But I am a goblin."

"Are you?" His blunt gaze locked with mine. "I thought that was one of those things you weren't ready to deal with."

Ouch. "Well played."

He didn't look the least bit sorry. "She wants you gone, and if you take that crown, you'll have power. Real power. I don't think you understand just how much."

He was right, I didn't. "Do you think I should take it then?" It mattered what he thought. I was two and twenty – older than Victoria was when she became queen – but I felt like a kid, young and frightened of the world.

Fortunately for me, I was a little like a rat when it came to fear. Back me into a corner and I'd claw and chew my way out.

"I think you should forget about the goblins and Her Nibs for the moment and concentrate on what's really important – making sure Val is safe. Let's go to Freak Show."

If I'd been tired before the peelers showed up, I was exhausted now. Still, I grabbed my key, made sure I had my dagger, and followed Vex out into the night. In a few hours the sky would begin to lighten and this neighbourhood would wake up, but right now, it was that damned quiet. Oh, there was the odd human stumbling about, but most of them were home, safely tucked up in their beds where night creatures couldn't prey upon them. Street lights and traffic lights seemed extra bright without the competition of passing head-lamps.

The night was just empty enough that I felt very insignificant and alone.

But I was neither of those things, I reminded myself as Vex opened the door to his vintage Sparrow motor carriage. It was silver and sleek, low to the ground, with tinted windows. I slid into the plush leather seat and leaned my head against the rest. He pressed a button on the front console and the engine roared to life.

We manoeuvred through the maze of narrow one-way streets and headed east towards Covent Garden. It wasn't very far from where I lived to the "neutral" territory where Freak Show and a host of other human- and aristo-friendly establishments did business.

"Do you believe that I didn't kill him?" I asked, tearing my gaze away from the passenger window.

Vex shot me a glance, but quickly returned his attention to the road. "I don't care if you did or not."

"Yes, but what do you *believe*?" Suddenly it was very important to me to hear the answer.

His lips twisted. "I didn't get to be alpha by being obtuse, sweetheart. I know you led him into that den knowing exactly what was going to happen. You'd never be free of him if you hadn't."

I was never going to be free of him as it was. But it was done and there was no point poking at the wound any longer. I didn't regret bringing on Church's demise. I regretted losing the man I'd adored when I was growing up. That man never would have put a silver tetracycline bullet into Dede.

The memory of my sister coughing up blood as she died on the ground in front of Buckingham Palace was enough to wipe away my guilt. I held on to that memory just long enough for rage to pull my head out of my arse.

Vex must have interpreted my silence as something else, because he glanced at me again, concern etched in his rugged features. "My hands aren't clean either. I'd be the last to judge you for doing what needed to be done."

I smiled a little. "Thanks." He was right, of course. The only thing I should regret about killing Church was that I hadn't done it before he could shoot Dede. Then again, murdering my sister was what had pushed me over the edge.

I consoled myself by thinking that Dede was in a better place. This world was too cruel for my fragile sister.

Freak Show stood on the site of an old theatre from the Regency period. The outside had been remodelled to resemble a circus tent, complete with old-style sideshow posters featuring staff and performers. As usual, there was a queue to get inside, even though it was the middle of the week. Before all this shit I would have just flashed my RG badge and bypassed the line. I didn't have that luxury any more. Fortunately, I had infamy and Vex, both of which were better than a laminated card with a bad photo on it.

The halvie at the door was dressed in a burlesque version of a ringmaster's costume, with her white hair cascading down her back in a mass of ringlets. Her heavily lined and lashed eyes widened at the sight of the two of us. She bowed – more to Vex than to me – and lifted the velvet rope so that we could go right in. I tried to ignore the murmurs of those waiting in the queue. I don't think it was egomaniacal to think people were talking about me when they actually were.

The music that had been a muted thumping outside turned into a full-fledged audio assault inside. More show posters and art filled the dim interior. The furniture was a mix of Baroque and Georgian, with bar stools that resembled delicate French chairs.

The skeleton of Joseph Merrick stood by the bar, encased in a protective glass case fitted with tiny lights to accentuate the deformation of the bones. Poor bugger. It wasn't the only skeleton on display; there was also that of a giant named Black Angus, who in life had been almost eight feet tall and perfectly proportioned, plus a skeleton of conjoined female twins, along with a photograph of them in life, and the bones of a "mermaid" found off the coast of Scotland one hundred and thirty years ago. To me it looked like someone had attached fish bones to a woman's torso, but that was part of the appeal, I reckoned.

On the centre stage of the club, surrounded by tables full of gawkers imbibing copious amounts of drink, a man and a woman performed amazing feats of body strength and control under the coloured lights. They seemed to entwine with one another with carefully controlled grace, supporting – in turn – their own weight and their partner's as they continuously moved, held, moved. I stopped for a moment to watch. For one blissful moment I didn't wonder if people were staring at me.

"Xandra!"

I winced. The cry had come at the end of the music, just before the audience could applaud for the duo on stage. At least fifty per cent of the heads in the club turned in my direction – including the contortionists. Fortunately, I was with Vex, and he always drew stares of his own.

I couldn't resent the person who had shouted my name. It was Val's maternal sibling Penelope, born Takeshi, otherwise known as Penny Dreadful, the most fabulous personage in all of London town. She was a tiny little thing, but in her outrageous heels she was my height, clad in a bright orange mini dress with an Elizabethan collar, purple fishnet stockings and a chartreuse beehive wig that framed her pretty face with garish ringlets. Only Penny could make such an ensemble work.

She hurried towards me with preternatural speed and grace. Penny was a halvie. She could have been a Royal Guard, but she'd decided her talents were better suited elsewhere. Plus, even in these enlightened days, there were those who didn't take well to girls trapped in boys' bodies, or vice versa.

Huge false eyelashes lifted to reveal blue contacts, but there was nothing artificial about the worry in her expression. "Did Avery speak to you?" she asked, grabbing my hand in hers.

I nodded. That she didn't flirt with Vex told me she was actually concerned. A flutter of anxiety tickled my stomach. Maybe Val really was in trouble. "Can you take a break?"

Penny grabbed the arm of a passing pink-haired boy dressed in jodhpurs, riding boots and a purple frock coat. I heard her ask him to cover for her for a few minutes. He cast a quick glance at me and Vex and nodded.

We followed her to the back of the club and up a set of stairs to the office, which looked exactly as it ought as the inner sanctum of a circus-style nightclub, with old posters pinned to the walls and bits of oddities scattered about. It smelled of coffee, with a faint trace of cigarette smoke. Penny closed the door, reducing the noise floating up from downstairs.

Then she promptly burst into tears.

Vex and I turned to one another, wide-eyed. It was obvious he wasn't going to be the one to comfort her, so the task fell to me. I put my arms around Penny and patted her narrow back. "It's all right, love."

Penny pushed out of my arms. Mascara ran down her cheeks, but no more tears sprang from her eyes. Her face was a mask of guilt and grief. "You don't understand. Val was taken because of me."

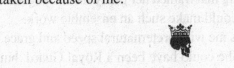

"Right," I said a few minutes later, as Penny dabbed at her cheeks with the handkerchief Vex had given her. Who even knew that men still carried such things? "Why do you think Val's been abducted? And how could it be your fault?"

She was perched on the desk, shapely legs crossed, looking dejected and lost. "Because it is. They never would have taken him if I hadn't got him involved."

I loved Penny as much as I was capable of loving another woman who wasn't family, but I was precariously close to slapping her silly. Why couldn't she just come out with it? "Involved in what?" I asked. My teeth were clenched. Vex nudged me with the toe of his boot, gave me a look that told me to take it down a notch. I sucked in a breath.

Penny sighed – rather exaggeratedly, I thought, but then I was hungry and peevish. And I was starting to worry about my big brother, who I had always thought of as somewhat invincible.

"Start from the beginning, love," Vex encouraged gently, leaning against the desk so that they were shoulder to shoulder. His voice was low, yet it filled the room with rich warmth that sucked the bitterness right out of me.

He seemed to have the same effect on Penny's inherent drama. She drew a breath, straightened her shoulders and looked me dead in the eye. She reminded me of Sayuri, her mother. "Do you remember after Dede disappeared I told you about other halvies who had gone missing from here?"

I did remember. "I was going to look into it, but I got ... well, rather caught up in my own shit." Fang me, today was turning out to be one of those days where I found it astounding I had any friends at all.

Penny nodded. "You do have a lot of shit, darling. Besides,

what could you do about it? I began keeping a list of people who disappeared, suspicious behaviour, all that kind of stuff you see on the box, right? Last week, this bloke I fancied asked me out for coffee after we closed. When I went outside to meet him, I saw him being hauled off by a couple of betties. I ran after them but they tossed him into a motor carriage and tore off."

"Two bad you didn't catch them." I meant it. Penny was a bit of a stereotype when it came to Japanese heritage and martial arts. She and Val were both extremely skilled fighters. She once kicked the snot out of me at the Academy, my old boyfriend Rye as well. But then Rye went on to break her records and I broke his.

Now that I thought about it, my records at the Academy probably wouldn't stand any more. After all, I wasn't really a halvie. Bloody hell, that hurt more than being kicked out of the RG.

"I would have fucked them up," Penny allowed. "I didn't know what else to do, so I called Val. I figured he could look into it – you know, check the number on the carriage plate and all that. I told him about the others and gave him all my notes. He told me he was going to start an investigation. The other night he came by to talk to me about what he'd found. When I went to meet him, he was gone, but his rotary was on the bar. I knew they'd taken him as well."

I cast a glance at Vex. He looked as worried as I felt. Val had been on a case. Whether or not it was official was another story. Had he gone willingly with those betties, or was he a prisoner? I found it hard to believe he'd let them take him without a fight. "Do you still have those notes?" I asked.

She nodded. Her wig bobbed. "I have copies at my flat."

I ran a hand through my hair. "You're taking the rest of the night off. The rest of the week maybe. And you're going to come and stay with me."

She looked horrified. "I can't do that! I need to work."

"Dearest, if your suspicions are correct, these people probably know exactly where Val got his information. I really don't want them coming for you next."

"I'll stay with you, but I'm not going to stop working. If they come back, I want to be here."

And do what, beat them into submission with her shoe? Penny was a scrapper, but she also dressed in clothing totally unsuited to fighting. Even I dressed for movement better than she did. Hell, Avery wore clothes more comfortable than Penny did.

"We'll figure something out," I allowed. "Come on. Go and tell your boss you're not feeling well." Her make-up was just enough of a mess that the manager would no doubt believe her.

"He's downstairs," she said, and reluctantly left the office to do as I instructed.

As we moved to follow, Vex stopped me. "Do you know what you're doing?"

"Not a farking clue," I replied. "But we need to see those notes, and if Penny's right, she needs to be protected. If those betties grabbed a Yard chief inspector who just happens to be the son of a duke, they'll have no qualms about taking a tranny whose father was a viscount."

His jaw clenched. I knew what he was thinking. Years ago Vex had had a relationship with a human woman who became pregnant. She was also a plague carrier. Their son, Duncan, had looked like a normal half-blood but could actually transform into a wolf like a were. He'd been abducted, tortured and killed in a brutal fashion. Vex never did find out who was behind it, though he suspected Church might have been involved.

I didn't say anything. I had no idea what words could possibly make him feel any better. I had no idea what it was like to lose a child. Losing a sibling had been bad enough. It was still bad. I reached out and took his hand, and held it all the way downstairs while we waited for Penny.

My gaze drifted back to the stage where the couple from earlier had been replaced by an Amazonian burlesque dancer who made me feel like a poor example of womanhood. Fang me, but she was all boobs and bum, with a tiny waist and enough feathers for six ostriches.

I opened my mouth.

"No," said Vex. It was nice to see genuine amusement in his face.

"You don't even know what I was going to ask."

"No, I don't wish you were built like her, and no, you don't need a pair of rhinestone pasties. However, I have no objection whatsoever to you doing a little fan dance for me sometime."

I grinned. "Okay, so you do know what I was going to ask."

He chuckled, slipped an arm around my shoulders and gave me a squeeze and a kiss on the forehead. For a few moments there were no thoughts of his murdered son, or the trouble Val might be in, or the fact that I had landed on Queen Victoria's shit list. That little bit of laughter made me think that everything just might be all right. Or at least it kept me from dwelling on the alternative.

Penny joined us a few moments later. She had a light cape and her handbag. "I'm ready."

We walked out into the waning night. There were still a

handful of hours of darkness left, and I for one would be glad to see the arse end of them. I needed sleep – a few hours of blissful oblivion.

The valet brought Vex's Swallow round. Penny climbed in the back seat and gave Vex directions to her flat. She lived in Soho, a neighbourhood friendly to halvies and humans alike, made up of predominantly artsy types who didn't care who you slept with or what sex you were so long as you weren't a bigot or boring.

The building had been put up within the last five years, part of the "new Gothic" movement that took elements from the previous century and made them light and airy as opposed to dark and dreary. Red brick and dark pointed spires with lots of windows made of bevelled glass.

We parked at a pay post in the street. As we walked to the front door, I had that slightly prickly feeling on the back of my neck – like we were being watched. I'd left my pistol at home, and I cursed myself for it.

I glanced over my shoulder as Penny fumbled with her keys, gaze sweeping up and down the street, searching the shadows. Nothing. Not even a neighbour watching from a window. So why did I feel so naked?

The door opened and Penny entered the building. Vex nudged me to follow. "It's fine," he murmured in my ear as I passed him. "Nothing smells wrong."

Scenting the air was exactly what I should have been doing, but I had forgotten just how incredible my sense of smell was now; it was one of those things you could ignore if you knew how. Still, I felt like a fucking rube. I was a freaking goblin – I should be the one determining if things smelled safe.

We followed Penny across the panelled foyer to the lift, and went up three floors before stepping out. Her flat was at the end of the corridor.

"My flatmate's still at work," she said, slipping her key into the lock.

The door swung open before she turned the knob. She froze on the threshold, mouth dropping open. I shoved her aside, every instinct I had screaming that something was very, very wrong.

I smelled copper.

"Fucking hell," Vex muttered, as we both looked inside.

The place had been trashed – quite literally ripped apart. But that wasn't the worst of it. Penny's flatmate wasn't at work – she was on the floor, face down in a puddle of blood.

Fucking hell indeed.

CHAPTER 5

DESPAIR IS OFTEN ONLY THE PAINFUL EAGERNESS OF UNFED HOPE

All that blood.

Thick, and so dark it was cherry-black in the lamplight. The copper-sweet scent went straight to my head. My vision narrowed, obliterating everything but the still body on the floor.

Meat. And I was so fucking hungry.

I crossed the threshold first, Vex at my heels, and went straight for the girl, dropping to my knees beside her slight still body. Glistening darkness matted her light blue hair. Her face was turned toward me, eyes closed. So pale. Pretty little thing. She smelled so good. The blood seemed to have come from her nose and a shallow cut above her right eyebrow.

"Is she alive?" Penny's voice was shrill, cutting through the fog in my brain.

Alive? I didn't know. I almost hoped she wasn't. She wouldn't miss a little bite . . .

"Xandra."

I lowered my head, closing the distance between my salivating mouth and that delectable little throat. Just a bite . . .

"*Xandra!*"

I snapped up straight, as though pulled by invisible strings. Clarity returned, razor sharp.

Albert's fangs. I'd been about to eat this poor girl, and she *wasn't* dead. I could see her back rise with every little breath. "She's alive," I rasped, stomach rolling.

"Oh, thank the fucking universe." Penny practically cheered. She and Vex lifted the now stirring girl and helped her to the sofa. I stared at the blood on the floor. It mesmerised me, called to me. I glanced at my companions. Penny had found tissues to wipe the girl's face, and they were cleaning her up, taking stock of her injuries and condition – asking her questions. They were paying me no attention whatsoever.

I gave in to the temptation. It was too great. Hunger pressed at the bones of my face. If I didn't do something, I was going to gob out, and poor Penny and her friend had been through enough trauma for one night.

Palms braced on either side of the puddle, I lowered my torso. My tongue shot out and I dragged the flat of it through the thickest part, lapping up cooling, sticky blood like a cat at a saucer of cream. The floorboards were rough, but a splinter was the last thing on my mind.

I had to force myself to stop. The cramping in my stomach had stopped, replaced by a warm contentment – very similar to that of a nice toddy. I rolled up to my feet feeling strong and light.

"We need to get her to hospital," I said, crossing into the living area. The entire flat looked like a dressing room for a burlesque troupe. I'd never seen a lampshade made out of a corset before, nor so many different shades of pink. The girl sat on the sofa – a deep fuchsia – with her head tilted back and a tissue to her nose. Her head wound had stopped bleeding.

Vex turned his head when I came to stand beside him. His brows drew together.

"What?" I asked.

He lifted a hand and wiped the pad of his thumb across the tip of my nose. It came away smeared with blood.

"Oh, fuck." I swiped the rest away with the back of my hand.

Vex didn't say a word. He simply pulled his rotary from a pocket in his kilt and dialled 999. He told the operator what we'd found and gave the address before hanging up.

"What happened?" I asked. I stared at the girl whose blood I'd just licked up, but whose name I didn't know.

"Betties," Vex replied. "She says there were two of them. They told her to give them the file, but she didn't know what they were talking about. They began to trash the place. When she tried to stop them, they punched her."

"They have to be the same ones that took Val." Penny gave voice to what I'd already thought. Shit. Val *was* in trouble. Ginormous trouble. Did Special Branch know what he was up to? If he'd been investigating the disappearances at Freak Show out of concern for Penny, then his superiors would have no more idea than I did of where to look for him.

"Go and find those notes, love," Vex urged as Penny fussed over her friend.

"Do you think that's what they were here for?" I asked, glancing anywhere but at the girl who I'd looked at as a snack just a few minutes ago. The wireless controller for the box was

on the coffee table. Someone had covered the thing in rhine-
stones.

"Perhaps. I think they were hoping Penny was at home."
What he didn't say, but we both understood, was that Penny
wouldn't have got off as lightly as her flatmate.

I expected Penny to return empty-handed, but she emerged
from the other room with a leather portfolio in her hands. Her
face was pale and fear rolled off her like a tangible thing. I
wanted to hug her, but I didn't trust myself, not after lapping
blood off the floor.

Vex took the portfolio from her and set it on the coffee
table. "Xandra, put the kettle on, will you? Penny, why don't
you get some cloths and water so we can clean Samantha up."

How the hell did he know the girl's name? He must have
learned that while I was ... busy. I dutifully went to the
kitchen. It was the best place for me at that moment, regardless of the fact that I resented being ordered about like a child
or a puppy.

I could hear them talking in the other room. Vex asked
Samantha if she could remember anything else about what had
happened, to which she replied that she'd heard a noise and
got out of bed, thinking it was Penny, but instead it was a
couple of betties. That was all she remembered. She was lucky
they hadn't killed her, or decided to have a little sport with her
while she was unconscious. It probably wasn't luck at all,
though. It was probably more a case of the betties being sent
here for something or someone specific – like Penny and her
notes on halvie disappearances. Given the circumstances, that
was a logical assumption.

By the time I had tea made, Special Branch had shown up.
Thankfully it wasn't Cooke and Maine. Also fortunately, the

inspectors didn't seem terribly keen on talking to me, so I let Vex handle them. I hung back in the tiny dining room and sipped my tea, watching and trying not to think about what those betties might be doing to my brother.

Vex never mentioned Penny's notes on the disappearances from Freak Show. He let the inspectors think this was nothing more than a botched robbery. We just happened to be at the club enquiring after Val when Penny took ill, and we offered to drive her home.

Bless us.

He also omitted the bit about suspecting the betties of being the ones in the photo with Val, and that was a good thing. If the Yard went after the betties now, Val would be killed for certain.

By the time the medics had taken Samantha away, the peelers had left and Penny had packed her bags, dawn was breaking, and I was so tired my normally charming disposition wasn't so charming any more. I was eyeing the congealed blood on the floor like it might be good on ice cream, disgusting as that was. I was going to have to do something about this hunger. It wasn't unusual for me to eat a lot, with my raging metabolism, but this craving for blood and for meat was getting out of control. Eventually I was going to go hatters from it and seriously hurt someone, because licking blood off a floor wasn't as low as I could get.

The three of us drove back to my place in relative silence. When we went inside, I took Penny to the guest room to get settled. Poor thing was pale, and her make-up was wearing off.

"You okay, dearest?" I asked, setting the smallest of her suitcases on the bed.

She nodded. "I wouldn't be if Sam wasn't going to be all

right, but at least now I know there really is something going on."

I knew that feeling, that dread-wrapped relief that came when you realised that you were right and things really were as shit as you thought they were.

"Penny, the missing halvies. Have any of them turned up dead that you know of?"

She shook her head, and reached up to remove her wig. It was a little shocking to see her standing there with a nylon cap on her head rather than a huge head of hair. All of a sudden she was like an actor after final bows.

"Doesn't mean anything," she said. "We both know bodies tossed to the goblins will never be found."

"That won't happen to Val." The gobs had come to me once after someone had dumped a friend of mine in their tunnels, I was sure they'd do the same if Val was left as an offering.

God, I couldn't think about my brother being ripped apart like Churchill.

Penny began peeling off her false eyelashes. "Are you really their queen?"

"They want me to be." I was too tired to discuss it. "You should get some rest. We'll talk tomorrow." I wanted to look over her notes as well, but more importantly I needed to sleep. I was no good to her or Val the way I was right now.

Penny hugged me. I gave her a good squeeze before leaving her to go to my own room.

When I walked in, Penny's portfolio was on my bedside table and Vex stood beside the bed unbuttoning his shirt.

"How is she?" he asked, voice low.

"Better than you might expect," I replied, pushing his hands out of the way so I could finish opening the buttons for him.

I enjoyed undressing him – there was a comfortable intimacy to the act.

"How are you?" He shrugged out of the shirt.

I chuckled and began divesting myself of my own kit. "Knackered. Fucked up. I licked that girl's blood off the floor, Vex."

He nodded, expression unperturbed. One of the things I loved about Vex was the way he seemed to accept me just as I was. "You're a goblin, Xandra. You need to start eating like one. And don't say you're not ready."

I closed my mouth. That was exactly what I'd been about to say. "Can we talk about this later? The last twelve hours have kicked my arse."

He didn't argue. I'd known he wouldn't. Vex was alpha for many reasons, his patience being one of them. He knew when to push and when not to, just as I knew that he wouldn't let me off that easily.

I washed my face and brushed my teeth before falling into bed. Vex was already between the sheets in the dark. He pulled me into his arms, our naked limbs entwining. He kissed me, and a few minutes later I wasn't so exhausted any more – not that I needed that much energy as Vex did all the work. All I had to do was try to be quiet so as not to traumatise Penny.

Afterward, my muscles and bones felt like they were made of lovely lead. Vex gathered me close and I buried my face in his shoulder, letting sleep come for me.

I dreamed of the goblin lair, of sitting around a fire in the flickering torchlight as gobs presented me with meat. I saw Church's face in the flames – pale in death, with unseeing eyes. I didn't protest when the goblins fell on his corpse. Then he turned into Val and the prince offered me his heart. I took it just as I had Churchill's, and sank my teeth in for a big juicy bite.

I wish I could say I woke up screaming, but I didn't. I didn't wake up at all.

Penny's notes went back almost six months. The first entries were in point form, pages from a calendar: "23 February – Jacob, sword swallower, never showed for work." Then, a fortnight later, "Still no sign of Jacob. No one has heard from him. Flat empty."

Around March and April she began keeping more detailed accountings. There were three disappearances in March, each on a different night of the week, but all three busy nights. The three were all patrons, and according to Penny, the kind of person that wasn't likely to be terribly missed. The Prometheus protein could lurk unnoticed in regular humans; that was what made courtesans so popular with aristocratic men. Sometimes aristos did the nasty with humans who weren't courtesans and didn't know they were carriers, and that was when these unexpected halvies were born. Often they were ostracised from their human families and left to their own devices once the social system was done with them. A few made it into the Academy, but many did not.

"Four disappearances in April," I remarked aloud when Vex refilled my coffee mug with French roast. "Albert's fangs, did no one notice?" It's not like half-bloods are so numerous.

"Penny did," he commented, sitting down at the table.

I looked up and met his gaze. "Besides Penny. Why didn't the rags run this?"

"People disappear all the time, Xandra. Four halvies in April, God knows how many humans. It only makes the papers when there are bones to be picked clean." He didn't like the press.

A bitter taste rose in the back of my throat. "I suppose they'd blame the goblins." But goblins wouldn't nab a halvie – it was against the treaty, and goblins had more honour than I would have given them credit for two and a half months ago. If a body was tossed into the tunnels, the goblins considered it carrion and the treaty didn't apply. It was only because they'd scented me on the corpse that my friend Simon's death became public at all. If not for the goblins' loyalty, he'd just be one of the missing.

"There are more monsters out there than just goblins. Humans torture and kill their own all the time. I'm not saying it's right, just that missing doesn't make a story."

"Some people run away," I murmured, thinking of Dede. "Some disappear because they don't want to be found."

"Do you really think that's the case with Freak Show?"

I shook my head. "No. It would help if we knew if there was anything special about these halvies."

Vex went still. "You mean like you. Like Duncan."

I nodded. I knew it pained him to talk about his son, so I wasn't going to dwell. "I'll have to talk to Penny. Maybe she remembers something she didn't write down."

My wolf frowned. "Special would mean these abductions aren't random."

I dumped sugar into my cup. A lot of it. "Val's certainly wasn't." I stirred my creamy coffee. "I should have taken all those files in Church's safe." He'd had a stack of folders on "different" halvies. One of those files was mine, and that had been my main concern when I broke into my dead mentor's office.

"You reckon his safe's been cleaned out?"

I shrugged. "Probably, but it wouldn't hurt to check, I suppose." Fang me, even from beyond the grave Church wouldn't let go of me.

"One of us should talk to Ophelia." From the tone of his voice, I knew which one of us he thought that should be. My half-sister had been abducted and experimented on, and she had a number tattooed on her arm to prove it. Our mother had rescued her from a facility.

A splinter of fear dug into my insides. If the people who took Ophelia, Val and Duncan were the same, then they were the sort who would love to get their hands on a goblin who could walk in the sun and looked like a half-blood.

What the fuck was I getting myself into? How much danger would looking for Val bring down on my head? How long before I was a target?

It didn't matter. The danger to me was irrelevant. I wasn't trying to be a hero; I simply couldn't live with myself if I didn't do everything I could to bring my brother home safely. I had failed Dede. I could not fail Val.

"I'll talk to Ophelia," I said. Hadn't she extended an invitation anyway? And if she could help me find Val, then I'd gladly apologise for almost killing her. "I'll ring her in a bit."

Penny shuffled into the room clad in a purple silk kimono and slippers, her short dark hair mussed and not a lick of make-up on her flawless skin. She was female to me and had been for years, so it was odd to see her with stubble, faint as it was.

"Good morning, sunshine," I quipped.

She smiled – it was tired but genuine. "It's not fair that you look so gorgeous without a face on. Morning, sexy." The last was directed at Vex.

He grinned and poured her a cup of coffee.

"There's French toast and sausage in the oven," I told her.

"You two certainly know how to treat a girl."

I waited until she was at the table and had eaten the better part of her plateful before asking her if she could remember anything unusual about the missing halvies.

"They didn't have any special powers or horns growing out of their heads," she replied, sitting back and crossing her legs. "At least nothing that I ever noticed, but then I never thought there was anything unusual about you, ducks. No offence."

"None taken," I assured her. I'd never known there was anything off about me either. Not really. Though the things I had noticed made perfect sense now that I knew the truth.

"Although …" Her brow puckered, but immediately smoothed again. She rubbed at her skin as though she could smooth out any wrinkling the expression might have caused.

"What?" I prodded when she didn't immediately go on.

"The two of you know about the private rooms at the club?" I got the impression this was something she could get into trouble for telling us about if we didn't already know.

I nodded. "I've seen the one where you can spy on aristos feeding. Vex has seen it too." Though he'd assured me that he'd never been on the other side of the glass.

Penny sagged in relief. "Several of them participated in the … entertainment. Aristos will pay good money to a halvie for a tickle and a pint."

She didn't mean beer. "Blood whores?" A crass term, but succinct.

"Not on a professional level," she replied. "It happens a fair bit – aristos see someone they like the look of and offer them compensation for opening a vein. They rarely take the same person twice."

I turned to Vex, my gaze locking with his. Sometimes a person's blood tasted different depending on diet, species, etc. It could be that the aristos were doing a little taste test to see if the halvies were unusual. It was a bit of a stretch, though. It would make more sense to take blood samples and send them to a lab for testing. It was what I had done with my own blood, and what had got Simon killed.

"A couple of them were related," Penny added. "If I remember correctly, there were at least two sisters taken, and another pair were brother and sister."

Vex glanced at me. "That supports your theory that these are unusual halvies."

It certainly did. Genetics was a grand thing.

I frowned. My maternal sister had been experimented on. My paternal sister had given birth to a fully plagued child. I was a goblin.

The blood rushed from my face.

"Xandra?" Vex frowned. "What is it?"

"What if Val wasn't taken just because he stuck his nose in where he oughtn't?"

His mouth tightened. "This is not because of you."

"No," I agreed. I didn't feel the need to shoulder this particular responsibility. "But it might be because of my genes. What if Ophelia was taken because our mother was turned into a were?"

"Your mother was what?" Penny demanded, wide-eyed.

"My mother was bitten when she was pregnant with me.

The change took. That's how I became a goblin – because she was special even for a courtesan. Dede said someone had come for her before she went into Bedlam." I didn't mention her baby. That wasn't something Penny needed to know. "Clearly some interesting genes run in both sides of my family, so maybe Val was taken to see if the pattern held true."

"If that's the case, why haven't they nabbed you?" Penny asked.

"Church had plans for me," I told her flatly. "I reckon I'm a little too high-profile for them. People are going to notice if I go missing. It would be in all the rags."

"Val's a copper. Isn't that high-profile too?"

"Cops go undercover. Sometimes they go missing. Sometimes . . ." I stopped.

"They die," Penny finished, saying the words I couldn't. "How much time does he have?"

"I don't know." I hated feeling this helpless. "Depends on how useful he is."

Tears filled her dark eyes. "We have to find him, Xandra."

I reached out and put my hand over hers on the tabletop. "We will." Val's disappearance might not have been my responsibility, but finding him was.

I just hoped that when that moment came, it wasn't in a goblin tunnel.

CHAPTER 6

KNOW THYSELF; KNOW THINE ENEMY

While in the Wellington Academy for Half-Blood Education, all students have a small tracking chip injected beneath their skin. This is, we're told, for our own safety. It's nothing quite that simple. It's an intrusion into our privacy, a way to keep tabs. However, it could also be quite useful in times of danger.

I'd had my chip cut out of me shortly after Church's death, and then I personally destroyed it. Right now, I was hoping that the people who had taken Val hadn't decided to do the same thing. It was a slim hope, but all I had at that moment. I'd called the Yard, but they refused to give me details on Val's case, or confirm that he was even on one that involved Freak Show.

Had my brother been poking about off the books? Maybe Special Branch didn't know any more about it than I did. I'd curse Val for endangering himself with a secret investigation, but even I was aware of just how pot vs kettle that would be.

Penny had a friend who was something of a techno-genius. Once she had dressed for the day – it took two hours for her to get ready – she climbed on the back of the Butler with me and we went to visit this friend while Vex took care of some pack business. I had called Ophelia and set up a meeting for later that night, so Vex decided he'd go to one of his clubs that evening and see if he could get information out of any of his cronies who took advantage of the feeding opportunities at Freak Show.

He also had the horrible suggestion that he look into whether or not there'd been an increase in horror shows here or abroad. I refused to think of my brother being bled and fed on to death on a stage for the enjoyment of a bunch of sick aristos. I didn't mention it to Penny either.

If I thought Avery a living doll, Penny was even worse. Her off-hours kit was a purple and green confection of ruffles and bows with a snug satin corset and high lavender boots that laced up the front and had bows down the back. In black and white striped trousers, black boots, white shirt and black corset, I felt positively plebeian next to her.

She had a parasol too – sunset wasn't for another three hours – but knew better than to put it up while the motorrad was in motion. The goggles I gave her pouffed up her blonde wig, but would help keep the false hair in place as we weaved in and out of traffic.

Her friend Lester lived near Covent Garden, in a brown brick and cream stucco building with a shop on the ground floor. I found a pay post for the Butler nearby, and slipped my goggles on to the top of my head once the Butler was stable. "Is that him looking out the window?"

Penny glanced up to where a sliver of a face peeked from between a narrow opening in the shabby curtains. She waved. "It is." The curtains jerked closed. "He's such a knob."

I didn't care what he was. He could spend the entire visit in a cupboard if he wanted, just so long as he could get a fix on Val's signal.

We entered the building through a narrow door and climbed a creaking set of equally narrow stairs to the first floor. The hall was dim, with a slant of sunlight through one window, catching dust particles. The place smelled of old age and mothballs.

A worn rug covered the dip in the floorboards in front of a door numbered 1A. Penny sashayed right up and rapped her rings against the wood. "Lester, darling, it's Penny. Do open up."

There followed the thunk of a deadbolt and the slide of a chain lock. The door opened a fraction, revealing a dark eye with a rather wild look about it set in a pale face. The eye shifted from Penny to me and back to Penny. Lester closed the door again, released the chain lock, then opened the door completely. "Come in."

I arched a brow as I crossed the threshold, unsure of what to expect when I stepped inside. A cross between a museum back room and a bird's nest, perhaps? Instead, I discovered myself standing on a freshly scrubbed floor in a space as sterile and tidy as an operating theatre. Everything was old and worn, but spotless. Paranoid and obsessive-compulsive. Wonderful combination.

I sneezed. Industrial cleaners were hellish on a nose as sensitive as mine.

Lester was watching me narrowly. He was a little man – shorter than my five foot seven – thin, with a thick head of curly dark hair that desperately needed to be cut. He wore a pair of khaki trousers with a crisp pleat and a starched white shirt, and highly polished oxfords.

He was human.

"I know you," he said. His voice was nasal, as though he had a cold. It was probably the fucking cleaning chemicals. Fang me, did he have a sense of smell at all? "You're the fucking goblin."

The? "Is that a problem?" My spine straightened.

"Of course not," Penny answered, looking from me to her friend. "Is it, Lester old chum?" Dear Penny, she knew I'd cheerfully chew off his face and spit it back at him.

He crossed his arms over his skinny chest with a petulant sniff. "I don't like goblins."

"That's too bad, because I bloody love humans," I shot back with a grin. "'Specially on toast."

He jerked back as though I'd pushed him. Penny shot me a filthy look. "No, she doesn't. Lester, don't be rude. We're here for five minutes of your time and we can pay you for it."

"Is it for her?" He jerked his chin towards me. I kept smiling. Really, he wasn't worth baiting, but I couldn't seem to help myself. Childish, I know.

"No, it's for me. My brother's gone missing and I need you to see if his tracker's still online."

That sucked some of the snark out of the little bastard. "Val?"

I wanted to ask how he knew Val, but keeping my mouth shut was probably the best course of action now if Lester was going to help us. Penny nodded. Her glossy lips were tight.

"Will you check?"

"Of course, Pen. Of course." Now that he was dancing to a new tune, Lester led us into his inner sanctum, which was a second bedroom with several desks crammed with logic engines. All of them were powered on. Some were running programs; others were waiting to be used, while the remainder were parked on individual aethernet sites.

Lester sat down in a chair with casters on the bottom and pushed himself across the polished floor to the opposite wall of machines. He situated himself in front of a keyboard and began typing. The screen changed, bringing up a search bar.

It was the SI-5 secure site. Fang me. Lester really did know what he was doing. SI-5 dealt with military security and intelligence for all of Britain. They didn't care if you had plagued blood or not; their concern was protecting the kingdom from enemies within and abroad. Just last year they'd broken up an American spy ring.

How the hell could he get into a government site so easily? I had been Royal Guard and I couldn't have got anywhere near it if I was given six months and a map.

"What's the transmitter serial?" Lester asked.

Penny pulled a slip of paper from her handbag, which matched her shoes. "752-01-3486-9."

Lester typed the number, his fingers a nimble blur. He hit the return key and sat back. It took maybe two seconds for the screen to change, bringing up a map of London.

When I was younger, we'd had scramblers to bounce our signals so our parents and instructors at the Academy wouldn't know where we were if we wanted to go clubbing or generally shag off. But I was thankful for the spyware now – if it would help find Val.

"Got it!" Lester announced a few seconds later.

I could have kissed the creepy bastard. "Where?"

He grinned as he lifted his head, then his gaze fell on me and a glare replaced the smile. "Between Queen Victoria Street and St Andrews by the Wardrobe."

Who the hell gave a church such a ridiculous name? I knew it had to do with a long-dead king and royal vestments, but couldn't they think of something more reverent? It was fortunate the church hadn't been built near a privy.

Lester brought up the exact location on his screen. I committed it to memory and bolted for the door, Penny fast on my heels. I didn't even try to convince her to stay behind. It would be like her trying to ditch me. Not going to happen.

"You're bloody welcome!" Lester shouted after us. The door to his flat slammed shut, locks clicked and slid back into place.

We must have sounded like elephants banging down the stairs, both of us were running so hard, and Penny's boots were so clunky. Outside I yanked my goggles down over my eyes and hopped on to the Butler. Penny jumped on behind.

It was late afternoon, the sun still high in the sky. Much of my skin was covered – either by cloth or a thick layer of sunscreen – but I felt hot, my flesh tender. Summer in England isn't that uncomfortable, but this one was unseasonably warm and I was more sensitive to sunlight than I used to be. I still fared better than any aristo, but I was going to need some blood after this.

Traffic was heavy, more so as we entered the predominantly human area of the city. They took up so much more space than we did. If the Human League succeeded in drawing people to their cause . . . I wasn't going to think about that. If the humans came for us, I'd fight, but for now Val was more important.

Finally, just when I was beginning to think I would cook in my own juices, we reached our destination.

The church was unimposing, yet stately. Like many buildings in London, it was older than God. The original had been decimated in the Great Fire back in 1666. There were rumours that the fire had been started on purpose, because even that far back, humans were starting to see the effects of the plague, and it terrified them. A mob didn't need much provocation in those days. However, most believed the fire was an accident, and by 1695 there was a new church on the spot – red brick with pale trim. There were a few public houses in the area, some shops and restaurants – even another church, only this one catered to a religion made up by a fiction author rather than the Anglican faith.

"Charming Lester said the signal was coming from here," I remarked as we cautiously – but not obviously – examined the area.

"He's not that bad," Penny responded, pulling her rotary from her pocket.

I glanced at her. She wasn't looking at me. "Fang me, did you shag him?"

The colour that rushed to her cheeks was all the answer I needed. I burst out laughing, couldn't help myself. "Tell me you were pissed when it happened."

"Of course we were!" she snapped. "You think it would have happened sober? Christ, he didn't even know I had a cock." Then she smiled. "You should have seen the look on his face."

We both laughed. "So, how was it?" I asked as she began to dial a number.

"One of the best I have had." Then, into her phone, "Lester, darling, it's Penny ... Yes, I'm sure this connection is secure ... No, there's no one around me but Xandra ... Of course she can be trusted. Lester, any chance you can activate that tracker for us, ducks? Maybe send the info to me? ... You're brilliant. Ta." She disconnected.

"Brilliant, eh?" I smirked at her.

"In all manner of ways," she replied saucily. Her rotary pinged. "Ah, here we are."

I joined her and looked over her shoulder at the small screen. On it was a map of the area, with a blinking circle about fifty yards from where we were standing.

There was nothing there but the back of a building and some bins.

My heart spasmed. My brother was not in one of those bins.

I ran towards the spot. Penny followed – fast despite her high boots. I pulled the covers off the bins and let them clatter to the ground, a terrible pounding in my chest.

It was all for naught. There was nothing in them but food scraps, packaging and a pair of manky boots.

"What the hell?" Penny glanced around. "We should be right on top of him."

It wasn't any sort of sixth sense that made me concentrate on the sounds around me and look; just her words. *Right on top of him.*

The blinking light wasn't very noticeable under the bright sun, but it was shaded just enough by one of the bins, and my tinted goggles made my eyes that much less sensitive to the daylight. I spotted the tiny gadget on the ground, near a discarded condom.

Charming.

"What is it?" Penny asked. Her hand went to her mouth as her lips parted and her eyes widened in horror. "Xandra ..."

I crouched down. I could smell my brother over the stench of garbage, the faint copper of his blood and the scent that was uniquely his. The transmitter was dry to the touch; it had been here for a little while. Had they cut it out of him and dropped it here? Or had Val dug it out himself?

I put the tracker in my pocket. At least now I had proof that Val was over his head in something. Maybe the Yard would be more cooperative.

"That means he's still alive, doesn't it?" Penny's expression was so hopeful it made my chest hurt. "If they were going to kill him, they wouldn't have bothered taking it out. Right?"

So hopeful. "No. They wouldn't have bothered." I didn't have the heart to burst her bubble. To be honest, I didn't want to burst my own either. Neither of us had any way of telling whether Val was alive or not, but this ... this wasn't good.

I needed to believe he was still alive. I told myself I knew it just as I had known that Dede wasn't dead when she faked her own death, but that was a lie. I didn't know. I just had to believe it.

But really, in the grand scheme, there were worse things than death. And for the people who had taken my brother, I was going to be one of them.

I called the Yard and left a message for Val's SI about his tracker. I'd be surprised if she called me back. I assumed that if they knew about it, the peelers would have it locked away as evidence. Maybe this would get them off their arses.

Penny's shift at Freak Show started at ten. She went off to start getting ready as soon as we returned to my place, fussing about like she had to hurry even though it was two hours away. I reckoned it took a fair bit of time to look as fabulous as she usually did. Plus, if it took her mind off Val it was worth it.

On the kitchen sideboard was a dark bottle with a note from Vex telling me to drink the whole thing. I uncorked it and sniffed. Blood – human blood. Bloody hell, it smelled good.

I should have been disgusted, and perhaps I would have been if I'd let myself think on it too long, but I grabbed that bottle and chugged half of it before my brain could stop me. By the time my mind caught up, instinct had a firm hold and my hunger simply would not be denied. I drank the rest of it a little slower, enjoying it. Then I had a cup of Earl Grey and the last of the vanilla cupcakes in the cupboard.

Sated, I went upstairs and brushed my teeth. I glanced at myself in the mirror. Albert's fangs, but I was pale now. It took a little getting used to, as did the amber in my previously completely green eyes. I reckoned the trade-off was the fact that my skin looked bloody amazing. Not a spot or dry patch in sight. Being goblin had some privileges.

"Xandy, help!" Penny yelled. She didn't sound like she was dying, so I walked rather than ran down the corridor to the guest room I'd put her in. She was in front of the cheval glass, in her underwear, five-inch platform heels and a skullcap.

"If I only had a camera," I remarked, earning a stuck-out tongue. "What do you need, dearest?"

"I lost an eyelash and I can't get down to look for it."

I thought about suggesting that she try taking off those ridiculous shoes, but kept mum. This probably had more to do with the fact that she didn't want to be alone than a lost eyelash.

I moved closer, then crouched to better survey the carpet. I found the caterpillar-like lash almost immediately, dusted it off and stood. "Crisis averted."

Penny smiled. "Thanks."

She applied glue to the lash and expertly set it on her lid. I studied the procedure with feminine appreciation. "Do you mind if I watch?" I asked.

"Not at all."

There was padding built into her knickers to give her a slightly more rounded bum and hips, and some in the snug-fitting camisole she wore. I watched as she applied highlight and contour to her chest to give the illusion of real breasts. It was amazing.

I helped her into her baby-blue silk Marie Antoinette-style gown. The layers of petticoats alone would have made me scream in frustration. Then I laced her into a pale pink brocade corset, cinching it tighter at the waist so her hips and torso looked noticeably fuller and rounder.

"It's none of my business, but have you ever considered surgery?" I asked. "Or hormones?"

Doe-wide eyes met mine in the mirror as she manoeuvred a gorgeous white wig into place. "Why mess with perfection?"

I laughed. "Indeed."

She turned to face me and I handed her the earrings that were on the dresser. "I like me as I am. I can be a girl or a boy – the best of both worlds."

"Brilliant." I felt a stab of envy, though. Yes, I looked like a halvie, but I was a goblin. I wasn't going to be able to pick and choose which I wanted to be whenever one served me better. Eventually I was going to have to choose.

Penny seemed to know what I was thinking. She patted my shoulder. "At the risk of sounding like one of those insipid cards my mum gets me every year on my birthday, it's not what you are, it's *who* you are. And honey, you are Xandra Vardan, gorgeous, vicious bitch."

I chuckled. "Yay me."

Her other hand came down on my opposite shoulder. There was nothing of the snarky, catty girl I adored in her eyes. At that moment, even though she was buried beneath layers of perfectly done make-up, I saw the resemblance to Val. "If anyone can save Val and destroy the fuckers who took him, it's you. I believe in you, otherwise I'd be a snivelling mess right now – and you know how I hate my mascara running."

As far as compliments went, I wasn't certain it was entirely flattering, but I'd take it.

I drove Penny to Freak Show and told her I'd be there when she finished. It was the best I could do when she refused to stop working. I was going to have to come up with something, because I wasn't confident she was safe so long as she was inside the club, especially since we'd found Val's tracker.

Then I sent a digigram to Vex on my rotary and let him know that I was on my way to Bedlam. I had a date to keep with Ophelia, but I was also hoping they had someone who could run a few tests on the transmitter. I doubted it would yield anything, but maybe they could see where he'd been if the memory was still active.

I am a nocturnal creature by nature, but there's something about London at night that fills me with energy and a sense of confidence. I don't know if it's the change in the tempo of life, or the lights, or the feeling that the city is a living, breathing thing. All I know is that I felt most alive in the shadows and darkness of London.

Traffic was light going over the bridge – I only had to drive illegally once – and I made it to Bedlam a few moments before the time Ophelia and I had agreed to meet. As luck would have it, there was an excellent parking spot available as well – not a lot of folks visiting mental hospitals after dark. They were somewhat like cemeteries that way.

Bedlam was a hulking beast of a building with a domed spire and wings that seemed determined to go on for ever. It had been built here in the 1800s, but the hospital had been around in other locations for hundreds of years prior to that. At one time it served the human community, but that was before my kind started showing up. Now it was a place where half-bloods – and the odd human carrier – went when their minds conspired against them.

Or when they'd been victims of grisly experiments. Dede had shown me some of those poor souls.

It was also the hideout for the so-called Insurrectionists – a group who rebelled against the current monarchy and wanted change. Though all of their known followers and conspirators had been jailed or executed in the years following 1932's Great Insurrection, they were gathering forces again. Were they anything to worry about? I wasn't certain, but Church seemed to think they were. He'd killed Dede to send a message to them as much as to me. As far as I knew, the truth about the Insurrectionists hiding in Bedlam had died with him, as had the identity of any spies he had within the ranks.

This bunch of traitors was headed by my mother, Juliet, and my maternal sister, Ophelia. My family covered the spectrum of patriotism in this country in broad strokes from one end to the other. My father had his head so far up Victoria's arse he was choking on shit, and his former lover was head of the group determined to bring about her downfall.

And then there was me, who didn't trust either side to look both ways before crossing the street.

The heavy iron gate with the word "Bedlam" above let out a low screech when I opened it. I jogged up the path and pulled the cord for the bell. They'd started locking the place up better after my last visit, smart cookies that they were. Used to be they only worried about people getting out.

"May I help you?" came a disembodied voice from the horn-shaped brass speaker on the wall. That was new too.

"I'm here for Ophelia Blackwood," I replied. "We have an appointment."

"Your name?"

I paused, a darkly humourless smile inching across my face. This was not going to go well. "Xandra Vardan."

Silence. I should have felt some remorse for this, but I didn't. I felt awful for what I'd done to Ophelia, but she'd made a full recovery, and I wouldn't have done it if she hadn't been so fond of antagonising me. Had she asked for almost getting her throat ripped out? Not really, no, but she'd intentionally baited me while knowing I wasn't . . . normal.

No, the loss of control weighed heavier upon my shoulders than taking a bite out of her did.

The door opened. A strapping young human in a black uniform greeted me with a stoic expression and a canister of Tetra-Sil in his hand. It was a tetracycline and silver aerosol that was quite effective against those of plagued blood. "Come in."

I crossed the threshold from slightly sticky summer night to the cool, dry interior of the asylum. At one time this place had filled me with fear. Now, it just made me weary. Old buildings like this were drenched in memories – moments in time – that lingered like a perfume. Death. Despair. Madness. Those three notes came together in a cloying, sweet scent that reminded me of opium smoke and funeral flowers. It was faint, but it was there, and I knew I'd carry it on my clothes and hair after I left.

There were two other guards at the hound – a gate-like machine that could sniff out dangerous chemicals and items such as guns. I had only my lonsdaelite dagger on my person, concealed within my corset. Lonsdaelite was a mineral and harder than diamond. It didn't set off any sort of security alarms. I always carried it with me, but rarely had cause to use it.

The two men and one woman – a halvie – watched me carefully as I went through the machine. They patted me down as well – the halvie being the only one brave enough for the job. Then she escorted me to the lift and came up to the first floor with me. The patient side of the building was locked down, but the wing that my mother and her followers kept to was well lit and inviting.

I was escorted to a door I hadn't gone through before. We had to walk past Dede's former room to get there. A lump stuck in my throat. I remembered barging into that room and finding her lounging on the bed without a care in the world, her copper hair dyed black. That was the true beginning of this mess for me. That was what had led me to eventually discovering that I was a goblin.

That had eventually led to her murder.

The guard rapped on the door to this new room and waited.

"Come in," said a voice I recognised as Ophelia's.

The guard turned the knob and gestured for me to enter. I stepped into a large area that looked more like a hotel room than a bedroom, with its sitting area, bar and refrigerator. A separate bedroom was beyond another doorway, along with a small en suite.

"I'm surprised you came."

I turned to face my sister. We were similar in height and build, but she had saltwater-blue hair and blue eyes rather than my red and green/yellow. I couldn't help but look at the base of her throat, where it met her shoulder; there wasn't even a scar.

"I'm surprised there wasn't a sniper on the roof," I replied. "You were the one who said we should meet here."

"I figured it was safest for both of us. Have a seat."

I glanced at the sofa. "I don't mean to stay that—" Well, fang me and chew the wound. There was a very large, high-calibre gun pointed at my face.

Ophelia pulled back the hammer, her gaze hard. "I said, sit the fuck *down*."

CHAPTER 7

THE WEIRD SISTERS, HAND IN HAND

I sat. I walked right over to that little sofa and plopped my arse down on it like any rational person with a gun pointing at her would. It was not my first instinct. That had been to make a grab for the gun and chew her face off.

I think it was only because of the blood I'd drunk earlier that I was able to think clearly and realise that Ophelia wasn't attacking me – she was simply taking necessary precautions against someone who had once hurt her very badly. I would have done the same. But then I wouldn't have invited that someone into my home.

No, I'd lure that person into the underside and eat their heart.

"I didn't come here to hurt you," I told her. "This was your idea, remember?"

She lowered the gun. The barrel trembled. "Can't blame me for not trusting you."

I frowned. "Beg pardon, but I came here trusting that you weren't trying to lure me into some sort of trap."

"Yeah, well maybe you aren't as smart as you think you are."

I met her blue gaze directly. "If you're going to shoot me, get it the fuck over with. I've things to do, and mucking about with you ain't one of them."

She hesitated. Was she honestly debating it? Finally she sat down on a chair facing the sofa. Not quite within lunging distance, but close. The pistol was at the ready, but no longer pointed directly at me. "I was surprised you called."

I shrugged. "Vex said you wanted me to give you a ring."

"I did. I thought you might like Dede's things." Her voice cracked a little, bringing a sad smile to my mouth. It was nice to know she was missed.

"I do, but that's not why I'm here."

The pistol came up a bit as my sister stiffened. "Why *are* you here?"

"My brother's missing. We think he was investigating the disappearances at Freak Show, that he might have been abducted by the people experimenting on halvies." Horrible thoughts of what they might be doing tried to flood my brain, but I denied them entry. "I thought you might be able to help me."

"Right. The lab I was kept in was burnt to the ground shortly after Mum got me out. They don't exactly put their address in the directory, so I'm not sure what kind of help you think I can offer."

The pair of us were like two hedgehogs trying to dance. The intent of harmony was there, but all the pricking and poking got in the way. I swallowed the urge to flip her off, and sighed.

"If he was taken by the same or similar people, you can tell me what they might be doing to him, and whether or not they'll keep him alive. You can tell me about the place where they kept you." I was betting that their operation needed substantial space in the right sort of environment. It wasn't like they could torture halvies in a flat above a coffee shop.

Ophelia – Fee – ran a hand through her tangled blue hair. "It was an old factory or something. They kept us in cells, separated so we couldn't talk to each other. They'll keep him alive as long as he cooperates and behaves."

I couldn't imagine Val being inclined to do either, but he wasn't stupid, and self-preservation ran in the family. "What are they doing to him?"

She shrugged, avoided my eye.

"Look, I understand you don't want to talk about this, especially not with me, but I have to find him. You may be able to tell me something that will help me save not only him, but anyone else they have held prisoner."

Her gaze jerked to mine. "Our mother spent weeks planning how to get me out. She had someone on the inside who helped her, and raided the place with a dozen trained half-bloods, and they still only managed to save a handful of people."

"She had to find you first. Tell me what I need to look for. Let me worry about the rest of it."

"You'll get yourself killed."

"I'm not abandoning my brother."

Her eyes narrowed. "If you had known about me, would you have tried to find me?"

I wanted to say no, just to be a bitch, but it would be a lie. "Yes."

She started. "Why?"

"Because you're my sister."

"You tried to kill me!"

I shrugged. "I didn't say it made sense. I've never met anyone who makes me want to punch them as much as you do, but if someone tried to hurt you, I'd hurt them. I'm sorry for what I did to you. I would take it back if I could, but I can't. If you want to punish me, fine, but please help me find my brother. I can't lose him too."

She swallowed. I heard a click as the safety on the pistol was switched on, and then she set the weapon on the coffee table between us. She either trusted me not to make a grab for it, or figured she was the faster of the two of us.

Either way, it was almost as insulting as it was a relief.

"Why do you think he was taken by the same people who took me?"

"He was investigating halvie disappearances from Freak Show when a couple of betties nabbed him outside the club. And earlier I found his tracker. It had been cut out of him. What?"

Fee had turned pale – more so than usual. It made me wonder just what had happened to her in that lab. "They use betties to abduct halvies. They're instructed to remove the tracking devices and deliver the subjects to the lab. In return, the betties are given the plague."

Betties liked to inject themselves with the plague, which they get from aristos. Some used a funky compound derived from aristo hormones that had a more subtle effect and wasn't as hard on the body. Others, I had learned, went right for injecting aristo blood straight into their veins. There was a more drastic effect in terms of strength, agility and speed. It was also more drastic in that it didn't take long for sores to appear and bits to start turning black. Those betties might be tough, but their lives were significantly shortened.

Her admission should have frightened me, but it didn't. I'd rather know Val was in the hands of Dr Frankenstein than not know at all. "Well, at least I'm aware of what I'm dealing with now. Tell me everything you can remember that might be useful."

"All right. I told you they'll need a large building. There were easily another dozen half-bloods where I was. The cells were in a separate area from where they did their tests. There was an infirmary area, a room where they tested our physical capabilities. There was an operating theatre, rooms where they conducted the sexual experiments, and a nursery."

I have to admit my stomach clenched at that. I'd heard about some of the sexual experiments from Dede – there was a halvie in one of the subterranean rooms here at Bedlam who had been raped repeatedly by a goblin in some facility. I'd never thought that there might have been children from such an atrocity. Not ones that lived.

How had they got a goblin? Did they abduct them as well? I could imagine a goblin doing terrible things to a human, even to a halvie if the mood struck, but not because they were told to. If a gob was hungry enough, or vicious enough, it would do whatever it wanted.

It was something for me to ask the prince about the next time I saw him. As much as I would rather not be a goblin, I kept coming back to it. I felt responsible for them, even though they'd done just fine without a champion for more than a century.

"So they need a structure with electricity, hot water, temperature control. Probably one situated where there's no nosy neighbours."

My sister nodded. "I don't remember hearing any noises other than ones from inside the building. No traffic, no outside voices. They had the windows boarded up."

Which led to my next question. "Fee, were they ... all aristos?"

"The ones running the place were, but most of the staff were human." She swallowed. "There were even a few half-bloods."

That really got up my arse. I could see humans wanting to poke at halvies; I could understand aristos too if they thought it might benefit them in some way. But halvies? What in the name of ruddy hell could inspire half-bloods to torture their own kind? How cruel did you have to be?

"They need equipment for what they do," Ophelia went on. "We monitor most pharmaceutical and medical supply companies in and around the city in our own efforts to find these labs. We've been trying to find one up north recently, but they've become better at eluding us. Mum would probably give you access to our information."

Why the hell hadn't she told me this to begin with?

"It's not that simple," she added, obviously seeing the tightening of my jaw. "This stuff is routed through other companies and holdings, both legitimate and bogus. These people know what they're doing and how to cover their tracks. The moment we expose one weak link, they change tactics. It's the reason we haven't been able to shut more of them down. The one I was in burned down, but not before they emptied it and took the remaining prisoners with them. They set up a new lab with the same amount of trouble it takes you or me to tie a corset."

"Well, that certainly makes me feel better, thanks." Sarcasm dripped from my tongue. How was I going to find Val?

"At least you know where to start looking," she said. "You know they're going missing from Freak Show, and usually from the private rooms. You hang out there long enough, something's bound to happen."

She had a point. I wouldn't have to worry about Penny so much either if I was there to watch out for her myself. Not like I had anything else to do. I was currently unemployed.

I fished the transmitter out of my pocket and held it out to her. "Do you think you could see if there's any useful information on here?"

Ophelia didn't take it. She just stared at it, her eyes strangely wet. "No."

"Why not?" I demanded. "You've done it before, surely."

"Raj was in charge of that." She met my gaze. "We haven't found anyone else who can do it."

If there was a scale measuring totally wankerness, I would be a solid ten at that moment. Raj had been her human lover. He'd also been a spy for Churchill, but Fee didn't know that. I would never tell her – it would serve no purpose other than to hurt her. Church had killed Raj when he was done with him.

"Right. Sorry." I put the device back in my pocket. Maybe the gobs would be able to analyse it for me. I should have gone there to begin with, but Ophelia had given me enough information to start with, and I could tell talking about it had brought up some unpleasant memories for her. As much as I wanted to find Val, I was loath to cause Ophelia more discomfort. Really, me stumbling into her life had brought her nothing but pain.

We went to Dede's room and Fee helped me pack up the things I wanted to keep. I think she was surprised when I told her to take what she wanted.

"Dede loved you," I told her, throat tightening. "She felt like she was home here, which is more than I was able to give her."

"She idolised you." Ophelia took a pair of black and purple striped stockings from the pile of clothing and set them aside. "She was always telling us – me and Mum – about things you'd done for her, or how you were always the best at what you decided to do. I envied her for having you."

If she'd made a noose out of those tights and hanged herself with it I wouldn't have been more stunned and horrified than I was right then. I was not the best at whatever I decided to do, except maybe when it came to violence and being an arsehole. "Then you met me and that envy turned to pity."

She shot me a droll look as she plucked a hairclip out of the pile as well. "You broke into a place that terrified you because you thought she needed to be rescued. I have three brothers, Xandra, but not one of them would have done that for me."

And I'd already told her that I would. "Turns out this place wasn't so scary after all – except for you, of course."

She smiled – not much, but it was a smile regardless. "Of course."

I don't know just what happened exactly, or what changed, but at that moment I felt like we were actually sisters – and in a good way.

Of course that was when my rotary decided to start shriek-
ing at me. I took it out of my pocket and checked the flip-slots
for the incoming number. I pressed the button to connect.

"Hey, Penny. What's going on?"

"Xandra, you have to get over here right freaking now."
Her voice was a shrill, shaking whisper that made my heart
try to jump out of my chest.

"What is it?"

"The betties that took Val," she said. "They're back."

I broke practically every traffic law on the way to Covent
Garden, some of them more than once. Ophelia clung to me
like a scab to a wound as the Butler screamed through the
streets so fast the resulting wind stung my cheeks. Thank God
I had my goggles, or I'd have been practically blinded by
watering eyes.

A big red double-decker omnibus chugged along ahead of
me, carrying the usual crowd of tourists – most from
America – who flocked to London and the rest of the UK to
see our ancient remains and our aristocracy. When I was
Royal Guard I'd get stopped occasionally for a photo.

I was going to give them something to show the folks
across the pond. I accelerated the motorrad and slipped
around the bus, barely fitting between it and a motor carriage
in the other lane. Flash bulbs went off above my head for a
split second before I whipped in front of the cumbersome
vehicle. Horns blared and I continued this pattern until there
was no one left in front of me, blocking my path. Then I
opened the Butler up, bent low over the steering bars.

Through all of this Ophelia never made a sound. She moved when I did, instinctively holding her body so that we were one with the machine. My opinion of her rose a notch or several.

We screamed to a halt outside Freak Show and jumped off before the engine had fully quieted.

"You can't park there," the halvie at the door told us.

I offered him a fifty-pound note. "Watch it for me."

There wasn't much of a queue, but the few people there were very interested in what was going on. I could hear their excited voices as at least two of them recognised me.

"Where are we going?" Ophelia asked as we turned the corner of the building.

"Back exit," I explained as we moved through the dark alley. I could really use my gun right about now, but all I had was my knife. Ophelia hadn't brought her firearm either – not smart to run around with an illegal handgun when you were a traitor to the Crown.

The alley widened at the back of the club, breaking into a small cobblestoned courtyard dimly lit by a light above the door. I could have driven the Butler round here, but that would have announced our presence, and we'd be spotted soon enough without roaring in like Waterloo.

There was a small, nondescript white lorry parked there with the engine idling. Its windscreen and windows were tinted, and even with my superior night vision I was only just able to make out the fuzzy outline of the driver.

Call me suspicious, but I didn't like that. Tinted glass meant two things in my world – that you were an aristo trying to escape the sunlight, or a human simply trying to escape.

The club door opened. A man backed out. I caught a whiff of him almost immediately. Some scents I could ignore, but there was no ignoring the scent of decaying human flesh. The Black Death had a bouquet all its own. In aristos, halvies and goblins it was a vaguely sweet smell, like vanilla or caramel. In humans it was something altogether nastier – a biscuit wrapped in rotting meat. Death.

He had a friend with him, who smelled almost as bad. This one had something over his shoulder. He turned as he stepped into the light, and I caught a glimpse of familiar five-inch heels.

Penny. How the fuck had they managed to grab her in a crowded club? She could have hidden from them, but knowing Penny, she'd tried to follow them. It didn't matter how they'd nabbed her. What mattered was that there was no way I was letting them take her.

I bolted for them, heedless of whether or not they had weapons. Behind me Ophelia swore, but I felt her at my heels.

The blare of a horn rent the air, obliterating the thump of music from the club.

The betties looked surprised to see us, but thanks to their friend's warning, they had a split second to react. I took a fist to the jaw. It was all I needed to bring the goblin to the surface – blood was a fabulous stimulant, especially my own. I reckon it was self-preservation.

Fangs tore free of my gums as the bones in my face ground into a new configuration. It hurt, but it was a good pain – like rubbing a bruise. I'd never looked in a mirror when this happened, so I had no real idea of what I looked like. Judging from the betty's reaction, I'd say I looked fairly terrifying.

"Put her down," I growled.

My betty pulled a shocker from his coat – a hand-held device that could incapacitate a half-blood for minutes at a time. He pressed a button and the prongs embedded themselves in my flesh. I felt the surge of electricity hit my body . . .

I was not a halvie. I was not human. According to many, I wasn't even an aristocrat. And apparently, the amount needed to bring down a goblin was pretty freaking high. I felt the surge from the top of my head to the tip of my toes.

And it pissed me off.

My head swam, and my nerves jumped, but I did not go down. I came at the betty with a roar, taking him to the stones, mindless of how hard my knees hit the ground.

Behind me, Ophelia dealt with the other one. I trusted her to hold her own until I'd dealt with this one. I trusted her with Penny.

"Where's my brother?" I demanded, shaking the betty like a dog with a new chew toy. "What did you do to him?"

I drew back my fist and jobbed the betty twice in the face. Something split beneath my knuckles, filling the night with the smell of diseased pus.

I gagged, my attention disrupted for that split second of stomach-rolling disgust. It was all the betty needed. Blackened fluid might be leaking from his flesh, but he was strong – very strong. He arched up, smashed me in the forehead with his own. I was more overpowered by the stench than by his strength, and so I wavered but I didn't release him.

Pain raced up my arm. Shaking my head to clear my double vision, I looked down and saw that the betty's teeth – both sets – were completely buried in my forearm.

I cuffed him on the skull but he didn't let go. Blood welled up around his lips. I could feel him sucking on the wound, even though his teeth were still in my flesh. I didn't try to stop him. He thought my blood would give him a boost of strength, but then he thought I was a half-blood. This camouflage of mine was becoming quite convenient.

It wasn't a well-known fact, but according to Vex, and the goblin prince, goblin blood was toxic – even to aristos. I had given Dede my blood in an effort to save her when Church shot her, and I ended up bringing about her death that much faster. I still had nightmares about it.

I would not feel the same guilt for this. Even if the Human League burned an effigy of me in the street and put a bounty on my head, I would not regret there being one less plague-fucked human in the world.

The betty's bite eased. I winced as his teeth came free of the muscle in my arm. My blood flowed freely now, entering his mouth even as he gasped and tried to pull away. I held him down, fingers forcing his lips apart so that more of my poison filled him.

He convulsed, eyes rolling back in his head. My blood, mixed with the tar-like pus drying on his cheek, ran down his jaw. Only when he began thrashing did I get up. Crimson erupted from his mouth – more than he'd ever taken from me. It sprang like a geyser of gore into the night. He choked on it, coughed up stuff that was too thick to be just blood. He convulsed one last time and then went still.

"Xandra."

I turned, focus shifting from the betty to Ophelia. I became aware of the sound of an engine – the lorry was driving away! I turned my head, frantically searching the area. The other betty was gone, and Ophelia was bleeding from a cut above her eyebrow.

"Where's Penny?" I demanded? I couldn't have lost her too. How would I face her mother? Or Avery? Was I totally and utterly incapable of protecting the people I cared about?

"Here," came a faint voice from my right. "Xandy, I'm here."

My shoulders sagged in relief. I didn't care that the other betties had got away, or that Ophelia had obviously taken a hard knock. All that mattered was that my favourite drag queen was sitting on the steps with a torn stocking and a lop-sided wig. Her left eye was swollen and her bottom lip was split – blood and lipstick smeared her chin – but at that moment she looked positively gorgeous.

I went to her and hugged her, pulling her hard against my stomach. I hadn't lost her. She was here. Safe.

"You're bleeding."

I glanced at my left arm – rivulets of blood dripped from my fingertips – then at Ophelia. "Yeah. Be careful. My blood's a little toxic."

She arched a brow – it was like looking in a blue-haired mirror. "Xandra, that tosser's dead."

Was that my conscience I felt poking me in the back of my head? "He wasn't long for this world anyway." Judging by his smell and condition, he probably wouldn't have lasted more than a few days.

My sister's lips quirked. "Wouldn't matter to me if he was. I'm not the one you've got to explain it to." She jerked her thumb in the direction of the street. The sound of sirens could be heard drawing closer, then stopped. Doors slammed. Voices and footfalls on the stone.

Two Scotland Yard officers walked into the light – one male and one female. I took one look at their faces and ground my teeth.

"Good evening, Your Majesty," said DI Maine in that flat tone of his. He didn't look surprised to see me. In fact, he appeared rather bored with the whole situation. "How lovely to see you. What happened here, then?"

I glanced down at Penny, who was staring up at me with wide eyes. "Fucking brilliant," I said.

Just what I needed when under investigation for murder – to be found with blood on my hands and a corpse at my feet.

CHAPTER 8

DANGERS BRING FEARS, AND FEARS MORE DANGERS BRING

Over the last couple of months, I'd decided that Fate despised me. This latest development only added to that certainty. A medic wearing a double layer of latex gloves cleaned and bandaged my arm. I thought about telling her not to bother, it would heal soon enough, but she squirmed in such a delightful way every time she had to touch me that I didn't have the heart to stop her. My blood would only hurt her if she ingested it, and it wasn't like I had consumption. A halvie with medical training should know that, right? Shouldn't be so skittish.

It was because she knew who – and what – I was. It was getting tiring – fast.

Special Branch had made it clear they wanted to talk to all three of us, including any witnesses inside the bar. I was hoping that eventually someone would tell me who the dead bloke was, but no one did. They took his body away in the ambulance without saying a word, and before I could search his pockets.

I had to admire Ophelia. Here she was, wanted in connection with the theft of halvie hospital records a couple of months ago, talking to the Yard without breaking a sweat, and it had to be close to thirty degrees – an unseasonably warm and muggy night for August. This summer had been so bloody hot.

"Thanks," I muttered when the woman was done with my wound. She squeaked a reply, but I didn't bother listening as I walked away. I went straight to Penny, who was sitting on the step with one of the club's performers. I recognised her as a contortionist I had seen perform several times. No idea what her name was, though.

"You okay, dearest?" I asked.

Penny nodded. Her wig was straightened now, and she looked more herself. She reached up and took my hand. "Right as rain. You?"

I sat on the edge of the step beside her. "Other than having been used as a betty's chew toy, and electrocuted, I can't complain." I was still a little twitchy – like the odd bug had crawled under my skin.

"Is it true you killed that betty?" the other girl asked, softly. She was looking at me as though she wasn't certain if she should be afraid or not.

"He was already on his way out," I told her. "I really didn't do anything to him." Except practically cave in his face and poison him, but she didn't need to know that.

She nodded, and I watched her spine visibly relax.

Ophelia wandered over to us, a carefully neutral expression on her face. "I'm going to take off."

I nodded. She'd already gone above and beyond by coming to Penny's rescue with me. "Do you need a lift?"

She shook her head. "Nah. The alpha's coming for me." Her expression turned to one of amusement. "Reckon he'll have some questions for you later."

I sighed. "You just had to ring him, didn't you?"

She grinned. "He would have found out anyway. I'm just saving you the trouble of telling him."

That was when the temperature seemed to go up several degrees, thickening the air, weighing it down. The entire scene quieted, like just before a thunderstorm. I knew without looking that Vex had arrived. I didn't have to see him. I could sense him, smell him. Every hair on the back of my neck stood at attention. I wasn't the only one. He commanded the attention of each person in that little courtyard.

I peeked around Ophelia and watched him stride right into the thick of things. He was dressed in fitted black trousers, shiny black knee-high boots, snowy white shirt and black frock coat. He didn't look the least bit affected by the heat either. Must be a wolf thing.

He lifted his head, as though scenting the air. Then he stopped and turned, his gaze locking with mine.

Fang me, it was like being shocked all over again. When he began to walk towards me, those pale eyes of his blazing with gold, I held my breath. It didn't matter that I was a goblin – the most terrible of beasts – he was impressive.

And I was in shit.

Ophelia bowed to him, bending one knee. I knew then that he was not impressed with either of us.

"Go wait in the Sparrow," he growled at her.

She didn't meet his gaze. She simply nodded, rose and

walked away without so much as a word. That bothered me, seeing her cowed. I stood up, meeting his gaze once more. "Don't be angry with her. She was only trying to help."

A muscle in his jaw flexed. "Are you all right?" His voice was even deeper than usual, quieter.

I nodded. "Got a bite, but I'll be fine." We hadn't been together long, but I'd never seen him like this. "Are you?"

He glanced away. "We can talk about it later. Do you want me to wait for you?"

Having him stand around in this heat, while his wolf hovered so close to the surface, was probably not a good idea. Never mind that Special Branch might think I needed the alpha to hide behind.

"No. Take Ophelia home. I'll bring Penny with me and meet you at my place later."

Vex nodded, face tight. "Fine." Then he turned his attention to Penny, and his expression softened. "You good, love?"

She nodded, offered up a faint smile. "You know it, gorgeous. I'll take care of your girl. You go do what you need to do."

His gaze came back to me. The gold was gone, replaced by a faint twinkle of amusement. I knew I wasn't going to get off this easily. "Don't get arrested."

Before I could respond, he turned on his heel and strode away. I wasn't the only one who watched him go. I noticed DI Cooke's gaze linger on Vex's back longer than I liked. When she spied me, she quickly turned away.

Special Branch talked to Penny next. I just knew that bastard Maine was going to make me stew as long as he could. Finally Penny came back to the step. Her friend had long since gone back inside the club.

"Do you want to wait inside?" I asked her. "It's probably

cooler in there." In the distance I heard the dull roar of thunder.

She shook her head. "I'd rather wait out here. With you."

Poor thing. I could have hugged her, but I didn't want her to think I believed her weak – and I didn't want to give that appearance to those few still hanging about. "I won't let them keep me long."

There was no one left to talk to but me – no one who had been involved in the altercation. I made a beeline straight for Maine. He might be a first-class twat, but at least he wasn't sniffing after Vex.

"I'm ready to give my account of events," I told him when he looked up at my approach.

"Perhaps I'm not ready to hear it," he replied, scribbling in his notebook.

"I'll be on my way, then. Unless, you care to arrest me for something?"

Maine arched a brow at me – didn't bother trying to hide it. "You're accustomed to getting your way, aren't you, Your Majesty?"

If that were true, Dede would be alive, and would have custody of her son. Val would be home with us and I'd still be sharing a house with Avery. My mother never would have been taken from me, and Rye – my first love – wouldn't have been killed by humans hell-bent on ridding the world of anyone of aristo descent.

"Yes, you have that 'I'm-privileged-and-I-know-it' air about you." Odd, but he made it sound like nothing more than an observation, rather than an insult.

"Your father was an aristo too, DI Maine."

He smiled – rather bitterly. "Yes, well I reckon you have the advantage of knowing who yours was. That's why you were able to go to school to train for the Royal Guard and I was never given the option."

Oh. I hadn't expected that. "I'm so—"

"Spare me your pity. I don't get invited to the palace, and I clean up the mess the rest of you make. I make sure half-bloods and aristocrats are held accountable for their actions, Lady Xandra. Queens, kings, freaks . . . it doesn't much matter to me. I will find out what you're hiding, because I know you're hiding something."

My jaw tightened. Wanted to play that way, did he? "If that's how you see me, DI Maine, that's your prerogative. Do you want to know what happened here or not?"

He pursed his lips. My knuckles itched to punch him. Hard. He held up his pad and pencil. "Do go ahead, ma'am."

I told him that Val had last been seen leaving this place with two betties – either by his own volition or by force. Then I went on to tell him that Penny had rung me when the betties returned.

"Why didn't she contact the Yard?" he enquired, rather suspiciously. Defensively. "CI Vardan is one of ours."

I shrugged. "I suppose she had more confidence in me." The expression on his face was almost as satisfying as jobbing him would have been. I continued with my story, leaving nothing out except for the fact that I'd been at Bedlam when Penny rang – and the truth about Ophelia. There was no reason to lie, and if the information helped Special Branch in their search for Val, then I wouldn't regret being honest.

When I was done, he continued to scribble on his pad for a few seconds before glancing up. "Death certainly seems to like you, Your Majesty."

I lifted my gaze to him, not bothering to look pleasant. "Does it?" This man had no reason to dislike me so much, but he'd come to my house believing I was a killer. I suppose that made him an excellent judge of character, but he didn't *know* I was responsible for Church's death. He was just very smart, and I despised him for it as much as he despised me – because I had been just smart enough in dealing with Church that he couldn't prove a damn thing.

"Your sister, Churchill, the man who shot at Queen Victoria, Simon Halstead. All in the matter of what? A few weeks?"

"He was killing himself, in case you haven't noticed. It's not my fault he bit me during the course of trying to kidnap me." I didn't know if the betty would have taken me as well, but I assumed it.

"Yes, I'm quite sure you had a terrible time of it fighting him off." Maine made a scoffing noise. "He's human. It was hardly a fair contest."

Straightening my spine, I pulled back my shoulders – posturing, that was what it was. "He's a betty, that makes it fair enough. He also left here with my brother. Purposely killing him before getting Val's whereabouts out of him doesn't make sense."

The officer closed his notebook and tucked his pen in the coiled spine. "But you did kill him. From what's left of his face, you can't tell me you didn't have every intention of hurting him."

"I was defending myself."

Maine smiled – it didn't reach his eyes. "No offence, but would you believe a lion who said it was only defending itself against a sheep?"

"He was no sheep. You can believe what you want, but all

the witnesses will tell you the same thing. I was trying to find out about my brother and rescue my friend – who was being abducted by your sheep. Your boy bit me and it did him in."

"And you tried to save him, of course."

"I tried to get him off me."

Shrewd eyes met mine. "You really don't care that he's dead, do you?"

"Actually, I do. He knows what happened to my brother, remember? The one you said was one of yours?"

"If CI Vardan was investigating this club, then you are interfering in that investigation. That's reason enough for me to take you to the Home Office."

I sighed. "I've told you what happened, and what I know. If you want to fuck about with me, that's fine. But if you make it difficult for me to find Val, you'll regret it."

Maine frowned. "Is that a threat, ma'am?"

Oh, I was so done with this. "Fuck off," I snarled, and turned my back on him. "If you need anything else, I'll be doing your job for you."

"I'll be watching you, Your Majesty," Maine promised.

I flipped him off. "Come on, Penny!" I called as I stomped towards the street, her heels clacking behind me. "We're done here."

I dropped Penny at my place. Vex wasn't there, so I decided to go to the den. The more time that passed before we saw each other again, the better. I didn't relish the tongue-lashing he was bound to give me for what had happened at Freak Show. Not only had I rushed in without thought, but I'd killed someone in the process.

It didn't matter that I hadn't meant to kill the bastard. I just . . . did. Was it instinct or plain cruelty that made me do it? It was one thing to call myself a monster and another to actually believe it. I could have stopped the betty from taking my blood. I could have tried to save him, if for no other reason than finding Val. Instead, I'd let him die and I'd felt a strange satisfaction with it. I'd done it out of a need for revenge, but I should have got the information out of him first.

Because of my actions, the other betties had got away, and my brother might suffer in retaliation. As if Dede didn't weigh heavily enough on my conscience.

This time I sent word ahead that I was on my way to the den. I didn't want surprises. It was one thing me for me to hear that goblins seduced drug addicts into being willing blood donors, sex partners and even the occasional meal, and quite another to see it first-hand. Part of me knew it was wrong and was very much horrified by the fact that another part of me didn't mind at all. Humans knew the risks of getting involved with gobs.

And that was all the thought I intended to give the matter for now.

I entered the den the same way I had the other night. Tonight there was a little music – a gob playing a mandolin while the pack sang along. They fell silent at the sight of me. Most bowed. Some looked at me with open resentment. I did not need more enemies, not with the Human League, the Bedlamites and Queen Victoria all gunning for my arse.

"Sorry to interrupt," I said as William the prince approached me. It was odd to refer to him, or any goblin, by such ordinary names. I'd never really given it much thought, but if asked I would have supposed that goblins gave themselves more tribal-sounding names. Names that were as strange and fierce as they were. "I wouldn't have come if I'd known you were busy."

He tilted his head, reminding me of a curious wolf. "Our lady does not interrupt. Our lady graces her plague." He took my arm and led me out of the great hall. "What troubles you?"

I took the tracking chip out of my pocket. "This belongs to my brother. I found it on the ground near the Wardrobe. Do you reckon one of your techies could take a look at it? See if there's any history left on it?"

"Not my techies," he corrected me. "*Your* techies. And yes. What the lady asks we will do."

I made a face. "I don't like that – and neither do some of the plague. I don't want you to do things just because I wish it."

He smiled. Fang me, but I will never get used to that. He reached out with long, nimble fingers and took the chip from my palm. That was when I noticed that his right hand looked decidedly different from his left, which seemed more paw-like.

He caught me looking – and seemed just as surprised as I was. "This is strange to you?"

I nodded, frowning. "Forgive me. I didn't mean to stare."

William held up both hands. I watched as the left one lengthened and became less furry, more slender. Bones and cartilage snapped and groaned. In a few seconds both hands were identical.

"Like our cousin wolves, the plague can change shapes."

That might explain why my face changed when I gobbed out. "Can you look human?"

He shook his head. "Look more human, yes. Be like human,

no. Too much plague to be furless and pale. Easier for old ones like your prince." He held up the chip. "Immediately this will be examined."

A huge wave of relief swamped me. "Thank you. I know I only seem to come here when I want something . . ." I faltered. This was the moment when he was supposed to shush me and tell me I wasn't at fault at all.

He didn't. Instead, he smiled again. "It is my hope that one day the lady will join us because *that* is what she wants."

I was such a tit. All I could do was nod.

After handing the chip over to one of the more tech-savvy goblins, I joined the prince and the others in the great hall. As much as I wanted to get home and check on Penny, I still wasn't keen on facing Vex. More than that, however, was the fact that I'd been raised to have better manners than I typically exhibited. I did only come down here when I wanted something. No wonder some of the goblins sneered at me.

I sat on my throne, and tried to ignore Church's skull just above mine. It was easier than it ought to be.

The music was good, and the crowd lively. I even sang along with some of the more chipper songs. He played everything from old folk songs to modern music I often heard on VBC radio.

Finally, after almost an hour, I took my leave. I'd left Penny alone for too long, poor thing. I felt a little better about facing Vex. He might take me to task, but it would be all right. I didn't reckon I'd done anything he wouldn't have done were the situation reversed.

When I exited cobbleside, my rotary chirped, letting me know I had a Britme waiting. I stepped to the side of the Met entrance and dialled the number to access the message.

It was Vex. "Something's come up. I don't know how long I'll be. I'll explain when I see you later. And then you can explain to *me* what the hell happened at Freak Show." I could hear a smile in his tone and it made me smile as well. "Try not to get into any more trouble before dawn, okay?" And then the message ended.

Like a lovestruck teen in one of those melodramatic American programmes, I saved the message so I could listen to it again later. Then I jogged across the street and returned to the Butler. It had rained while I was underside, and the night was much cooler than it had been. A lovely breezed whipped through my hair as I drove, and the smell of damp earth hung in the air.

I went to Avery's. I could have rung her and brought her up to date on what little I'd managed to find out, but I wanted to see her. She was my sister after all, and I loved her. It didn't matter that we fought as much as we laughed, or that she'd turned her back on me when I needed her. I had hurt her by not confiding in her, so that made us pretty much even.

She wasn't home, much to my disappointment. I let myself in and left her a note on the table. I'd left the house and just pulled my goggles over my eyes when headlamps in one of the Butler's side mirrors almost blinded me. It was a double-decker omnibus, and it was loaded with tourists.

What the bloody hell was it doing here? I knew there were evening tours for those who hoped to catch a glimpse of an aristo, or at least a few halvies, but I'd never seen one on this street.

A loud voice over a microphone answered my question. "And here we are, folks, Belgrave Square. This beautiful part of the Wellington district was home to many wealthy families in the Regency period, right up until the early 1930s. After the Great Insurrection, those survivors of noble birth relocated to Mayfair and the outlying counties. The goblin queen herself, Alexandra Vardan, lived here until just recently."

I was part of a fucking London tour? My life had become an annoying mix of the tragic and the absurd.

"There's a half-blood!" I heard a young voice cry. "On the motorcycle."

I wasn't terribly familiar with the American vernacular, but I knew motorcycle was the same as motorrad, just as I knew that the trunk of a motor carriage was the same as the boot. Not sure how they came up with that one, but it hardly mattered.

Flash bulbs went off as the large vehicle slowly pulled up behind and then beside me. It stopped, engine idling.

"You mean to tell me that you people let this goblin queen, this child-eater, roam the streets?" a man asked. He sounded florid and fat, and in need of a good bowel movement.

"Why yes," answered the guide. "She hasn't broken any laws."

"Son, where I'm from, a monster like that wouldn't be allowed to live."

I might have rolled my eyes if he hadn't sounded so sure. He was probably the kind of man who hunted for sport, but only when the entire operation was set up for the sole purpose of him killing something and he was practically handed his prey.

"Hey, little girl. You ever seen this *goblin queen*?" He said it like he might have meant "sack of shit". And he was talking to me. I just knew it. Fate wanted to fuck with me a little bit longer.

I turned my torso to look at him. He was exactly as I had imagined him. "I've seen her," I replied. In the mirror.

"What's your kind think of her?" My *kind*?

"She's all right." Really, what else could I possibly say?

"Would you trust her alone with your children?"

I looked at the man and his florid cheeks. Beside him was a haggard-looking woman and a young boy who I took to be his family. The top of the vehicle was full of tourists, and the lower half almost as packed. Faces watched me from behind glass, or poked out over shoulders and around those who were too tall. I felt like a model in an art class – naked and vulnerable in front of a group of people who were going to form their own image of me regardless of what I said or did.

"I would. She would never harm a child."

He laughed at me. "Sure she would. You put a rabbit in front of a wild cat and it's gonna get eaten."

My gaze locked with his. "Why settle for a rabbit when you could bring down a hog instead?"

His smile faltered. If I could have got away with leaping up on to the railing and scaring the living shit out of him, I would have, but I didn't want my photograph taken by every single tourist on board. And I certainly didn't want to end up being accused of threatening humans.

"You obviously don't know much about animals, ma'am. They bring down the small and the weak."

"Goblins aren't animals, sir." I forced a friendly tone. "They are intelligent creatures. And they're more likely to go after the biggest arsehole than the weakest link. You might want to stay above ground while you're visiting the city."

I started the Butler. "I hope you all enjoy your tour," I said loudly, convivially. "Do be careful and stay with your party.

London can be a dangerous city regardless of who or what you are, especially at this time of night." I smiled at the man as I toed the kick stand out of the way, flashing a hint of fang. "You never know when the goblin queen might decide to go big-game hunting." It was stupid, petulant and unapologetically cheesy, and I was pretty certain I wasn't going to regret it any time soon.

I drove away.

CHAPTER 9

THE SECRET OF FREEDOM IS COURAGE

Vex still hadn't shown up by the time I returned home. Penny was in a green peignoir set with feathers around the neckline and cuffs. She'd removed her wig but not her make-up, and bare feet peeked out from beneath the hem of her gown. She looked adorable, with her mussed short hair and big eyes.

I apologised for leaving her alone. She waved it away as though it didn't signify.

"Fancy a little something?" I asked.

Penny nodded. "I'm famished, but I didn't want to poke about in your cupboards."

"I'm not much of a chef, dearest, so you'd better get over that immediately."

I made us a cup of tea in the kitchen and a couple of corned beef sandwiches with thick fresh bread. Thank God I hadn't lost my love of food when my goblin genes fully kicked in. I had worried that all I would want was blood and meat. I did crave it, but real food still tasted grand. I suppose the gobs must be able to eat other things as well, otherwise more humans would go missing in the city – and the goblins wouldn't be so content to remain underside.

"Thanks for saving my arse tonight," Penny said as I plopped a plate on the table in front of her.

"I'm glad you called." I sat down with her. "And that I got there in time."

"Did Special Branch give you a hard time?"

"That Maine's got a bug up his arse," I replied, picking up my sandwich. "But for now he's no more annoyance than a pebble in my shoe." That was a fairly succinct way of thinking of the little bastard. He could try to make my life as difficult as he wanted, but he didn't have any real evidence on me and he never would. He'd have to go into the goblin den and analyse the soil, test every piece of bone there. That was never going to happen.

I chewed and swallowed. "I hate to say it, Pen, but I don't see how you can go back to work after this."

She made a face. "I have to work, Xandra."

I knew what this was about. Penny only took what she had to from her father. It was the law that aristocratic gentlemen had to pay for the care of their halvie children and provide an allowance. Vardan had bought us a house in the Wellington district and settled a sum upon each of us when we turned one and twenty. It was because of that money – and a sum from my mother's family – that I was able to rent this building and live comfortably now that I was no longer a member of the Royal Guard. Penny's father, however, had made it clear that while he would support his child and provide the necessaries, he would absolutely not pay for anything acquired for the continuation of her "lifestyle".

Custom-made frocks and wigs cost a lot of money, as did the pride of being able to send a big "fuck you" in the direction of your small-minded papa.

"Call in sick tomorrow night," I advised, poised to take another bite. "We'll think of something." Short of me spending eight hours following her every move, I had no idea what that might be. It would be the end of finding Val. Even if I put on a wig and coloured lenses in my eyes, I was still going to look and smell like me. The betties might not notice, but someone would. And they were already going to be cautious after tonight. They probably wouldn't come back for a while, so Penny was safe for the time being.

I had killed one of their mates. I was going to be a target too. I was no help to Penny if I had to keep watching my own back.

I didn't think the club management was in on what the betties were doing, or who they were doing it for. It just wasn't good business sense. Plus I thought I'd heard the manager telling Maine tonight that she was willing to offer a reward for information on Val. Everyone wanted to help when it was a Special Branch agent and the son of a duke who'd gone missing.

I needed to get someone into the club who no one would think twice about being there, who could hang out and keep an eye on Penny for me. Ophelia might do it, but she'd been seen with me.

It was something to discuss with Vex when he came home. *Home?* I took another bite of sandwich to cover my shock. This wasn't Vex's home. It was my home. I was not ready to think . . .

Vex was right – there were a lot of things I wasn't ready for.

I've never thought of myself as particularly weak, but I was starting to wonder. It didn't matter if I was ready for it, I already thought of home as wherever Vex was. I had fallen for him in a bad way from the very start, which was stupid, because he was expected to marry another were and try his best to produce at least one fully plagued heir, and some halvies.

No man of mine was going to screw courtesans, even if it was for the greater good. And the only thing he'd produce with me was a goblin – if we were lucky. Who knew what my freaky genes might come up with?

That wasn't something I needed to think about right now, and if I was good at anything, it was ignoring stuff I didn't want to contemplate. An example of this was my refusal to wonder why Vex hadn't shown up yet. Was he *that* angry at me for the scene at Freak Show?

Penny and I were watching a film on telly an hour or so later, sharing a huge bowl of crisps, when my rotary rang. I licked salt and oil from fingers before picking it up. "Hello?"

"It's Ophelia." Sirens and voices blared in my ear, almost drowning her out.

I didn't like the sound of those shouts. "What's wrong?"

The noise faded. She must have stepped into a building or a vehicle. "The alpha and I are both fine. There was an accident . . ."

Something wrapped around my heart and squeezed – hard. It didn't matter that Vex hadn't called or that he might be pissed off at me. Nothing mattered but his safety.

PleaseGodorAlbertoranyonelisteninglethimbeokay.

"What sort of accident?"

There was a slight hesitation on the other end of the connection. "We'll explain when you get here."

She'd better. "Where are you?"

"A pub called the Handsome Beggar, in Whitechapel."

"I'm on my way." And then a thought occurred to me. "Why didn't he call me himself?"

"He's a bit . . . busy at the moment, but he didn't want you to hear it from someone else. See you in a bit." The connection was broken before I could ask anything more.

"What's wrong?" Penny asked when I set the phone on the table.

"Not sure," I replied. I didn't want to worry her – either of us – any more than I had to. "I have to go and fetch Vex. Will you be all right by yourself for a bit?"

"I doubt anyone's going to come looking for me at the house of the goblin queen." She actually smiled, which was nice to see. "I'm going to take a soak in the bath. Relax."

"An excellent notion." I kissed her forehead. "Be back in a jiff."

I had a vague idea of where the Handsome Beggar was located. I'd never been there, but the pub had gained infamy back in the early thirties as a hangout for Insurrectionists. I didn't know what it was now, but if Vex was there it had to be reasonably safe for our kind.

The wind ran cool, damp fingers through my hair as I drove the Butler hard towards Whitechapel. This summer had been so strangely hot, it was nice to feel a little chill, however slight, in the air.

As I neared the pub, a sense of unease began to unfurl in my stomach, quickly turning to full-on fear. There were several fire engines, police carriages and ambulances just a little further down the street. Thick black smoke rose up into the sky as the firefighters battled a blaze that encompassed an entire

building. Several motor carriages parked in front of the building were burning as well.

One of them was Vex's Sparrow.

I parked illegally in front of the pub. Let them give me a
fucking ticket. I had barely kicked out the parking stand before
I jumped off the Butler and pushed through the small crowd
gathered to watch the entertainment down the street. I shoved
the door opened and stepped into a practically empty interior.
Those few heads lifted as I crossed the threshold. I didn't care
if the humans stared. My only concern was the gorgeous wolf
sitting at the bar. He had turned to face the door before I even
entered.

He was sooty and singed, and I could see traces of blood on
his face and hands. He smelled of smoke – not the clean kind
that came from wood, but the kind that reeked of burnt rubber
and scorched metal.

I might have thrown myself at him if not for the people
watching. Instead, I walked up to him and brushed some of the
black from his face. "You all right?"

He nodded, a wry smile on his lips. "The Human League's
bombs are as rubbish as they were a century ago."

The Human League? Again? They were really upping their
profile as of late. They'd started small in Ireland at the end of
the nineteenth century, and then grew until there were cells all
across Europe – wherever there was plague. I'm not sure how
much of the religious belief that all those of plagued blood
were evil creatures in the service of Satan continued today, but
the hate was still going strong.

"What were you doing over here?"

He cast a glance over his shoulder at the rest of the pub. No
one seemed to be paying us much attention now. The real

excitement was outside. "Ophelia and I came by to follow up on a lead I'd got about Duncan's death."

Duncan was his son who had been murdered. I looked around for my sister. "Where's Fee?"

"A friend came and got her a few moments ago. She's fine."

Judging from what I'd seen of the car, and where it was parked, the driver's side would have taken the worst of the blast.

"And you say I have a habit of being in the wrong place at the wrong time," I teased. I was just so damned relieved that he and Ophelia were unhurt. "Next time park in a car park, not next to a building targeted by fanatics."

His lips twisted as he took one of my hands in his. "A car park wouldn't have done any good, love. It wasn't the building they bombed. It was my motor carriage."

CHAPTER 10

BE WARY THEN; BEST SAFETY LIES IN FEAR

"Did they bomb you because of me?" I finally asked once we
were home. Vex was taking a bath in the claw-foot tub in my
bathroom, and I was perched on the toilet lid. Normally I'd be
in the tub with him, but not with the amount of ash that he'd
scrubbed off.

"Not everything's about you, sweetheart," he reminded me
without a hint of snark as he leaned his head back against the
tub. "Being alpha's sometimes just as dangerous as being
goblin queen. We're all the enemy to the League."

Forget that we'd never have a future because of genetics;
neither one of us was going to have a future, period. "Was it
just a trap? Or do you think there really was new information
on Duncan?"

He shook his head, damp hair curling around his ears. "It
was dodgy to begin with, but I followed up on it because there
was no way I couldn't."

I understood. I would have done the same thing if someone

had contacted me saying they had news on Val. "The League's been making itself a bit vocal lately." There'd been an incident not long after Dede's death. Someone had taken shots at the guards outside Buckingham Palace. Every once in a while the League had to re-establish themselves. I'd once taken a knife in the leg because of one of the bastards.

"Mm. They usually do around momentous occasions. The jubilee in June, you being a goblin – it's all the sort of news that makes certain humans jittery."

"So this *is* my fault."

He opened one eye. "Shall I fetch you a cross for you to nail yourself upon?"

When he put it like that, I felt like a total knob. "Fine, they have it in for all of us – I'm just a nice shiny target at present." I wasn't overly afraid, but I'd be a fool not to be wary. "Who's next? The Prince of Wales?"

Vex ran a hand through his hair. "Who knows? They could just as easily go for a church, or a human business they think caters too much to aristos."

"The Archbishop of Canterbury," I muttered.

"We haven't had one of those since—"

"Nineteen thirty-six. I know. Is it true Victoria ate him?" His death had really got the League riled up, but it had been just a few years after the Insurrection, and anyone even suspected of League/Insurrectionist sympathies was rounded up and jailed.

Vex's smile was wry. "He deserved it, the pompous wanker." Then he sat up and pulled out the plug. The water level in the tub immediately dropped. He rose to his feet, dripping. He was truly impressive naked – all long limbs and strong muscles. He wasn't naturally pale like so many aristos; he had a bit of a honeyed tone to his skin that wasn't the result of time in the sun, regardless that weres could walk around in the daytime easier than vamps. Feeding could buy a bit of UV exposure, but not a lot.

He had quite a few little cuts and bruises on him from the explosion. Fortunately for both him and Ophelia, they had stopped to talk about the fact that their informant hadn't shown up. The bomb placed under the Sparrow had been on a timer, and went off as they were walking towards the motor carriage rather than sitting in it.

When I thought of how close he'd come to being seriously injured, probably killed . . . My stomach heaved.

"Xandra?" Rubbing the beige towel over his stomach, Vex took a step towards me. "What is it?"

Unexpected tears spilled down my cheeks. "You could have died!" Oh, fuck me. I was *sobbing*. Of all the weak-kneed, foolish things to do.

Warm, damp arms closed around me, and I didn't care if I was an idiot. I leaned into an equally warm and damp chest and had a little cry. Vex said nothing, just held me.

When I was done, I lifted my head and swiped at my eyes with the back of my hand. "Sorry."

"Don't you ever apologise for caring. When Ophelia called me earlier and asked me to come and get her because you had just killed someone and Special Branch was there, I thought I might puke."

I gazed up at him. "Really? I thought you were pissed off at me."

He smiled. "That too. You're a wee bit hard to stay annoyed with, you know."

No, I didn't. "Other people seem to have an easy enough

time doing just that." Hell, I spent most of my time fed up to my eyebrows with myself.

He kissed me – a lingering and tingle-inspiring melding of mouths. "I'm not like other people."

"No, you are not," I agreed. "I'm sorry I made you worry."

He didn't say anything. He just kissed me again – until I was loose as a ribbon in the breeze – and carried me from the en suite into my bedroom. When he was done with me, my muscles were heavy and relaxed, and my brain was a sleepy, sluggish thing.

We talked about the evening. I told him about the tourists – he shook his head at me. I also told him that Penny refused to stop working.

"That girl's too stubborn for her own good," he remarked. "I don't want you hanging around there, not with the League being active and betties taking halvies from the premises. You'd be too tempting a target."

I stiffened. Was this the point in our relationship when he stopped treating me like an equal and started treating me like a weakling? A fragile thing to be protected? Never mind that I'd already decided not to hang about the club.

"Don't get like that now," he admonished. "I'm not handing out orders. I just worry about you."

And I was an idiot. "You know, for an alpha, you're incredibly agreeable."

He trailed his fingertips down my sternum. "Because I don't thump my chest and drag you about by your hair?"

"That wouldn't be the wording I'd use, but yes."

Those lovely fingers traced a path to my navel. I shivered. "Do you honestly think I'd need to do that to get you to do what I want?"

"No." He'd only have to ask.

Vex smiled – a tad smugly. *"That's* why I'm alpha."

Then his hand slid lower, and he demonstrated a particularly effective manner of getting me to do exactly what he wanted.

Shortly before dawn, as Vex and I prepared to go to bed to actually sleep after sharing an apple pie in front of the box, my rotary rang. I made a quick grab for it, hoping the shrill ring wouldn't wake Penny, who had toddled off to bed an hour ago. Poor thing was exhausted.

Before I could even say hello, I heard Avery say, "It's me. Am I calling too late?"

She knew she was, else she wouldn't have asked. "Almost. It's been a long freaking night. Did you get my note?"

"I did, thanks. I thought I'd fill you in on my evening."

"What's the news?"

"Sayuri didn't know what Val was up to and Special Branch doesn't have much."

"And neither of those things could have waited until this afternoon?" Yes, it was bitchy of me, but she was my sister and it didn't count.

"If you'd let me continue rather than cutting me off," she shot back, "I could tell you."

"All right, get on with it then." Out of the corner of my eye I watched Vex gather up our dishes and leave the room, giving me a little privacy. Not like he couldn't eavesdrop if he wanted.

"Like I said, it isn't much, but I went through the history on his rotary. There were several numbers that he called on a regular basis, one being his SI. You can imagine me trying to explain why I'd rung her without telling her the truth."

I smiled a bit at that. Avery didn't like to lie, but when the occasion called for it, she could spin a whopper without so much as a pause.

"Thing is," she continued, "she called him several times as well, around his disappearance. The messages she left didn't say much about what he was investigating, but she sounded worried. I think she knew more about what he was up to than we realised."

"Interesting. Did you find anything else?"

"Val rang an unlisted number several times over the two days preceding his abduction. It was a number he'd never used before and wasn't in his address book – which I checked after talking to his boss. I didn't want to repeat that experience again."

I watched Vex leave the room with the pie. I should have asked him to leave it. "What happened when you called it?"

"'Twas a recording with a bunch of nonsense on it."

I frowned. "What sort of nonsense?"

"I wrote it down. W1G – 7 – C Square – zero eight – twenty-two."

"W1G. C Square." My mind reached for the connection. "Cavendish Square?" It was the most obvious choice.

I heard Avery clicking buttons in the background. She was in front of her logic engine. "I'm looking at postcodes for Westminster. Number 7 Cavendish Square begins W1G."

I tried to remember what was at number 7, but I hadn't been to Cavendish Square in ages. It was an aristo-friendly zone, home to many aristo retainers, and humans descended from "good" families who hadn't been changed by the plague but had aristo connections.

That took care of some of the numbers. "Zero eight – do you think that's August? The twenty-second?" It was just three days from now.

"I have to tell Em."

"No!" I barked.

"Why not?" my sister demanded.

"Avery, if she tells her brother, the peelers will be all over the place." Emma's brother was also a copper. " Worse, word might leak out that the Yard's going to show up and they'll scarper out of there. We don't know what this is, but it's our one freaking lead on Val and I'm not going to fuck that up. Can I trust you with this?"

There was a moment of silence. I was asking a lot of her to keep this information from Emma, from the authorities. It meant she had to trust me.

"He could already be dead, Xandy."

"He's not dead," I replied with certainty. "I was right about Dede, wasn't I?" Wrong of me to bring it up, raw as it was, but it was true, and I had been the only one convinced she was still alive.

"How do you know?" she asked, ignoring the mention of our little sister altogether. There was an edge to her voice – she didn't want to think the worst, but she couldn't help it.

"Because he's one of us. There's something freaky about our family, Av. I'm a goblin. Dede had a fully plagued kid. Who knows what's up with you and Val?"

"We don't know that Ainsley's child—"

"I've seen him. There's no denying who his mother is. He has the Vardan eyes." All of my father's children had the same green eyes, though mine had taken on a ring of amber, and Dede's son had them too.

More silence, then, "Fang me." I understood. None of us had believed Dede when she said that her baby had survived. She'd been told it had died. In reality, Ainsley and his wife had raised the boy as their own. If we'd only believed her, things might have gone so differently for her. "Are you sure we're all freaky?"

I chuckled. "No. If it weren't for Dede, I'd blame what happened to me on my mother's transformation, but I think it's all on Father's side. It doesn't mean there's anything wrong with you, or with Val, but if he's been investigating people who like to experiment on halvies, and they've caught him, they'll want to fully examine him first." That was all I was going to say. There were any number of awful things that could be happening to my brother at that moment, and I refused to think of any of them.

"I want to come with you."

She did? "That's not a good idea. If you come with me, Emma will know you lied to her. I'm not putting you in that position, Avery. I'm not fucking up your life by dragging you into mine."

"He's my brother too."

"Yes, and he's going to need you when I bring him home." It hurt to say it, but Val might still be angry with me. "Please. I'll take Vex if I need backup, but I can't save him if I'm worrying about you too." It was a cheap shot – and an insult to her abilities – but it was true. I would worry about her.

"Fine," came her petulant response.

"There is something you can do for me."

"What?" Her suspicion practically slipped through the aether and smacked me in the ear.

"You're still on vacation, yeah?"

"For another week, until Lord and Lady Maplethrope return from the country." As Peerage Protectorate, Avery was assigned to an aristo family. Lord Maplethrope employed her for London protection, and for some travel, and had another PP at his country estate who knew everyone and every inch of the village in which they spent their time away from the city.

"Great. How do you feel about shadowing Penny while she's at work?" It was the perfect solution.

"Yeah, all right." I would have been surprised if she'd said no – she adored Penny as much as I did. "But why can't you do it?"

I sighed. She was going to find out anyway. It would probably be in the papers tomorrow. "Because I killed a betty outside the club tonight."

There was silence. I counted to five. "You what?"

I chuckled. No, it wasn't funny, but it was so bloody absurd I couldn't help myself. "I interrupted three betties trying to abduct Penny. One of them bit me. He was on his way out anyway, but the toxicity of my blood sent him on to his maker straight away." I intentionally didn't mention Ophelia. I didn't want Avery to think I was including my other sister in matters but not her.

"You're serious."

"Afraid so, yes. So if I go back to Freak Show and start hanging about, the betties won't come back."

"The rags are going to have a ball with this – you know that, right?"

"Indubitably. I just hope they mention my heroics as well. I did stop a kidnapping, after all."

"How can you be so flippant?"

"Because I refuse to be the alternative. So, you'll watch Penny?"

"Of course. Send me her schedule."

"Will do. While I'm at it, be careful, okay? A tour of Americans went by the house earlier, talking about the fact that I used to live on the street. Normally I wouldn't be concerned, but the League's been up to mischief as of late. They bombed Vex's car tonight."

Silence. And then, "Oh my sweet baby Albert! Was he hurt?"

"No, but he could have been. Just be on guard, all right? Carry your gun when you go out." Once upon a time, people in security and law enforcement didn't have weapons, but that, like so many other things, all changed after 1932.

"I will. You have a care as well."

Vex came back into the room – perfect timing. "I will. I'll call you later, all right?" She said something, but I was already hanging up.

"News on Val?" Vex asked, sitting down on the sofa beside me once more.

"Maybe. He rang a number before he was taken. It was a recording with a jumbled-up address and date."

Vex went very still. "Are you certain?"

"As I can be. Avery and I pieced it together. It's an address in Cavendish Square and the date is the twenty-second of this month. Why?"

"You're not going there. Not alone."

This was so much the opposite of what he'd said being an alpha was all about that I waited for him to thump his chest. But there was something in his eyes ... "Vex, what is it? Do you know what this is?"

He nodded. "I've heard of these recordings. I'm not telling you anything until you give me your word you will not go alone."

Okay, so the demanding, protective thing was a little attractive in a primal sort of way, but really . . .

He grabbed my chin in his hand, forcing me to meet his intense gaze. "Promise me."

I stilled. This wasn't about control or protecting me. This was fear. Dread. Whatever it was, it had my wolf agitated – and that was never good.

"I promise," I whispered. "Vex, you're freaking me out. What's going to happen in Cavendish Square on the twenty-second?"

He released my face and took my hand in his. He looked so damned sad.

"A horror show."

CHAPTER 11

WE ARE ALL FORMED OF FRAILTY AND ERROR

When Dede disappeared and we were told she was dead, I didn't believe it. I refused to. But when Vex told me that the message Val heard had to do with a horror show, all my certainty that my brother was alive evaporated.

My first memory of him was of a quiet boy who would help me up when I took a tumble. He seemed to always be picking me up. I cried when he went off to Wellington Academy before me.

He used to get teased for his name – Valentine. He despised 14 February, even though he was inundated with cards and chocolates. It became his day, and he loathed it. Then he turned sixteen, grew a foot over the summer and filled out, and suddenly girls weren't giggling any more. Or rather, they giggled for entirely different reasons.

My brother was smart and honourable, and when I started

dating Ryecroft Winter, a halvie of were descent, Val warned him not to break my heart. It was Val's shoulder I sobbed on the night I found out Rye was dead.

Avery and I had just lost our sister. We couldn't lose our brother as well. It wasn't fair. But then, I knew that fair didn't mean shit.

A horror show. It was a barbaric thing. They'd been popular years ago, and apparently still attracted substantial audiences in other parts of Europe. Basically it was a public execution, in which a halvie or human was drunk to death by aristos. They used to be held for sport, then for vengeance after the Insurrection. They'd been banned decades ago, but there were those who got off on them, and so they continued. You could even buy films of them in certain back-street establishments.

I asked Vex how he knew about horror show protocol, and he responded that an unfortunate side effect of living to his age meant that he had learned a plethora of things he wished he didn't know.

"Before they became illegal, they were only taboo and happened more often than I like to admit," he explained. "I never went to one – not because of a great sense of honour, but because I don't like to feed in front of an audience – or watch anyone else do it. Back then humans used to sell themselves, or their family members, to a show."

I made a face. "Really?"

He gave me a look that made me feel horribly young and naïve. "Poverty breeds desperation." Normally hearing him roll that many "r"s would have made me smile. Tonight, nothing.

"So does a missing sibling," I remarked. "Vex, what if—"

"Don't." He put his arm around my shoulders and pulled me close. "Don't think like that until you have to. It's no good."

The fact that he was speaking from experience made it impossible for me to think of a suitable response other than a nod.

"Too bad you didn't find out immediately that Val had been taken; you might have tracked him – or got one of your goblins to do it."

Goblins did have an incredible sense of smell. Unfortunately, there were a lot of odours around Freak Show, and trying to pick out just one that was days old would be difficult, especially without knowing which direction to take.

"I could try," I thought out loud.

Vex stood and pulled me to my feet. "Not tonight. It will be dawn soon and you need to rest. You're no good to your brother if you're worn out."

I let him drag me off to bed. Oddly enough, I was asleep soon after my head hit the pillow. Dreams came sometime after that. I dreamed that I was standing on the street outside my house in the bright afternoon sun, feeling it burn my skin as Churchill nailed Val to my door. "This is your entire fault," he told me. "You destroy everyone who loves you."

"No," I argued. "That's not true."

I felt a hand on my arm. I turned my head to see Dede standing beside me, looking as she had the night she died, except that her hair was its proper copper and not the awful black she had dyed it. She was very pale, tinged with blue, and dried blood clung to her lips and face. "Goblins can't walk in the sun, Xandy."

As she spoke, intense pain started in my feet and ran up my legs. I looked down to see my lower half engulfed in flames.

The fire ate through my clothes and skin, boiled my blood. Then Dede started laughing.

I woke with a start. Vex wrapped a strong, warm arm around me and pulled me against his chest. I snuggled there, dry-eyed, heart hammering. But it was a long time before I could close my eyes without seeing Dede's laughing face framed by flames.

I woke up just before four o'clock that afternoon. I got a pint of blood out of the fridge in my room for Vex so he could face the sun without too much discomfort. Being a were made him less sensitive to ultraviolet light, but it bothered him all the same. Summer was hell on aristos, with the long days and short nights.

I didn't like cold blood, but I downed a pint myself, grimacing as it slid thickly down my throat. If this was what I had to do to keep control of myself, then I'd do it. Didn't mean I had to ruddy like it, though.

When I went downstairs to make breakfast – a pint of the red stuff wasn't going to completely satisfy me – I found Penny at the table, having a cup of coffee and reading the day's rag.

"Morning, sunshine." I forced a bright tone. I was not going to tell her about the horror show lead if I could help it. And I wasn't going to tell her about Avery. If she didn't know she couldn't mistakenly tell someone, and she'd be more natural thinking Avery was just there for the hell of it. She'd probably get suspicious eventually, but it was only going to be for a bit.

I had three days to find my brother and pray they didn't

decide to kill him before that. Although I had the awful feeling that they were saving him for the horror show, if my suspicion about our family being unique didn't apply.

And that was the extent to which I was prepared to think of it. I'd go to the horror show and save his arse. Any other outcome was unacceptable.

"You made the cover," Penny informed me, closing the tabloid so I could see my own face in grainy colour. How had the vultures even got close enough to me last night to take a photo without me knowing?

"It's a good picture," I commented. The headline screamed: *GOBLIN QUEEN BOTCHES KIDNAPPING – KILLS HUMAN.*

At least there was no mention of me terrorising tourists. That would probably come tomorrow, after those who'd witnessed it saw this photo and connected the dots.

"It doesn't say how you killed him." Penny took a sip of coffee. "And it does say that the coroner verified he would have been dead within a day or two regardless."

I went to pour myself some coffee. "Does it mention you or Ophelia?"

"Not by name. I'm merely 'the victim'. Wankers. Good news is that they talk you up as a hero."

I poured cream into my cup. "And the bad news?"

"There's nothing about the fact that my attempted kidnapping wasn't the first. Nothing about Val or the others. It's like no one thought to mention it, or it wasn't important enough." She glanced up as I sat down. "It's like they don't matter."

I patted her hand. "But if they had mentioned it, then there'd be little chance of the betties returning, and we need to catch them."

"I suppose. I just feel so helpless."

"I know."

"Yeah, I reckon it's harder for someone like you who's used to kicking arse and taking names."

My brow tightened, then lifted. "Is that how you see me?"

She leaned back in her chair. She looked so young and . . . boyish without any make-up on. "Honey, those betties could have cut your lips off and the vultures wouldn't have called you a *victim*. There's nothing weak about you."

It was a compliment, but it didn't feel like one.

I drank a little more coffee and then got up to make breakfast for myself and Vex. Penny had already eaten, and once she finished her coffee, she left to go and shower. Vex eventually appeared, gave me a kiss, and took care of the eggs while I made toast. It was very domestic.

While we ate, I went through the post. There was a letter from Buckingham Palace.

"What the hell is this?"

Vex looked up, his gaze landing on the envelope in my hand. "That's a reminder about the faction head meeting on the twenty-seventh."

I wrinkled my nose – a flattering expression, I bet. "Do I have to go? I'm not sure—"

His fork clattered to his plate. I think he might have actually barked in frustration. "Enough. I adore you like mad, but woman, make up your fucking mind. You're a goblin, and no amount of whining and wishing it were different can change that. Do you think Victoria wanted to rule the Kingdom when she was but eighteen years old? The goblins want you as their queen – a position with decidedly more clout and power than the one you currently hold. I know you don't want to be a monster, but sweetheart, you don't need a crown to be a monster. You already are one. We're all monsters. Not many, however, get asked to be the ruler of the most feared and fucking loyal creatures on the planet."

I stared at him. Every word he said was true, but only three echoed in my empty skull. "You adore me?" It wasn't love, but I'd take it.

For a moment he looked as though he didn't know whether to throttle me or kiss me. "Is that the only part you heard?"

"No, I heard it all. That's just the part I liked best."

Vex smiled. "Eat your breakfast."

"Aren't you going to ask if I adore you?"

A shake of his head sent a lock of hair falling over his forehead. "I already know the answer," he informed me with a smile.

I grinned back. The man was infuriating. "Then I don't need to say anything at all."

"Not a word."

I turned in my chair so that I could lean over and kiss him soundly. He tasted like butter. "I adore you," I murmured. I think we both knew I meant more than adore. We both meant more, but this little confession would be enough for now.

What followed was a significant pause in breakfast while we celebrated our mutual affection in the tiny pantry – we didn't want to scar Penny for life if she came downstairs.

Afterwards, I put my bacon and eggs between two slices of bread and stuck the sandwich in the radiarange to heat it up. It was so good I made another one and ate it before going upstairs to shower. For a little while I didn't worry about my brother.

It occurred to me as Vex shampooed my hair that if it weren't for the people I loved, I wouldn't worry about much at all. I mean, I wasn't even all that concerned about Scotland Yard, even though I had just killed a man and didn't feel the least bit sorry for it. Probably because I didn't feel responsible for his death at all; it was all him.

The sun was slowly sinking by the time I was dressed in a dark red corseted waistcoat and snug black trousers that looked like bloomers. They were lightweight and had a ruffle hem that hit mid-calf. I hauled on a pair of high leather boots with an hourglass heel and was ready to go. I even put on a bit of a face. It wasn't as elaborate as what Penny did every night, but I looked good enough.

Vex was on his rotary to someone about the bombing, so I left him with a kiss on the cheek and the whispered promise to bring home something to eat.

I have no idea how Penny managed to perch on the back of the Butler dressed as she was. All I know was that she had to hike her frothy skirts way up and tuck them around her legs so they wouldn't get caught in the motorrad's moving bits. She had a scarf tied beneath her chin to keep her wig from flying off and a tiny hat that was a scale reproduction of a British frigate from the Napoleonic War in her handbag.

"You sure you want to do this?" I asked before pulling out of the drive.

She nodded. "They're not going to make me hide."

I felt better knowing Avery would be there to watch over her just in case. I doubted very much that the betties would make another appearance tonight.

After dropping her off at the club, I rang Avery to let her know that Penny had begun her shift, and then set off for home once more. The past couple of days had been so insane, I was looking forward to a little quiet time with Vex, just to talk.

Part of my mind insisted that I be terrified for my brother twenty-four hours of the day, but that was just too exhausting, and not at all conducive to rational thought. Hope persisted and kept me from dwelling too much on the negative. Sometimes being determinedly myopic played in my favour.

I would find Val, just as I had found Dede, and he would be all right.

I stopped at a little American franchise not far from my place to pick up some greasy but oh so very delicious fried chicken takeaway. When I stepped up to the counter to place my order – practically drooling from the delicious smell of frying meat – I was surprised to find David, the kid who had nailed the rat to my door, standing on the other side.

Fang me, but that was an unfortunate uniform they made these kids wear. Red and white really only looked good on children and Father Christmas.

His eyes widened when his gaze met mine. "Hi," he squeaked.

I smiled. "Hullo, David. Been behaving yourself, have you?"

He nodded, face white beneath a smattering of spots. "Yes. Did you come here to check up on me, ma'am?"

A frown pulled at my eyebrows. "Get over yourself. I'm here for food. Would you like to take my order?"

David shook his head as if trying to shake something loose. For all I knew, his little brain was bouncing from one side of his skull to the other. "Of . . . sure. What would you like?"

I glanced up at the menu board above his head. "A bucket of extra crispy, two large chips, coleslaw and beans."

"Will that be all?"

I nodded. What we didn't eat when I got home I'd save for later. He told me my total and I gave him my accrual card and waited for him to swipe it through the terminal. While the transaction wrapped up, my attention was drawn to the far side of the restaurant, where a young girl was being harassed by five boys old enough to know better.

One was a skinhead, another had a mohawk and piercings while a third sported dyed black hair and eyeliner. Another was dressed very dapper and the last had a ginger pompadour and a fag tucked behind his ear. It was as though they were a boy band and each member represented his favourite subculture. Tossers.

"Who are they?" I asked David, jerking my head towards the five.

"Dickie boys," he responded, as though I should know just what the fuck a dickie boy was. "They're always doing shit like that."

What exactly was "shit like that"? Did they just plan to harass the girl? Maybe make her cry? Or were they going to brutalise her one at a time?

"Why doesn't anyone stop them?"

He looked at me as though I was hatters. "No one can stop them. They beat the snot out of anyone who tries."

My first thought, I admit, was to take my food and just go home. Let the humans do whatever they were going to do – it wasn't my problem. But the girl reminded me a little of Dede, and I hadn't hit anyone today.

And yes, it occurred to me that if I stepped in, my popularity with the locals might improve, and that maybe saving a human girl would negate having killed a betty in public opinion. That would just be the icing, though. The real reason to get involved was because I couldn't stand bullies, especially five of them dressed like twats.

David handed me the receipt to sign. I scribbled my name, and slid the slip across the counter. "Be back in a sec."

If possible, the poor boy went even paler. "What are you going to do?"

"I think it's called 'the right thing'." I smiled at him. "Don't look so worried. I'm not going to kill anyone."

"That's not what the rags say."

"That guy committed suicide," I informed him. "He was a betty dying of the plague long before I ever met him." I left him with that to ponder and made my way to the other side of the restaurant.

The girl was crying now, and the dickies – what a bloody stupid name – were mocking her for it. One of them – the one with the pompadour – kept trying to grab her breasts. Meanwhile, twenty other customers sat and ate, pretending that nothing was wrong. Oh, but they all looked up from their meals to watch me saunter by.

"Oi," I called out as I drew closer. "Leave her alone."

The restaurant fell silent. It was an unnerving thing, silence. I could hear staff in the kitchen whispering that I was confronting the dickies, the oil bubbling in the fryers, the collective breath of everyone present.

"Mind your own fucking business," Goth Boy snarled.

At this point I was within arm's length. "This is my business. This is my neighbourhood." I reached out and flicked him in the eye. Not too hard, but hard enough that it started to water and his make-up ran.

"Bitch." Mohawk came at me, fists clenched. I jobbed

him in the nose with just enough force that cartilage crunched. He fell to his knees with a cry, hands trying to catch his blood.

His blood. For a pissant, he smelled divine. Fortunately, my brain grasped the fact that eating him would not win me the respect of these people. What my brain couldn't suss out was why I wanted their respect in the first place.

I heard the familiar snick of a switchblade release. Metal flashed as the knife arched towards me. My hand shot out, wrapping around Skinhead's wrist. I squeezed until he screamed. I had snapped it.

Dapper Dickie didn't make any sudden moves. He just looked at me with his pretty blue eyes. "Do you know who we are?"

"Yeah. You're dicks." I smiled. Potty humour got me every time.

"We're going to fuck you up," he informed me with an unsettling conviction. This boy – he couldn't be more than eighteen – would kill me if he got the chance, and he wouldn't even blink.

And I'd thought I was the only monster in this particular postcode.

"Do you by any chance know who I am?" I enquired.

"You're a cunt."

There were times when that word was utterly appropriate and flush full of lowbrow eloquence. This was not one of them. This was one of those times when the guttural coarseness of it seriously pissed me off.

I grabbed him by the front of his jacket and whipped him around so fast and hard that the tweed ripped beneath my hands. His back slammed into the wall and I released him quickly enough to get one hand under his jaw and lift. His toes dangled about my shins as he stared down at me in utter astonishment.

My fangs eased out of my gums, big and sharp. I felt the change in my eyes – the brightening of my vision that signalled the goblin in me coming to the surface. I managed to keep my face from changing too much. I wanted to be impressive to my audience, not terrifying.

"I'm the goblin everyone's been talking about, and I won't allow shits like you to hurt my neighbours any longer. If I hear of you so much as annoying anyone around these parts, I'll eat your liver while it's still inside you. Understood?"

A slight pressure on the hand beneath his jaw was the only indication that he had nodded, but it was good enough. I set him down. "Get out of here."

I didn't have to tell them twice. They scampered away with their injured tails tucked firmly between their legs. It might be the last I saw of them, but I doubted it. Someday, when he was older and more mental, Dapper Dickie was going to come looking for me, thinking he could settle an old score. Then I really would have to kill him.

A smattering of applause broke out once the door chimed shut behind them.

"That was brilliant," David enthused, some colour in his cheeks.

"It was necessary." I turned then and made for the door myself, but before I could leave, I was stopped by the girl the little bastards had been harassing. She didn't say anything; she just hugged me – a tad too desperately for my liking.

"There, there." I patted her awkwardly on the back. "You're all right." I wished she was smart enough to know to stay away from me when she reeked of fear and thankfulness. It was a delicious kind of vulnerability that appealed to my inner predator.

I had to peel her off me, and send her back to her friends, who started chattering away like birds the moment she was back in their booth. Like nothing had ever happened. Must be nice.

I walked out with my paper sack of chicken. I hoped it hadn't gone cold.

CHAPTER 12

THE SOUL IS HEALED BY BEING WITH CHILDREN

Vex's rotary smashed into the floor at my feet when I walked in the door. Bits of metal and plastic went flying. I jumped aside to avoid having a piece embedded in my leg.

He shoved a hand through his hair. "Bloody hell. I'm sorry. Are you all right?"

I could heal from a gunshot wound to the chest and he was concerned about rotary fragments. "Right as rain. Question is, are *you*?" I set the bag of chicken on the bar top.

"Lost my temper," he said, a little sheepish. "Sorry."

"Don't apologise to me. Apologise to your rotary." It was a lame joke, but Vex rarely lost it, and to see him so agitated was odd. Not just that, but he'd been distracted since returning to London. I didn't think our relationship was in trouble, but there was something going on with him.

I got plates and silverware from the little stash I kept behind the bar. "Come and eat."

He smiled. "You're not going to ask me about it, are you?"

I took the bucket of chicken out of the paper bag. "Do you want to tell me?"

"I want to eat."

So we did. I tried not to take it personally that he didn't want to talk right then. There had been a few times I didn't want to discuss things, and he always gave me the time I needed to sort my head out. The least I could do was offer him the same courtesy.

I told him about my adventure at the chicken place instead.

"I'm beginning to think you shouldn't be allowed to leave the house," he said with a smile. "I've only been back a few days and already you've had more things happen to you than most people have in a year."

"Reckon I'm just special." I popped a chip into my mouth and looked down at my plate. "This stuff is so awful, yet so very good."

"Better than haggis."

"One of the tyres off the Butler would be better than haggis."

Vex wiped his mouth with a paper napkin from the restaurant. He didn't argue. "So, how did it feel to defend a mere human?"

I rolled my eyes at his teasing tone. "Fairly good, actually. Though I'm beginning to think that as a race they have a great capacity to pretend that reality is exactly as they want it. After those tossers left the shop, the girl went back to her friends and all was right with the world. And the rest of the customers just sat there through the entire thing. They outnumbered those boys and could have easily overpowered them."

Broad shoulders shrugged. "Fear does that to people. Look at how terrified everyone is of goblins."

"With good reason," I informed him, with a little pride.

"But there are fewer goblins than there are aristos. Humans outnumber them by a fantastic degree, but they've yet to do anything about it."

"True enough. Though you'd not find many – or any – aristos who would go against the gobs either."

"No. The faction that aligns with the goblins wins." There was a touch of bitterness to his tone. Just enough to turn my head. I couldn't believe I hadn't figured it out, especially after my visit to Ophelia.

"Is the pack pressuring you to get an accord with me – with the goblins?" I wondered if Ophelia knew this and thought she'd butter me up so that I'd support her Bedlamites. I could see our mother putting her up to it. When I went to this faction meeting next week, would Victoria herself try to win my favour as well? That just might make going worthwhile – to see her suck up to me while trying to get rid of me at the same time.

Vex sighed. "Some arseholes are being fairly vocal about it, yeah. I had just finished talking to one when you came home."

Hence the destroyed rotary.

"These people do know I haven't decided if I'm going to be goblin queen or not?"

Grey-blue eyes turned to me. "I don't think it matters. The goblins will still look to you regardless."

He was right. "What would it mean if the pack and the goblins formed an alliance?"

"It would give us more leverage against the vampires." The weres and vamps were considered equal as aristos, but the vampires looked down on the wolves for being animalistic. The monarch being a vamp didn't help. It was an old struggle that usually amounted to nothing, but over the past few years the weres had been lobbying for change, as had the halvie and human parties. If push came to shove, the goblins would not only give a faction extra numbers; they would give them real physical power.

"There are a few suggesting I shouldn't be alpha if I can't get you to side with us."

I scowled. "You tell them that you being alpha is the *only* way I'd side with the weres." Bastards. How dare they try to pressure him like that.

"I'm not going to tell them anything. The goblins are their own race just as we are. I'm certainly not going to bring politics into my personal life."

I leaned over and kissed his cheek. "I'm sorry being with me has caused you so much grief."

His lips twitched. "I really am going to get you a cross so you can nail yourself to it."

Before I could respond, my rotary rang. When I glanced down at the flip-slots and saw the name and number, I frowned. "It's the prince." Weird timing.

"Hello?"

"Xandra lady, good evening. It is William." As though I wouldn't have recognised his voice or his unique elocution.

"Good evening, sir." I couldn't help but smile – not only at his formality, but at my own.

"Of you the plague has need. Will you come?"

This was new. "Now?"

"Please."

"All right." I glanced at Vex, who arched a brow – he could undoubtedly hear what the prince had said. "I'll be there as soon as I can. Vex will be with me."

"Your wolf is most welcome." That made Vex raise his other eyebrow as well.

I pressed the disconnect button. "What the hell was that all about?"

"We'll soon find out," Vex remarked gracefully leaving the stool.

"You don't mind coming with me?"

"Nah. I'd be miffed if you left me behind. We'll have to take the Butler, though; Ian hasn't brought the Panther around."

I didn't ask how many cars he owned, because I knew how much he'd loved that Sparrow – and now it was a scorched pile of metal and leather.

"You drive." I tossed him the keys from the foyer table. "We'll go through Mayfair."

He hesitated. "You sure?"

I shrugged. "No, but I'll be with you, so it's not like they can deny me entrance. Besides, Down Street is the official entrance to the den. If I have to, I'll pull rank."

"Pretty tough talk from someone who claims she doesn't want to be a queen."

I smirked at him through the V I made with my first and middle fingers.

It was a nice night for a drive on the Butler. The oppressive heat seemed to have finally moved on and a gentle breeze caressed the city. It seemed the rest of London felt the same way. Even though it was late for the daytime world, humans were out and about at pubs and clubs, or just out for a stroll or coffee.

The closer we got to Mayfair, the more the hair colours of those moving about changed to vivid hues. The odd horse-drawn carriage began to appear. This time of year, many aristos were at their country homes, but some preferred to stay in London year round. They found the gates and walls of Mayfair safe and comforting.

The guards at the Mayfair entrance did not seem the least bit happy to see me when Vex announced me as his guest, but they didn't put up a fuss. I might not be able to come and go as I pleased as before, but there was no reason not to let me in. When – if – I went through the official coronation as goblin queen, I'd be back on the list of those allowed all-hours access.

The walls followed Oxford Street, Regent Street, Piccadilly and Park Lane. The streets outside had been widened to allow a lane inside the walls as well. It was all one-way, so we entered at the junction of Piccadilly and Regent Street, drove north, then west to skirt around Berkeley Square, before meandering our way south to Down Street.

The buildings at the end of the street were empty, despite having survived the attack of 1932. This was where the humans had come up into Mayfair – those who lived. They'd sacked this area first in an effort to destroy the goblins snacking on their mates. Then they'd set off for the rest of the neighbourhood. Though there were ruins throughout Mayfair, left as monuments to those who perished, the area had undergone spurts of renovation over the past decades.

The building above the old station wasn't bad, and the brick town homes to the right needed a little work. The ones closest to the entrance of the lair weren't inhabited, but families remained in the spots a little further down. This was a popular spot for halvie housing – especially Peerage Protectorate.

Vex parked the motorrad right in front of the den entrance. I climbed off and hung my goggles on the steering bars. "Oh, nice." Someone had put a bar across the door – as if that would do any good if those goblins decided they truly wanted out.

Still, it pissed me off. I yanked it out of its brackets, and then kicked at them until they were turned back on themselves and useless.

"Feel better?" Vex enquired when I was done.

"If I could shove this up the arse of the person responsible, I would." I tossed the bar aside. It landed with a loud clang on the pavement.

The door itself was unlocked – the bar would only have prevented it from opening out, which made me further question the intelligence of the person who'd put it there to begin with. Even a young goblin could rip the door free of its hinges without effort.

Vex had remembered to bring a small hand torch to light the darker recesses of the tunnels. I didn't need as much light as he did – and he didn't need very freaking much. We didn't have to be careful or stealthy, as we were expected. I jogged down the first flight of stairs, then another, until finally we hit the old platform and hopped on to the tracks.

"Do you smell that?" I asked Vex as we neared the hole in the wall that would take us down even further into the den.

He sniffed the air. "Sage."

I'd take his word for it. "Why would they be burning sage?"

"A ceremony of some kind? Or they're roasting chicken."

If they were roasting, it would be something a mite bigger than a chicken. I remembered that the prince told me once that goblins didn't eat what couldn't fight back. I didn't think children would offer much sport, but I wasn't going to judge. To most aristos, humans were food for their blood; the goblins just took it one step further.

The smell of burning herb became stronger as we descended into the den. A goblin standing sentry saw us and ran into the main chamber with an excited yip. Vex and I exchanged bemused glances.

I flicked the switch on the torch to turn it off. There was plenty of light now. We turned the corner into the great hall, and stopped dead in our tracks. The place was packed – wall-to-wall goblin. Every freaking goblin in the country had to be there. Seeing them all, I understood why the other factions would want them. They were impressive, and more numerous than I'd first thought. That was a scary realisation. Still, there were fewer goblins than there were aristos, so the numbers weren't that startling.

I used to think they all looked like dogs, but they didn't. They didn't quite look like wolves either. They were something else, and there was an equal amount of the beautiful and the terrible in them.

At the sight of me, many dropped to one knee. That was when I noticed a female lying on a cot near the fire. She looked tired, her fur damp, and she seemed to be squirming under the blanket draped over her. What the hell was going on?

"Please get up," I said, a little peevishly. This bowing business was too weird. I liked it but I didn't.

The goblins rose in almost perfect unison. The prince approached me with a huge, teeth-baring smile. For once it didn't send my stomach to my toes. "Lady, you honour us!"

"If you say so," I replied, letting him embrace me. He offered his paw to Vex as well, and greeted him with great cordiality.

"Something to show you," the prince announced, taking my arm. "Come, come." I'd never seen him so animated. Fang me, he was happy. Joyous, even.

"What is it?"

He led me to the cot where the female lay, and said something to her in a guttural tongue. I didn't quite understand, but it sounded vaguely Welsh – if Welshmen barked.

She pulled back the blanket and the prince stepped in front of me, bending down to her. Then he straightened and turned. The thing in his arms made a noise . . .

He thrust a bundle into my arms. At first I thought it was something wrapped in fur, but then I realised that it was a baby. A baby goblin.

"Fuck me," Vex whispered, peering over my shoulder.

The furry little thing was almost the size of a halvie baby, a tad smaller. Its fur was dark, with faint caramel markings. Its eyes were closed, its muzzle tiny and its velvety ears were so new they only stood at half-mast.

It was – and I'm not lying – the most adorable thing I'd ever seen. And, from what I knew of goblin husbandry, something of a miracle. Goblins gave birth even more infrequently than aristos did. It wasn't impossible, but it was rare. Very rare.

Maybe that was changing. If that was the case, I didn't blame the cobblesiders for wanting to align with us. With them.

I turned my attention to the mother as I stroked the infant's muzzle. "She's beautiful ... I'm sorry, I don't know your name." I didn't know any of them really.

The goblin smiled. She looked so tired, and happy. "Medeira, and thank you, lady."

I looked at the prince. "Is this why you called?"

He nodded, still smiling. "Wondrous, yes? First in eight years. Would not be right without our lady to bless us. First you, now a live pup."

Until that moment, I hadn't realised just how these creatures saw me. To them, I was as much a gift as this squirming infant. I was hope for their race, for their future, for—

"Ow!" My head whipped around and I looked down at the baby. My finger was in its mouth. It had bitten me and was now sucking on the wound. Terror lashed through me as I jerked my finger free. The goblins gasped, but I grabbed the prince, horrified. "Will my blood hurt it?"

A few chuckles rose up from the crowd. Even Medeira, who I thought might attack me for possibly harming her child, was smiling. "No, lady. Blood is what a pup needs. The lady's blood is an honour."

They were all staring at me, waiting to see what I'd do next. A few months ago I would have run screaming for cobbleside. Now ... well, now I poked my bleeding finger into the baby's mouth and let it nip and lick away.

It was a good thing I hadn't known goblins were this cute when I was a kid. I would have begged my father to let me have one – and that would have been very wrong on so many levels.

"May I?" Vex asked, and the mother nodded. He ran his

thumb along the baby's glossy head. It made a small whimpering sound around my finger and then sighed.

There's nothing quite as odd as hearing an entire pack say the goblin equivalent of "aaah". It was like a high growl that bounced off the walls and pooled at the base of my spine.

"She likes you," William informed me as though it were a great honour. I had to admit, it did feel something like that, looking at her sweet furry face.

"She's a fine girl indeed," I pronounced. "What are you going to name her?"

Medeira and the prince exchanged a glance before she turned her amber gaze to me. "With the lady's permission, her name be Alexandra."

"Oh." Unexpected wetness burned the back of my eyes. "Oh, that would be lovely."

Reluctantly I gave the pup back to her mother so they could bond and the little mite could nurse properly. I had just straightened when growls rose from the pack. A familiar scent, mixed with some unfamiliar, assaulted my nose.

DI Maine sauntered into the great hall backed by six men in light armour carrying guns big enough to take down an elephant – or stop a goblin.

"Well," he said with a forced smile. "Isn't this a touching scene?"

I put myself between the little bastard and the cot. A growl the likes of which I'd never heard before tore from my throat.

"Careful, Your Majesty," Maine chastised. "I might perceive that as a threat."

Wait till I had my fangs in his throat and ripped it apart. See how much he mocked me then. The goblins moved closer behind me, each furry body vibrating with tension. If I gave the word, they would attack. What a head rush that was.

Vex put a hand on my shoulder. "Easy," he murmured. "DI Maine, I assume you have good reason for being here without invitation?"

The peeler produced a sheet of paper from inside his jacket. "I have a search warrant, signed by the PM on behalf of Her Ensanguined Majesty, Queen Victoria."

The prince growled as he came to stand at my side. "No authority has *she* here."

"Perhaps not." Maine offered the warrant to Vex. I reckon he thought neither the prince nor I could read. "But you signed an accord after the Great Insurrection to cooperate with the aristocrats in lawful matters, and this is a murder investigation. I think you'll see it's quite legal, my lord." The last bit was addressed to Vex.

I wanted to rip his smug head right off his shoulders. Vex was not the authority here. I was. But then, I was barely hanging on to my control. Any second it could slip and I'd fang out and that would be the end of DI Maine. Judging from the size of those guns, it would be the end of me as well.

Vex offered me the warrant. "It's official. They're legally allowed to search the den."

"For what?" I asked. My teeth caught at my tongue. They'd extended just enough to be a nuisance.

"Signs that Lord Churchill was murdered here," came Maine's easy reply.

I eyed him carefully, sniffed the air and caught his scent with startling ease. He wasn't as calm as he appeared. I could practically hear his heart beating against the ribs I longed to break. He reeked of bravado and smug pleasure. And fear.

He might be here to find evidence, but he'd been given that warrant to make a point – that Victoria could get to me. This was all a pretext to unsettle me, to make me give something away about what had happened to Church, or perhaps to goad me into doing something I'd pay dearly for – like killing a police officer. Victoria would love it if I did that.

"Does it say 'expendable' on your badge, Maine?" I asked sweetly, teeth back to normal size.

He frowned. "Come again?"

I shook my head. "Never mind. Go ahead, conduct your search. But mind your manners."

"Or what?" Maine challenged with a smarmy grin. "You'll eat us?"

"Not if we were starving," Vex said softly. "But do keep in mind that I'm a witness to whatever happens here tonight."

Maine shrugged, and Vex's eyes flashed gold – just for a second.

I turned to the prince. "Let them have their look. They won't find anything and then they'll leave."

That myopic gaze held mine for several seconds, measuring. This was the real test of his loyalty. He nodded. "Fine."

We drew back with the prince and the rest of the plague members. I stood by the mother and child on the cot as Maine and his men searched. There was nothing left of Church to find. His bones had been repurposed, and his blood so scattered over the floor that it was contaminated by the countless pints of other blood spilled over the years. Unless Maine took the throne that had been built for me – and he looked as though he'd rather not touch the thing – I had nothing to worry about.

His men postured and tried to disguise the fear that rolled off them in rank waves. Little boys hiding behind their big guns. The goblins were afraid too, and caught off guard. The difference between my goblins and these peelers, however, was that fear made goblins more dangerous, and they didn't have heavy gear on that would slow them down.

Maine was respectful, however. He didn't touch anything without asking. He was good at pretending to be relaxed, but his shoulders were so tight I could have used them as a straight edge.

When he came back around to us, the peeler stared at the female goblin on the cot. She stared back.

"What's this?" Maine jerked his chin towards the pup.

"A baby," I replied.

"A goblin pup?" His gaze narrowed. "What is it wrapped in? Give it to me."

The mother made a sound that was a cross between a growl and a whimper. I stepped forward. "Don't you touch her."

His gaze locked with mine. "Are you going to interfere with my investigation, Your Majesty?"

That was it. I was going to eat his face. Investigation, my fat arse. I took another step, only to have the prince inject himself between us. Maine's men stopped what they were doing and adopted defensive stances, weapons lifted. Fuck.

The prince spoke in a low voice, for Maine's ears alone. Vex and I could hear – probably the rest of the gobs could too – but Maine's men would have a more difficult time of it, especially since the rest of the den had taken their cue and begun to make low, guttural noises that drowned out all else.

"Touch that child you will not," the prince warned Maine. "You will leave this place and not come back."

Maine drew himself up. "It's illegal for you to stand in my way. I could have you arrested – or shot."

The prince drew himself up as well. He was a little bit shorter than Maine, but what he lacked in size he made up for in sheer power. "How many bullets have you? How many fired before each throat is ripped out? More of us than you."

"I'm not afraid of you." But Maine *was* afraid. He stank of it, just like his people. To be honest, I respected him a bit for it. Only a fool wouldn't be afraid of William.

The prince smiled, and Maine's scent soured a little. "I know you, Christopher Maine. Know your house. Your sister. Your nephew. Mother and father. 'Twixt my teeth bones will grind, and I will start with the youngest. If not me, then another."

I'd never seen such horror on a man's face before as that which dawned on Maine's. He went white – completely white. For a moment I thought he might have a heart attack. I moved closer, knowing this situation could end very badly if either one of them made the wrong move.

"Why are you here, Maine?" I asked softly.

He swallowed, gaze still focused on William. "Orders from up high. I was to bring a squad and search the plague den. Refusal wasn't an option."

"There's nothing here," I said, keeping my voice low. "You know it as well as I. Don't put yourself in the middle of whatever vendetta *she* has against me. Just go. Take your people and leave now, and all of this will be forgotten. Won't it, my prince?" I intentionally used his title as a sign of respect, and reached down so that my fingers curved around his paw.

Maine had a difficult time tearing his attention away from William, but when he finally looked at me, I made bloody certain he saw sincerity in my face. I did not want this to end in a bloodbath. Too many might get hurt, and there was a baby in the room. This was a time of celebration, not killing.

"He won't kill my family?" Maine rasped.

I shook my head. "He will not. No one will." William bowed his head in acquiescence, giving his word not only to Maine, but to me.

"We're done here," Maine shouted to his men. "Return cobbleside, now!"

The officers looked confused, but they didn't argue. I reckoned most of them were pretty relieved. They backed out of the great hall, Maine bringing up the rear. It wasn't until they were out of sight that I heard them turn and run.

"Well," I said with a grin. "That went well."

The prince – William – whirled on me, so quickly that I actually jumped. "It did *not*," he informed me hotly. "Our home invaded. Children threatened."

I sobered. "You are right. I didn't mean to make light of it. I brought this upon you and I am sorry."

He chuffed. "You are queen. Willingly we follow."

Yes, they did. The first time I came here, he told me how to find Dede. He sent for me when Simon's body was tossed underside. He, and the entire goblin population, had offered me nothing but assistance and respect. They'd killed for me. Named a child after me. And in return I called them monsters, feared them and forsook them. It was me who had brought Maine into their home.

I ought to be heartily ashamed of myself. I was.

I nodded. "You're right. I am your queen." I felt Vex's

fingers close over those of my other hand, and squeeze. I looked at the baby goblin, cradled against her mother's chest. For the first time I paid attention to what she was wrapped in – a man's shirt with a monogrammed collar – *WC*.

It was Churchill's shirt.

If William hadn't threatened him, Maine could have taken that shirt as evidence. He would have had me – or at least could have cast the right amount of suspicion.

"I am your queen," I repeated, voice stronger this time, carrying through the hall. "It's time I started acting like it."

CHAPTER 13

CURIOUSER AND CURIOUSER

We stayed with the goblins a little while – long enough to make sure everyone was calm, that no one was going to brave the lights of cobbleside and follow Maine home to eviscerate him. I held little Alexandra again before I left.

The prince walked us to the stairs leading out of the den. "Xandra lady?" I turned to him. "What was said about you being queen, was it truth?"

I nodded. I was pretty certain it would be a decision I'd regret some day, but not as much as I'd regret doing nothing. "It was."

"Your plague can plan a coronation?"

"Yes." I smiled. "Nothing too fancy, though."

He waved a furry hand. "Worry not."

I glanced up the stairs to the hole in the wall. Trouble seemed to follow me as of late – just how understated that thought was didn't escape me – and I didn't like that it had followed me down here. "I want you to put a door or gate in. I don't like that Maine and his wankers were able to waltz in."

"Nor do I." There was a low, dangerous growl to his voice that sent a cold shiver down my spine.

"Please do not retaliate. Let me deal with Maine." If the plague made a move, it might bring even more humans and halvies down here – armed to the teeth and ready to kill. It would be a bloodbath for all sides.

He bowed his head. "As you command."

"Cheeky," I muttered. I thought he smiled at that, but it was fleeting. I sobered as well. "Take care of that baby."

He promised he would – as if I could ever doubt it – then shook Vex's hand and kissed mine.

A train sped by as Vex and I climbed to track level, vibrating the ground under my feet. As we entered the tunnel Vex said, "You know I've never seen a goblin infant before. Cute wee mite."

"She is. I have a hard time reconciling how good they've been to me with the fact that they are still monsters. That cute wee mite is a monster."

He turned his head towards me as we walked, giving me that assessing stare he often wore when I said something he found particularly interesting. It was at times like this that I was painfully aware of the difference in our ages.

"She's your monster. They all are."

"I know. Makes me want to toss my pot."

He chuckled. "You'll get used to it – once you deserve their devotion."

That was the rub, though, wasn't it? Would I ever deserve it? It seemed like all I did was bring more trouble down on those I cared for. I reckoned I was going to have to work on that.

When we exited into Down Street, we found an RG standing beside the Butler, talking into a rotary. "Wait, they're here." He disconnected.

"Bennington," I said by way of greeting. I knew him, of course.

"Lady Xandra." Ohhh, my formal title – well aside from "Queen". So cool and detached – like we'd never gone to school together, or swapped stories over coffee. It hurt more than I cared to admit. "What are you doing with my motorrad?"

"Someone saw it parked outside the entrance to the den and reported it."

I frowned. "And the problem is?"

He cleared his throat. "You're not authorised to be here, ma'am."

"Not authorised?" Vex spoke before I could. "She's with me. She's also the goblin matriarch, or did you just crawl out from underneath a fucking rock?"

Obviously my banishment from Mayfair was a sore spot with my wolf.

Bennington swallowed. "I was just following orders, sir." Then, to me, "Is it true, then? You're their queen." He jerked his head toward the entrance to the station.

"Yeah, I am." Mentally, I dared him to have a problem with that.

He smiled a little. "Then I reckon we'll be seeing more of you round these parts. The two of you have a good night." He turned and walked away, returning to his foot patrol of the streets.

"That was surreal," I remarked.

Vex only grunted in response. He was still pissed off.

I watched Bennington walk away. "I don't think anyone reported anything. He was waiting here to ask me if I was really the goblin queen. I bet you ten quid he's got the *Sun* or *Good Day* on rapid dial on his rotary."

"He's a tosser. Let's go."

Vex drove home. We barely stopped at the gate on the way out – the kid controlling it almost didn't get it open in time – and Vex gave no indication that he was going to slow up.

Once outside of Mayfair, we tore through the late-night streets like the Great Fire was nipping at our heels. I didn't mind that Vex had the throttle wide open. I loved the wind in my hair, washing me clean of Maine's stench. I knew he thought of me as his enemy, but he would leave my goblins out of it or I would make him disappear just like Churchill. It was a cold and mercenary thought, but one I'd carry with me for the rest of my days.

I reckoned I had my share of loyalty as well.

When we finally arrived at my place, it occurred to me that Vex could have gone home after the den. I could have gone with him. He hadn't even suggested it. It had been a long time since I'd stayed at his house.

"How come we never sleep at your place?" I asked.

He ran his hands through his hair in an attempt to tame the thick, tousled waves. "I don't want my staff telling anyone our business."

That surprised me. "Is it really that bad?"

"Oh yeah. My second's been pushing hard for a pact with the goblins. I'm surprised he hasn't set a ladder outside your bedroom windows."

"It would be a quick way for him to find out what it's like to fall two storeys. I'm sorry being with me has made things complicated for you."

He shrugged. "He'll challenge me eventually. It's been brewing for a couple of years now."

The thought turned my heart cold. "Challenge? As in a fight to the death for leadership?"

"That's the one. Oh, sweetheart, don't look so afraid." He pulled me in for a tight hug. "That whelp couldn't beat me if both my arms were broken and I was blind in one eye."

My arms locked around his waist. "I've lost too many people, Vex. I can't lose you too." That was all the vulnerability I was comfortable expressing. It was more than enough.

He kissed my forehead. "I'm not going anywhere."

Oddly enough, I believed him.

We climbed the steps with our arms around each other. There was a package leaning against the door – one of those large padded envelopes that seemed capable of holding a small child, and were almost impossible to tear.

I picked it up – it had some weight to it.

"Who's it from?" Vex asked.

It had been delivered by a halvie courier service that I had used in the past. When I saw the name in the sender section, my stomach flipped. *Mr Fetch.* I only knew one person who had ever been called that, and it was not his real name. It was the one he used when he was in trouble. Fetch was the nickname I'd given him when we were children. I didn't even remember why.

"Val," I whispered. "It's from Val."

DEAR XANDY,

AT THE RISK OF SOUNDING LIKE ONE OF THE
BLOKES IN THOSE AMERICAN SPY FILMS WE USED
TO WATCH, IF YOU'RE READING THIS, THEN I'VE NOT
CHECKED IN WITH MY MATE IN A FEW DAYS AND
HE'S SENT THIS TO YOU AS I ASKED IN JUST SUCH
CIRCUMSTANCES. ENCLOSED ARE COPIES OF FILES
TAKEN FROM CHURCHILL'S PRIVATE SAFE, PAPERS
THAT PROVE THAT HE WAS NOT ONLY A TRAITOR,
BUT ONE SICK BASTARD. ONE OF THESE FILES IS
YOURS, ONE IS RYE'S. THE OTHERS BELONG TO
OTHER HALVIES, SOME OF WHOM WERE ABDUCTED
FROM FREAK SHOW, AND SOME WHO SIMPLY
DISAPPEARED. THERE'S ALSO A COPY OF ALL OF MY
OWN NOTES. NOW YOU KNOW WHAT I DO. IF I
HAVEN'T TURNED UP DEAD YET, FIND ME, XANDY.
THEY WON'T KEEP ME FOR LONG, AND IF THEY DO,
I MAY WISH I WAS DEAD. I KNOW YOU DID WHAT
YOU THOUGHT WAS BEST FOR DEDE AND I HOPE
YOU CAN FORGIVE ME. LOVE YOU.

VAL

After the night I'd already had, my brother's words brought
stinging tears to my eyes. Vex consoled me with a hand on my
shoulder before sitting down at the table beside me. "Do you
want me to go through them with you?"

I nodded. "Thanks."

He gave me a small smile and brushed the tangled mess of
my hair back from my face. "We'll bring him home, sweet-

heart. I promise you. And we'll destroy every last one of the bastards who took him."

It might seem naïve, but I believed him. I believed him because I planned to make certain that was exactly what happened.

I set my own folder aside – I'd already read it when I originally copied it in Church's office the night I realised just what he really was. Instead I went straight to the file of a halvie whose surname I recognised. She was the daughter of Earl Taft. Apparently she had extremely impressive regenerative abilities. The moment I saw her photo, I swallowed hard against a massive lump in my throat. I knew that face and bright yellow hair.

"I've seen her before," I murmured, running my finger over the image of her smiling Academy photo. I'd seen quite a different expression on her face through the small window in her cell door. "In Bedlam. They'd put bits of metal in her brain to see what would happen. I reckon they thought she'd heal around them."

"Bastards."

I glanced at him. "Bastards that hide behind a mask of gentility, pretending that they need halvies to keep them safe. They're laboratory rats and nothing more."

Her name was Georgiana and she was twenty years old. Younger than me. Damaged for the rest of her life unless they could get the metal out of her brain. They should have just killed her.

Did her parents know she was still alive? Did they care? An uncharitable thought, perhaps, but halvie production was more about business and duty than love.

There was an envelope and another five files after Georgina's. A boy named Andrew, two girls named Christina and

Vivian, and one belonging to Duncan MacLaughlin, Vex's son. We already knew what had happened to Duncan. He'd been able to transform into a wolf and they'd taken him. His headless body had been disposed of like garbage.

"Open it," Vex whispered, his voice rough.

I did, and my heart rolled over. Staring back at me was a younger version of Vex – a handsome young man with bright blue eyes that sparkled with mischief. It hurt to look at him.

Vex reached out and took the file from me. My throat closed painfully as I watched him stare at the photo, wetness filling his eyes. Finally he snapped the folder shut. He blinked and sniffed as he set it aside. "I'd like to take this one, if that's all right."

I frowned. "Of course." I rubbed his arm. I wanted to tell him that I was there for him – whatever he needed – but it seemed trite. I couldn't give him his son, and nothing could ever change that.

I picked up the envelope. Inside was a birth certificate with Dede's name on it as the mother. "Baby Boy Vardan" had been stillborn. There were a couple of pages of blood work and hospital information about the child – standard stuff for any birth these days. Everyone was checked for the plague. The process seemed so much more sinister now.

I couldn't bear to look at it, so I stuffed it back into the envelope for another time.

That left one more file. The name on it was as familiar as my own – Ryecroft Winter. My old friend and first love. Church had told me that Rye was murdered by humans during a trip to Germany. He had claimed that he tried to save him but had arrived too late. I knew the night I found this file in his safe that that was a lie.

I peeled back the cover. Nothing could prepare me for the sight of him. I had loved him with all the angst and drama of a young girl. It wasn't like the way I felt with Vex – the partnership. Rye always wanted to be the best at everything; he wanted to be my knight in shining armour. He hated it when I beat him in a fight. Sometimes I'd let him win just so he wouldn't pout. He'd feel so much better about it knowing I was a goblin.

If I trained properly, there was a chance I could best even Vex in a fight. Thing was, I wouldn't want to best Vex and I would never have to let him win – Vex didn't feel the need to challenge me.

"You loved him."

I looked up to find those well-lived and knowing eyes of his watching me without judgment or jealousy. "I did."

"He should have been in Edinburgh with the rest of the pack, but Churchill petitioned for him to remain in London. Said the boy had real promise to be an RG one day. His father didn't seem to care, so I let him stay. I should have taken him; you could have met him at another time."

"You are so fucking *good*," I told him. "You'd just let me be with someone else, wouldn't you?"

His face hardened. "If it was what you wanted, yes. But don't think for a moment that means I'd let you go without a fight. I'm a good man, Xandra. I'm a fucking honourable man, but I am a wolf and you are my mate."

Fang me. I don't know if it was the goblin in me or what the bloody hell it was, but *something* took that declaration with a growl of pure lust. In that moment I didn't care that the rules were against us – that Vex would be expected to marry one of his own kind and beget heirs with courtesans.

I set the file on the table and hopped over so that I perched on his lap. He caught me and pulled me closer, and our mouths came together hungrily.

He tasted of wolf and wet heat, life and promise. When he pushed back the chair and rose to his feet, I wrapped my legs around his waist and let him carry me from the kitchen, upstairs to my bedroom.

I didn't think again of the boy I'd once loved, and what might have been. All that mattered was Vex.

I had the files cleared away and hidden under the floorboards in my room by the time Penny came home. Vex and I had gone through the ones both of us were prepared to look at, searching for clues. We didn't find anything except the fact that Georgiana, Andrew and Christina had all been taken from Freak Show. No wonder Val had started to investigate the club; no wonder the people behind the disappearances wanted to shut him up. I actually hoped that he had unique qualities like Dede and myself – it would be the only reason they'd have to keep him alive.

We were sitting in front of the box, decompressing after what had been a bloody hatters night, sharing a huge container of ice cream. I didn't know the flavour, but it was chewy, with bits of toffee in it. If I had the funds I spent on food to spend on clothing, I would have a wardrobe so extensive I could change three times a day and still not wear the same outfit twice in six months. It was ridiculous. Vex often bought groceries for us. It wasn't that I wanted for money – I didn't – but he thought it was the right thing to do since he was here so much.

He really was the best thing that had ever happened to me. Because of him and his support, I felt stronger. He didn't think being a goblin was a bad thing, and that meant more than he could ever know, because I was still having problems with it.

Second thoughts and doubts be damned. I would accept the crown and make the best of it. I couldn't run from what I was. I didn't want to. Once I found Val, I was going to give serious thought to finding a more permanent housing situation closer to the goblin den. Not in it, of course – I needed to be cobbleside – but close. Once I was queen, and accepted formally into the plague, they wouldn't be able to keep me out of Mayfair. I'd have every right to be there.

Wouldn't that drive that old bat Victoria mad? Made me smile just thinking about it.

"Evening, gorgeous," I called when I heard the back door alarm go off. On the wide screen in front of me, a laughable American movie about a teenage werewolf playing basketball drew chuckles from Vex.

The alarm went quiet, and a few seconds later Penny minced into the room. "Greetings, darlings," she said wearily, plopping down on the other sofa. "What are you two eating?"

"Ice cream. How the hell do you stand all night in those ridiculous heels?"

She lifted a shapely leg, the last six inches of which was a pink glittery heel. "Because these shoes know how lucky they are to have me." Her little frigate hat was perched on top of her head. The sight of her never ceased to make me happy.

But Penny looked tired beneath her make-up. This situation with Val and her own near abduction had taken its toll. She glanced at the box. "What in the name of all that's fashionable and good in the world are you two watching?"

"Americans," Vex said by way of explanation.

"Ah." To my surprise, there was a wealth of understanding in that one syllable. "Right. I'm going to get something to eat."

I offered her the ice cream, but she turned it down. A few minutes later, she returned with a big bowl of salad topped with spicy chopped chicken and resumed her previous perch. She had removed the towering shoes.

"You're an insult to your kind," I told her, eyeing the bowl with disgust. "Salad?"

"Bugger off. It's healthy."

"You burn calories like dry tinder and are genetically predisposed towards perfect health."

She shrugged. "I like it. Sorry."

I shook my head. "At least tell me you put dressing on it."

"A third of a bottle."

"That's my girl."

She grinned. We watched the box for a bit – the teen wolf was going to something called a kegger. "Saw your sister Avery at the club tonight. Is that going to be a regular occurrence?"

"I wouldn't know," I lied. "I haven't talked to Avery since she told me about Val."

I don't know if she believed me, but she didn't push it and that was good. I didn't want her to think I was spying on her, but I had to keep her as safe as I could if she insisted on bloody flaunting herself in the betties' faces.

"They're lucky, you know – Avery and Val. To have you, I mean."

I stared at her. This was totally unexpected. "He's lucky to have you too."

She made a scoffing noise that startled me. Penny never

lacked in self-confidence; where had that come from? "Sorry. I reckon I don't see it."

It wouldn't matter what I said to her. She was obviously in a funk and not in the mood to hear whatever I had to say.

"I would have fought them, you know," she said. "If I'd been just a little faster getting to him, I would have tried to save him."

"I know you would." I resisted the urge to shoot Vex a what-the-fuck-is-this-about glance.

Her salad forgotten, Penny scooched closer to the edge of the sofa. "I mean, you can't save everyone, right?"

"I think Dede's proof that I can't save everyone, dearest." And then, because I couldn't help it, "Are you quite all right?"

"I'm fine," she said on a sigh. "Just tired, and feeling useless. Forgive me. I think I'm going to toddle off to bed."

I watched her stand and wished her a good night, as did Vex. She smiled wanly and wished us the same. Then she disappeared up the stairs, tugging off her wig as she climbed.

When I heard her bedroom door shut, I turned to Vex and whispered. "What the ruddy hell was that?"

He scooped up a spoonful of ice cream. "Sounded like guilt and desperation to me."

Yeah, it did, and that bothered me.

CHAPTER 14

ALL CRUELTY SPRINGS FROM WEAKNESS

I woke up late the following afternoon with Vex still sleeping beside me in the darkness. The heavy curtains over my windows blocked out the day so that Vex could wake up without having to feed to face the sun. As it was, it was a slightly overcast day, so it would be easier for both of us to be up and about.

I stretched and slipped from between the sheets. As I pulled on my black velvet kimono, I bent my neck to the side, getting a satisfying crack in return. Then I padded downstairs and dumped coffee grounds into the cafetière. While the water heated I nibbled on a piece of cheese to stave off the growling of my guts and spooned a glob of bacon fat into the frying pan on the hob. When that was hot, I slapped two steaks into the pan. They sizzled deliciously as I started up another pan of potato slices. I polished an apple on my robe and took a juicy bite.

When the steaks were done, I took them out of the pan and

cracked a couple of eggs into the hot cast iron. Vex still hadn't come downstairs, so I put his meat and potatoes on a plate and stuck it under the warmer. I took my own plate to the table and sat down with my portable logic engine to see what was happening in the world and check my messages – not that I ever had many.

I'd just polished off the last of my potatoes when someone rang the bell. I was sucking a bit of egg yolk off my thumb as I opened the door. It hadn't occurred to me until that point that it might be the Human League on the other side. Or even the press.

It was worse. Standing in the shade of my entrance hall were Ophelia and my mother.

"What the hell are *you* doing here?" Prior to a couple of months ago, I hadn't seen my mother in years. As far as I knew, she never left Bedlam, maintaining the ruse that she was an inmate there, and not a traitor to the Crown and a rare "made" aristo. She'd been turned with a bite, and so had I.

Juliet Claire – my mother – was a gorgeous blonde with porcelain skin and bright blue eyes. She looked to be a few years older than me, but in actuality was in her late forties. She wore a blouse, waistcoat and snug trousers tucked into high boots. Coloured spectacles concealed part of her face and a wide-brimmed hat covered her upswept hair. She looked like she should be riding about in a carriage in Hyde Park rather than slumming in Leicester Square.

She breezed past me into the house. Rude of me not to invite her in sooner, with the sun shining as brightly as it was. "Do I need an excuse to call upon my daughter?" she enquired, turning to face me.

Ophelia crossed the threshold and I closed the door. "Yes,"

I replied. "I reckon you have one else you wouldn't be here. Coffee?"

They followed me into the kitchen. "What an interesting space," my mother remarked in a manner that told me that "interesting" was a polite snub.

"People who live in asylums shouldn't comment on other people's homes." I took two mugs out of the cupboard, filled them with coffee and stuck them in the radiarange for a minute. I topped up my own cup as well and then joined them at my little table.

My mother had removed her hat and dark spectacles and studied me much like a hawk must study a young rabbit. "You look tense."

"My brother is missing, someone hired a kid to nail rodents to my door, I am under investigation for murder, and Vex was almost blown up. Can't possibly imagine what I'd have to feel tense about."

She turned that sharp gaze on Ophelia. "Did you know about any of this?"

"Some of it," my sister replied, looking as though she'd rather have her eyes gouged out than confess. "I was with Vex when the explosion took place."

I stared at her as well. "You were almost killed and you didn't tell her?"

Ophelia glared at me. "Would you?"

I thought about that. Probably not. I wouldn't want her to worry. And I wouldn't want to face the barrage of questions and demands for my safety that would likely follow.

"Exactly," she continued, correctly interpreting my silence. Then to our mother, "We didn't come here to discuss me."

Judging from the look on her lovely face, my mother

anticipated a full briefing from Ophelia later. It must be awful to live with someone who expected to know everything her loved ones were up to.

I made a mental note to apologise to both Avery and Val when I got the chance. The apple didn't fall far.

My mother wasn't done. "If you didn't spend so much time with that wolf, you wouldn't get into such trouble. It's always been his fault when you get hurt."

"*That wolf* is asleep upstairs," I informed her with a clenched jaw. "You're a fine one to talk – you're a were *and* completely hatters. If anyone found out what you're doing in that madhouse of yours, they'd put a silver bullet in your brain. Fee can take care of herself."

My sister shot me a startled and surprisingly thankful glance. I squirmed a little. "You came here for a reason. What is it?"

Juliet – sometimes it was difficult to see her as maternal – sighed. "I see that both of you are too much alike and I cannot win. Fine. Xandra, I came to speak to you about something important. Something only you can do that will change the world for ever."

I wasn't the brightest wick on the candelabra, but I didn't have to be to understand where she was headed, especially not after Vex's issues with the pack. "You want my goblins to align with you." It was a ludicrous thought. She might as well stick a sign that read *ALL YOU CAN EAT* above Bedlam's front gate.

"Did you tell her?" she demanded, accusing Ophelia.

My sister scowled. "No, but neither is she stupid. She knows that people are going to want to use her."

Our mother flinched. "I do not want to use Xandra."

She could start by telling me that and not my sister. "But you want to use my goblins."

She looked at me as though I'd spoken in tongues. "Well, yes."

Of course, because goblins didn't have feelings or intelligence. She'd take that back if she saw that room of monitors they had.

"For what? What could you possibly have planned that you would need the gobs to carry out?"

"I don't have anything *planned*." She was positively peevish. "But everyone knows that the side the goblins is on is the side with real power."

"Because everyone's afraid of them."

"Of course. If the goblins decided to come cobbleside and declare war, no one could stop them."

Maine and his big guns might give it a go.

"They have no intention of coming above ground, and if they did, it wouldn't be to fight someone else's battle."

"It's their battle too. I can't imagine they're treated fairly by the current regime."

I arched a brow. "Will the new boss like them any better?"

She flushed. "Of course."

I believed that about as much as I believed that Val was going to stroll through my door at any moment dressed in one of Penny's frocks. "Right. Look, I know change is coming. I reckon Queen V feels it too. Things can't continue the way they are, but the goblins will not side with people who think of them as monsters."

"*You* think they're monsters," Ophelia tossed in, reminding me of whose side she was on.

"Yes, but they're *my* monsters." The words fell easily off my tongue, surprising me as much as my mother and sister. "And I refuse to allow them to be used as weapons in your war."

"What are they if not weapons?" my mother demanded. "They are born killers. Animals with no sense of loyalty or right and wrong—"

"Mother!" Ophelia cried.

"What?"

I almost laughed, but Ophelia cut me off. "Xandra is a goblin."

Juliet frowned. "That's not the same. She was raised properly."

"I was raised as a lab rat," I informed her. "Born to a woman paid to breed with aristocrats, brought up to serve my betters and betrayed by almost everyone I loved. Does that sound fucking proper to you?"

High colour stood out on the apples of her smooth cheeks. "I did what I thought best for you."

"You let me think you were lost to me for ever. You couldn't even come and see me when I was shot. I almost died and you hid away in your fortress because your cause was more important. Yet when you think I might be useful to you, you turn up on my front step. All because you want to use and exploit the only beings who have shown me unconditional respect and caring. I've learned more about loyalty and honour from the goblins in two months than I ever learned from you."

For a second, I thought she might slap me. Gold flashed in her eyes – a sure sign of werewolf aggression. I let my own monster show just a little. If she wanted to get into a pissing contest with me, I was more than willing to discover which of us was more dominant. This woman was a memory to me, not a mother. Not any more.

Instead, the gold disappeared, replaced by wetness. She blinked it away. "You're right. I wasn't a good mother, but Xandra, you can help change our world. Don't you want to change it?"

Ah, maternal guilt. That was a potent weapon. "Of course I do. But I'm not going to speak for the goblins. I'm not going to sign them up for someone else's cause. Your flaw is that your crusade is more important than the people involved in it or even those you love. If I ever align with you, it will be because my plague wants to align, because we believe in what you're doing, not because you're my mother, and certainly not before I know I have your respect."

"Well said," came Vex's voice from the doorway.

I'd felt his arrival a second before he spoke. I think I could be dead and still know when he was near, even though he moved with astonishing stealth for such a big man.

Juliet – time to dispense with referring to her as my mother when she hadn't earned that right – leaped to her feet, squaring off against Vex as though he was the trespasser on her territory.

Two alphas, nose to nose. I was about to get pissed on.

"This doesn't concern you," she informed him, ice practically dripping from her words.

He folded his arms over his chest, shirt straining at the shoulders. "Anything that concerns Xandra concerns me."

She stiffened, but didn't stop staring at him. Brilliant – a battle for dominance in my bloody kitchen.

"Shit," Ophelia muttered. When I looked at her, she added, "Mum's not pack." As if that meant anything to me. "It means that she doesn't acknowledge Vex as alpha, but as her equal."

I rolled my eyes. "Figured that out already."

She scowled at me. "Fang me, don't you know anything? If Vex thinks she's challenging him, they'll fight. She's no match, but she'll fight him regardless rather than submit to his dominance."

Now I was scowling. "That's fucking mental."

"Isn't it?"

I turned my attention to the two wolves staring each other down. Vex didn't look like he was in any hurry to get violent, but he wasn't the type to take blatant disrespect for his position either. If Juliet didn't back off, he'd be forced to slap her down. And he could seriously hurt her. The only reason he hadn't made a move already was because she'd given birth to me.

Sighing, I rose to my feet and put myself between them. "I declare my house a no-pissing-match zone. Neutral. Now both of you step down or get the hell out."

Vex nodded. "As you wish."

Juliet smirked. "Some other time, MacLaughlin."

What the hell was her problem? She didn't like Vex because Ophelia was part of his pack? Did she blame him for Fee being abducted years ago and used for experiments? I didn't flatter myself into thinking it had anything to do with my relationship with him, though it probably didn't help that two of her daughters were loyal to him.

I took her by the arm, squeezing just enough to make my point. "If you ever put him in that position again, I'll take it as an insult, and I have no problem with kicking your arse. And I am just an animal – a born killer – remember?"

Her eyes widened, but she didn't push me. She nodded. "Fine." No apology or anything. What happened to the sweet woman I remembered holding me as a child?

"I think it's time for you to leave," I told her. I had things to do – like go to a horror show. "You've said what you came to say and I'm not interested."

I walked down the corridor to the front door and opened it. Beyond the shaded step the late summer sun was starting to mellow.

"War is coming, Xandra," Juliet said as she paused on the threshold. Ophelia shot me an apologetic glance from the pavement. "You're going to have to choose a side eventually. The humans are tired of living in fear. Half-bloods born to non-noble parents deserve the same respect and chances as those with the royal seal on their birth certificate. The vampires think they're superior, and the wolves want to dominate them. The goblins want to come cobbleside. There's no such thing as neutrality, or there soon won't be."

"I already have a side," I informed her as I crowded her out on to the steps. "Mine."

I shut the door in her startled face.

"I'm sorry about Juliet," I said to Vex a little while later as he ate his breakfast and I nursed another cup of coffee.

"She's not your responsibility. She's not mine either."

Hmm. "Why isn't she part of the pack?"

He cut into his steak. I eyed the pink centre with envy. "You don't know?"

"I don't know much of anything where she's concerned," I admitted. "She's been out of my life longer than she was in it." Blimey, wasn't that depressing?

Vex chewed and swallowed. "After she was bitten, I let her

know the pack was there for her should she turn. She told me in no uncertain terms to go fuck myself. I tried again when it was apparent she was indeed a were, with the same result. One of my wolves bit her and she blamed me for it as much as him."

"What happened to him?"

"He's dead." He bit into a piece of toast. "Why?"

"He's as much a part of me as Juliet and Vardan. I would have liked to have met him."

"No you wouldn't. A were who attacks a pregnant woman needs to be put down hard and fast."

"Were you the one who killed him?"

"Aye. Part of the job description." He watched me over the rim of his cup, checking for my reaction. His confession didn't inspire much more than minor disappointment that I'd never come face to face with the dog so I could kick him in the bollocks.

"I would think his death would give Juliet a little peace of mind."

"It didn't. I offered her sanctuary when I heard they were taking her to Bedlam. I don't have to tell you her choice."

No, he certainly didn't. She went to Bedlam, climbed into a bed of crazy and was lying in it till this day. "I'm still sorry for her being such a bitch. Remind me next time I move house to forget to give my relatives my address."

"You could always move in with me."

I froze. "You don't mean that."

Vex shrugged. "At least at my place you wouldn't have to deal with the League, the press or your mother. You'd have a little quiet."

A little quiet. Fang me, but that sounded good. I hadn't had quiet in a while – and these last few days had been a cacophony of shit. I'd cut out my own tongue – and be completely happy to do it – for a fortnight of being bored out of my skull.

The dust had to settle eventually, didn't it?

"You're a doll to offer, but I would like to continue our relationship, and moving in with you and the pack so I can avoid trouble is not conducive to that goal."

Another shrug. "Suit yourself."

Was he hurt by my refusal? Christ, he hadn't been serious, had he? And if he had been, why?

Maybe, said a little voice in my head, *because if you move in with him, everyone else will assume the goblins have joined the weres.*

If the goblins and weres joined, they would be an unstoppable brute force. If the Insurrectionists got the gobs, they'd be a formidable covert force. If the vamps were the winners, they'd be politically buoyed by the increase in numbers. The goblins were strong, loyal and smarter than they were given credit for. Any side who won them would have an advantage. Plus, my mother knew that goblins saw themselves as removed from the aristos, and would have no problem killing vamps or weres if it was necessary.

My mother also knew that the goblins' loyalty to me might easily extend to my family, just as Vex would know that that loyalty could also apply to my lover.

I ought to be ashamed for thinking it, but I couldn't help myself.

Or, whispered another voice, *perhaps he really does fancy you enough to share his house*. I opened my mouth to say something – anything – but he cut me off.

"We have to be careful tonight. Go in with guns blazing and we'll make more enemies than friends."

"I don't care about friends, I just want my brother."

Vex rested his elbow on the table. "Sweetheart, your brother's probably not going to be there. They'd realise the risk in killing such a high-profile halvie in front of witnesses. If you want to find him, you need to be patient. Violence will get you ostracised and might get Val killed." I must have pouted, because he continued, "I'm not saying you can't break a few heads – just be smart about it." *For once*, the little voice added.

I nodded. He was right, as was the voice in my head. I usually acted on impulse and had fucked things up as a result. I needed to keep calm. I wasn't the only one with something at stake. If I lost it, the repercussions would come back on Vex as well. He didn't need any more trouble because of me.

"My juice, is it worth the squeeze?" It was one of Dede's old sayings that I'd started using.

He stared at me. Blinked. "I'm trying to suppress my inner schoolboy urge to say something totally inappropriate. Are you asking if you're worth the effort?"

I nodded. "My life's been nothing but tits-up since you and I started."

"Being with you feels right. I can't explain it and I'm not about to try to justify it. You're the one who can't seem to accept it." He held up his hand when my mouth opened. "I know you've wondered if I'm with you for political reasons. That's shit and you know it. You'll grow out of this insecurity, because that's what this is. I'm willing to wait. And before you ask, I'll tell you – because I want to."

As answers went, it wasn't exactly what I was looking for,

but it was exactly what I needed to hear. No poetic declarations, no delicately worded half-truths. He knew me. Knew what and who I was. More importantly, he had never asked anything of me, even though I seemed to keep demanding from him.

If Vex wanted a partnership with the goblins, he would have made a move long before I entered his life. He was a sought-after bachelor. If he was with me, it was because he wanted to be. End of story. Why make a drama out of the one good and simple thing in my life?

"Thank you," I said.

He was still smiling. His life must have been dead boring before I showed up. "I need a shower. You need to wash my back. Come."

I didn't wait to be asked twice. I put my hand in his and stood, letting him lead me out of the room. A little slap and tickle was just what I needed to take my mind off things. A short break before we left to go to a seedy building and watch someone being murdered.

For the sake of all in attendance, it had better not be my brother.

CHAPTER 15

THERE IS NO GREATER EVIL THAN ANARCHY

Later that evening, Vex and I left my house to go and watch someone be exsanguinated. It was one of the prouder moments of my life, I thought, tongue firmly in my cheek.

Someone from the pack had dropped off another of Vex's motor carriages for us. This one was a sleek black Panther from the late 1970s. I slid into the leather seat and went over the plan for the evening in my head. When we arrived at Cavendish Square, Vex would go into the building while I skulked about outside, eventually finding my own way in. It might seem like unnecessary dramatics, but people would notice if I suddenly showed up at a horror show. Certain individuals – who Vex refused to name – had invited him to these evenings before, even though he always declined.

The point was, he'd been around long enough to know about these things and be trusted to keep his mouth shut. I, on the other hand, had not. And since the people who'd taken my brother might also be involved in tonight's entertainment, we decided it might be best for me to keep a low profile.

And that was fine by me. I'd rather not be seen at such an event. I wasn't a good enough actress to keep my opinion of it from showing. I wasn't a big fan of humans, but I wouldn't want to see one drained of blood just for sport. I certainly didn't want to see it happen to a halvie.

"Tell me again how these things got started," I said as Vex steered the Panther into the street. I was still not accustomed to this much road traffic. Humans felt secure in this part of town and stayed out well after dark, sometimes by themselves. That was a rarity the further west you went. The only humans you'd find in the area around Mayfair and Wellington district were cabbies and people who worked for aristos, or in aristo businesses. I was fairly certain most of them carried silver weapons, or portable UV torches.

Here, humans walked around like they were actually safe. A few months ago I would have agreed with them. I also would have curled my lip at the sight of them. Now ... well, I wasn't about to hug one of them any time soon, but I felt a little pity for them. They weren't safe. Not from aristos, or goblins ... not even from themselves.

"I don't know exactly when. The first one I heard of was when a young half-blood girl sold herself to the Earl of Bragstone for one hundred pounds. That was quite a sum in 1873. The money went to her sister, who was a widow with two small children. The earl was supposedly so impressed by the girl's sacrifice that he invited several of his closest friends to watch while he drained her. I've heard that he allowed them to join in, but no one's ever stated it for a fact."

I clenched my jaw. "Bastard." In those days halvies – long

before they saved the arses of many aristocrats during the Great Insurrection – weren't worth much more than humans. The earl wouldn't miss a hundred quid, and he probably thought it quite a joke that the girl would forfeit her life for such a sum.

Before finding out the truth about myself, and the world I lived in, I would never have believed such a story so easily. Now, I swallowed it like a bitter pill. "And they've been going on ever since?"

"At one time they were more commonplace. Prince Albert was instrumental in making them illegal. These days they're extremely rare – or so I've heard. There might be one every six months or so. They happen more often in France and Germany. Russia had a spate of them a few years ago, before the ring responsible got shut down."

Germany. Was that what had happened to Rye? Had Church given him over to be killed in front of an audience?

"I'm not sure I like how much you know about them," I admitted.

He glanced at me. "Live long enough, you learn a lot about many things you'd rather not."

"I know. It's just . . . disturbing to hear you talk about it as though you were reading it from a book."

"I haven't any personal experience, so I regurgitate what I've heard."

It occurred to me then that I was taking my apprehension out on him. This was going to be his first time at a horror show as well. Hopefully it would be the last for both of us, but the fact remained that he was only doing this because he couldn't let me go alone. And because he wanted to help me find Val.

"I'm sorry. I'm just foul tonight."

"I understand. That and the fact that you're cute are the only reasons you're still in the carriage."

I arched a brow. "Oh really? You think you could take me, wolf boy?"

He laughed. "I haven't been a boy for over a century, and I know I could best you. Maybe not in a few years, when you've reached your full potential, but I could more than hold my own for now."

No bravado or mockery, just plain speaking. "Allow me to apologise, then, before you call me out for impugning your honour."

"Apology accepted. Now, what do you say to directing all that anger at the people who took your brother instead?"

"An excellent notion." Truly, the man amazed me. It didn't seem to matter what I did or said, he'd let me know if I'd gone too far and then be done with it, like brushing dirt from his hands. Me, I came from a long line of grudge-holders and brooders.

Speaking of family, I hadn't heard from Avery yet this evening. I'd asked her to check in when she had the chance. I hadn't seen Penny either. I pulled my rotary out of my pocket and checked the call counter. I'd missed a call, but not from a number I recognised. Probably someone trying to sell me something, but they'd left a message on my Britme service, so it was worth checking into.

I dialled the number for the service. A few seconds later I heard a young male voice. "Goblin lady? Your Majesty? It's David – I work at the chicken place? You said to ring you if that vampire bloke showed up again. Well, he's at the front door—" He broke off as a loud crash sounded in the background. I heard the kid shout and then there was nothing.

"Shit," I muttered as I disconnected.

Vex didn't take his eyes off the road. "What?"

"The kid that nailed the rat to my door. I think vampires might have nabbed him."

"Tell me you're joking."

"Wish I could. He said the vampire that hired him was at the door. There was a crash, some yelling and then nothing. I think they took him – or they killed him in his flat." I highly doubted that. No intelligent vampire would want the media to get hold of an aristo-committed murder, especially not when the victim was human.

"You want to go to the kid's house?"

"No." I wasn't being cold – the message was from the night before. "If they were going to kill him, he's already dead. I might be able to scent the vamp who ended him, but I can do that after the horror show just as easily as I could do it now."

Bottom line: I couldn't do anything for David, but I might still be able to save my brother. I hoped finding Val would ease my conscience. The kid might have got himself into this mess, but I had made him my responsibility.

"Fuck it," I said after a couple of seconds. "Turn around. Please."

Vex did as I asked in a dazzling display of driving that would have done an American action film justice. It took what seemed like forever, even at a good speed, to get to the estate where David lived.

As we pulled into the drive, we spotted coppers on the terrace talking to a blonde woman I assumed was the kid's mum. There wasn't an ambulance anywhere to be seen, nor a hearse. I mentally crossed my fingers that we hadn't just missed one or the other.

I rolled down the window and listened.

"He's about five foot seven," the woman said tearfully. "With blonde hair and blue eyes. He's a good boy. I don't know why anyone would take him."

"He's not here," I told Vex quietly.

He nodded. "I heard. What do you want to do?"

I peered through the windscreen at the frightened woman. "I don't want to do anything with the peelers here. Let's go. I'll come back here later." It was the best I could do. If I got involved now, I'd be on the Yard's radar again, and Maine would find out about my connection to the kid. He'd probably suspect me of killing him too.

We drove away – hopefully without being noticed.

Cavendish Square was just north of Mayfair's fortified walls. The entire area was known simply as "Cavendish" these days. It was one of those areas that came more alive at night, but not because of aristo denizens. These people were human – some plague carriers, but still human – with connections to the aristocracy. Courtesans occasionally came from the area, having the right genetic make-up as well as the social requirements that made them good breeding material.

The inhabitants of this neighbourhood often worked for aristos – though not in the gauche manner of actual labour. They clung to the old ways, same as the ruling class, finding employment vulgar. Their positions were carefully chosen, as they were the "human" face of the aristocracy. They were barristers, surgeons, landowners who oversaw their own estates as well as those owned by their nocturnal relatives.

It was a lovely area – well kept and prettily appointed. Lots of greenery and manicured grounds. Stately buildings and well-swept walks. It was difficult for me to believe that one of these whitewashed brick structures was going to provide the setting for a murder. At least one.

Vex parked the Panther in a covered area not far from our destination. I noticed the section for horse-drawn carriages was almost full. Granted, it only held maybe a dozen vehicles at best, but that was still unsettling. Just how many aristos came to these things?

As though reading my mind, Vex turned to me after surveying the parking area to make certain we were totally alone. "I've heard of halvies and humans attending these things. Goblins too."

I didn't want to know that. It seemed so ... beneath the goblins that I knew. "I shouldn't be surprised. Death has always been something of a spectator sport in London." Public executions used to draw crowds now found only at festivals.

"I need you to know that I don't condone this sort of thing."

I looked at him. "I know that. You wouldn't even be here if not for me." I took his hand. "I want you to know how much I appreciate that."

His fingers squeezed mine. "All right then, let's get this over with."

Vex left the carriage park before I did. I pinned my hair up and covered it with a black scarf that perfectly matched the black of my snug trousers, corset and top. Even my boots were the exact same shade. I hadn't planned it that way; it was just a lucky accident of fashionable coordination.

I climbed a set of stairs to the next level of the parking structure. The heavy metal door groaned on its hinges as I pushed it open. I turned and headed for the low concrete wall that allowed me a good view of the street below – and the building across the way.

After a glance around to make sure no one was looking – and that there weren't any cameras watching from a concealed corner – I hopped up on the wall, bent my legs and pushed.

The edge of the wall crumbled beneath my boots, a few scant pebbles falling to the street below as I sailed through the air. This was what it felt like to fly.

For a split second I didn't think I'd make it. I'd never tried a jump this large before. It was too far.

And then my feet hit the roof and I landed in a crouch. Fang me, I'd made it. I turned and glanced over my shoulder at the carriage park, seeing just how far I'd jumped. Giddiness rose up in my chest.

I ran across the top of the roof as the sky continued to darken above me. I could see perfectly well as I skirted an oddly placed chimney. The next building was the one where the horror show was being held. Vex reckoned it would be below stairs. Many of these old building had lovely dark cellars with secret escape routes added after the Great Insurrection. I didn't know how cobbleside remained cobbleside with the maze of tunnels and catacombs beneath this freaking city.

At the edge, I didn't hesitate, just pushed off with my foot and sailed across the narrow alley to grab on to the wrought-iron gate across the lower half of one of the windows. My body dropped, jerked hard at my shoulder joints. I pulled myself up until my arms were straight down, and swung my legs over the narrow rail. Then, after making certain neither of my shoulders was dislocated, I forced open the window and slipped inside.

The attic was dry and dusty, smelling of old wood and rotted fabric. I sneezed, then froze. Had anyone heard? I strained my ears for the sound of footsteps. There were people in the building, but far below me, and with enough chatter that I doubted I'd been noticed.

A narrow door in the far wall was the only exit. I turned the handle and looked down an unlit staircase, below which was a hallway. I crept down the stairs, each creaking regardless of where I put my foot. Albert's fangs, was the entire place conspiring against me?

This must have been someone's house at one time, though now it seemed to be more of an office or some sort of shop. Old photographs hung on the faded paper – creepy-looking men and women, hand-coloured and stiff. I kept my gaze averted.

Wasn't I a piece of work? I wasn't afraid of sneaking into a horror show, but the back of my neck tingled at the sight of pictures of people dead at least eighty years. I didn't like early photography – it reminded me of a picture album I'd seen at the courtesan house. I'd gone through the pages hoping to find a photo of myself or someone I knew, only to find image after image of dead babies. I hadn't known they were dead at the time, not until my mother found me looking at it and took it away. There had been a photograph of her in there, holding a wrapped bundle, a lost and hollow look around her eyes.

And now that I remembered it, I felt sorry for her.

I pushed the memory away, ignored the unnerving photographs watching me and crouched in the shadows near the top of the stairs. From there I could hear the voices of people arriving. When Vex had called the number for the recording, he'd also got the password for the night's show. I reckoned it was a way to make sure no one just wandered in off the street, but it didn't seem like much of a security precaution to me.

After all, I was there to bugger things up, and I knew the bloody word.

When I heard Vex's voice, my heart gave a little thump. Silly, really. I hadn't felt like this since Rye and I first got together. I didn't have that teenage "oh, I'll die without him" feeling with Vex, and for that I was thankful. What I did have was fear. Fear that I'd lose him, because every part of me knew he was the best thing that had ever happened to me, and much better than I deserved. He seemed to see something in me that I couldn't, and while I wondered at it, I wasn't stupid enough to fight it.

His voice faded, along with the others. Eventually I heard the unmistakable sounds of a door being latched and then another opened. Instead of slipping down these stairs, I turned and looked for the servants' stairs that all these old buildings tended to have. Eventually I located a concealed door in the back wall. Clever. The wall swung open inwards, revealing a steep, winding staircase barely wide enough for one person.

The wall closed when I stepped over the threshold on to the first stair. There was just enough light from cracks and loose boards that I could see the faint path before me. Thank God for my improved vision, because I doubted even Vex would be able to see his hand in front of his face, though I'd wager William would scamper along sure-footed and nimble, the furry bastard.

There was a landing one floor down, and then the stairs continued. I kept going, following the muffled sounds of conversation. Eventually the stairs stopped and so did I – in the cellar.

As above, the exit here was another concealed panel. I brushed away a veil of cobwebs before searching for the release mechanism. When I found it, I held the door so that it opened just enough for me to peek out and make certain no one was skulking about.

The cellar floor was dirt, and the space smelled of earth, dust and death – not an altogether pleasant odour, but not terribly offensive either. Since discovering my goblin nature, I'd developed something of an appreciation for the smell of dirt – the soil kind. And death ... well, death didn't necessarily smell bad. It was shit and decay that made it nasty. To me, death smelled familiar – a memory I couldn't quite put my finger on.

Because scent was such a huge part of being a halvie or an aristo – a goblin – I'd taken pains to disguise mine by carrying a couple of small gauze bags filled with coffee grounds in my pockets. I'd laughed when Vex suggested it, but he said that in America they used coffee to hide drugs from narcotics dogs. If it could confuse a dog, it should work on vampires or weres. Maybe not on goblins, but I wasn't hiding from them.

I kept my back against the stone as I moved into the open room. Someone spoke on the other side of the wall, and I froze. I knew that voice.

"Two for the price of one tonight. Aren't we a lucky bunch? You boys would be in an entirely different situation right now if you'd just done what you were told. Still, you've served a purpose. When they find your bodies, Xandra Vardan will be the only name on the suspect list."

What the fuck? The man talking was coming closer. I hugged the wall, shoving myself as deep into the shadows as I could. He walked out of the little room without so much as a glance in my direction, but he didn't need to look for me to recognise him.

Ainsley. The man who'd broken Dede's heart. Broken *her*.

He'd used her, got her pregnant and then taken her baby and given it to his useless bint of a wife to raise as her own. I blamed him as much for Dede's death as I did Church.

A growl rose in my throat, and my fangs threatened to tear free of my gums. I took a deep, silent breath. I couldn't lose it just yet. I had to be calm. Had to stay in control.

A door closed behind Ainsley as he entered what I assumed was the theatre part of the cellar. That was where the voices were the loudest. From the sound of it there had to be at least twenty people in there. All waiting to watch the two prisoners die.

Well, not if I could bloody help it. I snuck into the smaller room. It smelled of old blood. Excrement. Piss. And very, very scared human.

There were two cages – one on either side of the room. Each cell was about five by five. My heart kicked hard against my ribs when I saw the faces of the two men staring at me with a mix of surprise and horror. One was David – rat boy.

The other was Detective Inspector Maine.

"Come to finish us off yourself, have you?" Maine demanded. He had a rather nasty-looking gash above his left eye, and that side of his face glistened with blood.

Warm, delicious blood. Would he be terribly offended if I licked him?

I glared at him instead. "Yes, because nibbling on your miserable hide is so worth putting myself in danger." Then, because I was curious, "How did you end up in a cage, anyway?"

For a moment I thought he wasn't going to tell me. He just

stood there, grinding his teeth. "I was looking for CI Vardan. I jacked his rotary records and found the number that gave details on this place. Guv told me to give it a look. They nabbed me out back."

I wondered how much Chillingham enjoyed being called "guv". More importantly, I realised that if Maine could crack the code for this event, I wasn't nearly as clever as I thought I was. Also, I realised that Val meant a lot to more people than just me.

"What are you doing here, Your Majesty?"

I didn't like his tone. "I'm here for the appetisers. Toss off, Maine. I'm here because I called the same number you did and thought it might lead me to Val."

He weaved slightly on his feet. He was most likely concussed. "Are you going to let us out or stand about jabbering all night?"

"I ought to leave your sorry arse for them to chew on, but Ainsley was right – I'm the first person the Yard would pounce on for it."

"Doesn't matter anyway." He sneered. "Special Branch know where I was going and had strict instructions as to what to do if I didn't check in on time. Backup will be here any moment now."

I froze. The Yard would shut this place down. Important people would be arrested. Once the human world got wind of this, there would be a cry for blood – aristo blood. That war that everyone said was coming would ignite much sooner than they expected.

War was another one of those things I wasn't ready for. Human numbers were so much greater, and now they had specialised weapons to use against us.

And damn it, Vex was out there in that room of twisted sickos. If he was arrested – at a horror show – he wouldn't have to be challenged by his second. He'd be ousted. And if someone bent on war took his place, a bloodbath would ensue. My goblins would get swept up in it. That pup wouldn't stand a chance. Avery and Val – if he was still alive – would be expected to fight. Expected to lay down their lives for the aristos. Humans outnumbered aristos. They outnumbered halvies. I wouldn't have any choice but to unleash the goblins on them ...

Whoa. I was getting too far ahead of myself, but it was a future easily predicted. Maybe war was coming. Maybe I couldn't stop it, but I could stop the man I loved from getting hurt.

The man I loved. Fang me. That was a shock. And it almost completely overtook the fact that Val wasn't here. Vex would have sent me a digigram by now if he was out in the viewing area. And he wasn't in the cages. I couldn't detect any trace of him – and I'd be able to smell him if he'd been here.

What the hell was I going to do? I pulled my rotary from my pocket and typed out a message to Vex. It was short and sweet: *GET OUT.*

I went to David's cage first. The poor kid was dirty and beaten and he had bite marks on his neck – someone had sampled the merchandise – but he looked otherwise unharmed. "You okay, kid?" I asked.

He nodded, but he was shaking. "I think so. Did you get my message?"

"I did. Lucky for you I was coming here anyway."

"Why are you here, Your *Majesty*?" asked Maine.

I glanced over my shoulder at him. He stood against the

bars, knuckles white where he was gripping them. "Same reason you are, Maine. I'm looking for my brother." That was the only reason he could be here. Unless . . .

His mouth thinned as he looked away. "I told Cooke we should keep a better eye on you."

Maybe he wasn't here because he was looking for Val. Maybe he was here because he'd outlived his usefulness. If he'd been set on me by Ainsley – who I now realised was the vampire who'd bullied David into murdering a rat – then he couldn't be allowed to live once he'd found out too much.

I turned back to the kid. "I'm going to get you out of here. Stand back."

I didn't have to tell him twice. Once he was clear, I lifted my foot and kicked the door of the cell. The impact shivered up my leg. The door didn't budge. I kicked again. This time the door groaned and I felt the jolt into my lower back. Fucking piece of shit iron door.

I was just angry enough that my monster raised its head. That was all the encouragement I needed to let the bloody beast out. Fangs burst free of my gums, the bones in my face shifted. *I* shifted. Claws sprouted from my fingers. My muscles tightened, felt heavier around my bones. It hurt, but it was such a delicious pain I didn't care. David whimpered. I kicked at the door again, pulling back just in time so that it didn't fly off its hinges – that sort of noise was bound to be heard.

I didn't bother to see if the kid came out. I was at Maine's cell, repeating the same process to free him as well.

The peeler stepped out with a fearful, cautious expression. He stared at me like I was something he'd never seen before. I reckoned that was exactly what I was. "What now?" he said.

"Got a flint?" I asked. He smelled like clove cigarettes, so I figured he had to carry something to light them.

He nodded and reached into his trouser pocket. He offered the small brass tool to me. I opened it and flicked my thumb along the wheel. Flame sprang to life. Excellent.

"Get the kid out of here," I told him. "When the Yard show up, tell them you rescued him. Till then, cover the entrance. They're going to pour out like rats from a sinking ship in a few minutes. The vampire who brought you both here is Lord Ainsley. More than likely he'll slither out of any charges you bring against him, but I'll make certain he doesn't come after either of you again."

"Why would you do that?" Maine demanded. "I know you don't like me any more than I like you."

I looked him in the eye. "I like Ainsley even less."

"Fair enough. For what it's worth, he's the one who told me to look into you for Churchill's murder. Told me I'd find blood in the tunnel below Buckingham Palace – Churchill's blood. Said the old man had followed you."

That was what everyone had called Church – the old man. Hearing it made my chest hurt. "Did you find his blood?" I asked, hoping my voice didn't sound as quivery to him as it did to me.

"No."

My shoulders threatened to sag under the relief, but I held them fast. "You still think I killed him?"

"I don't fucking care," he replied. "As far as I'm concerned the case is closed. Fucking mental vampires." He offered me his hand and I took it. I wasn't going to argue.

I led them to the concealed door and shoved them into the stairwell. "Go. It leads to the attic; you can escape from there."

It wasn't that far to the ground, and these old buildings had lots of ornamental details that made climbing easier.

As soon as they were gone, I quickly gathered up all the rags, papers and pieces of flammable debris that I could find. I made a nice little pile and doused it with lamp oil. These old buildings always seemed to have lamp oil. I doused the walls and floor as well. The cellar might be dirt and the walls stone, but the support beams were wood – old, dry wood. I flicked my thumb over the flint wheel again, and when it ignited, I tossed it on to the pile near my feet.

Flames roared up in front of me, so hot my face felt burned. I stepped back and watched, making sure the fire took before pulling my rotary from my pocket. There was a message from Vex: *ON MY WAY TO THE CARRIAGE*. I didn't know what he'd had to tell them in order to get out, and I didn't care. I shoved the phone into my pocket once more and ran for the exit just as the door to the theatre room opened. As I hit the stairs, I heard someone yell, "Fire!" I ran all the way to the attic, practically diving out of the window, and from there I pitched myself across the alley to the next roof.

Sirens and lights lit up the immediate surroundings. Scotland Yard had arrived as promised. Maine was good for something after all. Too bad he couldn't find Val.

Val. My thoughts were on him as I ran across the roof, heading for the carriage park. I saw Vex waiting for me on the other side of the cement wall.

I was no closer to finding my brother, but at least now I knew someone who might be able to give me information. Someone I wouldn't mind beating said information out of.

Ainsley.

CHAPTER 16

THE TRUTH IS INCONTROVERTIBLE

Vex and I stayed in the carriage park for a little while – it wouldn't look good for him to make too quick an escape. He was in enough trouble because of me – I wasn't about to bring any more to his door.

We stuck to the shadows, where we wouldn't be seen, a level above where all the aristo carriages had been stowed. A couple of men claimed their vehicles not far from us, but they didn't even glance in our direction, they were so hell-bent on getting out of there.

"I wonder if they arrested Ainsley," I murmured when we were alone again. I had already filled him in on what I'd seen and who I'd found in the cellar. "Or any of them."

"I'd be surprised if Maine didn't grab him," Vex replied, staring down into the street. There were still several police carriages in front of the building, as well as the fire brigade. The fire hadn't spread very far, and I'd seen there'd been no injuries from it – not that I'd be inclined to feel badly if there were. People who murdered for sport could use a little trial by fire in my opinion.

I liked to think of myself as non-judgemental, but who was I fooling? Judging was a hobby of mine.

"They won't hold him for long. His barrister will have him home before dawn."

"But he will have called attention to himself." Vex moved away from the wall and the lights below. "And you know how much Her Nibs despises scandal."

I pinched up my face and raised my voice to an obnoxious pitch. "We will not tolerate scandal or any behaviour that reflects poorly upon this great country." That was what she'd said when asked about allegations that Churchill was a traitor.

Vex laughed. He had the most brilliant laugh – big and almost sinister in its glee. I loved it.

I would not think about the fact that I also loved him. I would just enjoy it, and keep that secret to myself for the time being.

"How am I going to tell Penny I didn't find out anything about Val?" I asked when we were in the Panther heading back to Leicester Square.

"She didn't even know about tonight. There's nothing to tell. The fact that he hasn't turned up is good, you know. It means he's alive."

"Yeah, but what the ruddy hell are they doing to him?" I stared out of the window. There were decidedly fewer humans out and about than there had been earlier. It was late for them.

My brother was out there. Somewhere. Probably wondering what was taking me so bloody long to find him. If the situation was reversed, he would probably have found and rescued me by now. Knowing that the Yard had no more leads than I did made me feel marginally better at least. I wasn't a total failure.

When we pulled in behind my house, I frowned. "The light's out." I left the back light on to discourage anyone from snooping around, and so that I wouldn't come home to any surprises.

"Looks like it's busted," Vex said, peering through the windscreen as the carriage's motor rumbled to a halt.

I saw movement between the building and the privacy fence that gave me something of a yard. "Turn off the lamps."

He did, and the space between carriage and building went completely dark save for ambient light from the street, which wasn't much.

I opened my door and stepped out. Vex followed.

"You can come out," I said, in a soft voice. "It's just me and the MacLaughlin."

Not a sound came from the darkness, but within seconds a shadow emerged from the others, and then I caught a flash of glowing eyes. A young goblin, cautious on slightly bowed legs – limbs that didn't look like they should support bipedal motion but did. Buff-coloured fur, a short snout – more humanoid than I was accustomed to seeing. He had wide, doe-like eyes.

Now that I had spent time with them, I realised that goblins didn't look any more alike than humans did, or aristos. They had species-specific traits, but each was an individual. Some were very animalistic and others weren't.

I wondered how much of that was due to their shape-shifting abilities, such as William being able to change his paws into hands. It was a brilliant ability, and one that made sense of my own shifting. I was a new breed of goblin, and while I could look completely humanoid, I might never be able to shift into an entirely goblin form – which was sometimes disappointing because it meant I would never be quite as fast or quite as agile as a gob, or at least not in the same ways.

"Have we met?" I asked.

"No," came the slightly raspy response. A male. "I've seen you in the den, but we've never been formally introduced. I'm George." He held out his hand, and waved the other one in greeting at Vex.

I gaped at him. He was incredibly modern and well-spoken for a goblin. What kind of schooling did they get in the den? I made a mental note to find out and make certain education was offered to each and every one of them. If trouble was coming, and it was bound to eventually, I'd rather they be deadly and informed rather than dangerous and ignorant.

"Nice to meet you, George."

"Apologies for the light." He pointed at the back door. "It hurt, and I didn't want anyone to see me."

"Don't worry about that. Would you like to come in?"

He shook his scruffy head. His fur was long and silky, and he wore horn-rimmed dark spectacles to protect his wide eyes. He was just a kid – a teenager at best. "Thanks, but no. If I don't get back soon my dad will worry."

"Who is your father?"

"Dunno who my real father is – I'm a foundling – but the prince adopted me and raised me, so he's the only one that counts. He wanted me to give you this." He offered me a piece of heavy folded paper.

I opened it. It was a photograph, taken at the back door of Freak Show, the lights in the courtyard illuminating the couple so well I didn't have to squint at the grainy image. There was no mistaking Penny – no one else in London looked quite like

her. And the person with her was . . . a betty. One of the ones
that had got away the night I killed the third. He was also one
of the ones who'd taken Val. I was sure of it.

Icy fingers seemed to seize my heart and squeeze. "When
was this taken?"

"Got it off the camera about an hour ago," George informed
me. "I came here straight away. The prince tried to ring you."

I had my rotary set on silent and hadn't checked it since
escaping the horror show. Shit. "Thanks, George. You need a
lift anywhere?"

He shook his head. "Nah, thanks. I'll be on my way then."
He gave me an awkward bow and set off toward the street. I
watched as he checked both ways and then disappeared.

"There's a sewer opening not far from here. That's where
he'll go," Vex told me. "No need to worry about the pup."

I nodded. He was right, of course, but I did worry – a little.
Didn't matter that George could rip the arms off any human
who challenged him. Even goblins could get ganged up on. I
had to walk out to the street and look to make sure he was
gone rather than in trouble. Only then could I go into my
house and ring Avery.

"I'm bloody bored," she said by way of greeting. I could
hear music and talking in the background. "What happened
tonight?"

"I'll tell you later – nothing that got me any closer to finding Val. Are you still at Freak Show?"

"Where else would I be?"

I ignored her snippy tone. I should have known based on the
background noise. "Have you had your eye on Penny the
entire night?"

"As much as I could. What's going on?"

"Is Penny still there?"

"Of course she is. I wouldn't be here if she weren't."

"Did you see her talk to anyone?"

"She went outside during her break. I followed as closely as I could. Some guy was waiting for her. I didn't get a good look at his face, and Em called at the same time so I didn't hear what they talked about. She came back inside a few minutes later."

"Did she seem agitated or upset?"

"Not at all. Should she have?"

"A betty paid Penny a visit tonight."

A pause. Suddenly the background noise reduced drastically – Avery had changed locations. "One of the bastards who took Val?"

I glanced at the photograph in my hand. "Yes."

"You want me to ask Penny about it?"

"No. Then she'll know for a fact that you're watching her." I put the photograph down on the table.

"I met friends here tonight to throw her off a bit. You reckon the betty threatened her?"

"I have no bloody idea."

"She'll tell you about it when she gets home."

"Yeah, probably." I wasn't so sure about that. Penny had been acting strangely lately. Maybe she doubted my ability to find Val. God knew I hadn't much faith in myself as of late. Or maybe she knew I was keeping things from her. She could have decided to take matters into her own hands.

Avery and I talked for a few more minutes and then I hung up – after agreeing to tell her all about the horror show the next day.

I ran upstairs to change into a camisole and a pair of thin

baggy bloomers that came down to below my knees. On impulse, I prised up the floorboards covering my secret hiding spot. I removed the files and looked at them. So much information, and none of it did me any good. All it did was make my chest hurt.

I removed the pages about Dede's baby from the envelope and looked at them. When I read the first lines of the form on the second page, my heart skipped a beat. I flipped back to the first page and read it again, just to make certain I wasn't imagining things.

The first page was about Dede's baby – all the things the Prince Albert Hospital recorded when a halvie gave birth: child's name, sex, weight, length, blood type and race. Someone had initially checked the box next to "V" on the form – indicating that the baby was born vampire – but had then crossed it out, ticked "H" and written "stillborn" on the adjacent line.

The second page was for Ainsley's son with his wife. All the information was the same as on the first page – as though someone had copied it. Only this time the "V" wasn't crossed out. Even the accompanying documents on the genetic screening were identical. I had no doubt that the documents on file at the hospital had been tampered with to tell the story Ainsley wanted, but these were the original pages. Why had Churchill kept them? In case he ever needed to blackmail Ainsley? Or perhaps to convince Dede or myself to do whatever he wanted? I had no idea, and the old man was dead along with his secrets.

Why would Ainsley want me out of the way unless he knew that I had discovered the truth about his child? And why not just kill me to keep me quiet?

Unless he wasn't allowed to kill me.

Paranoia crept into my brain – it didn't take much for me to start wondering if there was some sort of great conspiracy afoot, not lately, when I'd had ample evidence that my life was built on bloody secrecy and intrigue.

I showed the pages to Vex. Earlier, in the carriage park, he'd seemed entirely calm, but now a muscle ticked in his jaw and his eyes shone bright with gold, reflecting the lamplight.

"I'm going to rip that fucking nancy's head off," he growled, "and piss down his throat."

Graphic imagery to say the least. "Get in line, wolf. I want to talk to him first."

"What the hell for?"

"He's not doing this on his own. The horror shows maybe, but it doesn't make sense that he'd want me locked up rather than dead. There's someone else behind all of this, someone who figures I'm worth more alive."

Vex frowned. "You reckon he's involved with the people behind the disappearances as well?"

"I do, though I have to admit that makes him even more of a prick than I originally thought. Smarter, too."

"You know, if he's been in on this from the start, there's a chance he seduced Dede knowing she might give birth to a fully plagued child."

The thought turned my blood to icy sludge. Could he have orchestrated the entire thing? No, aristocratic reproduction was too much of a gamble, even with modern fertility treatments – no doubt discovered because of these wretched experiments. Ainsley had got lucky in more ways than one. And when his wife delivered something not meant to survive, it was just a happy coincidence that he had a plan B in Dede. Literally inside Dede. Lucky indeed. Did he shit rainbows too?

"Regardless, Ainsley has answers I want." My jaw was clenched as I glanced at the papers, creased by the tightness of my grip. "I think it's time I asked him a few questions."

I couldn't get in to see Ainsley until the following afternoon. He was being held in daylight seclusion until sunset, when he would be released. As I'd predicted, it looked as though he was going to avoid being charged with anything. That was my own bloody fault. I was the one who'd released the prisoners and torched all the evidence of anyone having been held in those cellar prisons. I cursed myself for it, but kicking Ainsley's arse was not worth Vex getting in trouble or people dying for. Funny, not long ago I would have given the kid – David – up to his maker without a blink. Human life had never meant much to me. I'd been taught to fear and despise them. I reckoned that was mutual.

I managed to cross paths with Penny before I left. She slunk out of her room just as I came out of mine. She looked tired, thin and she needed a shave.

"You all right, love?" I asked.

She smiled wanly. "Morning, Xandy. I'm fine."

Fuck small talk and little lies. "Avery said she saw you talking to a betty at the club last night. Did he threaten you?"

Her back stiffened – the silk of her robe rippling. "So you have been spying on me, then?"

"Spying on you?" Where the hell had that come from? "I asked Avery to make sure no one tried to grab you again."

"I didn't ask you to do that, did I? I didn't ask to be involved in any of this!"

I started. This narrow-eyed creature scowling at me was not my Penny. "You tell me what the fuck is going on. Right bloody now."

Her shoulders sagged. "The betty said he had information on Val, but that he'd only talk to someone with the power to protect him – you."

"That's what's got your knickers in a twist?"

Her dark gaze darted away. "I offered myself in exchange for Val and he laughed at me. He said his employers were only interested in useful freaks."

I hugged her. "Oh, honey. That was brave of you. Stupid, but brave."

Penny's hands barely touched my back before she pushed me away. "What would you have done? Beat him to death like the other one? At least I found out what they really want."

Me. It came back to that – again. Was anyone else as sick of me as I was? Penny, apparently. Suddenly her anger and moodiness made sense.

"It's not my fault Val was taken." The truth of the words surprised me, given how much I delighted in blaming myself for everything.

She sighed, shoulders sagging even more. I hadn't realised just how much weight she'd been carrying. "I know. I don't blame you, ducks. I'm just so worried and . . . scared. I didn't want to tell you about the betty showing up last night."

"You did the right thing. When does he want to meet?"

"Tomorrow night. Midnight – at the club."

"Fine. I'll be there." But I wasn't going to be alone. I knew better than to trust that the betty just wanted to talk. At best he wanted to make a grab for me too. At worst he was going to dump Val's corpse at my feet. Either way, someone was going to have to be there to make certain I didn't kill him, because he had information I wanted, such as who was behind all of this.

Penny seemed surprised. "Really? You're going to do it? Even though it's probably a trap?"

I looked her in the eye. "You offered yourself to get Val back. The least I can do is show up." I pulled my pocket watch from my trousers. "I have to go. We can talk more about this later." I gave her a quick hug and left the house. I wanted to make certain she was all right, but I hadn't the time.

Right now I had to pay a visit to that piece of shit known as Ainsley.

Vex wasn't around to come with me, and that was good because he'd probably keep me from ripping Ainsley apart. However, he was gone because of pack trouble, which was never good. From what I gleaned, his second was kicking up a fuss over his leadership abilities and his absence from the pack, which I assumed was my fault.

How was I able to cause so much trouble without intent or effort? This nonsense with the pack wasn't my fault – I wasn't going to nail myself to that cross – but I was still the root cause. Just because I was a freak. That was all it was. I was a genetic abnormality. But then, every step in evolution had started in just such a fashion. I reckoned that was why I was so troublesome and yet so popular – because I might very well be a taste of things to come.

And I wasn't so bad. I might be a goblin who could walk about cobbleside – in the sun – but I'd yet to prove myself a dangerous, unpredictable killing machine.

Well, not entirely.

THE QUEEN IS DEAD

Still, it didn't hurt to be thought a little intimidating. I had dressed for the trip in head-to-toe black, despite the late summer heat. Nothing frilly or girlie – just a corseted waist-coat, black trousers and black high-heeled boots that made me several inches taller. I'd pinned my hair up with matronesque severity and painted my face with black winged eyeliner and glossy lips. I looked a bit like a dominatrix whose latex gear was out being hosed down.

Sunset was still several hours away as I drove the Butler towards the Yard. There were those who still called it "New" Scotland Yard, but the buildings along Victoria Embankment just east of St James's Park hadn't been new in more than a hundred years. A big red-brick and white building with grey stone at the base, it looked like it should be some sort of acad-emy, with its round turrets and neat trim.

I parked the Butler and walked into the main building like I owned it. It wasn't difficult – I could practically taste Ainsley's blood I wanted it so badly. I'm sure I projected a "don't fuck with me" menace from Westminster to Chelsea.

There was a set of hounds just inside the door. I walked through their frames with confidence. I didn't have any metal on me, or a gun. What I had was my trusty lonsdaelite dagger tucked into my corset. I should really carry more protection on me; claws and teeth weren't much help when up against a hand cannon with fragmenting silver rounds filled with tetra-cycline. I had yet to find out if I was faster than a bullet. Last time I hadn't been, but then I'd been shot in the back. Maybe I'd fare better if I saw it coming. Still, wasn't something I wanted to try.

The humans in this section stared at me. I didn't flatter myself that they all knew who I was. To several I'm sure I was just a dressed-up halvie. But it was clear when Val's superintendent came to greet me personally that I was not ordinary at all. Especially when the poor woman was pale and swallowed hard before offering me her hand.

"Lady Xandra, I'm Superintendent Chillingham." She was a little shorter than me, with thick cobalt hair and the kind of exotic beauty associated with people of Indian descent.

I accepted the gesture, careful not to squeeze hard enough that it might be seen as a threat, but how could I not hate such a gorgeous woman? "I've heard many good things about you from my brother. Might I have a word?"

"Of course. Come with me."

I followed her to the lift, aware of how all eyes followed us. The small box – I had a sinking feeling it was original to the building – slowly jerked us up two floors, and I then followed her to a small but tidy office.

"Would you like anything to drink?" she asked, then paled again.

I smiled at her. "Don't worry, I'm not going to ask you to tap a vein for me. Tea would be nice, if you have it."

"Earl Grey?" she asked, plugging in an electric kettle.

"That would be lovely."

She took two china cups from a small cupboard and fussed about with leaves and strainers. "I must apologise for my behaviour. It's not every day we have royalty descend upon us."

"Or a goblin," I added.

Chillingham returned the smile. "Or a goblin. I hope I haven't offended you. Valentine has told me many wonderful things about you."

Valentine, eh? "I've been looking for him."

All humour fled from her face. "As have I. Thank you for alerting me to his tracking device. We have our own monitoring system, which thanks to your find we now know was being bounced around the city. Many of our ranks have volunteered time to search. He is well respected in this office."

"Bounced?" I tried to ignore the rolling of my gut. "That sounds professional."

"Yes." The kettle whistled and she made the tea, but not before I spied a hint of tears in her eyes. She more than respected Val.

She was all composure when she gave me my cup and took the seat behind her desk. "What did you want to talk about?"

I followed her lead, pulled myself together and got right to the point. "I'd like to talk to Lord Ainsley, if he's still in custody."

"He's no longer being held, but he's in the seclusion parlours. May I ask why you wish to see him?"

I took a sip of tea. It was delightful. "It's personal."

"Lady Xandra, I cannot just give you access to a peer of the realm without knowing why."

I met her frank gaze. "I believe he knows something about Val's disappearance."

Chillingham put her cup down on her desk with a clatter. "What?"

I set my own tea aside. "Look, I don't have time or patience for games, and I suspect neither do you. It's obvious you care for my brother, so I'm going to be frank with you: Ainsley was involved with a horror show; not just that, but I think he might know about the disappearances at Freak Show – the disappearances Val was investigating." That was a bit of a stretch, but as a general rule my paranoia usually meant I was on to something. "If I don't talk to him now, I don't know if I'll ever get the chance." At least not one where he would be so vulnerable and off his guard.

"You think ..." Chillingham swallowed. Her eyes glittered, hard like stones. "You reckon Ainsley has information on Val?" She didn't bother to hide the emotion in her tone. This woman was involved with my brother – I'd stake my fangs on it.

I nodded. "I think he might."

She pushed back her chair. Her entire body was like a spring ready to snap. "Come on. I'll take you to the bastard myself."

CHAPTER 17

CONFESSION IS GOOD FOR THE SOUL

At that moment Superintendent Chillingham was my new best friend.

No need to tell me twice; I stood and followed her from the office. This time the lift took us down to the subterranean levels, where aristos would be kept if charged with a crime, or until the sun set or they contrived some way to get home during daylight hours.

We stopped in front of a door marked "3". Chillingham knocked, and politely waited until Ainsley spoke before entering. "You have a visitor, Lord Ainsley."

"Oh?" asked the ponce. "Who might that be?"

I stepped around the superintendent. "Me. Hullo, Ainsley." He was sitting on a very comfortable, very expensive-looking sofa, sipping what might have been tea, or blood, watching a football match on the box. He looked rumpled and tired, but still an arrogant bugger.

I swear on Prince Albert's grave, so long as I live I don't

think I'll ever see anything more satisfying than how he paled at the sight of me. Bastard was already downright pasty, but this . . . this was that beautiful moment when a bully realises he's not the scariest thing in the playground.

Ainsley was a pretty sort of man. A few inches taller than me, though in my heels I would be almost the same height, with golden hair and pale blue eyes. He wore his sideburns long, in a style that widened along his jaw. They were trimmed short and in a pattern of peaks and swirls that had to take his valet hours to achieve.

"Fifteen minutes is all I can give you," Chillingham informed me, and left the room without so much as a look at Ainsley.

"I'll have her job for this," he seethed.

"You won't." I stood in front of him. Sitting would put me at his level, and I refused to go there. "Would you really have killed poor David, Ainsley?"

He scowled. "Who?"

"The boy you threatened into nailing the rat to my door. You know, the one you were going to bleed to death last night. And what about Maine? It must have been a real pain in the arse to realise that he'd escaped."

Most people would have looked horrified that I knew. Ainsley just looked pissed off. "I don't know what you're talking about."

"Don't be like that, now. You know exactly what I'm talking about, because I'm the one who let them go and started the bloody fire."

Ainsley's eyes lit up like a struck match. The cup fell to the carpet as he sprang to his feet with an elastic grace that would have dropped a human's jaw.

I wasn't human, and I wasn't impressed.

"You fucking bitch," he snarled.

I flicked his nose – snapped the cartilage with my "fuck off" finger. "Manners, wanker. I want to know about the horror shows, and I want to know about the disappearances from Freak Show. I know you know about them."

His pink lips curved cruelly. What had Dede ever seen in this waste of flesh? He was pretty enough, to be sure, but so ... lacking in any sort of warmth. "You know nothing. You can prove nothing."

I pulled the pages I had copied from inside my jacket and handed them to him. "Thanks to Church, I can prove this."

I watched as his gaze scanned the pages and realised what they were. Even then he wouldn't admit defeat. He tore them into pieces.

"Those were just copies. I have others at home."

"You can't prove anything. They could be forgeries."

"Ainsley, does the blood on the 'official' record for your boy match the one your wife gave birth to, or the one my sister had? Because I'm pretty certain all it would take is a simple blood test to prove that that boy your wife dotes upon is not hers. And I'm pretty certain that I can make enough trouble for you that it won't even matter."

His jaw tightened. "I'll kill you."

That was when I smiled. "I just love the smell of desperation in the evening, don't you? Take your best shot, you miserable little clunge. My goblins will eat you in your bed." I also loved throwing my newly accepted status around. I should be careful, but I was simply having too much fun.

It was the mention of the goblins that seemed to finally get through to him. "What do you want?"

"Answers. Why did you want me arrested for David and Maine's deaths?"

"I don't care if you're arrested or not. I just did what I was told."

"By whom?"

His lips twisted. "Guess. Who would want you out of the way more than anyone else? It didn't matter if it was for Churchill's death or someone else's."

Fucking Victoria. I knew it – historically the queens of England did not react well to having another queen on the scene. I was so not prepared to go toe to toe with her. She had almost two centuries of backstabbing and deceit under her belt, and I wasn't three and twenty until November.

"Who's behind the horror shows?"

"That I can't tell you."

I straightened. "You can, or I'll eat your spleen myself."

He swallowed. "I can't tell you, because I don't know. I'm just the middle man."

"That's fucking convenient, isn't it?"

He stared at me, eyes widening. My temper was bringing out my goblin. I drew a calming breath. In the grand scheme of things that were important to me at that moment, the horror shows took a distant second. I had stopped one, but wasn't naïve enough to think I'd made that much of a difference. Val was what mattered.

"What do you know about my brother's disappearance?"

"Valentine?"

I nodded. "He was looking into the horror shows and the disappearance of halvies from Freak Show. I assume that some of those halvies have ended up as the star attraction in your charming little shows, but what about the others? What about the experiments?"

"I don't—"

I grabbed him by the lapels, hauled him close and bared my fangs. He jumped so high, I felt the pull of fabric against my fingers. I growled. "Don't. Fuck. With. Me."

Ainsley licked his lips, his face now completely bloodless. "The others – the ones that prove useful are taken to a laboratory, where they're experimented on."

"What sort of experiments?"

"Genetic mostly. It's all about propagating the aristo race; surely you've figured that out."

"Where are they taken?"

"I don't know."

I shook him, felt my face start to shift.

"I swear on Albert's grave, I don't know!" It was the panic in his voice that stopped me. As delicious as his fear was, I was still in control of my monster, and I knew a broken man when I heard one.

"I'm not sure I believe you, Ainsley."

"It's true. I'm not involved in that. I only know as much as I do about it because ... "

"Because of Dede," I supplied. I released him, her name taking all of the anger out of me. It didn't make sense. I should want to kill him for bringing her up, but his eyes had taken on a hollow look I'd never seen on him before.

"I did love her, you know." He didn't even step back or attempt to straighten his lapels. "I didn't deserve her, but I loved her as much as I'm capable of loving anyone. Not as much as she loved me – I don't believe there's anyone who could love quite so thoroughly as Dede."

If he'd punched me in the chest, I couldn't have struggled any harder for breath. "No." It was her love for him, for their child that had nearly crippled her, almost ended her, because even though they were both lost, she still loved them as though they were with her.

"I don't expect you to understand, but I was told to make a choice. I was told I couldn't have both Dede and our son, because if it got out that a halvie had produced a fully plagued child ... well, I don't have to tell you what it's like to be different."

"Humans have had full-blooded children. I don't know why it would matter."

"It would matter if it wasn't just a random act of God. It would matter if something had changed that made it possible for us to increase our numbers in a more substantial manner."

Yes. If the aristo birth rate suddenly went up, the humans would get scared. And when humans got scared, they did terrible and stupid things like burning down Mayfair and becoming an all-you-can-eat buffet for the goblins. We were stronger, but they still outnumbered us, and they had become a lot smarter over the decades. Smarter and better equipped.

I looked at Ainsley – pathetic creature that he was. I was probably the proverbial sucker born every minute, but I believed his pain. "So you chose the boy."

"What other choice did I have? If I hadn't, they would have given him to someone else. I couldn't let that happen and still look Dede in the eye. I had to do what she would have done. I chose my son. Sometimes I can't even look at him he is so much like her."

That might have been pouring it on a bit thick, but he seemed genuinely distraught, so I didn't challenge him on it.

He was still a tosser, even if he had done what he thought was right.

"Who made you choose, Ainsley?" All the anger I'd once felt towards him for breaking my sister's heart needed a new target or it would eat a hole in my chest. I needed to blame someone for all that had happened to my sister before that blame turned on me.

He looked away. "I can't tell you."

"Ainsley, we're beyond that. I know about the boy, and I know about the horror shows. I'm not going to ruin you, but you have got to give me something in return."

He scrubbed his hand over the back of his head, mussing his perfectly coiffed hair. "It was Vardan," he said softly, raising his gaze to mine. "Your father."

Fang me and chew the wound. What was it with vampires and duplicity? And why was I not more surprised to find out my father knew about Dede's baby? This was a man who had encouraged my mother to continue her pregnancy after being infected by a were just as some sort of . . . *experiment*.

No. I couldn't believe he'd be involved in Val's disappearance. He might have played with my life and with Dede's, but I couldn't believe he'd be part of something that might lead to one of his children being hurt – especially not his son. Sons were as important to men of his time and station as they had been centuries earlier. Names and lineage continued so long as there were sons. Vardan no doubt knew about the secret labs and whatever the bloody hell else was involved, but he could not have knowingly let his only son be taken.

And if he had, I'd break his neck and make a bracelet out of his teeth – and not necessarily in that order.

I left Scotland Yard with a brain travelling in so many directions it was tripping over itself. This was what it was like when I first found out what I was. I'd had a bit of peace after Churchill's death, but not much. Was this what my life was destined to be from now on? A never-ending series of questions, half-answers and unpleasant discoveries? There were times when I wished I'd just believed Dede had killed herself and never bothered digging around. Ignorance was bliss indeed.

I drove to the entrance to Mayfair. The RGs at the gate didn't want to let me in.

"I'm the goblins' queen," I explained slowly, jaw clenched. "How am I supposed to access the plague den if you won't let me in?"

Amelia Chesterfield – a little magenta-haired bitch I've never liked – shrugged. "That's not my problem, ma'am. The prince is still the registered representative of the plague and he hasn't put you on the list."

Ma'am? Fuck her. I pulled my rotary out of my pocket. "All right then. You just came on watch, right? I'll call the prince and he can come up once it's dark and resolve this matter."

She lost a little colour at that. Fang me, but this was a delicious power trip. I hoped the threat of goblins never diminished.

"Look," I said, willing to give her a chance. "I just want to go to the den. Sign me in. I'll be back within the hour. Put a tracker on my motorrad."

Her expression was dubious, but obviously sticking a tracking device on me and taking a chance on catching shit for it was preferable to chatting with the prince. Funny, but she didn't see me as that much of a threat, even though I could tear her apart just as easily as my furry brethren.

I was going to have to do something about that some day. I couldn't have these people I used to work with, who used to respect me, looking at me like I was less than them when in reality I was much, much more. Was I in danger of an ego trip? Probably, but this was about self-preservation more than anything else. Weakness was not something to show in my world. And not a word I ever wanted associated with me. How could I be the goblins' queen if I wasn't seen as at least their equal?

In the end she let me pass – a telltale red light blinking on the Butler's petrol reservoir. It would sound an alarm if I tried to take it off, but I had no intention of doing that. If I needed to travel in Mayfair, I'd do it on foot and underground.

There was a bit of a party going on in the den when I entered, reminding me of the first time I ever set foot in this place. Goblins carried trays of fruit and jugs of wine, while humans – strung out on the finest opiates the goblins could refine – danced to the beat of music that sounded almost tribal.

I didn't care. If humans were stupid enough to chase the dragon into the plague den, well then they were that stupid. I didn't want to think about it because I wasn't certain I wanted to know how these things played out. And when I saw a human woman being shagged by a male goblin and obviously enjoying it, I turned my back and made a mental note to check the calendar and avoid the den on nights when there was entertaining going on.

This was definitely not going to be the calming experience I'd hoped for.

"Our lady," came a familiar rasp.

I turned to face the prince. "Hullo, William. Quite a bash."

"If your coming had been known we would not have invited guests." He scratched the side of his jaw. "This looks badly . . ."

I shook my head. "Don't. You don't owe me an explanation, and I really" – I chuckled humourlessly – "don't want to know. I just came by to . . ."

"To what?" he asked.

I had no idea. Why *was* I there? Because Vex wasn't around and I needed to feel like someone was on my side. I needed to feel like I had friendship. Loyalty. I didn't go to my sister or my friends (what friends?); I came to the goblins.

William tilted his head and looked at me with his one amber eye. I forced a smile. "George brought me the photograph from Freak Show. I was hoping I might see the actual recording." I said it as an excuse, but once the words had left my mouth, I realised it was probably a sound idea.

"Of course. I will take our lady."

I stopped him. I could see Elsbeth waiting for him a few feet away. "I know where it is. You don't have to squire me about. Go and have fun."

He bowed, and I walked away. As I neared the monitor room, the sounds of the party diminished slightly. I leaned my back against the rough wall and exhaled a deep breath, forcing some of the tension from my muscles.

How much more of this was I going to have to take? More importantly, how much more whining was I going to have to do about it? I just wanted my life back. It didn't have to be the life I had before – I knew that was gone. I just wanted to feel as though I was in control of this new one.

I stayed against that wall for a few minutes, just breathing in and out, trying to relax. If I thought about things too much, it would make me hatters, and that wouldn't do me or the people who depended on me any good.

With a shrug of my shoulders, I straightened and continued on to the monitor room. There were two goblins in there, both of whom bowed when they saw me. I told them what I wanted to see and one of them sat me down in front of a monitor while the other lined up the recording. A few moments later, the courtyard behind Freak Show came into view on the screen.

I watched the grainy scene play out before me in varying shades of black and white. The truck I'd seen before pulled up to the back entrance and a betty slipped out. It was the one in the photo George had given me.

He went to the back door and rang the bell. A few seconds later he leaned forward to speak into the intercom. A moment or two later, Penny came outside. Had he asked for her personally? It sure seemed as though he had. She didn't look afraid.

On the screen, Penny said something to the betty. And then ... he laughed – just like she'd said. I felt for her, but more importantly, I felt relief. I wasn't proud of the fact that I had doubted, even suspected her, but I was glad to be wrong.

The betty got back in his vehicle and drove away. Penny remained on the back step for a moment or two longer. I watched her dab at her eyes with a handkerchief.

The betty had looked too relaxed. It was a trap, I was certain of it. I should take Avery with me, but I'd already lost one sister, and had a brother taken. If Avery was hurt while helping me, I'd never forgive myself. And neither would Emma.

No, if I was going to take someone with me tomorrow

night, it would have to be someone I knew wouldn't get hurt. I'd ask Vex, but he'd be tempted to rush in if he thought I was in danger. Plus, it might cause more trouble with the pack. I didn't want to make him choose between his people and myself. Mostly because I knew which one of us he was duty-bound to put first, even if his heart had other ideas.

"Is all well, lady?"

I turned. The prince stood in the doorway. He had blood on his muzzle and smelled of earth, smoke and sex. And blood, of course. He smelled of blood.

"All is fine. Do you have any plans for tomorrow evening, William?"

He shook his head, his one eye narrowing. "No. Do you wish something of your prince?"

"Could you come to Freak Show with me? I suspect I might be walking into a trap."

He bowed his shaggy head. "Of course. You need only tell me when."

I sighed. "Thank you. I'll ring you before I leave."

"Now, the lady will do something for me."

I arched a brow at his tone, but then it didn't take much for me to arch a brow. It was my second favourite expression. "What do you need?"

He extended his arm. Sometimes his hand looked more paw-like, but tonight it seemed incredibly normal, if a little furry. His fingers were callused and rough, but warm as I curled my own around them.

"The lady will come and eat with us. Eat with her plague."

"Eat what?" I asked cautiously as he led me from the room.

"Important it is for the plague to see our lady dine on meat. Those who disrespect her will change their thinking."

"What sort of meat?" I asked – my voice actually squeaked. Pathetic.

William turned his gaze to mine. "Warm. Bloody. Fresh."

Sweet baby Albert, my stomach growled at the words. Saliva flooded my tongue, wet and sweet. I knew what he was offering, and instead of being disgusted by it, I was filled with a ravenous hunger I'd rarely felt before. The last time I'd felt like this, I'd almost ripped Ophelia's throat out.

We entered the great hall, where there was still music and dancing going on. Humans reclined in clouds of sweet smoke that burned my lungs and muddied my brain. I felt as though the weight of my life had been pulled from my shoulders with every intake of breath. That was the beauty of opium, I supposed.

There was a long banqueting table against the far wall. We had to walk past all the goblins gathered in that room to get to it. They watched me closely, some of them drinking, some chewing on chucks of meat.

Was that a hand I saw one of them gnawing on?

I couldn't tell what the carcass on the table used to be, thank God. Only pieces of it remained, one of which was the heart.

The prince picked up the bloody organ and offered it to me, just as he had with Church's heart that fateful night a couple of months ago.

"Best part," he said. "Symbol of respect that it was left for our lady."

Swallowing hard, I took it from him. It was warm and sticky, but at least it had stopped beating. Hunger gripped hard at my insides as the smell of blood and succulent meat filled my head, more intoxicating than the opium. I needed this.

My goblin rose to the surface, lengthening tooth and jaw,

altering the bones of my face so that I became a more efficient predator. Saliva dripped from my fangs. The watching goblins began to chatter and cheer, and I realised that they'd never seen me fully change before. They didn't know this side of me. *I* barely knew this side of me.

The prince had been right to do this. He'd known exactly how I would react to the meat and how the tribe would react to me when I gave in. He was much more intelligent than I gave him credit for, and it shamed me.

But stronger than that shame was my hunger. I opened my jaws wide and bit down on the heart. Meat split between my teeth. Blood flowed over my tongue.

This was not the vengeance it had been when I took Church's heart into my mouth. This was not the justice I'd felt when I ended him as coldly as he had ended Dede. This was hunger. This was base and primal.

It was right.

I closed my eyes in bliss. Around me the goblins cheered, celebrating what I would forever remember as the moment I became one of them.

My point of no return.

CHAPTER 18

FIDELITY IS THE SISTER OF JUSTICE

My father was surprised to see me sitting in his private chambers in the dark. Or perhaps it was the blood on my face and hands that I hadn't been able to lick clean that surprised him in particular.

"Xandra." He straightened his shoulders. "My dear girl, how did you get in here, and what have you done?"

"I had to see you," I replied, rising from the chair I'd been in for the last thirty-three minutes. "I came from the plague den."

That seemed to be all the explanation he required, but then I would think the blood smeared around my mouth told enough of the story of what I'd done at the den. My father left me to go into his bathroom. I heard water running in the basin, and when he returned, it was with a warm, wet cloth that he used to wipe the blood from my face and fingers. It was a surprisingly sweet gesture, one that unsettled me.

He glanced at me as he wiped my palms. "You've taken your place as their queen then?"

"Pretty much." I watched the traces of rust disappear from my skin. "Does that bother you?"

"I suppose it ought to, but no. I always knew you were destined to be something extraordinary."

"And Churchill had the test results to prove it."

He hesitated, but continued cleaning. "Yes."

"What about Dede? Did you think she'd pop out a pureblood? Are you monitoring the kid too, just in case?"

My father lifted his head. His green eyes flashed as they met mine. "I can never lay claim to my grandchild; do you think that makes me happy? Do you believe for one moment that knowing one of my children is forever lost to me is a pleasant thought? That I don't pray and hope every day that Val will be returned safely? I have called in every favour I am owed; no one has heard where he is, or if they have, someone much more powerful than I has purchased their silence."

My jaw sagged. I'd never heard such emotion in Vardan's voice – ever. "You're a fucking duke."

"I'm a fucking eunuch!" I'd never heard him swear before, or raise his voice either. "Yes, I have some power, but there are schemes and secrets to which even I am not privy."

"Are you saying Victoria is behind this?"

"I'm saying I don't know." His shoulders slumped beneath the impeccable cut of his coat. "My involvement only runs so far as to unusual births, special children. Valentine has never exhibited any traits that would lead me to believe he is different."

"I'd wager Dede hadn't either until she gave birth."

He nodded, casting me a glum glance. "That is true. Both

your brother and Avery may have some sort of abnormalities that haven't shown up on any tests, and I am sick over it."

My eyebrows tugged together. "You blame yourself." I hadn't expected that.

"What father wouldn't?" He waved his hand when I opened my mouth to be a bitch. "I know I haven't been much of a father, but that doesn't mean I don't care about the four ... three of you. I care very much, and the fact that people want to poke and prod you because my offspring seem to exhibit fantastic abnormalities both shames and frightens me."

"Your offspring?" I tilted my head and studied him. "Have there been others?"

Vardan jerked his head. "There was a courtesan about a year prior to your birth who died while carrying my child. Another miscarried because there was something ... wrong. And my wife, the duchess, gave birth to a stillborn goblin."

As if I didn't know his wife's title, I thought wryly. "The courtesan that died, what happened?"

He turned his back and went to a small bar in the corner of the room. I watched as he lifted the hose-like tap of an oxygenating carafe – a device specially made to circulate human blood to keep it fresh and at host temperature. He poured a couple of ounces into a glass. "Would you like one?"

"No thank you." I was still feeling the effects of the heart I'd ingested. I felt like I could run a thousand miles, leap over buildings. Shag for hours. And that last one was not a feeling a girl wanted when in the company of her papa. I had to find Vex when I was done here. "Tell me what happened to the courtesan."

Vardan sighed. He looked old. Normally he appeared to be

a man in his late thirties, but tonight he wore the full length of his life in his eyes. "Whatever it was she was carrying ate its way out of her at seven months."

Fang me. I grimaced at the thought, my stomach and its contents rolling uncomfortably. "And yet you decided to give it another go with three more."

"Yes, well it was expected of me. And there was no reason to believe it would happen again."

And that was his opinion of human life. I would call him an arse if I hadn't shared that opinion for the lion's share of my own existence. I continued to share it, on occasion. I harboured no love for humans, but I didn't think of them as disposable either.

"You must have had a shit haemorrhage when that wolf attacked my mother."

He took a sip from his glass. "That she even survived it was a miracle. The fact that she changed, even more of one. That you also survived was something I could not ignore, let alone allow her to abort. I didn't know what you were, but I knew I did not want to lose you."

My throat tightened. I might shed a tear if I thought he wanted me to live because he loved me. "No, because the more buggered-up kids you have, the more Victoria thinks you're useful, right?"

Vardan made a face as he stared into his glass. "Yes, well that was an unfortunate side effect. I thought my children would be regarded as royalty, not freaks or lab rats."

"How about freak royalty? 'Cause I've got that one almost perfected."

He drained his glass and sighed as he raised his gaze to mine. "I've never claimed to be a good father, but I never wanted to see any of you hurt. I would never knowingly do anything to injure any of you."

"But you did. You let them take Dede's baby – that destroyed her. You treated her like she was hatters and lied to her. If you hadn't done that, she'd still be alive. She'd be happy. You locked up my mother so she wouldn't tell me the truth about what you'd done. About me. You let me think she was mad. You would have encouraged me to marry Church in the hope I'd pop out fully plagued gets, and never would have warned me that they might be goblin. If I had known why I was so important to him, maybe he wouldn't have lost his fucking mind, and then I wouldn't have had to—"

He jumped on that like a cat on a mouse. "Wouldn't have had to do what, Alexandra?"

Oh, I'd almost walked into it. I blinked. "I wouldn't have had to discover that the man I held above all was no better than my father."

He winced, and I congratulated myself on the barb. I refused to feel for this man. Refused to have any pity or sympathy for him when he had done so much harm for his own gain.

And above all else, I would *not* trust him.

"I suppose I deserve that," he said softly.

Cry me a fucking ocean. "You honestly don't know where Val is?"

A shake of his dark hair. "No."

I moved closer, so that we were within striking distance. He was taller than me, but he'd lived a soft and privileged life. Unlike Church, he had no idea how to defend himself. "You'd better not be lying to me about this, Your Grace. If I find out you played any part in my brother's disappearance, I will make certain you suffer for it, I promise you."

"Alexandra." His tone was placating. Patronising. "Dearest …"

I grabbed him by the throat and lifted him off the ground. My reach and his height wouldn't allow for more than a few inches, but it was enough to drive the point home. "I am not your dearest. I am the monster you hoped for when you forced my mother to carry me, but I am not *your* monster. Don't ever fool yourself into thinking otherwise. You lost me the moment you gave Ainsley Dede's child."

"It … couldn't … get … out …" His words were strangled by my grip.

I squeezed harder. If he could speak, I wasn't holding him tight enough. "I don't want your excuses or your lies. From now on, you stay the fuck away from me." I tossed him aside. He landed on his feet, but it was far from graceful. He clutched at his throat, gasping for air, staring at me with wide eyes filled with surprise and fear. Lots of fear. And disgust.

"I see now that we understand one another," I said before turning my back on him and making for the French doors that would provide my escape route.

"You won't find Valentine if they don't want you to," Vardan rasped after me. "He'll be lost for ever."

I hesitated, my hand on the door handle. I should just walk out, but I couldn't give him the last word. I looked at him over my shoulder. "Oh, I'll find him," I promised. "Even if I have to bring my goblins cobbleside and tear every inch of Mayfair apart looking for the truth. And I promise you – if I do have to resort to tearing the neighbourhood apart, I'm going to start with you."

I should have gone straight home after confronting my father, but I was too brassed off to simply toddle off and be by myself. Not to mention that my blood was still humming from my little snack in the plague den.

Thoughts of Church and his delicious heart flitted through my brain. Terrible as the old man had turned out to be, I couldn't think of him without a wealth of emotion washing over me. Sometimes it was anger or hatred. Other times, like tonight, it was loss. I missed him, even though he'd sought to control me and killed my sister. How ruddy pathetic was that?

So I risked remaining cobbleside, knowing full well there was a chance that the security cameras positioned all around Mayfair would spot me. I didn't care. I'd rather be outside in the dark, listening to the sounds of the night, catching the scents of horses and flowers, than stumbling about underside. I would be safer in the catacombs and more comfortable, but I didn't want to hide, and I didn't like the fact that part of me *wanted* to be below ground.

Vex lived on South Street, in a big red-brick mansion with white trim that had aged to a light grey. There were lights on inside, and one shining over the front door as though it was expecting me. It wasn't, of course, and neither was Vex.

That realisation made me pause, fingers already curled around the door knocker. What if he wasn't alone? I was fully aware that he might have some of the pack there, since they'd been giving him so much grief, but what if he had a woman with him? In comedic romance movies this was the scene where the plucky female lead discovers her cad of a boyfriend is having it on with another woman and then goes home to eat her own weight in ice cream and not gain a bloody pound.

"Fucking ridiculous," I muttered and gave the knocker a good hard tap.

When the door was yanked open, I had to take a second and reconsider my ridiculous pronouncement. The woman standing before me was about six feet tall, with long red hair and dark green eyes. She was a goddess and a full-blooded were. Perfect mate material. She and Vex would make gorgeous fat babies together.

She growled at me, full lips curling back in a snarl.

Instinct made me growl back. I held her gaze and refused to so much as blink. She was bigger than me, prettier than me, and quite possibly my superior when it came to sex – not like I had an abundance of experience in that quarter – but I'd rip out my own tongue before I'd let her dominate me. One of us was a bitch, and the other just a cute little puppy.

"*You*." Her voice was low and rough. "You're the cause of all of this."

"All of what?" I demanded, still holding her gaze.

She jerked her head towards the inside of the house. I focused all my attention on my ears and listened. There was a fight going on. I could hear the sounds of fist against flesh, the growling of wolves. One wolf in particular.

My wolf.

I took a step over the threshold. The female tried to block my way. "You're not welcome—"

I jobbed her hard and fast in the throat, effectively shutting her up, and pushed past her. "Unless something has changed drastically, I'm fairly certain I'm welcome in Vex's house." Could something have happened that I didn't know about? No. Vex wouldn't throw me over, though he hadn't said anything about a fight either.

His second. That was the only explanation. His second had challenged him.

I ran towards the sounds of combat. I could run incredibly fast, but such speed created great momentum and I didn't want to go tearing doors off hinges – not yet, at any rate – so I was slower than I wanted to be.

The house was grand, with highly polished panels of mellow wood and marble floors. I didn't stop to appreciate it as my heart began to thud heavily in my chest. Concern for Vex dominated all thought.

My ears led me upstairs, to a room with large double doors – the sort that signified a ballroom. I slammed my palms against the solid wood panels and shoved, flinging them wide open.

All but two heads turned at my dramatic entrance, and those that didn't belonged to the men fighting in the centre of the room. They were both caught in a half-transmuted state, a combination of man and wolf. One was Vex – I recognised him instantly, despite the feral change in his features and the abundance of fur. I'd seen his half state before, when Church had sent his minions to kill him.

I could only assume the other wolf was his second. I didn't even know the man's name. I didn't need to – the bastard had Vex's blood on his claws. My nerves began to tingle, gums aching. I wanted to dive into the fray and sink my own fangs into the other wolf's flesh and rip it from his bones for daring to injure what was mine. It wasn't necessary – Vex was beating the snot out of the whelp – but that didn't change my instinct.

"Your Majesty?" The voice was low and soothing – obviously male and Scottish. I turned my head and found a young man watching me with a friendly but wary expression. His eyes were an unbelievable royal blue. "I'm Argyle, the MacLaughlin's secretary."

"So?"

He tilted his head in that dog-like way I associated with every wolf and half-wolf I'd ever met. Assessing me, that was what he was doing. "I'm going to ask you not to intervene in the altercation between the alpha and his second. It's a challenge of succession and cannot be stopped until a victor is declared."

"Until one of them is dead, you mean," I retorted with a snarl.

He nodded once. "Or till someone concedes."

My gaze was on the fight. "How often does that happen?"

"Not very often. It's about honour, you see."

I got that. I understood it, but that didn't change the fact that I was scared for Vex – not as wolf and alpha, but as the man I'd come to prefer above all others. I knew that very few, if any, could best him in a fight, but that didn't stop me from fearing for his life. So I watched and held my breath.

It wasn't a long wait. Vex lifted his head and sniffed the air. His head turned and I got a good look at his golden eyes, shaggy cheeks and elongated fangs. He looked like something out of an American horror film, but I thought he was bloody marvellous. His gaze met mine – just for a split second – and then he turned, lunged and grabbed his opponent by the throat with his teeth.

The other wolf was a ginger, and big – almost as big as Vex. But he froze as those huge jaws clamped down on his neck. His big hands pressed against Vex's shoulders, but not with much force. The gold began to fade from his eyes, returning them to a bright green that was filled with fear and resignation. He grunted when Vex bit, and a trickle of blood ran down his shoulder from where my wolf had hold. I waited. The entire gathering waited, our collective breath held, our bodies statue-still.

And then Vex opened his mouth and stepped back, leaving the other man wounded and bleeding, but alive. The ginger was already back to human form, and Vex returned a few moments later, swiping the back of his hand across his mouth. It came away bloody.

The onlookers were still silent, exchanging stunned glances. I had the feeling that it wasn't because both men were impressive when naked, but because Vex had not killed his opponent.

"Fitz Sheridan," he said, his voice rough. "You are hereby banished from the pack. You will leave England, leave Scotland, and never return on penalty of death. Do you ken?"

Sheridan did not look particularly happy with his judgement. I reckoned there was more honour in death than in banishment. Gold flashed in his eyes and he bared his teeth with a saliva-dripping snarl.

A growl ripped from my throat as I pushed forward. Every head – including Sheridan's – turned towards me as my goblin fought for release. Strong hands caught at me. Not Vex, but Argyle, the secretary. Strong for a halvie. But it wasn't his strength that stopped me, it was those unnerving eyes. Seriously, did the kid have some sort of magic? His gaze calmed my aggression.

"Ma'am, are we to take from your reaction that you would fight for our alpha?"

I glanced at Vex. He was wearing that slightly amused

expression I recognised as one reserved just for me, only this time there was a hint of smugness to it, as though I'd pleased him greatly.

"Yes," I replied. "I would fight to my own death for him." Fang me, why not just admit that I was arse over tea kettle in love with the furry bastard while I was at it?

Now Argyle looked triumphant as well. Excited chatter filled the room, but I couldn't make out the words. Even Sheridan looked pleased – odd for a banished loser.

Sheridan bowed from the waist to Vex. "I accept my punishment, my lord." He was led by two halvies from the blood-splattered circle carved into the floor.

Vex came towards me, all blood and muscle. His hair was a mess of thick, damp waves. The wounds on his chest were nasty but not terribly deep. They'd already stopped bleeding, and once tended to would heal quickly.

"You have impeccable timing, sweetheart," he said in greeting, shrugging into the dressing gown Argyle held for him.

"Do I?" I glanced around, noting all the blatant stares focused on us, the foolish grins. "What the ruddy hell did I just do?"

"Come. I'll tell you." Then to the rest of the room, "Off with the lot of you. Show's over."

"Will you have need of me, sir?" Argyle enquired, hands behind his straight back.

"No, lad. Go out with the others and have a pint. I'll see you on the morrow." When Vex was in his role as alpha, or with his pack, he spoke differently than he did when it was just the two of us. Neither seemed less honest than the other, but I found it interesting all the same.

"Good night, my lord." Argyle bowed. "And my lady." The cheeky halvie winked at me before following us out of the room.

Vex led me down the wide, tall corridor to his bedroom. I'd seen it before, but the dark and ivory decor of it always impressed me upon entering. It was a gorgeous room, elegant and extremely masculine. It suited him.

"Dish," I commanded as soon as the door had closed.

Vex grabbed me by the shoulders and kissed me hard. "You are the most brilliant woman in the world."

I grinned, the bitterness of visiting my father wiped clean. I didn't even care that I could taste Sheridan's blood on his tongue. "If you say so, I won't argue. But what did I do to deserve such a title?"

"You allowed me to keep from killing one of my oldest friends."

"The guy who was trying to eviscerate you? No offence, love, but you need better friends."

"Bah. Sheridan's just a stubborn arse who doesn't know when to stop. Hardly an offence worth dying for."

"But you would have had to kill him had I not arrived?"

He grinned and ran his hands down my arms. Good thing I was wearing black, because I could smell blood – his and Sheridan's – on my shirt. "That's right. As soon as I saw you, I knew I wouldn't have to take his life. You jumped to my defence, brave and hatters that you are, and crafty Argyle knew exactly what to do."

"Which was?"

"Ask you if you'd fight for me."

The whole thing still didn't make any sense. "And I said yes ..."

Some of the amusement left his face. "You had no idea what you were doing, did you?"

"I believe I already said as much. No, no bloody idea."

He ran a hand through the mess of his hair. "You didn't mean it, then?"

Now he looked like I had just killed his puppy. "Albert's fangs, Vex, what the hell happened?"

His shoulders slumped in a manner I didn't like – he was hurt. "You declared yourself my mate."

CHAPTER 19

LIVE WITH WOLVES AND YOU LEARN HOW TO HOWL

So, apparently saying I'd die for Vex was not only the were-wolf version of "I do", but also had been taken by those present to mean that the pack now had an official alliance with the goblins.

Fuck.

"I know this means a lot to the pack," I told Vex after he explained, "but I can't just hand over my goblins like that. I need to discuss it with them first. There are some who aren't crazy to have a queen, and I don't want to give them more reason to eat my liver."

Vex turned to face me, an astonished look on his gorgeous and still bloodstained face. "An alliance with the goblins would be politically advantageous, but when you said you would fight to the death for me, politics was the last thing on my mind."

My heart gave a little thump. Pathetic creature. "Oh." I had been given lessons in deportment, manners, dancing and all things aristocratic. I always knew what fork to use – hell, I even knew the language of the fan, though I'd forgotten most of it. But I had absolutely no idea what to do at that moment.

Fortunately for me, Vex knew exactly what to do. He looked me right in the eye and said, "I love you."

Never mind a thump, my bloody heart stopped completely. And then, like a proper idiot, I burst into tears. My shoulders shook, my throat tightened and my nose clogged. I couldn't even see through the stinging wet.

Vex's arms closed around me, pulling me against his chest. He felt like safety and comfort – and it only made the tears come all the harder. "Shh, sweetheart. It's all right."

"It's not you," I managed to wail.

"I know it's not." He stroked my hair. "You go ahead and cry it out, and then we'll talk about it."

I carried on for a few moments before managing to get a hold of myself. Pulling myself together required pulling free of his embrace. I wiped at my eyes with the handkerchief he offered and then blew my nose. I didn't give the sodden linen back to him, but kept it balled up in my fist just in case I needed it again.

"Sorry 'bout that," I mumbled, as I sat down on the edge of the bed.

The mattress dipped as Vex sat down beside me. "What happened?"

What hadn't? It felt like days ago that I'd gone to see Ainsley rather than just a few hours. I told him about that visit, the goblin den and the altercation with my father.

"I'm sorry I punched your friend," I finished with a sigh. "She was only doing her job."

Vex's fingers curved over the top of my thigh, warm through my bloomers. "She shouldn't have denied you entrance to my home. You've had a rough night, haven't you?"

I nodded. My head had that foggy, heavy feeling that often followed a good bawling. "A rough few days."

"Rough few months." The hand on my leg squeezed. "What can I do?"

Tears threatened again, but I pushed them back, opting to lean into his shoulder instead. "Just do what you have been – be you." It wasn't as though he could fix any of this. I wasn't certain *I* could fix any of it either. Knowing the truth didn't help. So what if I knew what had happened to Dede's baby? It wasn't as though Ainsley's confession could bring her back or change the fact that my father was a knob.

"I ate a heart."

"I know." I could hear the smile in his voice. "Did it make you feel better at all?"

"A bit. Originally I thought I'd come here and shag you senseless."

"A splendid notion. Had I known, I would have kicked everyone out much sooner."

I covered his hand with mine. "I love you."

"I know that too."

Of course he did. He knew me better than I did. I moved my head so I could look up at him. "I thought you might like to hear me say it."

The strong lines of his face were relaxed, the skin around his eyes crinkled in a smile. "I do at that."

But I wasn't done. "You know no matter what, *you* always

have my support, and the goblins' too, if I have any sway over them." I couldn't say the same extended to the entire pack, but I could give him my loyalty regardless.

He kissed my forehead. "And you have mine. Come, let's get cleaned up."

We showered together, and had a needy encounter under the spray of hot water. I needed his strength right then, and I didn't care if that made me vulnerable. If I couldn't be vulnerable with him, I was shit out of luck.

"Are you really going to banish Sheridan?" I asked as we towelled off.

"Rather than kill him? Yes. I can't afford to look weak in front of the pack. It's a fair punishment."

"But he's your friend."

Vex shrugged. "I can't let that matter in such decisions. I have to do what's right for the pack. He would have killed me if he could."

That was a big if. I'd never seen anyone who could fight like Vex. He'd even defeated Church once, and Church had been a fantastic fighter. Until I had him killed, that is.

But Vex's words made me think of my father and what he'd said about never being able to claim his grandchild. Taking Dede's baby had been beyond wrong. More than cruel. But giving the child to Ainsley had protected the boy somewhat. He wouldn't be poked and prodded in a lab, and Dede hadn't been forced to undergo examinations of her own. Putting my mother in an asylum had protected her, as well as me – for the most part. Morally I was opposed to almost everything my father had done where his children were concerned, but it could have turned out worse, I suppose. Out of a list of bad decisions, he'd chosen the least awful.

Would I forgive him? Perhaps. Probably. I would never again trust him, though.

"Do you reckon I made the wrong choice?" Vex asked, pulling on a pair of clean trousers. He'd obviously taken my silence as disapproval, given the slight edge of defensiveness in his voice. Maybe I was hatters, but that peevish tone made me smile. He wasn't perfect after all.

I watched the muscles in his back ripple as he moved. "No. I think you did the right thing." I pulled my clothes on over my clean skin. I hated putting dirty clothes back on, but I didn't have anything of mine in Vex's wardrobe. I should probably remedy that.

I wasn't ready to move in with him, appealing as the idea was. I'd be too tempted to hide behind him, and I felt as though most of my life had been spent hiding. Certainly many truths had been hidden from me, and I was done with that. I'd uncovered things I wished I hadn't, learned things I didn't want to know, but there was something rotten going on in Britain, and now that I'd stuck my finger in it, I had to dig to the bottom.

Another reason not to move in, I realised as we went downstairs in search of food, was that the pack treated the place like their own private club. All the full-bloods had their own houses, but a few of them were playing billiards in the gaming room, while others made use of the library. Halvies milled about as well – Protectorate employees there because their aristos were, the rest Vex's staff and half-bloods with nowhere else to be. I couldn't imagine Queen V allowing halvies to hang about the palace. And other than me, I couldn't imagine anyone wanting to spend time with the goblins.

"I don't remember there being quite so many wolves here before," I commented as we entered the dining room.

"Waxes and wanes," was his reply. "Any time you were going to be here I made certain they all knew not to be."

Thoughtful, but still not something I wanted to deal with. For now, Vex and I would continue as we had been – me with my space, and him with his. No need to make the pack resent me more than they already did. There was no need to rush anything – it wasn't as though we were going to get married or spend the rest of our very long lives together. I didn't even know if my life expectancy was the same as an aristo's or still that of a halvie.

We were just finishing up a meal of fresh bread, sharp cheese and salty meats when a commotion rose from the front of the house.

Vex and I exchanged glances, both of us rising to our feet. We had guests, and the whole house was in turmoil.

"MacLaughlin!" someone shouted, but Vex was already on his way, me at his heels.

I smelled my sister before I saw her familiar blue hair. She was covered in blood that was not her own, holding another halvie upright. It was that halvie whose blood she wore. The poor girl was in bad shape – bleeding from multiple wounds and . . . I sniffed. Tetracycline.

Another were-halvie I recognised as a friend of Fee's – Ian – was wounded as well, though not as badly. All five of the halvies who had burst into the house were bloodied and dirty – and the four who were conscious enough to talk were trying to do so over the top of one another.

Ophelia spotted me and headed straight towards me. "Human League attack," she said as Vex took her wounded friend into his arms. "We were having a laugh at a pub, minding our own business, when a couple of hueys armed with automatics barged in and started shooting the place up."

"Albert's fangs," I responded. "That's ballsy. Was anyone else hurt?" By now, Vex had started to walk away with the girl and everyone followed him – Ophelia and me included.

"A few humans nicked with debris, but it was our table they attacked. We managed to take cover, but Annalise had already been shot. I don't know if the whole thing lasted even a minute."

"You're sure it was the League?"

She shot me a dry look as we climbed the wide staircase. "They used tetracycline bullets and shouted something about death to all freaks. Come to think of it, perhaps it was the Templars."

I scowled, more because that blatantly sarcastic remark was something I might have said than because I was offended. As far as I knew, the Knights Templar hadn't existed in England for centuries. "You okay, then?"

She didn't look at me, but gave a stiff nod. "I won't lie, I've spent a lot of time with humans. I've got a lot of human friends. I never expected to be on the opposite end of a gun from one, you know?"

Yes, I did. I never expected Church to turn on me. "You knew the shooters?"

She nodded. "One of them." Then, for my ears only, "She tried to join us several months ago. Juliet turned her away. Thought she was too unhinged."

"She'd know," I drawled.

"Bloody bastards are trying to start a war," she commented with a disbelieving shake of her head.

"I thought that's what you wanted."

Fee turned to me at the top of the stairs, strands of blue sticking to the blood on her face. We stood back so the others could pass by us. "We just want to end the bullshit. A democracy or something. These fanatics want our blood and they won't stop until we're all dead."

A shiver ran down my spine, and I'm not afraid to admit it. We of plagued blood were powerful and strong, but we had limitations. As far as I knew, I was the only one able to stand daylight for any amount of time. The humans outnumbered us by a vast margin, and if they were armed with silver and tetracycline, and attacked during the day, we were royally fucked – literally and figuratively.

But that was only if the entire human population rose up. I had to believe there were at least some who wouldn't be keen on taking the risk.

My rotary rang. Fee nodded at me and left to join the others who had followed Vex and the wounded girl. One of the halvies who brushed by me had a medical kit and what looked like an old-fashioned transfusion set.

"Yeah?"

"Xandy? It's Penny."

One of the last people I expected. "Dearest, now's not a good time."

"Oh. Sorry. It's just that I don't have a lift home from work and I've heard there's been some League violence tonight. I reckon a girl like myself might make a tempting target."

I closed my eyes. She was right, and Penny's blood was not something I wanted to have on my hands or my conscience.

"Isn't Avery there?" I asked, grasping at a last straw.

"No, she left."

"Why the fuck would she do that?"

All it took was a split-second hesitation for me to know that something wasn't right. Penny rarely hesitated. "Xandy, I need you to come and get me."

There was no mistaking the tremor in her voice. Shit. It was the betties, I just knew it.

"Sit tight. I'll come round as soon as I can." I disconnected, and stomped down the corridor towards the room into which Vex had taken the girl, only to meet him coming out.

"Is she all right?" I asked.

He shrugged. "Not sure. We've got to get the silver out of her, then flush the poison from her system, but she's young and strong, so hopefully that will be on our side."

"Penny rang – I think something's up at the club. Do you mind?"

"No. Go get her. Where's the Butler?"

"Fang me." I'd forgotten the motorrad wasn't parked outside. "Down Street."

"I'll drive you. Annalise is in good hands. Nothing I can do for the poor mite other than stay out of the way of those who can help her."

"You don't have to do that." But he was already on his way down the stairs. I had to hurry to keep up.

We took the Panther because it was the most readily available of his vehicles, which included a horse-drawn carriage. He had me at Down Street in record time.

"Come back to the keep when you're done," he instructed. "I want you where I can see you."

I smiled. "Love you too. I'll be back as soon as I can."

"Bring Penny. She shouldn't be alone. If there's trouble, call me."

I agreed, and gave him a kiss before sliding out of the motor carriage. I didn't even take the time to watch him drive away before hopping on the Butler.

The wail of sirens cut through the night in Westminster. I spied a news van as well. Special Branch would be all over the pub where the shooting had taken place, and ambulances would be on their way to help injured human patrons. I hoped they caught the hatters arseholes responsible.

I was very happy that Fee hadn't been hurt. I could admit that now that there was some physical distance between us. As much as she rubbed me up the wrong way at times, she was my sister, and I was honestly beginning to think of her with a degree of fondness, despite disagreeing where our mother's aspirations were concerned.

Freak Show was quiet when I arrived. The club closed at four in the morning – late enough for human partiers and early enough for full-bloods to get home before dawn. There were a few staff left, cleaning up and closing the place down for the day, and a couple of drunken humans huddled in the door lighting fags before staggering off down the street. I pulled into the alley and into the back courtyard.

Penny didn't immediately come out, so I turned the key in the ignition and let the motorrad rumble into silence. Before climbing off, I sent a quick digigram and looked up at the camera watching the courtyard. I waved at it, calmed by the knowledge that my goblins were watching, then dismounted and ran up the steps, knocking hard on the door. I should have been more gentle – my knuckles left marks.

"I just have to grab my bag," Penny said when she yanked the door open. Her eyes were wide, fearful. When she rolled them upwards, I knew we were not alone. "Come on in."

I stepped over the threshold, reaching for the dagger in my corset. It was eerily quiet. I'd never been here when it was this empty.

"Vex wants us to stay at his place," I said as I followed her to the office. If there was someone waiting to make trouble, he or she might think twice if they knew we'd be missed. "He wants us where he can see us, apparently."

Penny had stopped in the centre of the room and stood with her shoulders slumped and head low. Any second I expected her elaborate lavender wig to slide right off. "Penny? What's the matter?" As if I didn't already know – I could smell their stink the moment I crossed the threshold.

She turned, facing me with an expression that screamed of guilt and remorse, and fear. "I'm sorry, Xandra. They told me they'd kill Val if I didn't ring you."

The hair on the back of my neck rose, alerting me to danger. I whirled around, dagger slicing through the air, and betty flesh. I dodged to the side to avoid arterial spray. Penny wasn't quite as quick and ended up with crimson splatter on her wig. The betty fell to the floor, twitching out the remainder of his life.

Immediately I turned on the other one as two more came through the door. At least they'd sent enough to make it interesting.

A lank-haired blonde woman with black lumps on her neck raised her arm. I swore when I saw the gun in her hand and lunged for her throat.

Too late.

The dart pierced my neck. I pulled it out just as another struck me in the chest. A third bit into my thigh. I managed to grab the betty around the neck with my arm, taking her down with me and sliding the dagger between her ribs as we fell. Her eyes widened in shock and she squeezed the trigger again.

This one got me in the stomach. The betty and I stared into each other's eyes as we crumpled to the floor in each other's embrace. Every muscle in my body seized and seemed to turn to lead. My vision blurred as the betty's eyes went dead. Then the world grew black.

Fuck.

CHAPTER 20

STONE WALLS DO NOT A PRISON MAKE

My mouth tasted of aluminium, and my skin felt like a plague of bugs had burrowed in through my feet and out the top of my skull.

I'd been drugged. Hard. Probably tetracycline-laced laudanum; it was a common method of disabling halvies and aristos that didn't do any lasting damage, but took us out of commission for varying lengths of time. I'd obviously been out long enough to be transported somewhere, because I could tell without opening my eyes that I was no longer at Freak Show.

I was on a cot – a narrow, hard one – somewhere that smelled of dirt, antiseptic, blood and fear.

And Val, I realised with a leap of my heart. This place smelled of Val.

I sat up faster than I ought and my brain rewarded me by spinning wildly against the inside of my skull. For a moment I thought I might vomit, but then the spinning slowed, and my vision cleared.

The cell I was in was the type often seen in old pirate films – a solid stone wall behind me and bars on the other three sides where my prison connected to neighbouring cells. Beyond that was a dirt-floor dungeon sort of arrangement – dimly lit and damp.

Penny was on my left, still unconscious, and on my right, standing with his hands around the bars, watching me, was Val. "Fang me," I cried, leaping to my feet. I lurched across the floor on shaking legs, practically falling into the bars to cover his hands with mine.

"Are you all right?" I demanded.

My brother was paler than usual, dirty and perhaps a little thinner, but otherwise he appeared healthy. He nodded. "As well as can be expected. Xandy, how did they get you and Penny?"

"They told her they'd kill you if she didn't get me to come to Freak Show."

"Stupid brat," he muttered. He didn't mean it. He loved Penny, and no doubt felt responsible for her being locked up with us. I reckoned he felt responsible for me as well.

"They'd set up a meet for tomorrow night," I told him. "I expect they thought they'd catch me by surprise." But they hadn't, and I wasn't going to assume my captors were stupid enough to believe they had either. They'd got me because I'd gone in alone, thinking I could handle whatever they threw at me.

I was well aware of just how wrong an assumption that had been.

Still, I wasn't a complete dolt. That digigram I'd sent before going into the club was to Vex and William. If I'd told Vex earlier that it was a trap, he would have tried to stop me, or come with me. I couldn't let him put himself in danger, and I couldn't let him jeopardise my one chance to find Val.

So, now that I'd found him, what the hell did I do next?

"Have they hurt you?" I asked.

My brother shook his head, indigo locks falling over his forehead. He needed a shampoo – and a shower. "No. They've taken a lot of my blood. Made me toss off into a cup. I think I've been a bit of a disappointment to them really." His dry tone almost made me smile. They hadn't broken him.

"I got a bit of a thrashing the couple of times I tried to escape." He eyed me carefully. "They shocked me good. Drugged me when they first nabbed me."

I nodded. "Me too."

"Put me out for hours. Reckon your being a gob is why you're awake already."

"That's as good a guess as any." I glanced around the dimly lit cell. "Any idea where we are?"

"None. I hear water occasionally."

I strained my ears, searching. I could hear moaning, breathing. I could hear muffled voices, clangs and thunks – people going about their business. I could hear water, but I couldn't hear the city.

"We're underside. Deep." Somewhere along the Thames, or close to one of London's underground waterways that hadn't dried up. Could be a sewer for all I knew. The stink of shit hung heavy in this place, but it was the kind generated within rather than without. My cell was equipped with a lovely-looking bucket designed for just that sort of thing. I was not going to shit in a bucket.

"I'm going to get us out of here," I assured Val, but before I could ask him any more questions, the door to the dungeon opened, and several people walked in. Human. Halvie. Aristo. Each race was represented, an unsettling fact. It seemed the one thing we all had in common was a streak of immorality.

"I told you she was awake," said one of the human women. Like the rest of them, she wore a laboratory jacket.

"Fascinating," remarked a halvie man. He looked to be in his forties, which meant he was probably closer to seventy. I didn't recognise him. "Based on my calculations, she should have been out for at least another fifteen minutes."

One of the aristos stepped forward to peer at me through the bars. It took me a moment to recognise her. It was Lady Gadling. I remembered seeing her with Church. "You cannot apply expectations to this one. She's extremely unpredictable. And troublesome. Little more than an animal."

I lunged at the bars. They gave slightly under the force of my body. Fangs erupted in my mouth as I snarled at her, my goblin screaming to the surface.

Lady Gadling merely backed away from my cage. She smiled, a cold twist of her pale lips. Everything about her was pale – her eyes, her hair, her skin. She had been a reputed beauty in her day, but the bitterness of her soul crept out – like the picture of Dorian Grey, except the decrepit canvas was her actual face.

"Really, Xandra. Is that any way for the daughter of a duke to behave?"

"You fucking bitch," I snarled. "Does he know?"

A frown pulled at her smooth brow. "Vardan? Of course not. I wouldn't trust that idiot to organise a game of whist, let alone something of this magnitude."

"Why are you doing this?"

She smiled then – serene and yet condescending. "For my

people, of course." Then, to the others, "Drug her and take her to exam room three. She should be ripe."

Ripe for what? One of the humans pointed a small pistol in my direction. There was a soft *pfft* and a dart came flying through the air at me. I jerked to the left, my hand whipping out. I caught the dart and threw it back. It hit him in the neck and he went down almost instantly – a boneless sack of meat.

My triumph was short-lived. I barely had time to enjoy the look on his face before I felt stinging in my chest and thigh. I glanced down and saw two identical darts sticking out of my body. They'd got me again.

Slowly, I sank to my knees. My face hit the bars, but I barely felt it. I couldn't feel anything but the insistent tug of gravity. Even my brain felt as though it was being pulled down. My mouth opened, but only drool came out.

I could hear Val calling my name, but I couldn't look at him, couldn't respond as I toppled to the floor. My skull hit the hard stone but I felt nothing. My vision blurred. I was lifted, carried from the cell and tossed on to a gurney.

My brain struggled against the paralysis, but remained impotent. What the ruddy hell had they shot me with? It wasn't the same stuff they'd used at Freak Show; this was nothing I'd ever experienced before or ever wanted to again. I was a prisoner in my own body.

"I cannot begin to tell you how fortunate we are to have you, Alexandra," Gadling told me. Her voice echoed in my skull. "We've been studying your blood for years, but to actually have you . . .well, it's incredibly exciting."

"Fuck . . . you," I managed to croak.

It was a mistake. I saw the alarm on her angular face and realised I should have kept my mouth shut. "Give her more."

Something cold and sharp pierced my left arm, and then a flood of warmth rushed through my veins. They'd filled me with more of the paralysing drug.

At the end of the corridor they opened a large door and took me through. I stared at the stone ceiling and ancient lights, unable to even blink.

Finally I was taken to a room with white walls and bright lights that hurt my eyes. Hands roamed over me, removing my clothes. My legs were spread apart and something thin and cold slid inside me. What were they doing to me? I felt like I'd been slipped that rape drug I'd heard about, and was now being violated. I could hear them talking, but only certain words cut through the fog in my head.

" . . . only three . . . viable . . . good enough . . . "

My head rolled as I forced my lids open. Feeling slowly returned to my extremities, prickles of sensation. This time I did not mention it.

Across the room was a halvie male strapped to a similar table. I blinked. It couldn't be. I tried to lift my head as the pounding of my heart cleared the haze from my eyes. "Rye?"

"She's coming out of it!"

I pulled against the restraints pinning me to the table. I managed to snap one before I felt the bite of a syringe in the side of my neck. For one second I saw him clearly – thin and worn and not at all as I remembered, but I knew it was him. I would know him anywhere.

And then he was gone and so was everything else.

"Is she dead?" The question seemed to bounce off the inside of my skull like an echo through a cavern.

"No, I'm not fucking dead," I muttered with a scowl. The words were thick in my mouth and my head throbbed with the effort it took to frown. Slowly – very slowly – I opened my eyes, blinking against the film across my vision. At least the lighting in my cell was blessedly dim. I turned away from the brightness in the corridor beyond, and felt my brain slide to the other side of my head.

Whatever they had drugged me with had been powerful stuff, but it was starting to wear off, just as it had in the operating theatre. A little blood would sort me out.

Slowly, I pushed myself upright. They hadn't even taken me to my bed, just dumped me on the cold floor of my cell. I hadn't pissed myself, so that was good, but I needed to, badly. Looked like I was headed for the bucket after all.

I sat still for a moment, waiting for the dizziness to pass before glancing to my right and then my left. Val and Penny watched me with almost identical expressions – only Penny had mascara and eyeliner running down her pale cheeks. Her wig was askew as well. I might have laughed at it if our situation was different.

They turned their backs while I used the bucket, bless them.

Hitching up my bloomers – which had thankfully been put back on me – I turned to Val. "How long was I out?"

"Ten minutes? Fifteen tops. Where did they take you?"

"I don't know." It was as distant as a dream, but the twinge in my abdomen was not – a slight cramping. "Fang me." Bits of memory came flooding back. They'd put something inside me. What? And had they left something behind or taken something out? They'd mentioned something being viable.

And the duchess had called me ripe. That made me think of fertility.

Albert's fangs. Had they tried to impregnate me?

I was *not* a fucking laboratory rat. And I was not about to let them use my body as a bloody incubator for Christ knows what.

I rose to my feet, weaving slightly, but regaining more and more of my equilibrium. Rage began to churn in my stomach, the heightened emotion gnawing at the lethargy forced into my blood. I went to Penny.

"Give me your arm."

Her smudged eyes widened. "Why?"

"If I'm going to get us out of here, I need blood. You're going to give me some." It wasn't the nicest way to ask, but I figured we were beyond worry about delicate sensibilities.

Fear wafted off her like the scent of vanilla from a warm cake. Saliva flooded my mouth and my fangs itched to slide free. I had to be careful or I'd tear into her.

"Please, Pen. I need your help."

She slid her arm through the bars. I seized it and quickly sank my fangs into her wrist, ignoring her little cry. All those stories about vampire bites being pleasurable were based in reality. There is an enzyme in the saliva of all halvies, aristos and goblins that mingles with the blood when our fangs pierce flesh and turns what should be pain into sensual delight.

That I might be turning Penny on was not something I wanted to contemplate.

I took about half a pint, chugging the sweet, coppery stuff like a uni student with a cheap bottle of wine. Then I let her go, despite the desire to drink until she ran dry, and went to Val. I didn't have to ask. My brother offered his arm willingly. I took a bit less from him, because he was already weak.

The blood gave me strength and energy, overpowering the remaining drugs in my system. I walked over to the sliding iron door and gripped the bars in both hands.

"They're too strong," Val said. "Even if you could escape your cell, they'd see you." He nodded behind me.

I looked, and saw a security camera in the corner of the corridor ceiling. From the angle of it, I reckoned it kept tabs on the entire length of the cell block.

Correction – it was trained on the floor and the cell doors of the entire block. What it didn't watch was the ceiling and the back half of the cells.

I let go of the bars and walked to the back of my prison, then over to the bars separating me and Val. I ran for the opposite wall as fast as I could and leaped into the air, catching the bars near the top and bringing my feet up so the soles of my boots could catch against the metal.

"What the sweet bloody hell are you doing?" Penny asked.

I glanced down at her. "Hopefully getting us out of here." I knew from sneaking into Bedlam after Dede that I could climb like a spider. My strength and agility had increased since going off the supplements I'd been made to take to keep up the ruse that I was just a half-blood, so it was fairly easy for me to support my weight and creep sideways towards the front of the cell.

When I was close enough, I pressed my feet against one of the bars, so that I was holding my body parallel to the floor. I pushed, and the bar bent. It took a couple of tries, but it finally bowed. I repeated this process with the bar next to it, pushing it in the opposite direction, until I had a space just big enough for me to crawl through.

"Girl, you are one freaky-arsed bitch," Penny said. I might have imagined the awe I heard in her voice.

I grinned. Outside the cell, I clung to the beams and metal bits that ran along the ceiling, and crept towards the security camera. I hung above it like an insect, my right hand and knees keeping me suspended as I reached down and grabbed the electrical wires running into the camera. I pulled.

Sparks flew, but I succeeded in not getting burned or electrocuted. As soon as the red light on the device went out, I dropped to the floor, landing in a crouch. If I was lucky, the security folks would assume the issue was a short, or a logic engine error. They would attempt to fix it from their workstation rather than come down here.

If I was unlucky, I had a precious few moments to do ... something.

I ran down the corridor. Halvies shouted at me as I passed, all crying out for me to release them. The one goblin barked – as though it had forgotten how to speak.

There had to be a control panel for the doors. If I could find it, I could set them all free.

My focus jumped track when I reached the last cell. His scent overpowered me – not just because he smelled terrible, but because underneath the stench, he smelled of a sweet memory from years ago.

I stopped, practically tripping over my feet. The shouts of my fellow prisoners echoed around me, but I ignored them all. I stood close to the bars, peering in at the man crouched in the darkened corner.

"Rye?"

His head lifted. His bronze hair was way too long, and matted. His face was covered with stubble, and his clothes were nothing more than hospital scrubs. His feet were bare and dirty, but his eyes gleamed gold.

He growled at me.

"Rye, it's me. Xandra."

He tilted his head back and sniffed the air, then stared at me with those lupine eyes once more. This time the growl started lower in his chest. Slowly, he leaned forward, moving towards me on his fingertips and toes like a four-legged creature. Then he was at the bars, and only that iron separated us.

Did he even recognise me? Had they succeeded in ruining him?

"Xandra?" His voice was hoarse – rusty – but so very much as I remembered. My throat clenched at the wonder with which he said my name. And when he reached out to touch his dirty fingers to my cheek, I didn't flinch.

"It's me," I said, hot, embarrassing tears stinging the backs of my eyes. I reached up and wrapped my hand around his, holding both against my cheek. "I'm going to get you out of here."

"There's no escape," he whispered. "No getting out."

At that moment the door to my left slid open, and the Duchess Vardan walked in. I couldn't remember her Christian name. I'm sure I'd heard it once, but my father never referred to her by name, only by her title or as his wife.

"What the hell are you doing here?" I demanded, but I already knew. As soon as she walked through that door it all fell into place inside my head, like some kind of terrible jigsaw puzzle. Of course she was involved. Who else besides my father could know so much about his children? Who could make certain he didn't know anything other than what he was supposed to?

Who else would take pleasure in torturing his bastards?

"Alexandra," she said with that cruel smile as she pointed a pistol at my chest. "Look at you, out of your cell and looking positively feral. You gave them quite a scare earlier, but fortunately you were easy to subdue once more. In the future we'll have to remember how quickly you metabolise substances. No harm done, we got what we wanted from you."

From me. Did that mean they hadn't left something inside?

"I'm going to kill you," I promised her.

Her smile turned mocking. With her perfect blonde hair and painted red lips she looked like the model of nobility, but there was nothing noble about her. "That's sweet. However, I really don't think it's a realistic goal for you to set at this point, or ever for that matter."

As she spoke, a red light began to flash on the wall behind her head. She glanced at it with a frown. Then a voice crackled from a speaker in the back of my cell. "Attention, there has been a security breach in sectors C and F. The facility is on immediate lock— Arghhhhhh!" I winced, my eardrums cringing under the scream, but over the top of it I'd heard a familiar growl.

Goblins.

CHAPTER 21

LEST HIMSELF ROB THE PRISON OF ITS PREY

The duchess looked worried now, as she ought.

Her distraction was my advantage. I wrapped my fingers around the pistol in her hand and bent the barrel just enough to ensure the thing wouldn't shoot. She looked at me, then at it in shock.

And then she hit me in the face with it. My head snapped back, but I didn't stagger. She was strong, but she knew nothing about how to throw a punch.

It was my honour to instruct her, and I hit her hard enough that I felt her front teeth give beneath my knuckles. She fell back against the door, but didn't stay there. She came at me snarling and spitting blood. I ducked her fist and hit her again – this time in the nose.

I don't know which of us was more surprised when there was a buzzing noise and the doors to all the cells slid open. But she was the one who took off at a dead run, through the door she'd come through moments earlier. I would have gone after her, but I wasn't going anywhere without Val, and Penny.

And Rye, who was staring at the open cell like he couldn't quite believe his eyes.

I held my hand out to him. "Come on," I said. "Let's go."

At the same time, the door to the cell block burst open and in ran two of the most gorgeous creatures I'd ever seen – a huge wolf-man and a lean, snarling goblin – Vex and William. They were bloodied, snarling and beautiful.

I dropped my hand and ran to my wolf. Vex grabbed me and hugged me so tight I thought I might break. I didn't care that he was covered in blood, because none of it was his. "We have to get out, now," he told me. "The alarm triggered a security protocol."

"What kind?" By this time Penny and Val had joined us – other prisoners as well. God, there were so many, and that was only in this block. When I saw the old female goblin limp out into the corridor, something tightened in my chest. My own goblin responded by rushing to the surface so fast I couldn't even prepare for it. Some of the prisoners drew back in fear, but that old goblin came right for me and placed her paws on either side of my head, rasping something in a language I didn't understand. Gaelic, maybe? And how old did she have to be to look so ancient? Given the timeline of the plague mutations, she couldn't be more than a couple of hundred years old, but she looked much more than that, especially when compared to William.

"Lady of the Light, she calls you," William informed me proudly. "Great honour she bestows."

I could have asked who she was or how he knew this, but Vex began herding us towards the exit. "Out, all of you. Pretty soon this place will fill with a mixture of poisonous gases and tetracycline. If we don't get out now, we might never."

He grabbed my arm and I scanned the crowd for a glimpse of Rye. No sign of bronze hair, no familiar green eyes. I tugged free. "Vex, I can't."

I was met with a fierce scowl, made even more ferocious by his lupine countenance. "Why the hell not?"

Bodies pushed past me as Val leaped into copper mode and began taking charge of the evacuation. William handed the matron goblin to a younger one who had appeared to help lead the prisoners out. The young one draped a cloak over the old woman, and offered her a pair of dark glasses to protect her squinting eyes.

"Rye is here," I said in a low voice.

Vex's mouth tightened. "Where?"

"Last cell down."

"Come on." He grabbed my hand and started in that direction. His hand felt huge around mine, and slightly furry. He wore a large black shirt that hadn't ripped at the seams during transformation. I wondered if he'd planned for that. And then I wondered why the hell I was wondering. This place had mucked me up.

William flanked me. Apparently neither he nor Vex was about to let me out of their sight.

"Took you both long enough to get here," I commented drily.

The prince licked blood from his muzzle. "Saw the lady taken on security screen. Got licence of vehicle. Called for the MacLaughlin and tracked our lady with the wolves and city cameras."

A smile I had no inclination to fight curved my lips. "I knew you'd come."

A halvie wearing a laboratory jacket came through the door at the end of the corridor. He had an axe taken from the fire station raised above his head, and screamed as though he were an ancient Celt tearing across the battlefield. William slapped him with the back of his hand and sent the stupid tosser flying into the wall, where he landed in a twisted heap.

Rye was still there – crouched inside his cell. He looked bewildered and afraid. The sight was enough to bring tears to my eyes, but we hadn't time for that.

"Rye? I need you to come with me, love. I'm taking you home."

He turned his face towards me, pale and wide-eyed. "Really?"

"Really, but you have to come with us now. Can you walk?"

He laughed – a bitter, dry sound. "Dunno, but I can crawl. They made me do it enough."

A sob built in my throat, but I swallowed it down. I hadn't lost it yet and I wasn't about to now, not when it mattered most. I didn't have to say a word. Vex came into the cell and put an arm around Rye's back. Rye's own arm went around Vex's shoulders. "Come on, son. Let's get you home."

Rye teetered when his bare feet hit the ground. When his knees buckled, Vex gave up on pretence and picked him up in his arms. "We have to go. Now."

William led the way back through the cell block and out of the door. We ran up a flight of stairs, red lights strobing in the corners. A recorded voice announced that the primary defence system would commence in four minutes. That must be the murderous cocktail Vex had mentioned.

As we reached the next floor, I realised where we were. The

bloody Tower. The Tower of London. There was something strangely poetic yet incredibly twisted about that fact.

Four goblins and five weres ran towards us from the opposite direction, carrying bits of electronics and logic engines. Two vampires swept down behind them. One of them was the Earl of Stoke. The other was my father's duchess. Stoke raised a crossbow and pointed at the back of one of the goblins – it was Elsbeth.

What happened next was like something out of a film. William let loose a terrible roar, and dropped to all fours, shifting into something that was still goblin but much more terrifying. It was a creature made of muscle, tooth and claw, and it moved faster than anything I'd ever seen. One moment he was at my side; the next he was on Stoke in a snarling frenzy. Blood sprayed as the earl screamed. The duchess bolted for the exit along with the others. I lunged after her, catching her just at the threshold in a chokehold.

"Let me go!" she shouted. I squeezed her throat between my forearm and bicep, heedless of how she clawed at my arm, drawing blood.

"Shut your fucking mouth!" I warned. "Or I give you to the prince." That shut her up.

Stoke had stopped screaming. Out of the corner of my eye I saw what was left of him ooze across the stone floor. William had changed back to the form I recognised as his true visage, and licked the blood from his muzzle. He stared down at the mess of Stoke with grim satisfaction.

"William, we have to get out of here." The disembodied voice announced that we had but a minute left. Plenty of time, but I would prefer not to push it.

"What are you going to do with me?" the duchess asked as

I dragged her outside into the waning night. Dawn was fast approaching. I had to get my goblins underground immediately.

"Right now, I'm going to save your life," I replied, letting her go. I didn't want to do it. I wanted to kill her, but for some mad reason, my rational mind chose that moment to kick in. I couldn't kill her here. If I did, the Yard would snatch me up for certain. There would be witnesses. I couldn't drag her off for the same reason. People were rushing around us, and I couldn't risk it.

I couldn't turn her in either – not because of the scandal, but because if the Yard got her, I would never find out who she was working with. I couldn't stop anyone else present from giving her up to the coppers, but if she wasn't here when they arrived, an investigation would have to follow. It would buy me enough time to question her first.

And then maybe I could kill her.

She rubbed her neck and eyed me warily. Sirens approached in the distance as the Tower alarms rang around us. I watched as coloured smoke unfurled behind modern windows set in ancient stone. If there was anyone left inside, they wouldn't be alive for long. Goblins scattered as the noise and flashing lights drew closer.

"Why would you save me?" Duchess Vardan asked, still rubbing her neck.

I shot her a narrow glance as I turned to walk away. I didn't care if she was picked up by the peelers or not. She'd pay for what she'd done here. "So that some day I can make you wish I hadn't."

The next few hours were chaos. Special Branch made certain that all the prisoners who had escaped from the Tower were taken to hospital to be examined – questions would wait. I stuck around and gave my statement instead. I had no intention of telling them I'd also been a prisoner – no bloody way was I letting anyone at Prince Albert Hospital poke around inside me, not when they'd been the place that had kept a false file on me, or rather an empty one. I'd go to a doctor of my own choosing.

I told the Yard that I'd been looking for my brother, that Penny had rung me and that I'd arrived at Freak Show just in time to see her taken away by betties. I'd followed her here, and Vex and William had met me shortly thereafter. We'd set off the alarms to alert the authorities and had done what we could to save the prisoners. It was an easy lie, and close enough to the truth that all of us involved could remember it.

The goblins were gone, taking as many logic engines as they could with them. Only William remained, despite my telling him to get underside. He wanted the duchess's throat between his jaws, I could see it in his eye. He'd have to wait his turn.

"Yours, this is." He held out his hand.

It was my dagger. The blood had been wiped from the blade, and it glittered prettily under the lights – almost opalescent. "Thank you." I'd no doubt dropped it at Freak Show. To be honest, I was surprised to get it back. I would have thought a betty would have absconded with it.

He bowed his head. "The MacLaughlin would have retrieved it, but 'twas too intent on finding the lady. A most suitable consort is the wolf."

I had to smile at that. "Go home," I told him. "Clean yourself up and spend time with Elsbeth. Find out what's on those logic engines."

He bowed his shaggy, matted head and then did something that surprised me. He hugged me – hard. His fur smelled good. "Almost lost our lady," he said. "Never again."

It hadn't occurred to me that William might actually care about me. I thought much of his deference to me was because he saw me as the answer to the plague's prayers. That he was legitimately concerned for my well-being was enough to make my chest tight.

I hugged him back and then sent him away before the sun rose. He was cutting it close as it was, and even the dark glasses, hat and coat he'd retrieved when we came outside couldn't shield him. There were plenty of places for him to find underside access this close to the Thames, so I had no worries that he'd soon be safe.

The Special Branch agents surrounded Val, happy to see him. I let him have this time to answer their questions. There wasn't one of them who wouldn't be looking for the remaining betties who had taken him. They also needed to wait their turn.

Penny sat in the back of an ambulance, letting the Emergency Procedure Techs – the EPTs – check her for injuries or any side effects of the drugs she'd been given. Thankfully, she hadn't been hurt.

"Trouble has a rather pesky way of finding you, Your Majesty."

I turned towards the pain-in-my-arse voice. "Why, DI Maine, what an unexpected surprise."

He eyed me suspiciously. I guess saving his life didn't totally absolve me of all guilt in his estimation. "Your brother says he doesn't know who was in charge of this cluster fuck."

I arched a brow. "Eloquence is obviously your strong suit. I get the impression that you think I might have the answers he doesn't?"

"It would be very helpful if we had someone to hang this on, yeah."

"Sorry, mate. I don't have the foggiest."

He didn't believe me, and I didn't think it was because I was a shit liar, because I was actually pretty good at it when I wanted to be. The aristos unfortunate enough to be caught – there might have been two of them – had been hauled off in Black Marias along with the rest of the apprehended staff. Had one of them given my father's wife's name?

I didn't think the duchess was the mastermind, but she was obviously among the upper echelon. Could I end her? In a second, and not even blink. I would have mixed emotions about Church until the day I died, but not that bitch.

Of course, I couldn't say all of this to Maine. "I've given my statement. Might I go now?"

He shrugged. "I can't stop you. I may have further questions for you."

"You know where to find me." I turned to walk away. I was so tired I was ready to fall asleep on my feet. Even anger couldn't sustain me. I just needed for this night to be over. There were so many things I should do, people I should confront, but I couldn't think of a bloody reason to do any of it that wouldn't wait. Val was safe – alive – and that was all that mattered.

"Your Majesty?" This time it was said without mockery, as Maine fell into step beside me. Why wouldn't he leave me alone? Had saving his rotten life meant nothing?

"What?"

"Be careful."

It was on the tip of my tongue to tell him how sweet he was to care, but the caustic retort never made it to my lips as he pivoted on his heel and strode away, towards the rising sun. I squinted at it. Time for this goblin to get the hell home.

I collected Vex and we took his motor carriage as the Butler was still at Freak Show. I'd go back for it later.

Vex had ingested enough blood during the raid on the Tower that the sunrise didn't hurt him. I wondered if the duchess had made it to safety, and smiled at the mental picture of her getting caught in the sun and being reduced to a mound of bloody slush. I didn't know what happened to an unfed aristo under the full brunt of the sun – I'd never seen it happen – but for fantasy purposes, this would do.

Once at my place, I went straight to my room, stripped and crawled into bed. Vex did the same. We wrapped our arms around each other in the dark and drifted off to sleep without saying a word. Talking could wait.

When we finally crawled out of bed later that day, the sun was already setting. I got myself over to PAH – Prince Albert Hospital – which catered to halvies and occasionally aristos. It was located in Cavendish Square between the gardens and Oxford Street. Like many buildings of its generation, it was ostentatious red brick with white trim and high, narrow windows. It even had a bell tower on top, though I'd never known the bell to ring.

Vex was with me. I told him he didn't have to come, but he had pack members to check on – Annalise, the girl who had been injured in the League attack, and Rye, who was included in the pack simply by virtue of being born half-blood.

Most men would be jealous of me running off first thing to check on an old lover, but Vex wasn't like most men.

"Winter's going to need people he can trust to help him adjust to freedom. He's been a prisoner and abused for years. A man doesn't just recover from that. It takes time. He'll need you, and he'll need his pack."

I kissed him. "You're incredible."

He gave me a lopsided smile. "But if he touches you, I'll break his pretty face."

I laughed. I was fairly certain he was joking. Fairly.

He left me at the door to Rye's room. The fact that I'd been given credit for rescuing him got me inside. The guards were under strict orders not to admit anyone but authorised personnel.

There was only one bed in the small room, and Rye was in it. The blinds were open, letting in a sun that had come out after a drenching rain. He was staring at it, eyes narrow, as though he'd never seen daylight before. I supposed it had been a few years at least.

He was clean, his bronze hair brushed back from his gaunt face. His bones were too sharp, his eyes too sunken for him to be considered beautiful, but he was still finer than most. Once he gained some weight, he'd have girls chucking their knickers at him again.

It was good to see him – wonderful to know he was alive – but my heart didn't skip a beat at the sight of him like it used to. My stomach didn't flutter. This was why Vex wasn't jealous, because he already knew what I'd just figured out – I wasn't in love with Ryecroft Winter any more.

"I'm surprised you're awake," I said.

His head jerked towards me, eyes going wide. Hadn't he heard me come in? Or was he so adept at escaping into his own mind that he spent the majority of his time there?

"Xandy," he said, in a voice lower and rougher than I remembered. "I thought you were a dream."

I smiled as I approached his bed, tried not to notice how many tubes were running in and out of him, or wires he had attached. "Nightmare, maybe. How are you, Rye?"

"I don't know." His lips – he'd always had the most perfect mouth – curved slightly. "I'd given up hope of ever getting out. I'm having a hard time accepting that I'm free."

I reached out and wrapped my hand around his. "You are. And I'm going to make sure no one ever hurts you again."

His smile faded. "Xandy, it was Churchill . . ."

"I know. He's gone, Rye. He's dead."

"Dead? Really?"

I nodded.

"Fuck." Disappointment and anger flashed in his eyes, and tightened his features. "The thought of some day killing that bastard was the one thing I had to hold on to."

"Well, now you can hold on to something else."

The way he looked at me made me think he wanted me to be that something. I was the girl he'd loved, and I'd saved his life. I couldn't imagine what he was feeling, but I knew that as much as I wanted to be there for him, I was going to have to put a little distance between us if I didn't want him becoming too attached.

"They're going to let me out in a couple of days," he told me. "That is if the psych exam pans out. I reckon it could go either way."

I smiled at his attempt at humour. "Where are you going to go?"

"I don't know. Any suggestions?"

I couldn't take him in. Even if Vex didn't have plans to bring him into the pack, I couldn't give him the kind of help he would need. Who knew what sort of damage had been done to him in that place? Fang me, I didn't even know what they'd done to *me*.

"Yeah," I said. I pulled my rotary out of my pocket and dialled. A familiar voice answered. "Where are you? ... Fabulous. Can you meet me in Room 345 West?"

"Who was that?" Rye asked.

"Someone who can understand what you've been through and give you a place to recuperate. I think you'll like her."

We talked for a few minutes. Mostly it was me, bringing him up to speed on what he'd missed. I told him Dede was gone, and that Church had been the one to kill her. I did not tell him that I was a goblin. I didn't know how he'd react, and he'd been through enough. And I didn't want to see the look on his face when he found out I was queen of the very things we used to say we'd some day be tough enough to kill.

One of the guards knocked on the door. I opened it. "She's good."

Ophelia walked in. She was still bruised from her run-in with the Human League, but seemed otherwise healthy. She gave me a wary look. "You call me down here for a reason, pet? I was visiting my girl Annalise."

"Ophelia Blackwood, I would like you to meet Ryecroft Winter."

Her head whipped towards the bed. "They said you were dead."

Rye studied her. His gaze moved from my sister to me, and obviously made the family connection. It wasn't hard. "They were wrong."

"Rye's getting out soon, and I thought perhaps you might tell him why the pack would be a good option."

"Wouldn't the alpha be better qualified?" she asked, not taking her eyes off my ex.

I could stand back and let the two of them scrutinise each other and take the other's measure, but I didn't have all ruddy day, nor the patience. I grabbed Fee by the arm and hauled up her sleeve.

"Sod off," she cried, pushing at me, but I was stronger, and I managed to reveal the rust-coloured code tattooed on to her skin. She glared at me.

Rye looked at the tattoo for a long time before raising his gaze to Fee's belligerent one. Then he turned his left arm over so that she could see the underside of his forearm, and the similar markings on his own flesh.

Fee's expression softened, and I watched as the two of them became kindred spirits without exchanging a word. They formed a club I would never be part of, despite my brief time in the Tower. Was I jealous? Not bloody likely. Although I had to admit to feeling a tiny bit put out that I was no longer needed

"Yeah," Fee said. "I think I can help."

I smiled. "Brilliant." Then I gave Rye's hand a squeeze. "I'll poke my head in at you tomorrow, dearest."

Fee followed me to the door. "I heard what you did this morning. You saved a lot of lives."

I wasn't about to let her make me a hero. "Only because I am enough of a dolt to walk willingly into a trap. If it weren't for Vex and William, I might still be there."

"Well, remind me to thank them both." Before I knew what she was about, she wrapped her arms around my shoulders and hugged me. I froze. What I felt at that moment . . . I couldn't describe it. My chest was tight. My throat was tight. My eyes burned. The first time I'd met Fee I'd liked her instantly, but then I'd found out who she was and what she was up to – and there was that unfortunate incident with me almost tearing her throat out.

Somewhere in this whole mess Fee had started to mean something to me, and now I knew I meant something to her. We weren't going to be stealing each other's corsets any time soon, but it was a start.

I hugged her back – just a quick squeeze. "I've got to run. Ring me later."

Then I walked out of the room, and left behind that part of me that had never got over Rye.

CHAPTER 22

SUCCESS IS NOT FINAL

Since he'd only been held prisoner for a few days, Val didn't need to stay in the hospital, so we all congregated at Avery's that afternoon for breakfast and to do all the talking that hadn't been done last night.

Penny came with Val. She was different with me – skittish almost. She kept her distance, avoided my gaze. She might as well have got down on the floor and shown me her belly.

I hugged Val. "It's so good to have you home."

He hugged me back. Aside from appearing tired, he had shaved and showered and looked exactly as he ought. "I knew you'd come looking," he murmured in my ear.

I smiled. "Tenacity is a virtue."

He grinned back. "For you, perhaps." He offered his hand to Vex. "Thanks for providing the cavalry."

"You're welcome, but it's the prince who deserves the most thanks. He's the one who came to me."

I owed William a substantial debt – one I wasn't sure I could ever fully repay. Thank God for the goblins and their nosiness, or my disappearance – and Val's – might have ended on a far less happy note.

Val's dark eyes came back to me. "I'd like to thank him."

There was more to that declaration than just good manners. "Honestly?"

He nodded. "I want to see the plague den, and I want you to take me. I think it's time your old family met your new one."

"I can arrange that." I smiled. "But don't say 'old'. That makes it sound like I'm choosing one over the other." I hoped it never came to that.

"Fair enough." Then he hugged me again. "I'm sorry I was such a prat about the goblins and Dede."

"I should have handled it differently. You and Avery were right to be upset."

"It wasn't right of us to turn our backs on you when you needed support. You would never have done that to us. It was bad form."

I appreciated that and told him so as we walked together to the table.

Avery wasn't much of a cook; in fact she didn't cook at all, and with Emma gone, her ice box was next to bare. She was brilliant, however, at pastry selection. She also made a mean pot of coffee, so we all sat around the table with steaming mugs, and four boxes of sweet goodies to select from.

Val spoke first. He started by saying that he had indeed begun to look into what Penny had told him about Freak Show. After questioning Fred, one of the part-time bartenders, he was nabbed by the betties.

"Where's this Fred now?" I asked casually, wishing the bastard was close by so I could rip his legs off.

"A cage," Val replied. "Special Branch picked him up this morning. He claims he was working alone, that no one else at the club was involved. Apparently management was clueless. They thought the betties were coming round for a fix."

"And that's okay, is it?" I shook my head.

"I suppose they thought the little bastards were getting their blood from a willing aristo or halvie. There are dealers who make a living that way. I know of three impoverished aristos who manage to keep up the façade of wealth by selling their own blood. It's not illegal, so the Yard can't do a bloody thing about it."

"What about the horror show?" Vex asked. "How did you find out about that?"

Val glanced at me, then down at his cup. "I found the number in a digigram on Churchill's logic engine."

My chest pinched. You'd think that I'd feel better about his death the more I found out about him, but it only seemed to make it hurt all the more.

"I'd intended to investigate, but of course you know why I didn't make it."

"I went," I told him. He didn't look all that surprised, and I wondered if Maine had told him. "Ainsley was there."

That got a reaction – from both Val and Avery. After Dede's affair with the earl, the two of them had shared my dislike of the rat bastard.

"Why isn't he in custody?" Val asked.

"Since I freed the would-be entertainment, there was nothing to arrest him for. Besides, he's the only one who can give us access to our nephew."

My brother and sister fell silent, and exchanged a guilty glance. They hadn't believed Dede about the baby. Neither had I in the beginning.

"You think he'd let us know him?" Avery asked softly.

I shot her an arch look. "If he wants to keep his liver he will. Vardan knew about it. It was his idea." I didn't relish telling them that, felt no satisfaction in it at all, but they needed to know what I did. No more secrets – unless I absolutely had to.

Avery covered her mouth with her hand, while Val's brow furrowed. They didn't say anything, and I knew they wouldn't until the three of us had a chance to be alone.

"Nephew?" Penny asked.

I turned to her. I'd forgotten about her, she'd been so quiet. "Dede had a child with Ainsley."

She glanced at Val, then back to me. "I thought it died."

"So did we." I snagged a cheese Danish from one of the boxes. "We were lied to."

"How awful." She pressed a hand to her chest. "Poor Dede."

"You can't tell anyone," Val informed her. "Okay, Pen? No one."

She scowled at him. "Of course I won't tell anyone, you daft git."

Avery took a sip of coffee. "So Ainsley's involved in horror shows and was behind the rats nailed to your door?"

"At least one of them. I'm not convinced the Human League wasn't involved as well. Ainsley was just trying to goad me into doing something stupid so Queen V would be rid of me."

"You'd think she'd be trying to woo you," Penny remarked. "Since everyone seems to have a hard-on for the goblins."

"Eloquently put, Pen." Val smiled sardonically. "Very descriptive."

"It's true," she protested with a flutter of false lashes. She turned to Vex. "Right?"

My wolf turned a droll gaze on my brother. "It's true. I have an erection right now."

Laughter flew out of my mouth as my jaw dropped. I wasn't the only one caught off guard by Vex's sincerely delivered ribald remark; we all chuckled.

"Do you reckon Vardan knew about the duchess's involvement?"

"No," I said. "The night I confronted him, he was sincere. And Lady Gadling confirmed that in the Tower. She told me he wasn't part of their scheme. I believe that in his twisted way he really thought he was doing what was best for us."

"Surely he knows the truth now, though." Avery looked from me to Val. "She can't hide it from him for ever."

I shrugged. "She might confess, but I suspect she'll plead her innocence and get the family solicitors on to it. The law hasn't changed that much in the last two centuries – it's still biased towards the powerful. If she is found guilty, she'll flee to the continent. I doubt he'll go with her."

"What about Rye?" Avery asked, effectively changing the subject to something more positive. I could have kissed her for it. I really didn't want to think about the duchess right now.

"He's in Prince Albert," Vex told her. He had taken care of all the arrangements. "Two of my halvies are on guard by his door – boys he used to know. When I checked this morning, he was asleep. Had a bit of a spell earlier, apparently, but once he realised he wasn't a prisoner any more, he calmed down."

"We're going to go by when we leave here," I added. I'd already seen him, but I wanted to go again. It wasn't a need to be with Rye that drove me, but guilt. I was certain Churchill had got rid of Rye because of me. Of course, Church never came right out and admitted his motives, but I'd loved Rye and Church had wanted me. He'd tried to have Vex killed, so it seemed logical that he could easily have betrayed a boy who thought of him as a mentor.

It wasn't my fault Rye had been handed over to those sadistic bastards, but I felt the weight of it regardless. I'd found him and he was my responsibility. I couldn't just hand him over to Ophelia and walk away.

"How are you doing, Val?" Vex asked.

My brother nodded slowly. "Fair, considering. They didn't do much to me. I think they figured out pretty quickly that they could use me to get their claws into someone much more . . . interesting."

"That would be me," I said.

"Obvious much?" Avery asked sweetly. "God, Xandy. It's not always about you." Her overly obnoxious tone made everyone chuckle. I appreciated the levity, and not being allowed to take on even more guilt. At this rate, Vex really would have to get me a cross and a handful of nails.

The phone rang and Avery got up to answer it. I snagged a doughnut from the box closest to me and bit into its iced goodness. Fang me, but I loved sugar. It was almost as delicious as blood – and made me feel almost as good.

"By the way, Xandy," Val began. "Maine wanted me to let you know that the investigation into Churchill's murder has been officially dropped. Seems there's no evidence to support the claim and he's been re-established as a missing person. A bloke in Vienna claimed to have seen him there a fortnight ago."

I resisted the urge to look at Vex. "He always liked it there," I said. What else could I say?

Avery shuffled back into the room, her face chalk-white. I dropped the doughnut into my napkin and stood up. Val rose too. "What's wrong?"

She looked from one of us to the other. "That was Father. He was rather distraught."

I went to her and put my hands on her shoulders. "Dearest, what's happened?"

"It's the duchess," she said, eyes wide. "She's dead."

CHAPTER 23

FEAR MAKES US FEEL OUR HUMANITY

All I could think was, *That was fast.* I wondered if she had indeed wished I hadn't let her go when her murderer came calling.

Of course she'd been murdered. I'd never known a vampire to die of any sort of natural causes. The fact that she'd been ended so soon after the raid on the Tower told me that the people in charge were scared she might give them up. And I flattered myself a bit by going even further in assuming that they were also afraid of me finding them.

That didn't change the fact that now I would never get any information out of her.

It took balls to kill a vampire in her own home, and a duchess at that. Had one of the staff done it? Maybe. But if it were me who wanted someone dead, I wouldn't trust anyone but myself with making sure it got done.

Vex didn't join me and my siblings when we went to my father's house. He dropped me off and then returned to his own home to start making arrangements for the were halvies recovered from the Tower.

He wasn't impressed that I'd asked Fee to help Rye. Apparently she'd convinced him that he'd be better looked after at Bedlam than in the pack. "That's not your decision," he said. "It's mine. I'm alpha and Winter is my responsibility."

"I love that you take such care of your people, but he needs to be made to feel safe. Bedlam has doctors who can help him and aren't linked to the aristocracy."

"I could bring in physicians to treat him," he protested with a frown.

"Ophelia knows what he's been through, as do many of the patients there. No offence, Vex, but he wouldn't trust you, and having the pack coming and going all the time at your place would only make him fear someone was going to grab him again. You know Fee will keep you apprised of how he's doing. You have so many other people to worry about; let me and Fee take this one."

His mouth thinned. Maybe he was a little jealous after all. The thought almost made me smile, but I thought better of it. Vex was not in the mood to be teased. "Fine, but I'm going to check in on him myself from time to time, and when he's ready, he'll be brought back into the pack."

"If he's ready," I amended. "Vex, they had him for years. What if he's broken beyond repair?"

"If they'd broken him, sweetheart, he'd be dead." He reached across and opened my door for me. "Ring me when you're done. I'll come and fetch you if you need me."

I kissed him. "Are we okay?"

A faint smile tilted his mouth. "No, because I can't stand that you're good-hearted and only want what's best for someone you once cared about. Frankly, I don't know how I can stay with you after this." Even though his tone dripped with sarcasm, my heart clenched at his words.

"Honestly," I tried again. "Are you angry with me?"

Warm hands cupped my face. "Foolish girl. If I was angry, I'd tell you I was angry." He kissed me firmly. "Now off with you."

I smiled and slid out of the motor carriage. Avery and Val were waiting for me on the pavement.

"I'm glad you and the MacLaughlin are still together," Val said, shoving his hands in his trouser pockets. It was a warm night and he wasn't wearing a jacket.

I shot him a surprised glance. "Reckoned I'd have run him off by now, did you?"

To my chagrin, he nodded. "Something like that, yeah." When he saw my expression, he continued, "What? Even you have to admit you're not the easiest person to get on with."

"Vex and I get on just fine – not that it's any of your business," I retorted. "And I don't comment on your love life, Valentine Vardan."

"What of it?"

"Superintendent Chillingham." That was all I needed to say. His jaw dropped.

"How do you know about that? No one knew."

"I certainly didn't," Avery joined in, clearly annoyed. "Thanks for telling me, Xandy!"

I rolled my eyes from her to Val. "I met the woman. Saw her face when she talked about you. Didn't take much to figure it out. I can't imagine you're a peach to live with either, but I reckon she's happy enough to have you home."

My brother actually flushed. "She is at that."

"It's not fair that Xandy met her and I haven't," Avery announced peevishly. "Both of you know Emma."

"We'll make dinner plans," Val promised, putting an end to a conversation he obviously did not want to have. "Now, can we deal with the situation at hand?"

One of the servants had already hung a black wreath decorated with small red crosses on the door as a sign of mourning a full-blood. The plague doctor's carriage was parked out front, its black lacquer gleaming under the street lamps.

"I hate those bloody tossers," Val muttered.

I took his arm and steered him towards the front door. "I'll protect you from the beaked man, Fetch. Don't you fret."

He snorted, but didn't shrug me off. Many halvies were afraid of the plague doctors from seeing them as children. They were morticians for the most part, collecting the bodies of halvies and aristos. They continued to wear the ridiculous masks for reasons that were entirely theirs. Some believed it was out of respect for the dead. Others said it was because the masks resembled ravens or crows, which were once thought to escort the dead to the other side. And then there were a few who said they clung to the old belief that the masks would somehow protect them from the Black Death.

I reckoned the last was the closest to the truth, but only to an extent. At one time the plague doctors had been human, and they would have sought to protect themselves, but the role was mostly filled by halvies now, so what was once protection had now became tradition.

The door was answered by a footman we didn't recognise – not that any of us had spent enough time at our father's house to become familiar with his servants other than the butler and housekeeper. However, said footman recognised each of us, so we were taken immediately to Vardan.

He was in the duchess's suite with the plague doctors. It was like crossing a threshold into another world. The room was decorated in a style that would have been popular a century and a half ago – delicate feminine furniture with fabrics in lavender and white. A ball gown hung on the wardrobe door – something princessy and better suited for a younger woman. A wedding portrait of the duchess hung above the mantel. I stared at it.

"Is that a smile?" Avery whispered in my ear, catching the direction of my gaze.

"Frightening, what?" I whispered back, fighting the urge to giggle. Of course I wasn't upset that the old bitch was dead, and yes, a small part of me hoped that some day I might shake the hand of whoever did her in, though since that same person would probably try to end me as well, perhaps a handshake wouldn't be the wisest course.

My only regret was not getting information out of her. I should have questioned her as soon as we got out of the Tower. I should have hauled her arse home and forced her to give up her cohorts.

A bad smell permeated the room. I didn't have to guess what it was. It made my nose itch. I glanced at my siblings; neither of them seemed too bothered by it, lucky sods. This was not one of those times when goblin senses came in handy.

Vardan came out of a second small room attached to the suite. He looked like hell. His face actually crumpled slightly when he caught sight of us. Fang me, he truly loved the witch.

He went to Val first. I heard a small sob and immediately turned to Avery, who had turned to me. I'm fairly certain both of us wore identical expressions of horror and helplessness. What did you do when your distant father broke down?

Thankfully, I didn't have to find out, because Val had gone into copper mode, asking Vardan what had happened. Avery joined them and held our father's hand. I went straight for the room with the plague doctors in it.

The two of them looked up from the portable gurney where the duchess lay. They were disconcerting with their long black robes, tall hats and masks. I've always found the masks somewhat pretty, though – some of the ones in the Victoria and Albert Museum were quite ornate. These ones were fairly plain, bone in colour, the eyes beneath rimmed with black.

They didn't speak. If I was there, I had a right to be there, and it was my understanding that they didn't speak unless spoken to. What if I put on my goblin face, would they speak then? Run screaming? It would be uncouth of me to find out – not to mention disrespectful. Though who I was worried about disrespecting, I didn't know.

I approached the gurney and looked down at the duchess. She was a horrible sight. Clad in a silk peignoir set, she was stiff, eyes open. Her long blonde hair hung almost to the floor, shiny and smooth. But beyond that, there was nothing pretty about her. Her skin was mottled – ivory, grey and black. Her fingertips were ebony, as was the flesh around her mouth. She stank – putrid and rotting, with a faint tang similar to fish. Only one thing could cause this sort of disgusting package. Tetracycline poisoning.

I turned to the plague doctor nearest me. "Injection site?"

He – or she; as with goblins, it was sometimes difficult to tell – reached out with black-gloved fingers and opened the dead woman's mouth. Underneath her sore-covered tongue was an angry red spot ringed with black.

I frowned. She didn't look like she'd been restrained with ropes or shackles. Whoever had done this had controlled her with sheer strength. That meant it had to be an aristo, or a gang of halvies. But whereas a gang of halvies would call attention, an aristo would not.

"Thanks," I said to the beaked man, then turned on my heel. My attention snagged on the small French writing desk against the wall. The chair was knocked over and there was a piece of paper on the blotter. I picked it up by the corner with a tissue so as not to contaminate any evidence.

Dear Vardan,

I simply cannot live with myself any longer. I have done terrible things for which I fear I can never be forgiven. I hope you will at least forgive me for this.

All my love,
Imogene

I made the great leap and assumed that Imogene was the duchess's name. This was a fairly rubbish attempt to make a murder look like a suicide. Of course, that was exactly what it would be called, because the witch had been killed by someone higher up the food chain.

When I entered the main area of the bedroom, the remaining members of my immediate family turned their gazes on me, as if they expected me to make everything better – or perhaps burst into song.

"You know she didn't really kill herself, don't you?" This was directed at my father.

"Xandy, perhaps now is not the time ..." Avery began.

"This is important," I told her. "She was killed because she fucked up at the Tower. Your Grace, did you know about the Tower?"

Our father shook his head. His eyes were red and he looked like shit. "I knew she was involved in something, but she never confided exactly what. I just supposed it was something Victoria got her into."

I arched a brow. "As in *Queen* Victoria?"

He frowned. "Who else?"

"Indeed," I drawled. "I don't suppose Her Nibs was here last night or earlier this evening?"

"Of course not."

"Did you have any visitors?"

"I already asked him," Val chimed in. "Father and Her Grace went out for a ride in Hyde Park. Her Grace seemed distracted, depressed. When they returned home, she came up here to change, and when she didn't join him downstairs for a drink, he came up and found her slumped over a suicide note on her desk."

"This wasn't suicide, unless she somehow managed to inject herself with tetracycline and then hide the syringe that delivered it." I looked at Vardan. "If you don't want Special Branch investigating you for murder, I'd suggest you try to think of someone who could have got into your house without alarming the staff."

My father's eyes widened. "Murder? I would never murder my wife! Insolent child, how dare you!"

I scowled at him as Avery patted his hand. "I know you didn't kill her."

"That's good to hear," he chuffed.

"You don't have the bollocks to kill anyone," I added. "But the fact remains that someone did."

His shoulders sagged. "I have no idea what she was doing or with whom she was doing it. If I'd known she was involved in those awful experiments, and that she'd violated my boy—"

"And your girl," I interrupted. "They were very quick to violate me."

Vardan rose to his feet and lunged towards me. His shirt was untucked and his cravat was a limp mess. I'd never seen him so out of control. "What did they do?"

My brow pulled. I was tempted to tell him to fuck off. "I don't know for certain, but it was gynaecological in nature." Not the kind of thing a girl chatted about to her papa.

He blanched. "Are you ovulating?"

"What? No! Maybe. What are you suggesting?"

"Eggs," he replied. "I think they took your eggs."

"What would they want my eggs for . . . ? Shit."

The funeral was the next night. I didn't want to go, but there was no getting out of it. It was my duty, and I'd been taught that appearance was more important than reality. I had to act the dedicated child, else it looked bad for my father and for me. Wouldn't be seemly of me to embarrass the family.

So I decked myself out in a proper black gown with a skirt of feathers, and hat complete with veil, and let Vex drive me to the church, where I sat and listened to people blatantly lie about how wonderful the duchess was. Then we went to the Vardan crypt in Kensal Green.

I went inside afterwards, but not to pay my respects to the duchess.

There was a fine layer of dust on Dede's coffin. I wiped away as much of it as I could, soiling my gloves. I didn't speak – there was nothing to say. I just stood there and stared at the box that held what was left of my sister until I couldn't stand to look at it any longer.

Vex was waiting when I came out. I let Avery and Val take our father home and didn't try to invite myself along. I'd rather stab myself in the eye with a fork than spend another minute watching him mourn, or listen to him speculate as to what his wife might have planned to do to me.

Earlier today I'd gone to a gynae doctor Ophelia had suggested for an exam. Apparently everything looked normal, but I was becoming increasingly aware of just what a relative term that was. At least I knew they hadn't left anything in there.

If the duchess and her butchers had taken eggs from me, they were still in the laboratory, which was now being ripped into by Special Branch. Whatever embarrassment might be caused by the thought of Val or one of his cronies seeing my harvested bits was mitigated by relief that the duchess wouldn't be able to do anything with them.

Of course the duchess wouldn't be doing anything at all – not any more.

"Okay?" Vex asked as I approached.

I nodded, and we left the cemetery hand in hand.

Vex drove. The press had cleared out, no doubt chasing my father like a flock of vultures after a zombie. The duchess's death had been all over today's tabloids, which of course was all the prompting they needed to dredge up Dede's death as well. And my being a goblin. One paper even speculated that the duchess's death was related to Churchill's disappearance.

The Human League had been in the news as well. Someone

had dumped a lorryful of dead rats in front of the gates of Buckingham Palace. I had no idea how they'd managed it, but they'd done it at night, when the guards would be less diligent. No one expected humans to be brazen enough to attack in the dark, when there was more chance of immediate retribution.

It was little more than a student prank, but it sent a message.

So did the press vehicles, lights and picketers outside my house.

"What the bloody hell?" I asked.

Vex slowed down. The narrow drive that led behind my place was blocked. I was tempted to tell him to turn around, but that wasn't really an option. He parked the Panther and I stepped out.

"There she is!"

Bright lights swung in my direction as I approached. I held up a hand to shield my eyes. This would be the perfect time for some fanatic to plug me full of silver and tetracycline.

"Lady Xandra, how do you respond to recent allegations that you were among the full-bloods found conducting experiments on half-bloods and humans at the Tower of London?"

I squinted at the woman holding a microphone in my face. She was of Indian descent, polished and impeccably put together in a peplum suit. "I beg your pardon?"

"Witnesses say that both you and the Lord Alpha were at the scene."

I frowned. "And because I was there, I automatically have to be a villain, right?"

The reporter looked confused. "You're saying you rescued those poor creatures?"

Creatures? "No. I'm saying that the MacLaughlin and the prince rescued them."

She obviously wasn't interested in hearing about that. "What about reports that you attacked human boys at the local Southern Fried Chicken shack?"

I actually had to think about that – so much had happened since. "Those boys were harassing a teenage girl."

"Don't you think it's rather unfair of someone with your strength and speed to pick on a young boy?"

"No more unfair than for a group of young men to pick on a lone girl." I met her gaze, daring her to challenge me.

She gave me a chiding look. "Really? I wager you could have thrashed each and every one of them."

She was not going to get me with this. "What do you reckon they were going to do to her if they had a chance?"

"Nothing like what a goblin could do."

Someone in the background yelled, "Go home, freak!"

I looked into the camera. "Those boys walked out of the restaurant. I didn't hurt anyone."

"Not even Lord Churchill?"

I forced myself to remain calm. "Not even." It wasn't exactly a lie.

"Didn't you recently kill a man outside the club called Freak Show?"

Vex cut in. "This interview is over. Her Majesty has nothing more to say."

People started shouting at me as we approached the building. A rock sailed by my head, so close I could feel the breeze. Another smashed the front window. A cheer went up.

"Look out for pitchforks," I told Vex drily.

He didn't look amused. "Get inside. Now. This is going to turn ugly."

"Monster!" a man shouted.

"Killer!" This time a woman.

"Get out of our neighbourhood!"

Something struck me hard on the temple, knocking my head to the side. I looked down, and through the stars blurring my vision saw a brick, glistening with blood, fall to the pavement. Wetness trickled down the side of my face.

I didn't think. I gave into instinct and my goblin came rushing to the surface with a growl that tore through the noise of the crowd and brought silence raining down.

Lights burned my sensitive eyes. Blood ran down my neck from the gash by my eye, and I stood my ground, waiting for the first one to come at me. I was ready for them, and I would fight, even as the knowledge that it was futile washed over me.

For the first time in my entire life I was suddenly aware of just why the full-bloods were so afraid of humans. They were many and we were few. I could take on a handful of them and win. With Vex by my side the odds went up, but there had to be at least fifty people gathered in front of my house, armed with lights and God only knew what else.

Strength in numbers. That was what they had that we didn't. And the overwhelming arrogance that we were the monsters.

The woman reporter was there again, her companion shoving his camera in my face – a good close-up of the monster for the folks at home. I closed my fingers over the lens and squeezed until it shattered against my palm.

The reporter gasped. Vex grabbed my arm and pulled me towards the house. Another rock sailed by, followed by a bottle.

"Get her!" someone shouted.

The entire mob surged forward. Albert's fangs, this was not how I thought I was going to die.

"Stop!" Suddenly a young man shoved in front of me, blocking the crowd's path. It was David.

"Get out of the way, son," said a man with a cricket bat. Seriously? Did he just walk about with the thing? Because it seemed to me that perhaps he'd come to my house *looking* for a fight. And weren't there laws against this sort of thing? Where the hell were the police? Oh, there was one at the back of the crowd. Watching. I wasn't in the West End. No one was going to come to my rescue here.

Except for a scrawny kid.

"She's not a monster," David yelled at them. I wished then that I hadn't busted the camera – this was something I wouldn't mind the good people of London seeing on the box tonight.

Fortunately, there was another camera. Joy. Why did they need lights that were brighter than the bloody sun?

"Shut up!" screamed the kid when the crowd disagreed with his assessment of my nature. They fell silent, shocked by the violence of his outburst. "She saved me," he informed them, voice now harsh and dry. I watched his gaze dart around the crowd. "I got into trouble – the sort I couldn't get m'self out of. She found me. If it weren't for her I wouldn't be alive right now, and those guys she were said to have roughed up? They would have done a lot worse to that girl. She " – his thumb jerked in my direction – "ain't done nothing wrong."

The mob didn't seem to know what to do with this information. I watched them glance at each other in confusion. It was clear that they didn't know how to react to a human kid singing the praises of one of the very monsters he'd been taught to fear his entire life.

It might have been coincidence, or perhaps he had simply

been waiting for the right time to assert himself, but that was when the copper at the back yelled, "All right, people, let's break this up then! Time to get back to your homes." He and a female partner that I hadn't noticed earlier began herding the crowd away from the building. Reluctantly, the humans did as they were told.

I have to admit, I breathed a sigh of relief. Fear wasn't an emotion I felt very often – especially not where my own personal safety was concerned – but I'd felt it too many times in the last few days.

I was not going to live my life like this. There was an old saying about dancing with the devil you knew. I was beginning to think I was better off taking my chances with the Marlborough House set, as the haughtiest of aristos had once been known.

"Thank you," I said to David.

He turned to face me. I noticed the reporter still had the camera on us as she backed away. I hoped she stepped out into the street and got clipped by a taxi.

"It's not safe for you here any more," he said, face pale and drawn. He had a black eye and I wondered if he'd got that from Ainsley or because he'd defended me to the wrong person.

"Looks like it's not safe for you either."

He shrugged. "I'll be all right, but you ... you should go. The League's been around here lately stirring people up. If I was you, I'd get out."

It was sound advice. I nodded, and offered him my hand. He accepted the handshake and then took off across the street. The reporter stopped him on the other side.

"Can you call some of the pack, do you think?" I asked Vex as we went into the house.

"It might be a good idea to have some extra bodies on guard duty tonight, just in case."

I stared at the broken glass all over the floor of the bar area. I was going to owe my landlord for that. "I don't want guards. I want them to help me move." I glanced over my shoulder at him. "For once, I'm going to do the smart thing and get the hell out of here."

CHAPTER 24

THOSE WHO DO NOT REMEMBER THE PAST ARE CONDEMNED TO REPEAT IT

I wasn't joking. By dawn I'd packed up all my belongings and had them carted off to storage, thanks to a group of enthusiastic halvies who wanted to please their alpha. Fee was one of them. I was happy to hear that she and Rye were getting on okay, and that not only was there a room for him at Bedlam, but also a counsellor who would help overcome the trauma of having been a prisoner for so many years.

The thought of it made my chest hurt. If the duchess were alive I'd beat her senseless for the part she'd played in his torture – and would have played in mine. The field day the press was having with her suicide made it a little easier to stomach.

Of course, the press was also having a field day with me. By the time the morning papers hit – just as I was about to leave Leicester Square – my face was all over them. My *goblin* face. I didn't even recognise myself at first.

Vex peered over my shoulder at the copy I held taut in my hands. "I think you look sexy," he commented with a grin.

I tossed the rag on the step where I'd found it. "Thanks." I thought I looked ... horrifying. By this evening it would be my face human children – and some halvie – would think of when their parents warned them of the monsters lurking in the dark corners of London.

I shouldn't care. I generally liked being thought of as scary and intimidating because it kept people out of my way, but last night I'd realised that fear was a powerful motivator for hate.

I'd been taught to despise humans because aristos were afraid of them, but I thought I was scarier. June had marked the eightieth anniversary of the Great Insurrection, and I was truly afraid that another one was coming.

I packed a valise and a trunk with the essentials and took that back to Vex's house, where I was going to stay until I found a place of my own. Avery probably would have welcomed me back to the house we once shared, but I felt something of a walking target and didn't want to bring that down on her.

When William found out that I was homeless, he sent me a digigram – I had a hard time imagining him typing – asking if I'd like to take a look at the rooms above the old Down Street station building. It was also goblin property.

The place wasn't in great shape, but it was large and had a lot of character. It hadn't been touched since 1932, so it was going to need some work, but it had high ceilings and gorgeous mouldings. Unfortunately, it also had some mould. William organised the goblins into shifts for cleaning. The windows were boarded up, so it would be dark inside, even during the day, and additional dimming precautions were also taken. He told me the place would be ready in less than a week. Vex's offer of cohabiting was still good, but I wanted my own space. I think he understood – probably better than I'd want him to.

It wasn't that I didn't want to be with him – I did. That was what scared me. He would be too easy for me to lean on, and I just couldn't afford to be weak.

That didn't stop me from enjoying our time playing house. It even made me less anxious about the faction meeting we had to attend.

It was at Buckingham Palace, of course. Queen V hadn't ventured outside the palace walls in ... well, I don't know how long. I reckon she kept quiet about it when she did.

As with all court appearances, we were required to dress accordingly. I had no intention of mourning my father's wife, and thankfully mourning wasn't required these days as it was in the past. Still, I'd had decorum drummed into me from a young age, so I wore a grey silk gown with a tattered skirt and embroidered bodice that required me to wear my corset underneath it rather than on top.

I pinned my hair and donned a tiny hat. I tucked my dagger in my corset. I felt more secure having it on me. Dropping it at Freak Show that night had been something of a blessing. If I'd had it when the betties took me I might have lost the dagger as well as the contents of my ovaries. There was no contest over which I would miss more.

Vex was dressed in the MacLaughlin tartan, with a linen shirt and frock coat on top and black boots on the bottom.

"We're going to melt," I told him as we exited the house. It was raining.

"I might because I'm so sweet, but you'll be fine," he joked as he opened the motor carriage door for me.

I shot him a wry glance before sliding inside.

We stopped at the Mayfair gate to sign out. Did someone actually study the comings and goings of the Mayfair set? I reckoned they did. I was going to have to become more familiar with the tunnels and catacombs beneath this city if I wanted to keep even a shred of privacy once I took up residence inside these walls.

It was a short drive to the palace. We didn't talk much on the way. At the gate, an armed member of the Royal Guard checked our identification and made us prick our fingers on the blood-scanning system. Our DNA would be checked against our records to confirm that we were indeed who we claimed to be. Victoria had installed this extra security after a human took a shot at her a couple of months ago. I'd taken the bullet and then got another for my trouble. Only the second one had come from Church's gun.

It was in the private train tunnel beneath the palace that I had challenged Church and led him to his demise. I'd been here once since then for a meeting similar to this. My stomach didn't roll quite so much this time.

Inside the palace we were escorted to a room underneath the grand staircase on the right. It was a large room with pale blue walls decorated with white plaster scrollwork. The carpet was old but in excellent condition, and portraits of stately ancestors hung on the walls.

There was a table in the centre of the room – not huge, but big enough to hold a dozen or so people. At the head was a very ornate chair. A similar one sat at the foot. That would have been Albert's seat. I suppose it belonged to the Prince of Wales now.

Were the rumours that Victoria had killed her husband because of his sympathy to humans true? Or had he really been killed by humans? If humans had killed my husband, I wasn't so certain I could try to work with them as Victoria did, but then I supposed she wanted to avoid more bloodshed.

We were the first to arrive, and William appeared shortly afterwards. The human prime minister, Lavinia Wellesley – descendant of the great man himself, the Duke of Wellington – and her companion arrived next. Vex hadn't appointed a new second yet, so he was the sole representative of the wolves, which might be an issue if we planned to vote on anything, though I doubted it would be a problem tonight.

The Prince of Wales arrived just before his mother. He was a fairly handsome man – if you liked facial hair and weren't put off by the fact that he looked like a male version of the Queen. He was certainly cordial enough. He shook all of our hands, and told me it was a pleasure to meet me. I didn't remind him that we had met before.

Finally, Victoria arrived. Only twenty minutes late. Obviously she was in a hurry.

We all bowed as she entered. "Thank you for coming," she said as she took her place at the head of the table. As I suspected, Bertie took the seat at the opposite end. Vex and I sat side by side, with William across from me. The humans sat opposite each other on the other side of Vex.

I caught the PM staring me and forced a smile. She didn't return it. Bitch. Then again, I don't reckon I sold it with the right amount of sincerity. That was when I noticed that she had a stack of scandal rags on the table in front of her – my face on the cover of every one.

Dear me, but it seemed I was about to get properly scolded. Bollocks.

"Several concerns have been brought to our notice," Victoria began. She looked tiny, but she had a powerful voice, and a gaze that promised your head on a spike if you didn't pay attention. "The first of which is the unfortunate death of the Duchess Vardan. We had no idea the poor woman was so ... troubled."

I fought the instinctive urge to arch a brow. V actually sounded sincere, which made me wonder if perhaps she really was ignorant about these experiments.

"Do you have anything you would like to say, *Your Majesty*?"

I winced. Her Nibs had this tone to her voice that made me think of the matron at the courtesan house. "The duchess has never been the same since the loss of her child, ma'am." The lie rolled easily off my tongue. For all I knew, it could be true.

Cool blue eyes locked with mine. "And what of this debacle concerning the Tower? You and the Lord Alpha were there?"

"Yes. I was ... abducted and put into a cell in the Tower. The MacLaughlin and the prince rescued me and everyone else held prisoner."

She arched a brow. "You were a prisoner? The papers neglected to mention that."

"I didn't tell them, ma'am. We tried to keep the entire situation as quiet as we could, but of course that proved impossible."

"I find this really quite astonishing," V remarked. "Who took you and to what purpose?"

"It was a betty, ma'am – a human who—"

"I know what a betty is," she interrupted, curt and sharp. "Continue."

All right. "I don't know what they intended to do with me. I only know that they were conducting some sort of experiments in the facility."

"Yes, we have recovered much in the way of scientific apparatus, but the electrical systems seem to have been compromised and many of the logic engines are missing." Her gaze slid to William. "You wouldn't know anything about that, would you?"

The goblin shook his shaggy head. "Nay." He was good – looked her boldly in the eye and held her gaze as he lied.

"Hmm." She was not amused. "I am quite distressed about the recent increase in human violence against the aristocracy."

"It will blow over, Mama," Bertie insisted with a wave of his perfectly manicured hand. "It always does. The sheep will calm themselves."

Victoria looked like she might pop her top. Was it the fact that he called her "Mama" in front of us, or that he dismissed her concern so casually?

"Human violence does seem to be escalating," I heard myself remark.

Victoria seemed as surprised as I was to find us on the same page. "Do you have any theories as to why?"

I shrugged. "Maybe because of me. A goblin who can walk about cobbleside during daylight probably has them scared. Or maybe they've just been waiting for the right time to strike."

She slowly shook her head, dark hair shining under the light. There was tension in the lines of her face. "Horror shows and abductions. Strange experiments and traitors popping up at every turn. If the humans have been waiting for the best time to strike at us, they surely have chosen well. How can we stand against them when we are so fractured?"

"Hit them where it hurts," Bertie advised. "Force them into submission."

"That could make things worse," Vex said, shooting the prince a sharp look. "You might force them into desperation."

Bertie made a face. "Impose a city-wide curfew. At least then we'll have fewer of them to contend with after dark."

"You cannot be serious!" The PM looked stunned. Surely this wasn't the first time she'd heard aristos talk about humans in such a way. "You want to broker peace by taking away their basic human rights?"

"They lost those rights after the Great Insurrection, remember? The humans signed a treaty with the full-bloods. They promised never to rise up again in return for privileges few countries can offer. Now they spit on our generosity. They should be horsewhipped."

Bertie was full-on fucking hatters. Completely mental. Listening to him was akin to watching a train derail. I couldn't stop it, didn't want to witness it, but couldn't turn away. It was brilliant.

"There will be no horsewhipping." Victoria's smooth brow pinched as she regarded her son. "We will not respond with violence. We are sure Queen Xandra can attest to how futile that would be."

The PM slid the stack of scandal rags across to me so that I could see my goblin face up close and personal once more.

William reached over and picked up the top one. "Beautiful," he rasped. "Ferocious with charms is our lady."

Fang me if that wasn't almost poetic. "They ambushed me outside my home. They threw a brick at me. There were enough of them that I was worried about our safety. A few days ago Vex was in the vicinity of a Human League bombing."

"Even more recently," Vex continued, "a girl from the pack was seriously injured in what appears to be a random League attack on a West End pub."

Victoria directed her attention at the PM. "Have your people arrange a press conference. We wish to address the human population. You will speak as well. We must prevent any more violence."

Bertie gaped at her. "Mama—"

"We have made up our mind, Bertie," she snapped. "What would your father have done in such a situation?"

Bertie looked sullen – not an attractive look on a grown man. "He would have tried to bring peace."

"And that's what we will do. Prime Minister Wellesley, see that it is arranged."

The PM inclined her head. "Of course, ma'am."

"Excellent. Meanwhile, we will want extra security on the Mayfair and palace gates until things have settled. Queen Xandra, we wish to have you attend the press conference as well."

I started. "What the bloody hell for?"

She looked at me as though I was dim-witted – and far too coarse for her liking. Fair enough. "If the truth of your ... nature is indeed what has frightened the humans, we must present you in a more flattering light."

Fang me, I hadn't expected this. "I don't think—"

"Do you or do you not wish to prevent a second insurrection?"

Just the thought made me shudder. "Fine. I'll do the

conference." Now I was the one being sullen. It probably wasn't a fantastic look for me either.

The meeting continued for another hour and a half. We discussed what Scotland Yard had determined about the horror show and the Tower – nothing I didn't already know – and a few other items before we adjourned.

"Queen Xandra, might I have a word?" Victoria asked as we all rose to depart.

I turned to Vex. "I'll wait for you outside," he said, bowing to V.

"He is a good man," the Queen remarked when we were alone. "You've chosen well."

"Thanks." It came out so dry, I was surprised I didn't spit sand in her face.

"If you were to marry, it could create quite an alliance between wolves and goblins."

She was as subtle as a needle to the eye. "We are both aware of an alpha's duty to the pack, ma'am." Vex would marry a wolf, no matter how much that pained me.

"If not the alpha, you could have a prince."

It took me a second to realise that she meant Bertie rather than William. To be honest, I'd take William before I would Bertie.

Fang me, but she'd just offered me her son – the future King of England, if his mother ever had the good grace to die. That would keep me close, wouldn't it? And what better place for one's enemies?

"You flatter me, ma'am." Oh, I sounded almost sincere. "But when I marry it will not be for political reasons. I should like to have a partner as you had." That was probably laying it on a bit thick, and I felt as though I were a heroine in a Jane

Austen novel, but it was better than the "fuck no!" that had been my initial reaction.

A faint smile actually curved her lips. "I do not wish to like you, Lady Alexandra." I didn't miss that she'd said "I" instead of the royal "we". "I do not wish to think favourably of you at all, but I find I must trust that you wish to avoid conflict with the humans as much as I do."

I nodded. "I do. For what it's worth, I'm not ready to trust you either."

"No. However, I suspect it's in both our interests to forge a kind of truce – at least where the humans are concerned. I believe we are headed for a war. You will need to decide which side you are on."

"Are you insinuating that I'm a traitor?" Because I'd job her right between the eyes, sovereign or not.

"I'm saying that you have connections to every faction involved in this conflict, and that those connections might cloud your judgement."

"I judge just fine, thank you."

Her smile faded. "Be flippant if you must, but have a care, young queenling. You are not the first to be offered the goblin crown. I do not suspect you will be the last. Your Prince William is the not the amiable old hound you believe him to be."

"You don't have any clue what I believe." And if she thought I was going to start distrusting the prince, who had never done anything but help me, on her word alone . . . well, then she had an incredibly inflated sense of self.

"You are right, of course. Forgive me." She rose to her feet. "Good evening, Your Majesty. I will see you at the press conference. I trust you can find your own way out?"

She glided from the room, leaving me standing there alone like the last kid on the playground to be picked for sport.

I did find my own way out – stomping and silently swearing the entire way. Vex was waiting in the motor carriage. One of the footmen opened my door for me. I tossed myself inside with such force, the Panther rocked.

"She still alive?" Vex asked with a smile.

"Yes." More's the pity.

"You okay?" The smile was gone, replaced with genuine concern. God, he was fabulous.

"I'm fine. I just want to go home, eat and lie in front of the box for a few hours. Want to join me?"

"Sounds perfect."

As he manoeuvred the motor carriage out of the palace compound, I leaned back against the seat and stared out of the window at the world I'd grown up in and thought I knew so well – but really didn't know at all.

And I wondered what Victoria had meant when she'd said that I wasn't the first to be offered the goblin crown.

CHAPTER 25

EVERY NEW BEGINNING COMES FROM SOME OTHER BEGINNING'S END

I officially became the goblin queen three nights later. The press conference was scheduled for the next evening, but I tried not to think about what I might be asked in front of the entire VBC viewing network. I was nervous enough about the coronation without thinking of being on camera – and not crushing it to bits.

The ceremony took place in the den, deep below what was now my new home. The place looked amazing – two floors, spacious and clean. All my furniture was arranged – I used some that had belonged to Dede as well, which made it feel even more homely. I was almost right up against the great wall that separated Mayfair from the rest of the city, so I got a little street noise, but it wasn't too bad. Plus, this area of the street, known as Gob Lane, was extremely quiet. I was pretty much the only person living there – above street level, that was.

I dressed up for the occasion, in a gorgeous tea-coloured gown I'd bought just for the evening. William had informed me that as queen, I could access the goblin treasury, which contained a ridiculous amount of money. I still had funds from the sum my father had settled upon me when I turned eighteen, but it was nice to know I didn't have to worry about it in the future.

Vex wore his kilt, and Avery and Val dressed up too. William came wearing a once fine but now somewhat shabby and ragged frock coat of rich wine colour, with gleaming armour that looked Roman underneath and at the shoulders. Even Ophelia was there. My mother wasn't, but then I didn't invite her. I didn't want her in the den, not when she wanted to use me and my goblins for political pull. Her presence would be disrespectful to William and the entire plague.

Rye wasn't there either. He still didn't know about me, and I had no idea when or even if I was going to tell him.

"He's doing well," Ophelia told me before the ceremony began. "Last night he only woke up screaming once."

My chest squeezed. Poor Rye. "Can I visit him?"

"I don't see why not. Just make sure I'm around first. The staff are protective of him, and you're not exactly known as Miss Congeniality at Bedlam."

I rolled my eyes. "Go for a girl's throat once and they never let you live it down."

She laughed, which was a relief. I hadn't meant to attack her that day – I just lost all control. William told me I needed more blood or meat in order to keep myself in check. The idea of eating raw meat both disgusted and intrigued me. I knew I'd like it, but when I thought about the whole process, I couldn't bring myself to do it just yet. So I drank instead. Thank God for blood bags. And not just blood bags, but blood that was delivered right to my door.

I had good reason for not venturing too far out of Mayfair, not on my own. The day after the meeting at the palace, my former abode in Leicester Square was torched – the inside of it gutted. They'd burned it during the day on the wrong assumption that I was a typical goblin. If I were, and had continued to stay there, I'd have been charred right now. But luck had been on my side and I finally got to be the one who was one step ahead.

The goblins were still working on sorting out all the information from the Tower logic engines. Hopefully we'd soon have some useful information. Meanwhile, we continued to pretend that the duchess's death was a suicide, because the truth would make the human situation all the worse and probably paint big targets on the rest of the family – not that we weren't already marked. My desire for the truth, however, came second to my desire to live a little while longer. Not the most heroic of goals, but that was the reality of it. I'd lost a lot of that bravado I'd gained with being a goblin. Mortality was a bitch.

My family stood at the front of the crowd in the great hall. Avery looked a little nervous with so many goblins around, but she tried to hide it. Beside her stood Elsbeth, and then the mother with the new pup – baby Alexandra, who was already growing like mad. Even the gobs who were assigned to the monitors for the night were allowed to take a break for the ceremony.

There were a few goblins, I was told, who refused to come. They were the ones who didn't believe I should be queen, or didn't approve of me in general. That was fine. I was just glad there weren't more of them. As it was, it was only three or four. I might be able to win them over eventually. Or not.

Just before we were due to start, William brought another goblin to me – it was the old female from the Tower. She took both of my hands – her own were more like paws – and squeezed them gently, smiling up at me with glossy amber eyes. She was missing a few teeth and her skin had lost some elasticity, but she appeared to have a good few years left in her.

She spoke to me in a language I didn't recognise. I looked at the prince.

"Gaelic and old German," he explained. "It is the language of the plague. Says she thanks you for saving her. Prayed she did for the day our lady would come to save the plague. Fifty and two hundred years she has waited."

"Two hundred and fifty?" I stopped. I could feel my heart beating in my ears. "She's more than two centuries old?"

William nodded. "Three is closer."

"But . . . but that pre-dates even George the Third." The Mad King was said to have been amongst the first aristos to exhibit any signs of the plague mutation.

The prince smiled. "Yes. We were first here, lady. Before vampire, before wolf, there was goblin."

Fang me. Slowly, I sank on to the throne that was to be mine. This changed everything, didn't it? Or did it? My brain couldn't make the jump, though I was certain there was one.

"For you she has a gift," William went on, seemingly oblivious to my shock.

The old girl was still smiling as she took something from the prince and offered it to me. It was a small black box. I opened it. Inside was a beautiful pair of ruby earrings that glittered in the torchlight.

"Oh," I said, proud of being able to summon even that much articulation. "They're beautiful. I couldn't possibly . . . ."

William stopped me when the old female spoke. "You must, she says. They belonged to our first."

"First what?" The hair on the back of my neck tingled.

"Our first lady."

"There really was a queen before me?" I had come to the conclusion that Victoria had only said that to make sport of me.

He nodded. "In her day, yes. Many years ago there was one."

"What happened to her?"

Sorrow clouded his good eye. "She was ended by the leech queen."

"Victoria?"

"Aye. Took her head. But we took it back. It is now yours."

It took a second for his words to sink in, but by then he had taken up the crown and placed it on my head. So much for pomp and circumstance.

Had he really just said that I was wearing the first queen's head? Was that a fanged skull set in the bloody thing?

"Our lady!" he cried, and a chorus of bark-like yelps filled the cavern. Baby Alexandra howled in response. Vex and Ophelia both joined in with howls of their own, starting the goblins up again until my head vibrated with the animalistic sounds.

Vex came over and crouched beside my throne as the goblins began to celebrate. There was music and food. I saw Ophelia waltzing with George. It was just surreal enough to make me doubt my sanity.

"Did you know anything about this other queen?" I asked.

He shook his head. "Not that I'm aware of, but I do remember hearing something about Victoria executing some would-be usurpers way back when."

Had this other queen tried to take the throne? Was that why Victoria had killed her? Was that why she felt so threatened by me? And how had she managed to not only kill this queen, but take her head without the prince ripping out her spleen?

"Hey." Vex nudged me. "You okay, sweetheart?"

I nodded. "I'm fine." I pushed all thoughts of anything but this moment out of my head. That someone had come before me didn't matter, nor did her death have any effect on me taking the crown. I was not going to let anything ruin this occasion. I deserved a fun night that was all about me. Not that every night wasn't all about me, but this time everyone else felt the same way. I could ask William about this former queen tomorrow.

Val pressed a glass of champagne into my hand and offered one to Vex as well. Then he took one for himself from the small table set with glasses and several chilled bottles.

"A toast," he said, raising his glass. "To Xandra – queen of the goblins. Long may she reign."

Vex raised his glass as well. "The queen is dead. Long live the queen."

Our little circle drank to that, and I tried to pay attention as they congratulated me and studied my macabre crown – all bone and gleaming metal.

The queen was dead. Slain by a jealous Victoria. Was it a threat when she told me I wasn't the first? If so, it was a pretty cheeky one. And I'd thought she truly wanted to be allies, united against a human uprising. I had no doubt that if the humans attacked tomorrow, she'd toss me to them like a bone to a pack of ravenous dogs.

I smiled as my brother and sisters hugged me. Laughed as I wrapped an arm around Vex's waist and snuggled against his side. I was not about to be intimidated by a woman who barely stood above my shoulder, who wasn't even aware of everything going on underneath her slightly hooked nose.

Yes, the former queen of the goblins was long gone, but I had the crown now and I intended to keep both it and my head. This queen had no intention of dying, and certainly no intention of going quietly. Whether it was humans who came for me or aristos, I would be ready. I was not going down without a fight.

Long live the queen.

GLOSSARY

AC/A-cylinder – audio cylinder. A small metal tube used to store music and other electronic data.

accrual card – card given out by banks to extend credit to customers, which is then accounted for and paid every month to avoid interest charges.

aether – slang for airwaves, usually applied to telephone, telegraph and video communications not broadcast over private channels.

aethernet – term for the international network of logic engines that share government, education, personal and commercial information using the same protocols.

Albert's fangs – a curse seen as taking the late Prince Consort's name in vein . . . er, vain.

aristocrat – collective term for vampires and werewolves, particularly those of noble birth.

box – television.

Britme – electronic service provided by Britannia Telephone and Telegraph where people can leave a voice recording for the person they're trying to reach via stationary line or rotary.

bubonic betty – human who injects aristocrat hormones to gain enhanced senses, strength and speed.

cobbleside – above ground.

courtesan – human woman employed by the aristocracy to breed half-bloods. These women are plague carriers, their blood rich with the Prometheus protein necessary to full-term healthy pregnancies.

digigram –electronic text-based message sent between wireless devices and logic engines.

digital processing machine – device that scans and transmits documents' digital files.

fang me – being fanged means being used for food by an aristocrat – a practice beneath most halvies.

job – to hit or get violent with. Associated with the violence often attached to halvie occupations. "He really did a job on that human." "She jobbed the betty hard in the kidneys."

halvie – a half-blood. Half vampire/were and half human.

hatters – derived from "mad as a hatter". Slang for crazy, insane.

horror show – illegal spectacle at which vampires or weres consume a human or halvie victim for the audience's titillation.

huey – slang for human.

logic engine/log en – electronic device that stores and processes information, and allows for many kinds of digital communication over the aethernet.

meat – goblin term for anything warm-blooded, and therefore edible.

merk – short for "merkin", formerly a genital wig used by prostitutes. Now a human slang term for a cute but promiscuous girl.

Met – name given to the Metropolitan Underground Railway.

mice – derogatory goblin slang for humans. As mice and rats don't cohabit, neither do the plagued and humans.

motor carriage – transportation. Modern carriages propelled by an engine rather than horses.

motorrad – a two wheeled vehicle similar to a bicycle but with an engine, bigger frame and thicker wheels. In America they are called "motorcycles".

pay post – receptacle for money in exchange for a place to park a motor- or horse-driven carriage. The proceeds go towards paying government expenses.

peeler – slang for a Scotland Yard officer, taken from the name of the founder of the police force, Robert Peel.

plague – responsible for the Prometheus mutation that made vamps and weres and goblins. Also the term the goblins use to describe a group of themselves. The London plague is used to refer to all the goblins in London.

privacy box – tall red box that affords the user privacy to make a wireless call or anything else that strikes his/her fancy.

radiarange – counter-top oven that cooks food using non-ionising microwave radiation.

rotary – portable wireless telephone. Has a rotary dial.

rut – vulgar, but slightly more polite than "fuck".

tango – halvie slang for a fight.

underside – underground.

VC – video cylinder. A cylinder used to record and play back video, such as films.

Yersinia – from *Yersinia pestis* – the bubonic plague. The name of the goblin city.

extras

www.orbitbooks.net

about the author

Kate Locke is a shameless Anglophile who wrote her first book at age twelve. Fortunately, that book about a British pop band is lost for ever. When not experimenting with new hair colours, Kate likes to hang out with her husband who, while not from England, can do a pretty convincing accent. She spends her days being bossed about by five fur kids and making stuff up – often while wearing a "uniform" that looks suspiciously like pyjamas. During "off" hours Kate often screeches along to *Rock Band* (being a rock star was her second career choice if the writing thing didn't work out), watches BBC America, or plays with make-up. She loves history, the paranormal, horror and sparkly things. The author's website can be found at www.katelocke.com

Find out more about Kate Locke and other Orbit authors by registering for the free monthly newsletter at www.orbitbooks.net

if you enjoyed
THE QUEEN IS DEAD

look out for

THE IRON WYRM
AFFAIR

by

Lilith Saintcrow

PRELUDE

A Promise of Diversion

When the young dark-haired woman stepped into his parlour, Archibald Clare was only mildly intrigued. Her companion was of more immediate interest, a tall man in a close-fitting velvet jacket, moving with a grace that bespoke some experience with physical mayhem. The way he carried himself, lightly and easily, with a clean economy of movement – not to mention the way his eyes roved in controlled arcs – all but shouted danger. He was hatless, too, and wore curious boots.

The chain of deduction led Clare in an extraordinary direction, and he cast another glance at the woman to verify it.

Yes. Of no more than middle height, and slight, she was in very dark green. Fine cloth, a trifle antiquated, though the sleeves were close as fashion now dictated, and her bonnet perched just so on brown curls, its brim small enough that it would not interfere with her side vision. However, her skirts were divided, her boots serviceable instead of decorative – though of just as fine a quality as the man's – and her jewellery was eccentric, to say the least. Emerald drops worth a fortune at her ears, and the necklace was an amber cabochon large enough to be a baleful eye. Two rings on gloved hands, one with a dull unprecious black stone and the other a star sapphire a royal family might have envied.

The man had a lean face to match the rest of him, strange yellow eyes, and tidy dark hair still dewed with crystal droplets from the light rain falling over Londinium tonight. The moisture, however, did not cling to her. One more piece of evidence, and Clare did not much like where it led.

He set the viola and its bow down, nudging aside a stack of paper with careful precision, and waited for the opening gambit. As he had suspected, *she* spoke.

"Good evening, sir. You are Dr Archibald Clare. Distinguished author of *The Art and Science of Observation*." She paused. Aristocratic nose, firm mouth, very decided for such a childlike face. "Bachelor. And very-recently-unregistered mentath."

"Sorceress." Clare steepled his fingers under his very long, very sensitive nose. Her toilette favoured musk, of course, for a brunette. Still, the scent was not common, and it held an edge of something acrid that should have been troublesome instead of strangely pleasing. "And a Shield. I would invite you to sit, but I hardly think you will."

A slight smile; her chin lifted. She did not give her name, as if she expected him to suspect it. Her curls, if they were not natural, were very close. There was a slight bit of untidiness to them – some recent exertion, perhaps? "Since there is no seat available, *sir*, I am to take that as one of your deductions?"

Even the hassock had a pile of papers and books stacked terrifyingly high. He had been researching, of course. The intersections between musical scale and the behaviour of certain tiny animals. It was the intervals, perhaps. Each note held its own space. He was seeking to determine which set of spaces would make the insects (and later, other things) possibly—

Clare waved one pale, long-fingered hand. Emotion was threatening, prickling at his throat. With a certain rational annoyance he labelled it as *fear*, and dismissed it. There was very little chance she meant him harm. The man was a larger question, but if she meant him no harm, the man certainly did not. "If you like. Speak quickly, I am occupied."

She cast one eloquent glance over the room. If not for the efforts of the landlady, Mrs Ginn, dirty dishes would have been stacked on every horizontal surface. As it was, his quarters were cluttered with a full set of alembics and burners, glass jars of various substances, shallow dishes for knocking his pipe clean. The tabac smoke blunted the damned sensitivity in his nose just enough, and he wished for his pipe. The acridity in her scent was becoming more marked, and very definitely not unpleasant.

The room's disorder even threatened the grate, the mantel above it groaning under a weight of books and handwritten journals stacked every which way.

The sorceress, finishing her unhurried investigation, next examined him from tip to toe. He was in his dressing gown, and his pipe had long since grown cold. His feet were in the rubbed-bare slippers, and if it had not been past the hour of reasonable entertaining he might have been vaguely uncomfortable at the idea of a lady seeing him in such disrepair. Red-eyed, his hair mussed, and unshaven, he was in no condition to receive company.

He was, in fact, the picture of a mentath about to implode from boredom. If she knew some of the circumstances behind his recent ill luck, she would guess he was closer to imploding and fusing his faculties into unworkable porridge than was advisable, comfortable ... or even sane.

Yet if she knew the circumstances behind his ill luck, would she look so calm? He did not know nearly enough yet. Frustration tickled behind his eyes, the sensation of pounding and seething inside the cup of his skull easing a fraction as he considered the possibilities of her arrival.

Her gloved hand rose, and she held up a card. It was dun-coloured, and before she tossed it – a passionless, accurate flick of her fingers that snapped it through intervening space neat as you please, as if she dealt faro – he had already deduced and verified its provenance.

He plucked it out of the air. "I am called to the service of the Crown. You are to hold my leash. It is, of course, urgent. Does it have to do with an art professor?" For it had been some time since he had crossed wits with Dr Vance, and *that* would distract him most handily. The man was a deuced wonderful adversary.

His sally was only worth a raised eyebrow. She must have practised that look in the mirror; her features were strangely childlike, and the effect of the very adult expression was ... odd. "No. It *is* urgent, and Mikal will stand guard while you ... dress. I shall be in the hansom outside. You have ten minutes, sir."

With that, she turned on her heel. Her skirts made a low, sweet sound, and the man was already holding the door. She glanced up, those wide dark eyes flashing once, and a ghost of a smile touched her soft mouth.

Interesting. Clare added that to the chain of deduction. He only hoped this problem would last more than a night and provide him further relief. If the young Queen or one of the ministers had sent a summons card, it promised to be very diverting indeed.

It was a delight to have something unknown, but within guessing reach. He sniffed the card. A faint trace of musk, but no violet-water. Not the Queen personally, then. He had not thought it likely – why would Her Majesty trouble herself with *him*? It was a faint joy to find he was correct.

His faculties were, evidently, not porridge *yet*.

The ink was correct as well, just the faintest bitter astringent note as he inhaled deeply. The crest on the front was absolutely genuine, and the handwriting on the back was firm and masculine, not to mention familiar. *Why, it's Cedric.*

In other words, the Chancellor of the Exchequer, Lord Grayson. The Prime Minister was new and inexperienced, since the Queen had banished her lady mother's creatures from her Cabinet, and Grayson had survived with, no doubt, some measure of cunning or because someone thought him incompetent enough to do no harm. Having been at Yton with the man, Clare was inclined to lean towards the former.

And dear old Cedric had exerted his influence so Clare was merely unregistered and not facing imprisonment, a mercy that had teeth. Even more interesting.

Miss Emma Bannon is our representative. Please use haste, and discretion.

Emma Bannon. Clare had never heard the name before, but then a sorceress would not wish her name bruited about overmuch. Just as a mentath, registered or no, would not. So he made a special note of it, adding everything about the woman to the mental drawer that bore her name. She would not take a carved nameplate. No, Miss Bannon's plate would be yellowed parchment, with dragonsblood ink tracing out the letters of her name in a clear, feminine hand.

The man's drawer was featureless blank metal, burnished to a high gloss. He waited by the open door. Cleared his throat, a low rumble. Meant to hurry Clare along, no doubt.

Clare opened one eye, just a sliver. "There are nine and a quarter minutes left. Do *not* make unnecessary noise, sir."

The man – a sorceress's Shield, meant to guard against physical danger while the sorceress dealt with more arcane perils – remained silent, but his mouth firmed. He did not look amused.

Mikal. His colour was too dark and his features too aquiline to be properly Britannic. Perhaps Tinkerfolk? Or even from the Indus?

For the moment, he decided, the man's drawer could remain metal. He did not know enough about him. It would have to do. One thing was certain: if the sorceress had left one of her Shields with him, she was standing guard against some more than mundane threat outside. Which meant the problem he was about to address was most likely fiendishly complex, extraordinarily important, and worth more than a day or two of his busy brain's feverish working.

Thank God. The relief was palpable.

Clare shot to his feet and began packing.

CHAPTER ONE

A Pleasant Evening Ride

Emma Bannon, Sorceress Prime and servant to Britannia's current incarnation, mentally ran through every foul word that would never cross the lips of a lady. She timed them to the clockhorse's steady jogtrot, and her awareness dilated. The simmering cauldron of the streets was just as it always was; there was no breath of ill intent.

Of course, there had not been earlier, either, when she had been a quarter-hour too late to save the *other* unregistered mentath. It was only one of the many things about this situation seemingly designed to try her often considerable patience.

Mikal would be taking the rooftop road, running while she sat at ease in a hired carriage. It was the knowledge that while he did so he could forget some things that eased her conscience, though not completely.

Still, he was a Shield. He would not consent to share a carriage with her unless he was certain of her safety. And there was not room enough to manoeuvre in a two-person conveyance, should he require it.

She was heartily sick of hired carts. Her own carriages were *far* more comfortable, but this matter required discretion. Having it shouted to the heavens that she was alert to the pattern under these occurrences might not precisely frighten her opponents, but it would become more difficult to attack them from an unexpected quarter. Which was, she had to admit, her preferred method.

Even a Prime can benefit from guile, Llew had often remarked. And of course, she would think of him. She seemed constitutionally incapable of leaving well enough alone, and that irritated her as well.

Beside her, Clare dozed. He was a very thin man, with a long, mournful face; his gloves were darned but his waistcoat was of fine cloth, though it had seen better days. His eyes were blue, and they glittered feverishly under half-closed lids. An unregistered mentath would find it difficult to secure proper employment, and by the looks of his quarters, Clare had been suffering from boredom for several weeks, desperately seeking a series of experiments to exercise his active brain.

Mentath was like sorcerous talent. If not trained, and *used*, it turned on its bearer.

At least he had found time to shave, and he had brought two bags. One, no doubt, held linens. God alone knew what was in the second. Perhaps she should apply deduction to the problem, as if she did not have several others crowding her attention at the moment.

Chief among said problems were the murderers, who had so far eluded her efforts. Queen Victrix was young, and just recently freed from the confines of her domineering mother's sway. Her new Consort, Alberich, was a moderating influence – but he did not have enough power at Court just yet to be an effective shield for Britannia's incarnation.

The ruling spirit was old, and wise, but Her vessels ... well, they were not indestructible.

And that, Emma told herself sternly, *is as far as we shall go with such a train of thought*. She found herself rubbing the sardonyx on her left middle finger, polishing it with her opposite thumb. Even through her thin gloves, the stone prickled hotly. Her posture did not change, but her awareness contracted. She felt for the source of the disturbance, flashing through and discarding a number of fine invisible threads.

Blast and bother. Other words, less polite, rose as well. Her pulse and respiration did not change, but she tasted a faint tang of adrenalin before sorcerous training clamped tight on such functions to free her from some of flesh's more ... distracting ... reactions.

"I say, whatever is the matter?" Archibald Clare's blue eyes were wide open now, and he looked interested. Almost, dare she think it, intrigued. It did nothing for his long, almost ugly features. His cloth was serviceable, though hardly elegant – one could infer that a mentath had other priorities than fashion, even if he had an eye for quality and the means to purchase such. But at least he was cleaner than he had been, and had arrived in the hansom in nine and a half minutes precisely. Now they were on Sarpesson Street, threading through amusement-seekers and those whom a little rain would not deter from their nightly appointments.

The disturbance peaked, and a not-quite-seen starburst of gunpowder igniting flashed through the ordered lattices of her consciousness.

The clockhorse screamed as his reins were jerked, and the hansom yawed alarmingly. Archibald Clare's hand dashed for the door handle, but Emma was already moving. Her arms closed around the tall, fragile man, and she shouted a Word that exploded the cab away from them both. Shards and splinters, driven outwards, peppered the street surface. The glass of the cab's tiny windows broke with a high, sweet tinkle, grinding into crystalline dust.

Shouts. Screams. Pounding footsteps. Emma struggled upright, shaking her skirts with numb hands. The horse had gone avast, rearing and plunging, throwing tiny metal slivers and dribs of oil as well as stray crackling sparks of sorcery, but the traces were tangled and it stood little chance of running loose. The driver was gone, and she snapped a quick glance at the overhanging rooftops before the unhealthy canine shapes resolved out of thinning rain, slinking low as gaslamp gleam painted their slick, heaving sides.

Sootdogs. Oh, how unpleasant. The one that had leapt on the hansom's roof had most likely taken the driver, and Emma cursed aloud now as it landed with a thump, its shining hide running with vapour.

"*Most* unusual!" Archibald Clare yelled. He had gained his feet as well, and his eyes were alight now. The mournfulness had vanished. He had also produced a queerly barrelled pistol, which would be of no use against the dog-shaped sorcerous things now gathering. "*Quite* diverting!"

The star sapphire on her right third finger warmed. A

globe-shield shimmered into being, and to the roil of smouldering wood, gunpowder and fear was added another scent: the smoke-gloss of sorcery. One of the sootdogs leapt, crashing into the shield, and the shock sent Emma to her knees, holding grimly. Both her hands were outstretched now, and her tongue occupied in chanting.

Sarpesson Street was neither deserted nor crowded at this late hour. The people gathering to watch the outcome of a hansom crash pushed against those onlookers alert enough to note that something entirely different was occurring, and the resultant chaos was merely noise to be shunted aside as her concentration narrowed.

Where is Mikal?

She had no time to wonder further. The sootdogs hunched and wove closer, snarling. Their packed-cinder sides heaved and black tongues lolled between obsidian-chip teeth; they could strip a large adult male to bone in under a minute. There were the onlookers to think of as well, and Clare behind and to her right, laughing as he sighted down the odd little pistol's chunky nose. Only he was not pointing it at the dogs, thank God. He was aiming for the rooftop.

You idiot. The chant filled her mouth. She could spare no words to tell him not to fire, that Mikal was—

The lead dog crashed against the shield. Emma's body jerked as the impact tore through her, but she held steady, the sapphire now a ringing blue flame. Her voice rose, a clear contralto, and she assayed the difficult rill of notes that would split her focus and make another Major Work possible.

That was part of what made a Prime – the ability to concentrate completely on multiple channellings of ætheric force. One's capacity could not be infinite, just like the charge of force carried and renewed every Tideturn.

But one did not need infinite capacity. *One needs only slightly more capacity than the problem at hand calls for*, as her third-form Sophological Studies professor had often intoned.

Mikal arrived.

His dark green coat fluttered as he landed in the midst of the dogs, a Shield's fury glimmering to Sight, bright spatters and spangles invisible to normal vision. The sorcery-made things cringed, snapping; his blades tore through their insubstantial hides. The charmsilver laid along the knives' flats, as well as the will to strike, would be of far more use than Mr Clare's pistol.

Which spoke, behind her, the ball tearing through the shield from a direction the protection wasn't meant to hold. The fabric of the shield collapsed, and Emma had just enough time to deflect the backlash, tearing a hole in the brick-faced fabric of the street and exploding the clockhorse into gobbets of metal and rags of flesh, before one of the dogs turned with stomach-churning speed and launched itself at her – and the man she had been charged to protect.

She shrieked another Word through the chant's descant, her hand snapping out again, fingers contorted in a gesture definitely *not* acceptable in polite company. The ray of ætheric force smashed through brick dust, destroying even more of the road's surface, and crunched into the sootdog.

Emma bolted to her feet, snapping her hand back, and the line of force followed as the dog crumpled, whining and shattering into fragments. She could not hold the forcewhip for very long, but if more of the dogs came—

The last one died under Mikal's flashing knives. He muttered something in his native tongue, whirled on his heel, and stalked toward his Prima. That normally meant the battle was finished.

Yet Emma's mind was not eased. She half turned, chant dying on her lips and her gaze roving, searching. Heard the mutter of the crowd, dangerously frightened. Sorcerous force pulsed and bled from her fingers, a fountain of crimson sparks popping against the rainy air. For a moment the mood of the crowd threatened to distract her, but she closed it away and concentrated, seeking the source of the disturbance.

Sorcerous traces glowed, faint and fading, as the man who had fired the initial shot – most likely to mark them for the dogs – fled. He had some sort of defence laid on him, meant to keep him from a sorcerer's notice.

Perhaps from a sorcerer, but not from a Prime. Not from me, oh no. The dead see all. Her Discipline was of the Black, and it was moments like these when she would be glad of its practicality – if she could spare the attention.

Time spun outwards, dilating, as she followed him over rooftops and down into a stinking alley, refuse piled high on each side, running with the taste of fear and blood in his mouth. Something had injured him.

Mikal? But then why did he not kill the man—

The world jolted underneath her, a stunning blow to her shoulder, a great spiked roil of pain through her chest. Mikal screamed, but she was breathless. Sorcerous force spilled free, uncontained, and other screams rose.

She could possibly injure someone.

Emma came back to herself, clutching at her shoulder.

Hot blood welled between her fingers, and the green silk would be ruined. Not to mention her gloves.

At least they had shot her, and not the mentath.

Oh, damn. The pain crested again, became a giant animal with its teeth in her flesh.

Mikal caught her. His mouth moved soundlessly, and Emma sought with desperate fury to contain the force thundering through her. Backlash could cause yet more damage, to the street and to onlookers, if she let it loose.

A Prime's uncontrolled force was nothing to be trifled with.

It was the traditional function of a Shield to handle such overflow, but if he had only wounded the fellow on the roof she could not trust that he was not part of—

"*Let it GO!*" Mikal roared, and the ætheric bonds between them flamed into painful life. She fought it, seeking to contain what she could, and her skull exploded with pain.

She knew no more.